"I think I should tell you something," he confessed.

Charlene propped her arms on his shoulders. Their warm bodies touched intimately, separated by only threads of clothing and discipline, while their thoughts ran wild every which way.

"I've been in love with you since the first time I ever saw you."

She didn't know what to say. His expression was serious and anxious, studying her for a reaction.

Struck to the core, she pulled away from his embrace and raked a hand through her hair. "Oh, Mason."

"I wanted to tell you so you would know how I feel. That this isn't some passing attraction. I love you, and I want to marry you."

"Curtiss Ann Matlock blends reality with romance to perfection."

—*Romantic Times*

Curtiss Ann Matlock

DRIVING LESSONS

ISBN 1-55166-599-9

DRIVING LESSONS

Copyright © 2000 by Curtiss Ann Matlock.

Visit us at www.mirabooks.com

Printed in U.S.A.

For Lou, my angel, my teacher, my friend.

"If you keep on going, you will eventually
get where you want to go, no matter
how many wrong roads you go down."
—Cowetta Valentine

One

Charlene had made tomato pudding for this Sunday's dinner. Normally that was considered more of a fall and winter dish, but she had made it this hot day anyway for her husband Joey, in case he got home in time. Joey loved her tomato pudding so much that he might just smell it up there in Missouri and come home faster.

She burned her fingers getting it out of the oven. Plunking the dish on the counter beside the ham, she rushed, shaking her fingers, to the sink and stuck them in the stream of cold water. She wondered why people shook burnt fingers. Maybe it was about the same as blowing on them. She did not think either action helped all that much.

It was the every other Sunday when Charlene had dinner at her house for the family—her husband and three children, and her father and his two boarders were the regulars. Sometimes one of the kids had a friend over, and every once in a while her sister and brother-in-law, Rainey and Harry, drove down from Oklahoma City to join them. On very rare occasions her brother Freddy and his wife Helen bent themselves to show up, although not in the months

since Freddy had suffered his breakdown and pulled a gun
on the IRS agent and wound up in the hospital.

"Mama…" Danny J. sauntered into the kitchen and
went straight to sniffing over the food "…is Dad comin'
home today?" He got to the chocolate cake and scooped a
fingertip in the icing.

"Quit that!" She smacked at his hand and kissed his
head at the same time. He pulled away; he was thirteen
now.

"When's Dad comin' home?"

"Tonight sometime, I think."

"Then why'd you make tomato puddin'? No one else
likes it." His eyes focused on her.

"I like it," Charlene said. She stuck her fingers back
under the water. She didn't want Danny J. to see her hands
shaking. She felt her whole body shaking. "Now, take the
trash out for me."

He frowned and slumped his shoulders all over but did
what she asked. As he went out the back door, Charlene
reminded him to put the lids tight on the trash cans so the
raccoons wouldn't get in them. Joey kept saying he was
going to have to shoot those raccoons, which upset Jojo
considerably. Charlene had to take her aside and tell her,
"You know your daddy isn't goin' to shoot those raccoons.
For one thing, he doesn't have a gun." Joey wasn't a man
who could kill anything. He made sure the barn doors were
open so birds could fly in to their nests. Joey was like that.

She was patting her hands dry with her apron, when she
heard the sound of a vehicle. She raced to the window.

But no, it wasn't Joey.

She stared at the car coming like gangbusters—her
daddy's maroon Oldsmobile. Daddy and his girls—that was
what everyone had started calling Charlene's father and his
elderly women boarders. For the past four months there had

only been two, but he'd had as many as four at times the past year.

The big Oldsmobile rolled up the concrete drive and came to an immediate and jerky halt, enough to throw them all through the window had they not been wearing seat belts. Her father was awfully proud to still be driving at his age. Charlene was a little worried.

She stood there holding her fingers in her apron and watching as Rainey and Larry Joe went out to greet the new arrivals. Rainey escorted the elderly ladies toward the house, and Larry Joe stood beside his grandfather to chat. Daddy liked to stand out there and smoke a Camel before coming inside.

Charlene turned back to the stove and then just stood there, head cocked, the babble of feminine voices floating to her from the living room.

Someone said her name. Footsteps were coming toward the kitchen.

Snatching up a Tupperware bowl, she hurried out the back door, closing it softly behind her.

On the back step, she put her arm up against the glare of the bright sun. Good-golly it was hot. She looked around for Danny J., only just then remembering him. The trash can lids were firmly in place, showing that he had made quick work of his job and scooted away before he could be assigned another.

As she went down the path to her little garden, grasshoppers jumped here and there, startled by her movements. Her garden was pretty much burnt right up. She had tried to keep it watered, but morning and night, day after day, had just gotten too much.

This summer was one of the hottest and driest on record. There had been no rain since the first of June, and temperatures had soared over a hundred for days on end. Creeks

and ponds were going dry, pasture grass was withering and
concrete cracking. It had been reported in the *Valentine
Voice* that there was a doubling in county-wide arrests because of people all over the place getting into fights over
portable air conditioners and yard sprinklers. Some eve-
nings lately Charlene had begun to feel that if it did not
rain, she was going to go crazy.

In the garden, cucumbers were barely hanging on. She
found one that was not too shriveled, and a handful of
cherry tomatoes. The tomato plants were pretty much giving up the ghost. She bent and rooted around in the weeds
for the thin salad onions. Her daddy and the kids liked to
put salt in a saucer and dip slices of cucumber and the salad
onions in it and eat them. Daddy had taught the kids that.

She came up with three pitiful-looking onions and slowly
walked back toward the house. Her burned fingers had begun to throb, and the skin was getting quite red, starting to
bubble up, too. Inside at the sink, she stuck them under
cold water again as she washed the vegetables. Voices high
and low floated from the living room.

Rainey came in and over to Charlene's shoulder. "Do
you know Mildred brought her own margarine? Country
Crock in those little singles. She pulled it out of her purse.
Does she always do that?"

"Uh-huh." Charlene nodded. "She carries all sorts of
stuff in her purse. Once she brought out Hellmann's mayonnaise."

"Good grief. She might get food poisoning. Did you
burn your fingers?"

"Just a bit." Charlene was wrapping them in a wet paper
towel. "Joey didn't come in, did he?" She thought it possible she had missed him. Maybe he was parked over by
the barn, where he had to unload the horses.

"No. Let me see your fingers."

"Never mind."

"Oh, don't be silly, Charlene. Let me look at your fingers."

"Leave me be, Rainey."

Rainey stared at her. Charlene told Rainey to please go get the cloth napkins from the buffet drawer. "It's a special dinner," she said, giving a smile to try to make up.

Rainey studied her.

Charlene turned quickly to get a frying pan from the cupboard. "And use Mama's good silver. There's eight settings."

She heard Rainey leave. Pushing stray hair from her face with the back of her hand, she went to the refrigerator for flour and milk to make gravy. The biscuits would be out of the oven in five minutes. There was a big ham with pineapple slices over it, cornbread dressing and gravy, fresh green beans, corn on the cob, a gelatin salad, the tomato pudding and a chocolate cake. She had managed to turn out a really good meal.

Jojo came in. "Maa-maa?" she said, dragging it out in the way children seemed to enjoy saying the name just to be saying it. After a minute, she repeated with a definite tone, "Mama?"

"Yes, sweetie?"

"Aunt Rainey's gonna tell everyone about her baby at dinner, isn't she?"

Charlene looked down into her daughter's upturned face and cupped her small chin. "Yes. Don't let out the secret."

"I won't," Jojo said, as if wounded. Then her blue eyes searched Charlene's face in the worried fashion that had become her habit in the last months.

"Take that plate of garden veggies in to the table for me, won't you, sweetie," Charlene said.

"Okay, Mama." She very carefully took the plate. Jojo

had been trying so hard for the past year to be good. To make her world right by her goodness.

Charlene stirred the gravy, an activity that caused her to swing her entire body in pleasant rhythm, and remembered when she had told everyone she was going to have Jojo. Her mother had held a dinner just like this one. Charlene had been thirty-seven, and Freddy, Mr. By-the-book, had made a lot of comments on that. Rainey was only a year younger now, and this would be her first. The years just flew past. Here Jojo was nine years old. Charlene had so wanted another child. But God had not seen things her way, and He knew best, although sometimes how things turned out was really hard to take.

Realizing she'd gotten lost in thought, she had to stir the gravy hard; it was starting to stick.

"Table's all set," Rainey said, striding into the kitchen. "Ready for me to take this stuff out?"

"Yes. Oh, let me carve the ham in here."

She again splashed cold water over her fingers in the paper towel. It was tricky slicing the ham while holding those fingers out. She heard her family gathering in the dining room, heard Danny J. and Larry Joe roughhousing. They didn't do that so much anymore. She thought she heard a vehicle...but no, it was just the wind picking up, she guessed.

She arranged the ham neatly on two big plates that could sit at each end of the table. It was easier for people to serve themselves that way. When Rainey came in to fill ice tea glasses, Charlene told her to set out the wineglasses, too.

"I have a bottle of wine I've been saving for a special occasion."

With a cocky grin, Rainey breezed out of the kitchen with the walk she had adopted that appeared to accommodate a belly she didn't yet have.

"Where's Joey today?" Daddy asked, when Charlene carried in the ham.

"He's up in Missouri at a horse show. He went up on Friday."

She shouldn't have tried to carry both plates at once. Feeling pressure on her burnt fingers, she almost dropped one plate right on Ruthanne, one of her father's elderly boarders, who had already sat down. Ruthanne's place was always the same. It was important not to confuse Ruthanne, who was having a little trouble remembering what year it was. The doctors said it was a form of senility, but as long as she remained in familiar surroundings, it would likely progress slowly. Sometimes Ruthanne would have to be reminded of who people were, but she was such a sweet thing that no one minded.

"Daddy, you go ahead and sit there at the end of the table, and Rainey can sit at this end today."

Whenever Joey wasn't present, her father would sit in the big chair at the end of the table, but he always waited to be told. There was not a hurried bone in her daddy's tall and lanky body. He had iron gray hair, more iron than gray, and there was an air of old gentleman about him in his white short-sleeved Sunday shirt. After the matter of where he would sit was settled, he would help Mildred into a seat on his right or left.

Mildred Covington had finally gotten what she wanted, being able to hold on to Daddy. Since she had had her stroke, she used a cane and very often Daddy's arm. The woman managed to be within a foot of him at all times. Charlene had noticed that when Daddy wasn't present, Mildred managed fine on her own, but when Daddy was around, she made good use of him.

Mildred had her big purse right with her, of course, white vinyl, with lots of pockets. As soon as she got sat down, she pulled out three pink packets to sweeten her tea and a small cloth to wipe her dishes. As she wiped her ice tea spoon, she said, "It all looks so good, Charlene, dear, but did you remember I can't have any of that dressing if there's celery in it? I just can't tolerate celery."

"I made you some without, Miss Mildred. Larry Joe and Danny J., you boys come on now," Charlene called.

Jojo was giving her granddaddy a hug and whispering in his ear. He whispered back in hers, and she danced and rubbed her ear. He picked up the wineglass in front of his plate.

"Are we celebratin' something?"

"Yeah, Grandaddy," Danny J. said. "That you're alive another day."

"Remember to respect the elderly, boy," his grandfather shot back.

The remark came to Charlene as she went back to the kitchen. Somehow her father never quite seemed to fit the term "elderly." Although he was. He was eighty-seven this year, she thought. All of them just getting older and older.

Charlene got the bottle of wine from the bottom of the refrigerator, where she'd halfway hidden it beneath a bag of flour tortillas. It had red curly ribbon around the neck and a note that said: For Charlene and Joey on their twenty-first anniversary. It had been a present from Rainey and Harry, but she and Joey had never gotten around to drinking it. They'd gone out to supper, but Joey had been too tired when they came home to open the wine. Charlene tore off the note. Likely Rainey wouldn't notice it was the same bottle.

Charlene never had used a corkscrew, and she ended up breaking off the cork. Larry Joe came in and dug it out with his pocket knife. Rainey teased him about where that knife had been.

Charlene made a flourish out of the announcement. "Everybody, our Rainey has big news," she said, and stood back from the table while all eyes turned to Rainey, who sat glowing appropriately like the star of Bethlehem, her joy so bright that Charlene had to look away.

Rainey said, "Harry and I are gonna have a baby."

While congratulations were exchanged and Rainey explained how Harry hadn't been able to get away to have dinner with them, and how she was extremely healthy and all was proceeding correctly, Charlene went around the table filling the wineglasses. A splash for the children and a swallow for Rainey. Half a glass for Ruthanne, who looked a little vacant, if pleasantly so.

Charlene raised her glass. "To our Rainey and Harry and their rare and special union, and to this very lucky child that is come to bless their hearts and teach them all sorts of things they never imagined."

Daddy said, "Here, here! God bless Little Bit," which was what Daddy always called Rainey. His nickname for Charlene was Daughter, which had always hurt just a little because it sounded so simple and flat.

There was a lot of grinning and to-do about clinking the glasses together. Jojo looked at her glass wide-eyed and took a sip and made a face. Danny J. was quick to swallow all of his and then hold up his glass, as if Charlene might refill it. "Dang," he said, when she took the glass away.

Ruthanne was very demure, sipping and saying in her lovely soft voice, "Congratulations, Rainey dear, to you and your husband Charles."

"That is Harry, Ruthanne," Mildred corrected in the loud voice she always employed with Ruthanne, as if Ruthanne was hard-of-hearing instead of confused. "Let me get a picture of the mother-to-be," and she pulled one of those little disposable cameras out of her purse.

Charlene disappeared into the kitchen, taking the bottle of wine. Standing at the sink, looking out the window to the drive where Joey's blue truck would be seen if it were coming, she tipped back her head and downed her first glass, then poured what was left in the bottle and finished that, too.

She looked at the clock and out the window again. She told herself that Joey would be home soon. Likely one or two of his horses had done really well and had to show again today. And it was a long drive. Silly of her to expect him before night.

But she knew, the way a woman can know things, especially about a man she has been married to for twenty-one years, that Joey wasn't coming home. He had been leaving her for the past year, and now he was long gone.

The City Hall thermometer reads 96°

That evening at sundown, when she and Jojo were the only ones at the house and went out to feed and water the horses, Charlene wasn't too surprised to find every one of Joey's saddles and all of his bits and bridles gone from the tack room.

She stood in the door and stared at the little dusty room, until Jojo came up and asked, "What is it, Mama?"

"Nothing, hon. Let's get the outside waterin' done and get in out of this heat."

They went inside, and Charlene went back to her bedroom closet and saw that all four pairs of Joey's favorite boots were gone, as were each of his Mobetta shirts. The only remaining jeans were ones Charlene was supposed to hem.

She had not seen all of this before because she had been afraid to look.

"Mama, will you paint my fingernails?" Jojo asked.

"We'll paint our fingernails *and* our toenails," Charlene told her and got her manicure supplies. The two of them sat at the kitchen table, where Charlene put Wild Plum on Jojo's fingers and toes, and Coral Sunset on her own. It took her a little longer than usual because of her burned fingers, which she kept wrapped in a wet bit of paper towel. Jojo laughed at Charlene's little half reading glasses.

"Don't make fun of your mother," Charlene told her and gave her a kiss.

Her father was getting older and so was she. This was what happened to women growing older: they lost their eyesight, their hormones and their husbands.

Then Jojo wanted to watch a movie—she wanted to watch some thriller called *Scream,* but Charlene wouldn't let her and put in the videotape of *The Wizard of Oz.* She sat on the couch with Jojo lying in her lap and the cordless phone on the end table beside her. Jojo fell asleep halfway through the movie, but Charlene continued to watch. Dorothy was just clicking her heels to fly home to Kansas when the telephone rang. Charlene answered it before the first ring ended. She didn't want Jojo to wake.

It was Joey, and she asked him to hold on while she got Jojo slid off her lap. She walked with the phone into the kitchen and listened as he said he wasn't coming home.

She said, "Oh, is the show runnin' on? I thought it was just a weekend show."

She didn't think she should jump to conclusions. He might have meant he was just not coming home that night. She wanted to give him every opportunity to reconsider.

"I meant I'm not comin' home at all, Charlene."

That sent her sinking down into a kitchen chair. She changed ears with the phone, as if that would help her to find sanity and make sense of the words jamming her throat. What she ended up saying was, "I made you tomato pudding for Sunday dinner. It's in the refrigerator."

The line hummed for long seconds after that, and then he said, "Thank you. I'm sorry to have missed it."

Silence again. Charlene's throat seemed to swell shut.

"I'm sorry, Charlene, I just can't come home."

"Well, why not? Why not just come home, Joey?" She didn't think her tone was encouraging.

Silence, and then Joey said, "I've called my customers to come pick up their horses still in the barn. Will you please feed them until then? It'll only be a couple of days. You can just go to feedin' them hay, if you want."

She kept her voice even and said she would feed the horses. Maybe she should tell him she wouldn't, she thought, but that sounded so mean, and he would know very well she wouldn't take things out on innocent animals.

"I'll talk to you about this soon, Charlene. When I get it straightened out in my mind."

Her ears were ringing. "What?"

"I said I'll call you. When I can get things straight."

What could she say to it? She wanted to beg him to come home, wanted to scream at him and bang the receiver on the table and scream at him some more. But that would be out of control.

"Okay," she said faintly, having lost her voice.

"You have my pager number, if you need me."

"Yes." Tears started, and she was melting down on the table.

"Goodbye, Charlene."

She didn't say anything, just tried to find the button to cut off the phone. She had trouble seeing because of her tears.

Immediately regret washed over her. She should have said something more to him. Something to make him stop the craziness and come home. She should have asked him if he was sure of what he was doing. She should have instructed him to get himself home this instant.

She should have told him that she loved him.

After a few minutes of sitting there and staring, she got up and went to the sink and ran cold water over her wrapped fingers. She thought maybe she should look at them, but she didn't have the energy. She went to the refrigerator and pulled out the casserole dish of tomato pudding. There was one scoop out of it where she had sampled it at dinner.

She got a spoon and sat at the table and proceeded to eat right out of the casserole dish. She thought it was some of the best tomato pudding she had ever made. Joey had never had tomato pudding until they married and she made it for him. He had liked it so much that he'd requested she make it for him all the time; once they sat in bed after making love and ate tomato pudding, feeding it to each other. What made Charlene's special was that she used hamburger buns instead of sliced bread. Usually she made it from her own home-grown and canned tomatoes, but with the heat demolishing her plants this year, she had used Del Monte's instead.

Two

The City Hall thermometer reads 84°

Winston Valentine's house sat up a hill from the town named for his own family. In reality the house had belonged to his wife, but after living in it so long, he thought of it as his own, and most everyone referred to it as the Valentine house.

Whenever he came out of his front door, the first sight he saw was the town laid out below. He could also see the roof of his son's home at the north edge of town, and before his eyesight got so poor, he'd been able to see all the way across to the cluster of buildings that was Charlene's place out on the far side of town.

This morning when Winston came out on the front porch, bringing the flag, just as he did first thing every morning, after half a cup of coffee, the town was awash with the faint golden glow of a sun ready to burst over the horizon.

"Hey, Mr. Valentine!" The paperboy was pedaling right along on down the street, tossing newspapers into yards with practiced ease.

"Hello to you, Leo."

Perry Blaine, in his black Lincoln, drove slowly past the boy. He was on his way to the drugstore, where he would sit and have coffee and work the crossword puzzle in isolated peace away from his wife and thirty-year-old daughter Belinda, who showed no signs of moving out of his house.

Across the street Everett Northrup was coming out onto his front porch with his flag, too. Already a few steps ahead of him, Winston hurried to get his flag set in the holder on the post before Everett, who was ten years younger but not nearly so agile as Winston.

When the flag was set, Winston paused and waited for Everett to glance his way. Then he pulled the string and the flag gracefully unfurled. Snapping to attention, Winston saluted the cross bars and stars of the Confederacy waving from his porch.

Across the street, Northrup let his flag unfurl. The Stars and Bars of the United States came halfway down, but then got tangled.

Northrup, all red-faced, jumped to get it straight, while Winston, thoroughly satisfied and whistling "Dixie," went down his steps and out across his lawn to get the Friday edition of the *Valentine Voice*. As he retrieved the rolled paper, he saw Northrup saluting. He waved his paper at his neighbor, who saluted him in place of coming over and knocking his block off.

It could be a sad commentary on his life, Winston thought, that irritating his neighbor had become a major highlight of his day. But then, he was fairly certain his irritating Everett helped to keep the man's heart pumping, and so he could consider it in a noble light.

"Mornin', Winston!"

It was Mason MacCoy coming along and casting a wave out the open window of his pickup truck. Mason's place was east down the road about four miles. He often passed at this time, on his way to the IGA bakery or the Main Street Cafe.

"Good mornin'," Winston called and waved back. He

liked Mason. He didn't treat Winston like an old codger, as so many did.

As he headed around to the side of the house, here came another truck. Busy street this morning. Why, it was Joey in his new blue Dodge—only pickup in town that color—Winston saw with surprise, and he instantly thought, Coming into town the back way.

Instinctively he raised his hand in a wave. No need not to wave; Joey's and Charlene's disagreements were their own, and he'd always liked Joey just fine.

Joey saw him and looked startled. Then he cast a brief wave and seemed to speed up going down the hill.

Winston stood there a moment watching the rear of his son-in-law's truck and feeling all manner of great sadness and pity. By not coming home, Joey had made an ass of himself, as men will on occasion. Things did not appear to be improving on that score.

Raising his eyes, Winston looked across at what he took for his son Freddy's rooftop and then on farther to about where Charlene's rooftop would be, if he could see that far. The town was starting to stir. Another day going on, people loving and arguing and living and dying.

"Well, I'm not dead yet," he muttered.

Around the side of the house, he went to tending his dead wife's rosebushes, which was what he always did after the flag raising. The fragrance of twenty blooming rosebushes swirled around him as he turned on the faucet and checked to make certain the soakers were dripping at the base of each bush. Pulling clippers from his back pocket, he pruned stems where necessary and cut blossoms just beginning to open, flowers of yellow and red and pink.

"Good mornin', Coweta," he said in a hushed voice, feeling someone looking at him.

Sometimes his wife came and visited with him. When it

had first happened, he had been very worried about his faculties, but as all around him seemed perfectly normal— he could still see and hear everyone else just fine and didn't confuse them and hadn't started peeing in his pants—he figured he was okay and Coweta really was there, as she assured him that she was. In fact, in the course of their visits, she had explained all sorts of things about the soul and earth and heaven.

Of course, he didn't go around telling people he visited with Coweta. They would think he was looney, just the way they thought Ruthanne was because she forgot the year and often talked to her sisters, who'd passed away a long time ago. Actually, Winston, too, thought Ruthanne was a little looney. But since he could see Coweta, he figured it was a good bet Ruthanne could see people others couldn't, either. There was a guy over in Tillman County who claimed the Virgin Mary came to a hill on his place, and he was making a bit of money off it. Some people got called crazy, and others made money.

This minute, however, when he looked over his shoulder, Coweta was not there.

Straightening, Winston looked up and down the street. There wasn't a soul in sight, except for Dixie Love's little black cocker let out in the front yard to do his business.

This was somewhat disconcerting. Winston hoped he was not losing his faculties after all. The older he got, the greater became the fear of ending up sitting in a nursing home hallway, peeing in his pants.

Winston was not losing his faculties. It was Vella Blaine, watching him with Perry's binoculars pressed up to the venetian blinds of her dining room window.

Just then Vella saw Mildred come around from the back. Mildred was in a robe—a flowery silky kind such as fancy women wore—and her hair was wrapped up in a flaming pink turban. She ought to be ashamed wearing such a get-up at her size and age. She said something to Winston, and the two went back inside. Mildred at least seemed in a hurry.

When all she gazed at were the blooming rosebushes, Vella lowered the binoculars and went into her own kitchen, where her daughter still sat in her robe and slippers, drinking coffee and reading the paper. Vella wished she would leave. She couldn't call Minnie with Belinda sitting there.

"Well, something is goin' on over to the Valentines'," Vella said. "Mildred just came out, and she looked in a state, and she and Winston went hurrying back inside. I wonder if Ruthanne's broke a hip or something."

Belinda lowered the newspaper and eyed the binoculars. "Are you spyin' on the neighbors again?"

"I am not spyin' on the neighbors. I was just watchin' birds, and I happened to see."

"Oh, Mama, you are never in this world watchin' birds. You're watchin' the neighbors."

"I am not. I have my book and everything."

Vella reached around to grab her bird book for evidence, but it wasn't on the end of the counter. "I was watchin' blue jays this morning. One went after Dixie Love's dog. Dived right down at him." At last she found the book, under a couple copies of the *Conservative Chronicle* and a *Ladies Home Journal* on the microwave cart.

Belinda had the paper up in front of her face again.

Vella refreshed the cup of coffee she'd left to go peer out the window and sat down at the table. "Winston was clipping a bunch of rose blossoms again this morning. I just can't understand it. It has been over a hundred every day. My bushes and everyone else's have only put on a bud here and there. My Fragrant Cloud may even die, and I've kept it watered and shaded.''

"Maybe you've got those nematode things in your soil," Belinda said, not looking out from her newspaper.

Vella looked at the newspaper and wished her daughter would get some gumption.

She said, "If I've got nematodes, then Winston is the only one in town that doesn't have them, because he is the only one with rosebushes blooming like there's no tomorrow." She added silently to herself, And he is the only old man in this town livin' with a bunch of women.

As soon as Belinda went upstairs to dress, Vella telephoned Minnie Oakes to give a report on Winston's activities, on Mildred running out dressed like a dancer in a forties picture show. Minnie agreed with her that Winston and the women needed watching. Women were coming and going at his house, and that just wasn't right. A couple of times Vella had mentioned her puzzlement over Winston's getting all those blossoms from his rosebushes, but Minnie wasn't interested in this. Minnie only did vegetable gardening.

Three

The City Hall thermometer reads 102°

Charlene felt as if her skin were too tight and might at any moment tear apart. It was very hard work, trying to appear normal and not like someone who wanted to get a gun and go shoot her husband. If she shot Joey, then he never would be able to come home.

And Charlene very much wanted Joey to come home. She didn't care about him running off, if he would just come home. She believed the heat was the biggest cause of Joey up and leaving. As a horse trainer, Joey worked outside in the sun a great deal. It was hard for a person to hold up under such persistent heat, not to mention the heavy pile of disappointments twenty-one years of marriage managed to accumulate. She considered his wild behavior now something akin to heatstroke that caused him to go a little crazy, but when the episode was over, and the temperatures dropped, he would regain his senses and come home and take up their normal life again, just like none of this had ever happened. What she had to do was hold on until then.

She managed to do that all week, until Friday afternoon when she came out of the IGA and looked up and saw her husband, his cowboy hat set back like he wore it sometimes, sitting at the new stoplight in his new, bright blue one-ton Dodge, with black-haired Sheila Arnett in the seat beside him.

Charlene, clinging to the grocery sack of two dozen eggs, quart of orange juice and pound of bananas, stopped and stared.

"Charlene? What...? Oh."

It was Rainey's voice, coming to her dimly, while she could not tear her eyes from the sight of Joey and that woman in his truck. She thought that the moment was like something that would happen in a soap opera. She wished heartily that she looked better. None of those women in a soap would be looking like she did when this happened to them. They would have all their makeup on and certainly wouldn't be wearing old jeans and a sleeveless shirt, with their pudgy arms stuck out, and their hair pulled back carelessly into a ponytail.

She ducked her head. Oh, Lord, please don't let him see me. She would just die if Joey saw her. Maybe she would just die anyway. It would be easier.

"Come on, Mama."

Her eldest son's voice broke through the fog of despair, and she looked over at him. With a pained expression, Larry Joe took her sack, shifted it and the one he carried onto his right arm, and put his left arm around her shoulders. "Bubba, come on now," he called to Danny J., who was over at the soft drink machine at the corner of the store.

With a bit of alarm, Charlene saw her younger son beating up the Coke machine. She knew she should reprimand him, but she was too preoccupied with watching her husband and his girlfriend drive on past. She didn't think Joey saw her.

Rainey called out, "Jojo, you get right to the truck and stay there."

Charlene saw her little girl crossing the blacktopped lot. Jojo was gazing down the road. Likely she had seen her father driving with another woman, when she needed to be watching for traffic.

"That machine took my money, Mama," Danny J. complained, trotting up to her.

"Just get on to the truck," Larry Joe said, his arm pressing Charlene to walk along beside him.

"Just because Daddy's gone, you ain't the boss of me," Danny J. said.

Charlene got up voice enough to say, "Danny J., please go on to the truck and watch your little sister."

He peered at her, then ducked his head and shuffled off, mumbling, "Watch her do what?"

Daddy's gone. The words echoed in Charlene's mind.

"Good golly this blacktop is hot," Rainey said. "It just soaks up the sun. It's all this blacktop ever'where raisin' the temperature. My baby's gonna come out parboiled."

Rainey had stayed to help Charlene at this time of crisis, which was very welcome, but more and more Rainey was working on Charlene's last nerve. Rainey had become obsessed about avoiding the heat and cranky when not in an air-conditioned space. This annoyed Charlene, who thought a straying husband of a whole lot more significance than the heat.

"You didn't have to come with us, Rainey," Charlene said. "You could have stayed at the house, in the air-conditioning, with all the curtains pulled, too."

The attack took Rainey by surprise. "I didn't mean anything by it, Char. It's just so dang hot there isn't any point to walk slow over this parking lot. It's not healthy, hon."

Clamping her jaw tight, her eyes flashing, Charlene broke into rapid steps and walked straight to the rear of the Suburban.

"Charlene…"

Charlene got to the rear of the Suburban and had to wait for Larry Joe, who had the key. He came jogging over, and she said brightly, "Tie that bag closed, Larry Joe. I just hate these plastic bags. If we put them in right, the ones with the milk won't fall over. Those milk caps do leak. Danny J., hon, stop wipin' that car with the back of your T-shirt. You and your sister get on in the truck.

"The seats are burnin' hot, Mama," Jojo said in that worried voice she'd used all week.

"We'll just wait a minute," Rainey suggested, "and let Larry Joe start the engine and get the air conditioner cooling things off. I wished I'd remembered to put towels on the seats."

Charlene ignored them and walked up to the front passenger door, took hold of the handle and felt it burning her palm. She slipped into the front seat, and while Larry Joe started the engine and the air conditioner, she sat perfectly straight, feeling the heat of the seat through her jeans and the beads of sweat break out on her skin, run down her temples and between her breasts. She felt each bead of sweat deliberately and gave anticipating thought to having heatstroke and dying, but then who would take care of her babies, since her husband was off driving around with his black-haired girlfriend?

When her sister and younger children got into the back seat and closed the doors, Charlene said, "How 'bout if we go to the Dairy Freeze and get an ice cream? That'd be nice in this heat."

She looked around and found everyone staring at her. Larry Joe's jaw was so tight that he might be in danger of breaking a tooth. Her gaze went to Rainey, who was frowning deeply and wiping the hair from her forehead, and then over to her two younger children, who were staring at her in that odd way she'd seen on their faces so often the past week. An accusing and painful way.

Jojo shook her head and dropped her chin to her chest, while Danny J. went and turned his face right out the window.

Rainey said in a very practical voice, "Charlene, we just bought ice cream in the store. We might as well go home to have it in the air-conditioning."

"Well, okay."

Charlene faced forward as Larry Joe headed for the street. The afternoon sun was so bright, bouncing off the hood. Confusion filled her chest, made it hard to breathe. She felt as if she might scream.

Oh, my gosh, she really might scream, she thought, feeling a peculiar fury welling up in her chest. It was possible that she might start screaming and smack out the window glass. She gripped the armrest to keep control of her hand, but she could not seem to swallow the emotion that had now swelled into her throat.

"Larry Joe," she said, all of a sudden. *What are you thinking, Charlene?*

"Yes?" He cast her a curious, questioning look.

"Just turn right and let's see if we can catch sight of your daddy. I have something I need to tell him."

Larry Joe looked at her for a long second, and then he hit the pedal and sent them out on the road.

"Oh, Mama....Mama, our ice cream's gonna melt," Jojo said.

"It'll be all right for a bit," Rainey said quickly. "That boy packaged it right in that freezer bag. Here...I'll move this vent so the cold air is blowin' right on the bag with the ice cream. It'll be fine, sugar."

Charlene kept her gaze out the windshield, her eyes searching like revolving radar for her husband's blue truck.

She didn't see it anywhere on Main Street. Like it had disappeared from the earth, in the same manner as he had from their lives.

That was how it was, no more pretending he had not gone. No more pretending that what she feared had not come about. No more pretending that he could come back as if he'd been away on vacation. They were too far past that now, since she herself had seen him with Sheila Arnett.

Why did he have to leave me, God? What's wrong with me? Why did he stop loving me?

"Rainey, do you have a lipstick?"

Rainey could always be counted on for a lipstick, and she produced one instantly. "Here—Burnt Sunset. It's perfect for you."

Charlene peered into the mirror on the visor and applied the lipstick. It helped a little, but her eyes were still the eyes of a forty-six-year-old woman who had been crying every night into her pillow. And there just wasn't anything she could do about her hair. As she smoothed stray strands, she caught sight of her rosy painted fingernails. At least she had her hands looking good, womanly. She'd done her nails at three o'clock in the morning, when she couldn't sleep and couldn't stand to wrestle the sheets and pillows anymore.

She caught Jojo's worried little angel face in the mirror, then flipped up the visor.

She looked at Larry Joe's hands on the steering wheel, the rough hands of a man now, and wondered if she should tell him to stop and just go on home. She didn't want to have a scene in front of her children.

"There's Daddy's truck at the feed store," Danny J. said. His nose was pressed against the window glass.

Charlene saw Joey's blue truck sitting out front of MacCoy's Feed and Seed. Then Larry Joe was whipping the Suburban around and heading back toward it. He glanced at Charlene with a questioning eyebrow.

She looked at him and then at the blue pickup gleaming in the sun.

"Just pull over here to the side," she said, a sense of wild determination coming over her. "Here. Stop here."

She wanted the children far enough away so they could not hear, should she lose her temper and yell. Children should never see their parents acting rudely. *Thank you, God. Sheila Arnett is not in Joey's truck.* She must have gone inside the store with him. Just running around with him, bold as brass.

"Y'all stay here. I'll only be a few minutes," Charlene said, as if she were running into the Texaco for a cold drink.

"Just go on." Rainey shooed her with her hand and spoke in a tone that said, Do it, do it.

Charlene got out and slammed the door of the Suburban and stood there a moment, her hand pressed on the door, sort of stuck there. Staring at the feed store, she thought, I cannot go in there.

But she couldn't stand there hanging on to the Suburban, either, so she started off toward Joey's blue truck. Her feet crunched on stray gravel. She should have brought her sunglasses. She fought hard not to squint, which she knew did nothing but accentuate the wrinkles around her eyes. It was almost impossible not to squint, though, with the glare coming up off the white concrete parking lot. Brand-new paving. The MacCoy brothers owned the elevator and had money. She sure wished she looked better. Wiping a dribble from her temple, she thought, Back straight—a woman always looks in business when she walks with a straight back. That was what their mother used to tell them. Their mother had had a straight back until the day she died, and their daddy had never left her.

The City Hall thermometer reads 103°

One second Mason MacCoy had been taking a big drink of ice tea from a foam cup, wishing Fayrene Gardner over at the cafe would learn he liked lemon in his tea so he didn't have to ask every time, and the next he had turned his head and absently looked out the yawning door of the feed store warehouse like he did a hundred times a day, and he saw the woman walking across the lot in the bright sun.

He took a second look, moving forward to the loading dock.

She seemed familiar, and he hadn't expected to see anyone familiar. Not a familiar woman. Certainly not in the heat of the day, when nothing was stirring.

Why, it was Charlene Darnell. He knew that shiny-penny colored hair and that way of moving that was sort of a glide.

He took a few more steps forward and peered hard into the brightness of the lot, his gaze followed the line from where she had come, and he saw her faded red and white Suburban. He could see shadows inside, possibly her kids.

Ohh, buddy.

He watched her slow down, round her husband's blue truck and then stand there uncertainly.

Darnell had to be inside. Everyone knew about Joey Darnell getting crazy and leaving his wife and kids and shacking up over there at Sheila Arnett's place. Darnell claimed it was business, but no one believed him.

It occurred to him that Charlene Darnell might have come to shoot her husband. Or Sheila Arnett. That was how these things happened, normally sane people going all crazy. He himself had done that, gone crazy over a woman once. And it had been hot like this then, too.

Uh-oh, buddy. He didn't see a gun in her hand. Okay.

He watched her place a hand on the open window of Darnell's truck, look inside, and then lean back against the door. She was sort of in the shade there.

She might have a gun, he thought, one of those small ones, tucked into the waistband of her jeans. Her full breasts caused her shirt to hang out enough to hide a gun, if it were tucked into her jeans.

Mason gazed at her full breasts.

He thought Charlene Darnell had some fine breasts, the way they were so upright and womanly.

And then he thought how small she looked there. Like she might melt away. While her husband hid from her inside.

The way she looked caused a wince deep down inside Mason. It was a shame…and she *could* have a gun hidden in her waistband. If so, someone had to stop her before she did something foolish…someone needed to see to her.

And almost before he knew it, he had taken hold of the hand-truck he had piled with feed bags and started down the incline and across the lot to Darnell's pickup. When he hit the lot, he began to whistle; that seemed a good thing to do to cover what he suddenly realized might be a really foolish action on his part.

She heard him, and her head swung around. At the sight of her lovely face, the wisps of hair blowing round it, his heart sort of jumped.

"Hello," he said, casting her a smile.

She sent him a return smile, but it didn't reach her eyes. Her expression was on the verge of tears. That really unnerved him. He wouldn't know what in the hell to do if she broke down crying.

He jumped right in with, "Well, it is another scorcher, tenth in a row now over a hundred." He checked out her waist and didn't see any evidence of a gun.

"Yes, a hundred and three, the thermometer on City Hall said a minute ago." Her voice was sort of faint.

The worry that he'd made a mistake in coming out here swept him hard. He had butted into someone else's business, which was never a good idea. He sure hoped he had not gone and gotten himself into a fix. Lord, please don't let me have gotten in a fix.

"I wished they'd never put up that stupid sign," Mason said as he set about loading the feed sacks into Darnell's truckbed. "They still can't get the clock to work, and that thermometer just makes everybody hotter. Ever'body's always readin' the temperature and talkin' about it."

The sun lit her hair like a halo. Mason couldn't quit looking at it.

He slammed the tailgate closed, saying, "People try to make like this heat is something unusual. Like this sort of heat hasn't ever happened before. Global warming and everything. We've had droughts before, though, and likely we'll have them again. Had a bad summer some ten years or so ago, no rain from June to September."

"I remember that," she said. "It was eleven years ago. My son was only two, and over the summer he'd forgotten what rain was like. He went out in the yard and just stood there in it." She brushed stray hairs from her face and glanced from her Suburban to the store door with a worried expression.

It was a poor situation, Mason thought. Someone in there needed to shove that lily-livered Darnell out the door.

He couldn't think of anything else to say about the

weather. He ought to ask her if she wanted him to go in
and get her no-'count husband. He couldn't just go back to
the warehouse and leave her standing out here all alone like
she was. He didn't want to do that. He didn't see anything
else for him to do but go into the store. That was what he
would have to do. He'd go in the store, and probably all
he'd have to do was look at Darnell. He would speak if he
had to, though.

Watching the man take hold of the dolly, about to leave,
Charlene came out with, "They're ready to seed the clouds.
They reported it on the news last night. The governor came
on and said the airplanes are ready to go up and seed whenever the conditions are right."

She felt a sense of panic. She did not know what in the
world to do if he went off and left her standing out there.

"That's a tricky deal, that seeding," the man said, relaxing and leaning on his dolly. "One minute can be dry,
and the next you can end up with flooding." His eyes were
on her intently. Really bright blue eyes.

"I always thought that was a tale, about the seeding, but
I guess it's true." She felt silly not being able to think of
his name. One of the MacCoy brothers, the youngest. He
often delivered feed to their place, and he always spoke to
her when he saw her. He knew manners. She remembered
his blue eyes.

"No...it's true. Conditions have to be right, though.
Can't seed just any clouds."

She couldn't think of what to say to that. It was time to
quit all this, too. She would just have to go in the store to
get Joey, because she couldn't leave now.

Right at the moment the MacCoy man nodded at her and
moved to leave, the glass door to the store opened behind
them. Charlene glanced over her shoulder to see Joey step
out.

He came down the couple of steps, keeping his head pointed downward, showing the crown of his hat. He didn't raise his head until he reached them, and then he didn't look at Charlene, but at the man beside her.

"I don't believe I ordered any cattle feed, Mason," Joey said. "I told Adam I wanted the fourteen percent pellet horse feed. Thirty sacks of it." Charlene had always marveled that Joey could speak as if all was normal, even if a tornado was about to sweep them away.

"Oh?" The MacCoy brother—Mason—raised his eyebrows. "Well, I guess I got your order mixed up with someone else's. I'll just unload 'em."

"No. I'll drive over to the warehouse in a few minutes, and you can unload them there," Joey said in a short manner Charlene didn't think was called for.

"Well, okay, if you're sure. I don't mind takin' them back now. I got the dolly."

"I'm sure. You can just go on."

Mason MacCoy's blue eyes came over to hers, and he smiled with them and nodded again, same as tipping his ball cap. She nodded back, and then he rolled his dolly off toward the warehouse, walking with easy strides.

Joey looked from Mason back to Charlene. He had a peculiar sense that something was going on here that he didn't understand. For some reason Mason had been jerking him around. But it seemed to Joey like he couldn't understand a lot these days.

"What do you want, Charlene?" he asked, finally looking at her.

By the look on her face, he knew immediately he had said the wrong thing. It seemed even more of a crime on his part, since he had meant very much to say the right thing. Or to at least avoid saying anything really wrong, and here he'd gone and done it right off.

"What do I *want?*" she said.

The hairs on the back of his neck prickled. He imagined Sheila and the others in the store watching, and this did not help his thought processes.

"What do you think I want?" She was yelling now, and gesturing wildly. "You called me on the phone to say you were leaving me. On the *phone,* Joey."

He didn't know why using the telephone so they didn't have to go through a scene was a bad thing. He didn't think he should say so, though.

"You are just runnin' around with her in front of everyone. How can you do that? How can you carry on with her right in front of your children?" She was leaning forward and looking a little wild-eyed.

"Carryin' on? I'm not carryin' on," he said, feeling prodded into speech.

He didn't think he had ever seen Charlene this mad. And he sure didn't want her to get hysterical right here, but then he followed her pointing hand and was startled to see the old Suburban sitting there off the side of the road. He'd been so jolted by seeing Charlene that he hadn't given a thought to how she had arrived.

"They saw you drivin' her around. How do you think that looks to them…their daddy with his new girlfriend, and he hasn't even spoken to them in a week."

"My girlfriend? She isn't my girlfriend, Charlene." He lowered his voice, hoping to encourage her to lower hers. He sure didn't want Sheila to hear him. "She was just ridin' in the passenger seat. I wasn't touchin' her or anything."

"Fine," she said. "You are drivin' her around in the passenger seat and you have not bothered to come see your children in a week."

She was throwing the accusations at him, and he didn't know which one to answer first.

"I told you I would come by, Charlene. I told you I knew we had to work it out, but that I needed some time to think things through. We agreed we both needed time, and you said that was okay," he reminded her.

She had folded her arms in a way that pushed her breasts out. He wished she wouldn't do that. Looking down into her accusing eyes, he had the shocking urge to take a hold of her and shake her. He didn't think she should have done this right here. This was not the place. There was the telephone.

"I said okay when you said a few days. When were you really plannin' to come? Ten years from now?"

"There isn't any need to yell about this, Charlene. Not here."

"You're worried about me yellin'? You have left us, and my yelling is your main worry right this minute?"

"Look...I don't want to fight," he said. "I didn't think you'd want to see me, is why I haven't been around. And I figured we'd get in a fight, and I didn't want that, especially in front of the kids." They never argued in front of the kids—if Charlene was going to bless him out, she would wait until they were alone.

"I thought I would wait awhile for things to settle down before I came around. I need to get myself a little straightened out first, Charlene. That's all." He wanted her to understand, but he didn't know how to explain. "And you know you can page me if there's an emergency. I'll call you back."

He thought for one horrible moment that she was going to hit him.

Then she took a deep breath and put her hands on her hips. "What are we supposed to do in the meantime, Joey, while you're gettin' yourself straightened out? Are we just supposed to sit and wait?'' Her angry eyes demanded an answer.

"I guess not," he said, and clamped his jaw tight. His mind was whirling, and he was afraid he was either going to cry or punch her. He simply had no sense of control over himself these days. It was a safe bet he wasn't going to say anything right.

"Oh, Joey." Charlene rubbed her upper arms. Joey looked so lost that she had an urge to hug him. Then, squinting in the bright light, she looked out at the Suburban.

"Well, I suppose it doesn't matter about me. You can leave me, write me off like I never existed, but are you just going to let your children feel like you've abandoned them? That you don't love them anymore?"

His eyes came up.

Her panic had given way to righteousness for her children. She grabbed it and held on to it. "No matter what you do, you cannot deny those are your children, and they need their father."

"Charlene…I know they are my kids. I love them, but right now they are fine with you. You've always been a much better mother than I have a father."

Her tender inclination vanished. "I didn't conceive those babies by myself," she said.

He blinked and looked away.

"Joey, no matter how you think you don't measure up as a father, that doesn't mean you get to quit being one. You are their father, and they need to know that you still love them. That just because you've left me, you are not leavin' them. I suppose they'll survive without your constant presence, but they won't be able to get over it if they believe that in any way they caused you runnin' off."

He frowned and gave that shake of his head that was really annoying Charlene. She waited, but he didn't say anything. Joey could do that—wait her out. Most of their arguments had always been one-sided, because Joey would just shut up, and she felt called on to speak and get things out. He was putting it all on her now, just like he always did.

"What are you going to do, Joey?"

He shrugged, pulling inside himself in the way that made Charlene so mad that she wanted to turn around and walk off. She wondered if she should just tell him what to do; maybe she should say to him: "Joey, just get in your truck, we are goin' home."

She said, "Joey, can you come speak to them right now? Just talk with them, set up a time to go out for pizza or something. Show them you will always be their daddy. Make some sort of explanation to them, Joey, and assure them that you love them."

His blue eyes came up to hers. "Do you think that Larry Joe is gonna go along with that, Charlene? He hasn't said two words to me in three months."

She bit her bottom lip, then said, "He's your son, Joey. You two may not see eye to eye, but he *is* your son. They are your children, and you need to come over there now and speak with them."

She turned then, trusting he would follow, and he did. The back door window on the Suburban went down, and Jojo poked her head out and said in her worried little voice, "Hi, Daddy."

"Hi, pumpkin."

As Charlene slipped into the seat, she saw a relieved smile on Joey's face. It was a smile that made her hurt.

He crouched and talked to Danny J. and Jojo through the window for a couple of minutes, asking how they were and what they were doing and would they like to go for pizza tomorrow night.

He never said anything to Larry Joe, who wouldn't even look around at his father. Larry Joe kept his face straight ahead and rubbed the beginnings of his mustache, and every thirty seconds he gunned the motor to keep the air conditioner working effectively, no doubt thinking of his aunt Rainey's delicate condition. Charlene just gripped the armrest and kept her lips shut tight.

Four

The City Hall thermometer reads 104°

When Larry Joe pulled into the drive, the empty corrals were spread out in front of Charlene. The scent of dust came in the window Jojo lowered in order to call to the three horses that came running up to the pasture fence. "Hello, Bo…Dog…Lulu. Hello!"

Gazing straight ahead, she watched a dust devil go twirling past the gaping barn door and the training pen, where the gate was hanging open, one corner snagged on the ground. Joey was always going to fix it.

Larry Joe followed the curve to the house and parked, as they always did in the summer, beneath the cooling shade of the big elm. While the rest of them got out, Charlene sat there, staring at the house. At the door where Joey had swept her into his arms and carried her across the threshold. She had slipped from his arms just inside the door, and, trying to catch her, they'd both ended up on the floor.

Larry Joe bent and looked at her through his open door, rubbing his hand over his short-cropped, sun-kissed hair.

"I'm goin' over to Randy's, Mom, until we have to go to work," he told her. "You'll be here to drive Mom anywhere she might need to go, won't you, Aunt Rainey?"

"I'll be here until Monday, hon."

Looking to Charlene again, he said, "Guess I'll go on, then. I have my pager, if you need me."

Charlene gave him a hurry-away wave, saying, "Be careful," and kept from flinging herself at him and holding on.

Her eyes lingered on his wiry shoulders as he strode away and got into his bright yellow truck. The engine roared, and he sped off down the driveway, leaving dust billowing up around the Ford logo on the tailgate.

Jojo stopped at her window and looked in. "Maa-ma?"

"I'm just going to sit here awhile, honey," she told her.

"Come on in, y'all," Rainey said, "Your mother just needs some peace and quiet for a few minutes. I'll make us some milk shakes. The ice cream will be perfect for that now."

Charlene didn't seem to have the energy to move. She had this fearful feeling that she might simply fall to pieces, her arms and legs scatter all around, if she got out and moved. She felt guilty; mothers weren't supposed to come undone. And one thing she had always been was a good mother. She might have failed in the wife department, but no one could say she had failed motherhood.

Opening the glove box, she got out several 7-Eleven napkins, to be ready in case she started crying. While she was rifling around in there, she found the vehicle insurance verification—the date to expire was two days away, which startled her a little. She generally kept on top of these things.

She sat there, staring at the form. She had always kept the checkbook and paid the bills. That wouldn't change for her. What was Joey going to do? He hadn't written but about five checks in all their married life, and those were when Charlene had been in the hospital having a baby. Maybe Joey intended to go off and live his life while she continued to write checks for him.

Lifting her eyes, she gazed out the windshield, her mind going through all the imaginings a woman in her situation was prone to.

She blamed Joey; she blamed herself; she blamed God; she blamed "the slut"—and she blamed herself again. She went through every single thing she had said, cursing her stupidity and Joey's idiocy, and then went through every single thing she wished she had said. This involved arguments dating back twenty years.

She planned revenge. She wanted Joey to suffer as she was suffering. She planned to mark him out of the family Bible and to shred the Mobetta shirts he had left in the closet. She planned what she would wear to court. She planned to drop dead to show him how he had hurt her; and to be done with the shame of being a woman who could not keep her husband. She planned how she could flaunt herself with other men to show him. She planned what she would say to the "the slut" when she ran into her at the IGA. She planned how she could get "the slut's" black hair to fall out. She planned what she would say and do when he showed up at her door and begged to be allowed to come home. She planned with all the fury and relentless accusation of a brokenhearted woman who has been set aside.

Once she looked down and saw that she had shredded not only the napkins but the insurance form.

"Mama's still out in the car, Aunt Rainey."

Rainey was coming in from the laundry room. Jojo sat on the kitchen counter, looking out the window while finishing her milk shake, sucking and making noise with the straw. Rainey noticed that her niece watched her mother continuously in a manner of a little puppy that doesn't want to let its human out of sight.

"Yes, she is, sugar." Rainey glanced at the clock. Charlene had been sitting there thirty minutes now. "I'll take her out a milk shake. Bet she needs it."

Rainey, who had suffered only a brief week of nausea, had in her pregnant state become quite cognizant of her own nutritional requirements, and since this crisis with Joey, she had begun to worry greatly over her sister's diet, which had in the past week consisted mainly of coffee, ice tea and bags of Murray cookies. She feared Charlene might now be in such an emotional state that she could have a breakdown, or even a heart attack. Plenty of perfectly healthy people had heart attacks under stress, and after sweating great heaps of calcium and magnesium out of their bodies. Hoping to insure against such a catastrophe, she ground up a couple of her own calcium and magnesium tablets and added them to the drink, along with a smidgen of cod liver oil.

Charlene was gazing right out the windshield, but Rainey didn't think she really saw her come up. She sort of jumped when Rainey spoke to her.

"I brought you a milk shake." She passed the glass through the window. "You need something nutritious and cool."

Charlene's face was pale as buttermilk, and the wisps of hair curling around her face were wet with sweat.

Rainey said, "You've been sittin' here for a half an hour, hon. Why don't you come on in and cool off?"

Charlene's golden-green eyes looked up at her and then at the house. "I don't think I can go inside," she said. "It's like I know I'll be goin' in without Joey."

Rainey's throat got all tight. "Well, it isn't like Joey was in there that much," she said, with some aggravation because Charlene was scaring her. "And until today, you haven't laid eyes on him in a week."

She watched Charlene's manicured fingertips shake as they played with the straw in the glass.

"Honey, let's go sit on the porch, where it's cooler."

Charlene shook her head.

"Charlene, you could get heatstroke." Rainey considered opening the door and pulling Charlene out.

"It's not so hot in the shade here," Charlene said in a voice that sounded as if she was sort of fading right away.

Feeling as if her presence was needed to keep Charlene here on earth, Rainey went around and slipped into the driver's seat.

Looking for something to say, she began, "Do you know the sight I saw last week? Helen out in her yard in these little shorts that show her fanny every time she bent over. She's had her eyes lifted—does she think that the job went all the way down to her thighs? Her face may look forty now, but her thighs still look a worn fifty-two."

"Helen's havin' a hard time right now, with Freddy like he is," Charlene said in a sad voice that put Rainey to shame.

"Well, I know. I shouldn't be so judgmental." Rainey worried her fingernail in a slit on the leather steering wheel cover. "I don't think that runnin' around looking purely tacky is a great help to dealin' with a husband who's had a nervous breakdown, though."

She was of the opinion that Helen and Freddy drove each other crazy; this seemed to be a general consensus with everyone, really, even her Harry, who was a psychiatrist. Harry put it nicer, however, saying that Helen and Freddy were codependents, which Rainey said was a fancy way of saying they made each other crazy.

She saw Charlene absently playing with the straw she'd stuck in the milk shake. Rainey told her to just take a little sip. "It'll make you feel better, hon. You haven't hardly had anything all day."

"Well, some good's comin' out of this. I'm losin' weight."

"You do not need to lose weight," Rainey said. "It is never good to go losing weight when you are under stress."

Rainey wanted to cry for Charlene. Mostly, she guessed, she wanted to cry for herself, because seeing Charlene like this made her very shaky. It seemed like all of her loved ones were sort of falling apart. Her brother Freddy had cracked up; her sister-in-law Helen was turning to tacky; and their daddy had taken up flying the Confederate flag with zeal. Now Joey had let them all go, and Charlene was barely holding on. This was all very frightening to Rainey. For most of her life she'd been the one who couldn't seem to get it together. Now that she had pretty well straightened her life out, everyone else seemed to be going to hell in a handbasket.

Charlene held the milk shake on her thigh while she stared at the dashboard. Rainey reached for the glass and took a couple of good sips. She didn't see a need for the healthy drink to go to waste.

"I keep thinking the silliest things," Charlene admitted. "I was thinking that maybe if I went into the shower, I'd have a good cry."

"I don't think that's such a silly thought," Rainey said. "The shower is good for cryin'. The water washes the tears away and covers the sound. I cry in the shower all the time."

"You do?"

"Well, not lately," Rainey admitted, giving a little smile.

Charlene looked away out the windshield. Rainey saw in an instant how it must appear to her sister: Rainey with her whole life just blossoming out, while Charlene's was withering and dying on the vine. She felt suddenly very guilty over her good life. And afraid, too.

"Talk about silly thoughts," Rainey said, "you know what I've been thinkin'? I've been thinkin' that Harry is my third husband, and I wouldn't have gotten the courage to marry him but for looking at how you handle things, Charlene. Sometimes I get scared. Sometimes I think it is impossible to stay happy forever, and what if someday it all falls apart with Harry and me."

"It won't. You'll have ups and downs, but you and Harry are made for each other. He's your third and last."

"I'm not certain people are made for each other." Now that she was thinking of it, she was beginning to feel really badly. "If you and Joey can't make it after twenty-one years, that doesn't bode well for the rest of us."

"Rainey, you are my dear sister, but right now I am in my own crisis, and I don't need to share in a fantasy crisis with you." Charlene fairly shouted at her.

"I'm sorry," Rainey said, contrite. "I just want you to know I understand. You aren't alone."

Charlene looked at her, squeezed her arm and sighed greatly as she again gazed out the windshield.

They both sat there for a few silent minutes in which Rainey felt helpless, but then Mason MacCoy popped into her mind.

"What were you and Mason talking about this afternoon?" she asked.

Charlene looked startled. "Who?"

"You and Mason, when you were waiting for Joey to come out of MacCoy's Feed and Seed Store?"

"Oh, he'd just brought some feed he thought Joey had

ordered. We were talkin' about the weather. You know. He
was just bein' nice."

"Well, it sure looked like you two were having a full
conversation. Mason is a real polite person. He used to
come in to Blaine's when I worked there—came to get his
grandaddy's medicine, and Lord, that was a bill. He paid
for a lot of it, too. I guess he lived with his grandaddy and
took care of him. The rumor is that he's been in prison
but I don't know if that is the truth."

Charlene said, "I just thought we would work it all out
and Joey would come home." She apparently had not been
listening to Rainey.

"I sort of thought so, too." Rainey was really surprised
that Joey had not come home. She was surprised that he
could possibly make a move without Charlene helping him.
"And he still might."

"Why do you think Daddy never left Mama when she
had that affair? Even when she had you, he never left her.'

Rainey had to look down, and her heart beat fast. "I
don't know. People just do things differently."

"I was really scared then that Daddy might leave. I
would hear them talking sometimes. They'd fight, and
Daddy would storm out, and Mama would make chicken
pot pie or maybe just biscuits, and eventually Daddy would
come home to eat it. I'd ask her, 'Mama, why are you
cookin' so much?' and she'd say 'I'm makin' enough for
your Daddy, when he comes home.'"

There was a tone in Charlene's voice that made Rainey
shiver.

"I made those two chocolate cakes last week for Joey,
tryin' to be ready if he came home," she said. "He loved
my chocolate cake from scratch."

Rainey knew this, even though Charlene hadn't said it
at the time. Then she realized she was playing her fingernail

in the slit on the steering wheel cover. The truck was wearing out.

Rainey was getting really hot and thinking of getting out and going into the air-conditioning, where she could call Harry and make certain he was still there and being her husband, when Charlene burst out with, "I just don't know what I'm goin' to do, Rainey!" Her eyes were wild. "I really don't know what I'm going to do."

"Oh, Charlene, divorce is not the end of the world. Life does go on, and you are not alone. Me and Harry and Daddy are here." It seemed a little silly to make any mention of Freddy, who even when he wasn't crazy had never been a great help. "And you have the family house. Mama left that house to you, and it is yours, so you're not without resources. There's plenty of room for you and the kids and Daddy."

"Oh, good grief," Charlene said. At least her panic had turned to annoyance. "I can just see it. Me and the kids and Daddy and all those old women he keeps taking in nowadays. It's like an old women's home. I don't know why he can't take in old men."

"He does. It's just that they keep dyin' faster than the women."

Charlene stared at Rainey, and Rainey stared back.

"Well, I do not want to go back to that house," Charlene said emphatically. "I don't care that Mama left it to me. As long as Daddy's alive it is his house, really. And how would I move everything? Just look at that garage."

Rainey looked and had to agree it would really be a job. The garage was so stuffed the door had to be left open.

Charlene said, "You know what I've done for the past fifteen years? I've been a mother and a homemaker. The most I've done that I could put on a resume was that I've substituted up at school, minding a classroom of kids. I can't *do* anything. I have no education. It would take months to get my beautician's license again. I can't even drive, Rainey.''

''You can drive. You just won't drive,'' Rainey felt called on to point out, although she felt vaguely sorry for doing so at this moment.

Charlene had not driven for almost six years, since the time she had collided with a drink truck, giving Rainey a hard enough jolt to cause her to lose her baby. The doctors had thought at the time that Rainey would have lost the baby anyway, but no one had ever been able to convince Charlene of that.

''Would you want me to drive you right now?'' Charlene asked. For an instant her depressed state seemed to fall away, and she gazed at Rainey's belly with that raised eyebrow that, as always, said she knew some things.

''I would ride with you after you have a little practice,'' Rainey said.

She realized then that she was holding her belly, and she moved her hand and smoothed her shirt. It was a little distressing that she was not bigger in the belly. She was not a skinny woman, but she was a hard-muscled one. Harry loved her body, she recalled with a pleasurable warmth. He liked to run his hands over her and say, ''You are beautiful.'' Harry was the most open, honest man she had ever known.

''You know what is the worst?'' Charlene said, demanding.

''No...what?''

''The worst is that I've loved Joey since I was twenty-two years old. Any time I felt angry at him, I'd pray for God to help me love him. I would think of how Mama had hurt Daddy so much, and how I used to lie in that bed and pray for Daddy to come home. I never wanted Joey to leave me, so I've worked and worked and tried to be the best wife in the world, and I've still messed it up.''

Charlene went to crying mad then. She had to open the glove box again to find more napkins for her runny nose. That was the awful thing about crying—a runny nose. Here one was having a major heartbreak, about to go crazy, and one had to deal with hardly being able to breathe and snot running everywhere.

''I have to get myself together,'' she mumbled to Rainey around the napkin at her nose. ''I have to take care of my children. They can't have a mother comin' apart.''

Blowing her nose, she straightened up to go inside and be cheerful.

Five

The City Hall thermometer reads 82°

Saturday morning, when Winston came in the back door after the flag raising and tending the rosebushes, he found Mildred sitting at the kitchen table in her fuchsia silk bathrobe and white sleep turban, her face powdered and blushed and lips colored brightly.

"Northrupt's got a new flag," he told her as he laid her rose on the table. "He's gone to half a size larger."

Mildred was digging into her purse, pulling out things one by one. She seemed to take this inventory on a regular basis. She paused, looked at him and blinked. "A bigger flag?"

"Yes. He just had to beat me out. That's why he did it. A whole new rig that rolls straight down."

"Well, that's nice." Mildred had returned to digging in her handbag.

"It almost touches the ground. He's gonna have to raise his holder if he wants to be sure it doesn't touch the ground."

"Here they are...my coupons! I have one for Jimmy Dean sausage. Vella gave it to me."

Winston gazed at her.

"Jimmy Dean Sausage, hot, medium or mild," Mildred

read from the coupon, then said, "Vella says Belinda has real high blood pressure."

Winston wondered at the woman.

"Ruthanne's blood pressure isn't so good, either. What are we going to have for breakfast, Winston?"

He sighed and said, "I imagine we'll whip up somethin'." By we, he meant him, because Mildred never did anything but pour orange juice and maybe get toast out of the toaster, and they didn't let Ruthanne near the stove.

He threw out yesterday's flowers and placed the new blooms in the green vase. Then he poured himself a cup of coffee.

"We only have two eggs and no sausage," Mildred said.

He snapped open the newspaper. It was thin today, always was on Saturdays. The top headline read More Glitches in the Time and Temperature. They were sure having a problem with the new sign. The time still did not display, which probably was a blessing, because it wasn't keeping the correct time, anyway. They finally got it to bong on the hour, only the few times it successfully bonged, most thought it was cannon fire from up at Fort Sill. The mayor was taking a lot of flak over this sign.

Mildred said, "We have this coupon, but the sausage is still down at the store. Oh, yes, it's still in date. Expiration 12-31. It doesn't have a blood pressure warning. Maybe it should have."

He looked up from the paper. Mildred's own blood pressure was no great shakes, but it didn't stop her from eating. Food had become a main reason for Mildred's living. He probably should be glad. Once sex had been her focus, but since the stroke it was food, and that really was easier to deal with.

She was again digging into her big handbag. "We could

have a small breakfast and go out for a big lunch,'' she suggested and stopped to look up at him.

"Okay. We could drive up to the Squire's Cafeteria in Lawton. How 'bout that?'' In Lawton he could buy a new flag at the army surplus store. Northrupt had raised, and he was going to call, by golly.

"Oh, yes…'' Mildred fairly glowed. "And I have some packets of Thousand Island dressing in here somewhere, I'm sure I do.''

Winston moved down to the next headline, Heat Wave Takes Toll. He hoped it wasn't anyone he knew. No, they were talking about the condition of the roads.

"Squire's makes a really good green salad, but I don't much like their dressing. That dressing Charlene makes is really good—she should bottle it. Do you think now that she and Joey are broke up, Charlene might like to have Sunday dinner *every* Sunday?''

Mildred's question finally got through, and he looked up to see her gazing hopefully at him.

She added, "It might take her mind off her troubles, you know, to keep busy. She is such a good hostess.''

This was not the first time she had suggested Charlene should have dinner every week. No restaurant was able to please Mildred quite as well as Charlene could.

"For all we know Charlene and Joey might be back together. I don't think we need to jump to conclusions.''

"They weren't yesterday. You know that. When we saw Larry Joe, I asked, and he said they weren't. Larry Joe needs new shoes. Why does he wear those beat-up boots? Maybe you could buy him new ones.''

Winston gazed at her. She was not looking at him but at the array of coupons and food packages in front of her.

"I don't see how they can ever get back together,'' she

said, her voice turning sharp. "Not after all that Joey has done."

"Well, maybe it isn't so much what Joey has done," Winston inserted, "as what they both do about it. And it isn't anyone else's business."

"No...I suppose not. But he has just humiliated her."

"He's just run off, not dunked her head in a puddle."

"How can you say that? Oh, here's that Thousand Island dressing. I knew I had it. Are you going to ask Charlene about this Sunday's dinner?" She lifted hopeful eyes.

Winston said, "I imagine Charlene might better like it if we asked her to come out to a restaurant and eat with us once in a while."

Her face fell. "Oh...yes, I suppose she might."

"Have you smelled your rose?" he asked, giving up and folding his paper under his arm.

"Oh...no." She held the rose up and inhaled deeply, and a slow smile came over her face. "Oh..."

"I'll go get showered, and then I'll come down and make some toast or something."

Leaving Mildred happily returning to surveying the contents of her purse, he took his coffee and the vase of fresh blossoms upstairs.

The sounds of splashing and Ruthanne humming "Amazing Grace" came through the partially opened door of the hall bathroom as he passed. Ruthanne wasn't being provocative; she just tended to forget. He shut the door for her, and she called sweetly, "Thank you," as if to some stranger off the street come in to shut her bathroom door.

Winston continued on down to his own room, where he set the vase of roses beside the photograph of Coweta atop the dresser. "Where are you?" he asked the photograph.

His wife had not paid him a visit in a good many days. He thought this rude. And he thought she needed to be here for this new crisis with one of their children. She was the one everyone had always turned to in a crisis.

He had begun to feel someone looking at him outside, and now he wanted to see his wife, and she wouldn't show up. He thought about calling out to her, whispering around, maybe, but that seemed to be too close to the narrow line between full and lost faculties.

Six

The City Hall thermometer reads 101°

Charlene spent most of Saturday in anxious anticipation of Joey's arrival to get Jojo and Danny J. that evening. By the time he came, she had done a major fix-up. She had washed her hair, using a lemon rinse and brushing it dry in the sunshine to bring out the shine. Rainey had repainted Charlene's fingernails and toenails to go with her dress. Charlene had the house downright cool so her makeup wouldn't melt, and she had her hair curled and piled atop her head, earrings dangling at her ears, and was dressed in a cotton floral print sundress that was cut to accentuate everything she had—which was in generous proportion up top—and camouflage some of which she had too much of a little lower.

In the privacy of her bathroom, she stood in front of the mirror and tugged at the dress's bodice.

The cut of the dress was not the motherly sort she normally wore; it barely covered what it was supposed to, which had been the idea when she'd bought it—when she'd been so desperately trying to capture Joey's attention. On the two occasions that she had worn the dress, however, Joey hadn't really seemed to notice at all. This memory dampened her faith that she might succeed in making him sorry for what he had left behind. But, still, she was driven to try.

In a further attempt to provoke a subconscious sensual aura, she bent over and whipped off her panties. She had read of this little trick in one of the women's magazines out of New York City, which was always having stuff like that in it—how to be more alluring and sexy, all stuff that didn't much relate to the life of a middle-aged housewife in middle America, but she read it at the doctor's office anyway, wondering what went on in the lives of beautiful New York City women, who probably never had to clean a toilet. Each time she had tried the little stunt of going without panties, she felt quite bold and pleased with her secret; however, she always worried what might happen should she get caught in a wind that lifted her dress or have some sort of accident.

When Joey arrived, she peeked through the curtain of the window beside the door. She watched him get slowly out of the truck. He stood a moment as if uncertain which door to approach. As if maybe afraid to come to the door at all, and this was highly annoying. Was she such a frightening woman?

Hand grasping the knob, she whisked open the door and greeted him. "Hello, Joey."

This threw him into a startled look, which she immediately handled by welcoming him inside with all the grace of a founding member of the Junior League.

"Come on in. Jojo and Danny J. are ready and waiting with anticipation."

She smiled her warmest smile and spoke in her most charming voice. As she moved, she was conscious of the dress swirling around her bare legs.

"Here they are," she said, as if presenting him with a gift.

She swept her children to their feet and out the door with their father, and stood on the front step waving them off. She stood there next to the scrubby climbing rosebush, waving while the truck drove down the drive and turned onto the highway, until it disappeared around the corner.

Then she came back into the house, slammed the door and flopped down on the couch, saying to Rainey, "I felt like the faithful family dog, left behind."

Joey slipped into one side of the booth, while his two youngest children slipped into the other, both of them staring at him. He had the feeling they were looking into the deep shame of his mind.

He reached over and took the menu from behind the napkin holder, and in the process he managed to knock over the saltshaker. He set it straight, then brushed the spilled salt into his hand, and then he didn't know what to do with it. He finally just brushed it off his hands under the table. Jojo bent and looked underneath.

Joey opened the menu. "Do you want the works?" he asked.

"All right," Danny J. said, with a nod. He was slouched in the corner of the booth in a manner that looked obnoxious. Joey thought maybe he should tell Danny J. to sit up, but he didn't know why the boy shouldn't slouch if he wanted to. He thought maybe good fathers would know, but he didn't.

He looked over at Jojo. She stared at him with her large hazel eyes. She had not said a word since he'd picked them up. She had sat very close to him, though, and smiled at him.

"Jojo, is that okay with you?" He felt as if he had to keep his voice real low or she might jump up and run like a skittish colt.

"I don't like the olives."

"You can pick the olives off," Danny J. said.

"We'll just get it without the olives," Joey said, smiling at Jojo. "That okay?"

She nodded and gave a little grin that made him feel good.

"I like the olives," Danny J. said with some force, causing Jojo's grin to disappear.

Joey looked at him. Danny J. stared back for just an instant before turning to look out the window. Joey saw a teenage girl getting out of a car. Her midriff down to below her belly button was bare, and he didn't think she had a bra on. And he knew his son was watching this girl.

"How 'bout we get two pizzas?" Joey said, feeling pleased to have come up with the logical idea that he was fairly certain Charlene would have started out with.

Just then, at the very moment of that thought, he glanced again out the window and was startled by seeing Charlene's Suburban driving slowly past. Charlene, her face with dark sunglasses staring right at the restaurant...Rainey at the wheel.

Checking up on him, he thought with irritation. But then he wondered if she was coming to join them. Charlene could hardly let the children out of her sight. No, the truck went on past. She was just checking on him, and his irritation slipped a little into disappointment.

"Daddy...Daddy, I have to go to the bathroom." Jojo was scooting out of the booth.

"Oh...okay. You know where it is?" Joey looked around with some confusion.

"Yes."

Watching her go, he felt a little at a loss and experienced a strong longing for Charlene to turn around and come back inside and handle everything. He turned back in the booth, and Danny J. was gazing at him again.

The City Hall thermometer reads 99°

After making certain of the whereabouts of Danny J. and Jojo, Charlene had Rainey drive over to Stidham's Texaco, so she could see Larry Joe, too. He worked at Stidham's part-time. Norm Stidham wouldn't put him on full-time because then he'd have to pay him benefits.

"Don't you think you're bein' a little neurotic?" Rainey asked.

"Well, I think it could possibly be expected," Charlene said. "Just go on over there and get some gas. I like to keep the tank filled, in case of an emergency. And I'm not being any more neurotic than you are driving careless. I wish you'd watch where you're driving. I didn't wear any panties."

"What?"

"When we got into that argument about whether to take your car or mine, I forgot to go back in and put on panties." Charlene didn't like to ride around in Rainey's—really Harry's—little Mustang. It sat too close to the ground for her comfort, and she thought Rainey's driving required more metal around them. "I don't want to have a wreck and have the paramedics show up, or maybe get sprawled out for all the world to see."

What Charlene really felt was an anxiety about being away from home. Almost as soon as Rainey had sped out of the driveway and onto the highway, Charlene had begun to experience a rather desperate urge to go back home, and now it had a strong hold on her. She felt as if she had lost her husband, and she might therefore lose her children, and her home might somehow disappear, too.

Rainey drove over to the Texaco. Randy Stidham was pumping the gas, and Larry Joe was in the garage working on an engine. He wasn't one bit surprised to see her. Charlene gave him a hug. Larry Joe never seemed to mind that she hugged him right in front of anyone who happened to be around. He would hug her right back. It always flitted through her mind that this might be some part of the conflict between her son and his daddy.

She felt much better when Rainey pulled back out on the road. She knew exactly where her children were, and Joey, too—for the time being anyway.

"How about barbeque from Blaine's?" Rainey asked with a certain eagerness. "They've started serving barbeque sandwiches that are real good."

Charlene told her fine. She really wasn't hungry, but all the way there Rainey kept talking about the barbeque sandwich like it was the last food on earth, and she whipped into an empty parking space so fast, Charlene thought she might take the front off a little Nissan that appeared to challenge her for the space.

"Rainey, I know my truck is a little beat-up, but it is the only one I have," Charlene said. "I don't need you to wreck it."

"That guy's car was littler than us. He should know that we have the right-of-way. The bigger vehicle always has the right-of-way."

"Maybe he doesn't know that, because that is a rule you made up."

"It is a commonly understood rule," Rainey said matter-of-factly. "And if he doesn't understand it, he shouldn't be drivin'."

Rainey was focusing a worried eye on the drugstore. "Look at this crowd. There's always the Blaines' table, though, and they still let me sit there, even though I don't work here anymore. Mr. Blaine hopes I'll come back. Belinda drives him crazy.''

Charlene removed her sunglasses and looked around. She had noticed the activity all up and down Main Street.

"I don't think I want to go in," she said.

This statement upset Rainey, who had become quite hungry. "What do you mean, you don't want to go in? The whole point of comin' up here was to get you out and about, Charlene. You've been cooped up in the house all week.''

"Yes, and look what happened to me when I finally got out—I saw my husband with his girlfriend.''

"You needed to see Joey. You needed to see the truth of it and to speak to him.''

"And I did that. That was enough.''

Rainey calmed herself. Force never worked with Charlene. "You'll enjoy it, hon…a nice change of scene, maybe say hello to some nice friends.''

"I don't want to run into Sheila Arnett." Charlene was gazing at Blaine's Drugstore as if it might at any moment blow up.

Rainey said, "I've only seen Sheila Arnett in Blaine's once or twice. She's the type that goes up to Lawton to get everything. It'll be all right.''

"I didn't wear any panties, and I don't want to see anybody.''

"Oh, for goodness sake, Charlene. No one can see you don't have on panties. That dress is not see-through. And lots of women go without underpants. Men, too. Harry does all the time, says it is very comfortable under jeans.''

Charlene was a little surprised by this. Harry had never seemed quite as freewheeling as Rainey.

Rainey said, "I'll bet if we stopped people and asked them, a fourth of these people are not wearing underwear,

and it is no sin. Now, come on." She grabbed her purse
and opened the door.

"You go on in and eat in there if you want. I'll wait."
She looked out the windshield and held tight to the armrest
in the middle of the seat. "I feel like if I get out I'm just
so bare…like I'm right out there for everyone to see, and
they'll come up to me and want to say something about me
and Joey, and the whole time they're thinkin', 'There's that
woman who couldn't keep her husband satisfied at home.'"

Rainey said in a patently patient manner, "Lots of men
and women fool around. And it is because of an unfulfilled
need somewhere, but it is not the fault of one or the other.
My Monte played around. I don't really think it was my
fault, unless it was that I mothered him too much."

"I just don't want to get out, okay?"

Rainey blinked and then said, "Do you want coleslaw
with your barbeque sandwich?"

"No."

Rainey got out and stepped up on the sidewalk and
walked the few yards down to the drugstore in her long-
legged, big-belly-that-she-didn't-have fashion, sidestepped
the drip from the air conditioner in the transom and disappeared inside.

Charlene looked around out the windows of the Suburban. Valentine was quite lively on a Saturday evening in
summer.

The cafe and Blaine's Drugstore and Soda Fountain had
started staying open until nine o'clock, trying to compete
with the new chain places out on the highway. All through
the summer months there was Saturday night bingo at the
Senior Center that had moved into the old Western Auto
two doors down from Blaine's. Tucked between the drugstore and Senior Center, Grace Florist kept later hours to

catch customers on their way into either. Across the street was the Family Pool Hall that was trying to give teens somewhere to go, and the Little Opry, featuring a lot of local musicians, had opened in the old Starlight Theatre just last month. Charlene had wanted to go one night, had dressed up to go, but Joey had had a horse get injured, so they hadn't made it.

Just then she saw a couple of women from her church approach along the sidewalk. She reached down and tilted the seat, laid her head back and closed her eyes; if she pretended to nap, she wouldn't have to act like she saw them. Through her slit eyelids, she saw the women pass on by, their heads tilted toward each other, as if they were whispering to one another: "She didn't keep him happy in bed." "When it's cold at home, the husband goes looking for warmer pastures." "If he doesn't get it at home, he'll get it somewhere."

She found her sunglasses and put them on. Maybe people might still recognize her, but she could pretend she didn't see them.

It was so hot. The temperature on the City Hall sign still read 98°, and here it was near seven o'clock.

She rolled down her window and then scooted over to roll down the window on the driver's side, letting a breeze that smelled like hot concrete and dust blow through.

Funny how such a breeze could be nice simply because of being familiar. Made her remember being a child and her thighs sticking to the plastic seat of the big winged-fender Plymouth her mother used to drive. Mama had liked to drive. Mama would put her foot down on the accelerator and send that car flying so fast it pushed a person into the seat cushion.

Blinking, she jerked her foot off the pedal where she hadn't realized she'd placed it and dropped her hands to her lap, turning her gaze out the windows to watch people, mostly the women, whom she studied, noting their various stages of fix-up. A teenage girl hurried across the street toward the Little Opry. She wore a short skirt halfway up her thighs.

Rainey sometimes wore skirts like that. Charlene lifted her dress and examined her legs. Her legs weren't bad, although they weren't twenty-five anymore, either.

Time had passed her by. She wore long dresses and long hair, and all around her women were wearing their skirts above the knee and cutting off their hair.

She had noticed the short hair trend first on television news anchorwomen, then on the soap opera stars, especially those turning into their fifties, who whacked their hair right off.

Sheila Arnett had sleek chin-length hair, bobbed and tucked behind her ears. She looked really modern, like those models in the western-wear catalogs. Sheila Arnett was no more than thirty-five, Charlene guessed.

Reaching up and twisting the rearview mirror so she could see herself without really appearing to, Charlene mentally tried on a number of different shorter styles.

Activity in front of the Senior Center drew her attention. The senior citizen van pulled up, and people got out. Then there was Daddy getting out. Daddy was one of the number callers for the bingo. That surprised everyone. He wasn't much of a talker, but here he'd started calling those bingo numbers in a booming voice. And he'd started looking after old people, after Mama had taken care of him for sixty-five years. There he was this minute, helping old ladies out of the bus. Just went to show people changed, or else it was inside of them all along and just came out one day.

Watching all the old people go into the Senior Center, Charlene wondered what would happen to her when she got old. Would there be someone like her daddy to step in and take care of her? Would she have to take up playing bingo?

Suddenly the appearance of a woman at Charlene's elbow at the window caused her to jump.

"Hello, dear," the woman said with a tender smile.

"Hello."

The woman had hair so white it shone like a halo. It was swept back from her face and in big curls on top. She wasn't young, but she didn't look terribly old.

"You sure do favor Winston," the woman said, smiling so beautifully that Charlene had to smile in return.

"I do?"

The woman knew her daddy. But Charlene was certain she had never seen the woman before. Where had she come from?

"Oh, yes. You have Winston's lovely green eyes."

The woman had a bouquet of red roses in her hand, so she must have walked out of Grace Florist, probably while Charlene had been watching all the seniors.

"I just love the scent of roses." The woman lifted the bouquet of roses and inhaled. "Don't you?"

"Well...yes. Those are lovely flowers," Charlene said, being polite, yet wondering why the woman was standing there beside her, and thinking that maybe she should ask who the woman was, if she could find a polite way to do it.

"I think the scent of roses calms a person, just like a tranquilizer. Here, dear. You try this rose. There aren't any thorns on it. They have this little tool that cuts off the thorns, and if they're careful, they won't hurt the stem at all. I don't think roses last as long without their thorns, though. It's not natural. Everything in this life has a thorn or two. Now, inhale deeply. That's it."

"It is nice." A sort of feathery peacefulness seemed to wash over Charlene. She sniffed again.

"Yes, it is," the woman said, herself again inhaling from the bouquet. "This summer has been hard on roses, I'm afraid, but they're a tough species. They'll survive, and the struggle makes them produce even more beautiful blooms. The ones with the most thorns are the toughest, and the most fragrant, too."

Charlene didn't think hothouse cultivated roses cared one whit what the summer brought.

"Well, now, here comes your sister. So lovely to have seen you, dear."

"Oh...goodbye."

Charlene was already turning her gaze out the windshield to see Rainey coming out of Blaine's, sidestepping the drip, carrying two paper bags. A man was coming with her.

Why, it was that MacCoy from that afternoon at the feed store. Mason MacCoy. Coming right along with Rainey.

And then he was looking right at Charlene. She could not really see his blue eyes at this distance, but she remembered them clear as day.

He nodded and touched the brim of his ball cap. And Charlene smiled at him and nodded in return. He didn't come over with Rainey, though, but kept on walking past and on down the street, and went into the police station at the corner.

Charlene realized she was staring after him when Rainey slipped into the truck. She also realized she still held the single rose. She looked around, starting to point out the woman who had given it to her, and to ask Rainey if she knew who the woman was, but she didn't see her anywhere.

"Well, she was right here just a minute ago, right when you came out of Blaine's."

"Daddy knows a lot of women," Rainey said.

Then they sat there, gazing at each other.

"Well, aren't you gonna take us home?" Rainey asked.

She was poking fun, because Charlene was still sitting on the driver's side behind the steering wheel, and Rainey had gotten in on the passenger side.

"Good heavens, no!"

They had to get out and trade places.

"You are gonna have to start driving again, Charlene, now that Joey's gone."

Inhaling the rose, Charlene let the comment pass.

Seven

The City Hall thermometer reads 90°

It was dark when Joey returned with the children. Charlene walked out to meet the truck when it pulled into the drive. She felt more stable now, at home where she belonged and wearing jeans and a denim shirt. She'd left her hair put up, though, and her earrings on. And she had these hopes fluttering around in her chest, too.

Danny J. said a quick but friendly goodbye to his father. His eyes came around to Charlene, and then he ducked his head, turning. She reached out and touched his hair before he was away and hurrying into the house in the manner of a son who didn't want to hear private things between his parents.

Joey lifted Jojo from the truck seat, and she hugged him with one arm while clinging to the small box of leftover pizza with her other arm. As Joey lowered her to the ground, she hugged and kissed him again and let go with the reluctance of Velcro, turning to wave at her daddy half-way up the walkway.

"Pizza in the refrigerator," Charlene reminded her, feeling the need to say something, make some contact with her daughter.

The door closed, and Charlene and Joey were left standing there. She looked at him, and he looked back. The silvery moon shone on his thick hair and fell over his shoulders. Joey Darnell was a handsome man.

She averted her eyes and managed to say, "They seem to have had a good time."

"We did okay, I guess. Didn't do anything but eat pizza and play video games and pinball."

He toed the concrete drive with his snakeskin boot. He'd dressed very nicely for the occasion with his children. Charlene thought of this and felt warmth wash all over her.

"It was being with you that they needed," she said. "You showin' them that they matter to you."

"Well, of course they matter to me, Charlene."

He glared at her, then dropped his gaze and rubbed the back of his neck.

"I know they do," she said. "I know you love them just like I do, but we have to keep showin' them. Sometimes in such a mess like this the kids get to wondering. We need to make certain they know none of this is their fault."

He nodded, and then he went to again toeing his boot on the drive. The action irritated her. She wanted to kick his foot and shout, Look at me!

Oh, God, help me. Help me to do right. To say whatever I should.

She wondered what he would do if she said, "Joey, come home now."

And then Joey was saying that he was sorry.

"I didn't mean any of this to happen," he said in a low voice, still looking downward. Then slowly his eyes met hers. "I never meant to hurt you, or the kids, Charlene."

Quite surprised by his words, it took Charlene a long moment to answer.

"I know you wouldn't hurt us on purpose, Joey. I know

that." She almost touched him, then stopped, possessed of all manner of nameless fears.

"Yeah...well."

"Joey, I wouldn't hurt you either. I love you."

He glanced at her, then away.

When he didn't respond, she said, "What did I do wrong? What does she give you that I didn't?"

"Look, Charlene, I'm not sleepin' with her," Joey said in a low voice. "I'm not havin' an affair with her. It only happened one time with Sheila. That's all."

"I see."

"I'm stayin' over there at the trailer she has, not in her house. She's exchanging the trailer and her arena and horse barn for me training her horses, so I'm not spendin' any money on it."

Charlene's mind had several moments of pure incoherence, and then she said, "Well, what do you want, a medal?"

"What?"

"For sleeping with her only one time, and now savin' money in a business deal with her. Do you want a medal for all that? Am I supposed to be grateful?"

"I was just tryin' to explain how it is."

"And how is that? Do you even really know? Let me tell you what the facts are. You are over there with her, and I'm here alone, that's how it is. Why, Joey? I'd really like to know what is so wrong with me that you had to run away from me. We've had twenty-one years together and produced three children, and I never wanted to be anything other than your wife." She stopped, clamping her mouth shut.

"It isn't you, it isn't her. It's me. Okay? You didn't do anything...but look at the last year, Charlene. Have you been happy? We've been arguin' and tryin' to patch it up, but we haven't managed to do that, have we? Don't you think I wonder what's wrong with me every time I look at you and see you can hardly look at me?"

"I just knew you were mad at me, and I didn't know what to do about it. But I kept trying, Joey."

"I can say the same thing, Charlene."

"But I'm still here. I'm still tryin' to understand. I'm not running off and havin' an affair."

"That's right. You're still hangin' in there. Well, I got tired of that. I got tired of these arguments that never get us anywhere. I got tired of seein' myself disappointed all the time. I think beatin' a dead horse is about as useless a thing as anybody can do. It's time to try somethin' else now."

"Then you should have said that!" she screamed at him. "You should have told me that from the beginning. You didn't have to desert me."

With that, Joey threw himself into his truck, slammed the door and started the engine. Charlene, humiliated by losing her temper, clamped her mouth tight against further crude yelling.

Whirling, she strode for the house. Reaching the safety of the doorway, she looked over her shoulder and saw Joey roaring away down the drive. Running away from her. *Leaving her again.*

She went into the house and slammed the door. Danny J. stared at her from the hallway, and Jojo and Rainey from the dining room. Charlene burst into tears, causing Danny J. to turn and head back to his room, while Jojo and Rainey came to put their arms around her.

Joey drove straight to Sheila Arnett's place. When he came up the drive, a light glowed from the living room. The next second he let up off the gas, pushed the head-

lights down to parking beams and crept past the house as
quietly as possible. He stopped the truck out front of the
little travel trailer. Dust billowed in the dim yellow lights
and sifted in the window. His shirt stuck to his back when
he got out, even at nearly ten o'clock. The air conditioner
jutting out of the trailer window was going hard, spitting
out hotter air into the night heat.

"Jo-ey?"

His head whipped around. She always said his name like
that, dragged out slowly. Her voice was always a little surprise. It was high-pitched and didn't quite match the smoky
way she looked.

He saw her step off the porch and into the moonlight.
She moved like a cat, drawing a man's eye and making
things happen inside him.

"Good evenin'," he said, stuffing his hands in his back
pockets. Sheila scared him a little.

"I almost didn't hear you drive up. Didn't see your
lights."

"I dimmed them. I didn't want to wake you, if you were
already in bed." He caught her scent, some womanly perfume that wrapped around him like a summer night.

"I was reading. I never get in bed before midnight.
How'd it go with the kids? You were gone awhile. You all
must have had a good time."

He nodded. "It's pretty easy to please kids with pizza
and video games." He shifted a step away, while an inner
voice was saying, Go ahead and be with her...go ahead....

"Would you like to come in for a while? I just opened
a bottle of wine. We could talk."

He stood there a moment, on the edge. But then he just
felt tired of everyone's expectations.

"I thank you all the same, Sheila," he said, "but I don't
have a thing to say right now."

He turned to the camper trailer, holding himself to measured steps, while inside he was running for all he was worth. Entering the trailer, he closed the door and leaned on it, as if trying to hold back the world. What he really wanted to do was go get a horse and ride out down the valley in the moonlight, but he was too afraid that Sheila might see him and come after him.

The City Hall thermometer reads 85°

Mason rode in the police car with Neville Oakes. Their images reflected in the night-dark windows—Neville in his policeman's uniform and Mason in a tan denim shirt. Even in the midnight hours, it was still so hot that they had the windows up and the air conditioner running. Neville was twelve years younger than Mason and almost a hundred pounds heavier. He sweated easily, and Mason sometimes got so cold in the car, he had to lower his window, which he did now.

"Whew." Neville pointed at the digital thermometer out in front of City Hall. "Do you believe it? After midnight and it is still eighty-five degrees."

"I wish they had never put that thing up there," Mason said. "Are they ever goin' to get the clock workin'? Then we can all obsess about the time along with the temperature."

"They're callin' in some guy all the way from St. Louis," Neville said. "No one seems to be able to figure out the problem. Oh, the clock keeps time, but it runs ten to fifteen minutes behind, so they fixed it so it won't show at all.

"And they really did a nice job on that old buildin'. The thought was to bring up City Hall and set a standard for everyone to match. It's workin'. Look at the *Valentine*

Voice—Miss Porter is cleanin' off that brick and puttin' in new windows. And Blaine's got a new awning."

He turned the corner and drove down a tree-lined street. The fresh scent of mowed lawn came through the window.

"There's Winston, right on time," Neville said, slowing the cruiser.

Mason saw Winston Valentine in white T-shirt and dark sweatpants. Neville lowered his window and greeted the old man, and Winston said, "Good evenin', boys," without breaking his slow but rhythmic stride.

"Gettin' out from the women, Mr. Valentine?" Neville asked.

"Gotta get out and keep what I got of my mind and my body," the older man said. "Gotta work at it, boys, or women and the Feds sap it all right out of you. Least ways that Fed gov'ment can't tax me for this walkin' yet."

"No, not yet, anyway." Neville gave him a wave and drove off. "I'd like to be able to jog when I'm in my eighties," he said to Mason.

"You don't jog now."

"Yeah, but I'll take it up. Winston didn't jog when he was my age, he told me. He said that back then he smoked up to two packs of cigarettes a day and drank a six-pack of beer. Do you think the women in his place really pester him, like he claims?"

"I haven't spent much time speculatin' on that."

Neville shook his head. "My grandmother and Vella Blaine sure have. Mrs. Blaine is not at all happy about those women that come and go at his place." He pressed the accelerator and headed out the highway east of town. "I wonder if men his age really can get it on. Could your granddaddy do it when he got old?"

Mason slid his eyes to Neville. "I never had occasion to ask, and Grandpap didn't never say. He'd been widowed three times, and he wasn't very inclined to have anything to do with women. He said he didn't want to have to bury another one. You sure are powerfully interested in the sex lives of the elderly."

"I'd just like to know what to expect for when I get there."

"I think it is an individual thing." Mason offered.

"Well, they sure don't want them foolin' around at the nursing home. My mom said that a few of the old men and women there are nutty about sex, and she'd like to get programs to give them some activity to divert the energy. My dad and the mayor are workin' on getting some outfit to come in here and build a senior living community for people that don't really need the nursing home. Duplexes and apartments, golf course, maybe."

"We could use it," Mason said, remembering how his grandfather would have been shuffled off to a home, until Mason moved in with him. His grandfather ended up dying in his own bed, where he wanted to be.

"Well, buddy," Neville said, shifting his large bulk, "you thought any more about becomin' a full-time deputy?"

"Answer's still no."

Mason was serving as a special deputy. Valentine now had a force of three and a half, that was the joke. His duties entailed driving around with an official officer three nights a week and wearing a pager to be on call twenty-four hours. Mason rarely slept more than four hours a night, and he liked to put his waking hours to good use. Liked to keep himself busy, even if it wasn't much more than walking around checking doors, helping Lodi, the town drunk, to a bunk at the jail for the night, or getting Vella Blaine's cat out of the elm tree.

"I could use you, you know that." Neville, who had quit

the army and taken over from his father, Mickey, as Chief of Police back in the spring, took his job seriously. "This town's growin' whether we want it to or not—we'll get that senior living center by and by, and there was a guy in here the other day talkin' to the mayor about building one of those juvenile detention centers. I don't much like the idea, but it could bring upwards of a hundred new jobs with it. We're not hardly the little rural burg we used to be. I'm gonna have to hire more men to deal with stuff like what's been happenin' around here lately."

He was referring to two recent situations—one had been a farmer going crazy and threatening to shoot all his cattle, and another had been an altercation right in the middle of town at the Main Street Cafe, which also served as the bus station, where a young hoodlum high on this and that—not one of the Valentine boys but a young fella from up north somewhere—had pulled a gun.

"Oh, Neville," Mason said, "those were just a couple of fluke happenings. People here are human, just like everywhere else, and sometimes they get a little out of sorts. I don't think we're lookin' at a crime wave in Valentine. It's the heat, most of it. It'll all calm down when this spell breaks."

"I know we aren't any Oklahoma City, but I'll tell you, buddy, I don't know what we'd have done without you in that mess at the cafe. No, sir."

"That boy did not intend to shoot anybody. The gun wasn't loaded. It was all a mistake." The boy had broken down crying like a baby in Mason's arms. He thought of it. He needed to get himself up to the county jail to visit the boy.

"Nobody knew it wasn't loaded," Neville said. "And the point is, what if it had been loaded? By golly, I think Midgett would have gotten himself and maybe me shot.

"I never in my life thought I'd be facing a .357 right here in Valentine. That's why I came home here, so I wouldn't have to face stuff like that."

Neville went on in that vein for some time, about how Valentine had always been a peaceful place with no crime. About how neighbor looked after neighbor, and old men like Winston could walk the street safely at night. About how, if he could, he would pull Oklahoma out of the United States and put a wall around it because the rest of the nation did not deserve Oklahoma.

Mason listened, staring at his reflection in the black glass, seeing vague pictures of his own violent past that he never could completely erase.

"You have a lot more experience than the rest of my force in dealin' with violent situations," Neville pointed out. He seemed possessed of the opinion that because Mason had been in prison, he had good experience with violent offenders. "You'd be a real good deputy for us."

"You know I don't want to carry a gun," Mason said. "And I'm not all that fond of khaki, either." As a part-time special deputy, he wasn't required to wear a uniform or allowed to carry a firearm. He liked that.

Neville cast him a frown. "It was a boot you used to kill that boy, and you still wear boots."

"They're on my feet," Mason replied, not letting himself be perturbed.

Neville breathed deeply, looked at his watch and pronounced it time to head back to town. "Juice'll be pullin' the first of those red chili pepper bagels out pretty soon now. I like to get them when they're soft."

"Those aren't real bagels...not like bagels are supposed to be."

"They're Southern bagels. What would you expect?"

Mason said he could use a cup of coffee. It occurred to

him that the night sort of had its own inhabitants, such as night patrolmen, and the bakers and the nurses at the nursing home, and a few senior citizens, like Winston Valentine, who walked up and down the streets at night.

Neville had turned around and was heading back toward town when suddenly a yellow truck came flying into the glow of their headlights. The pickup was going so fast that its tires never touched the ground as it crossed the road in front of them. A boy hanging out the window yelled, "Yee-ha!"

"Oh, geez," Neville said. "I want my bagel." But, flipping on his blinking lights, he turned left onto the gravel road and followed after the truck.

Mason sat up in the seat. He recognized the truck. It belonged to Larry Joe Darnell. Charlene's son.

He thought of her sitting in the Suburban that evening, gazing at him.

Neville said, "That's Larry Joe. He's got that truck souped up, too."

Mason reminded Neville to remember eighteen, and Neville said he had never been eighteen because his daddy had been the police chief.

The yellow truck stopped, or Neville might never have caught it. Neville pulled up behind it. The patrol car's headlights caused the chrome bumper to gleam and illuminated three male heads.

They'd been at the lake. Young men cutting up on a Saturday night, filled with beer and cocky as God allowed. Mason stood back and watched as Neville had the three get out of the truck and line up beside it. He knew Randy Stidham by first name. Randy pumped gas and fixed cars at his daddy's Texaco and had taken his own apartment that summer; Ralph Stidham was proud of the boy. The past spring Larry Joe Darnell had started working part-time at the Texaco, mostly nights. The third one was Jaydee Mayhall's son, Clay, who didn't work anywhere that Mason had ever seen. He pegged Clay Mayhall as a trouble-maker, and Mason had learned to spot such when in prison, where survival often depended on being able to judge people with one look. Mason felt certain Clay Mayhall was destined for prison down the road, or at least to be a heart-break for a lot of people. Unless God intervened, but likely the boy would be calling on the aid of his daddy, Jaydee Mayhall, who pampered the boy straight down the wrong road.

"Are any of you boys of age to be consumin' alcohol?" Neville asked.

And right off the Mayhall boy said, "We ain't been con-sumin' no fuckin' alcohol. Search us. We don't have none," and sort of laughed.

Neville leaned close and said, "You watch your mouth. I don't like such language."

The boy, tall as Neville but skinny, grinned and said a mock, "Yes, sir."

The other two boys were decent and looked downward.

Neville came over to Mason and said in a tired, annoyed voice, "They're not sober enough to let 'em go drivin' around. Be my dang luck they'd crack up and kill themselves or someone else. Well, dang. I don't want to take them to jail," he added miserably.

"You mean you don't want to chat with Jaydee Mayhall?" Mason asked, teasing.

"That dang Jaydee'll be all down my back, and I'll have paperwork out the ying-yang." Neville didn't believe in swearing, although he managed by making up his own acceptable words. He sighed. "I guess there ain't no gettin' around talkin' to Jaydee, but if I get him out here to get his boy, I won't have to do paperwork."

Mason looked over at the boys. At Charlene's son, seeing Charlene that afternoon in the sunlight.

Almost before he knew it, he said, "Let me drive the boys to wherever they're stayin' the night. I'll keep the truck and drive myself on home."

Mason got behind the wheel, and the three boys squeezed in the single seat next to him, Charlene Darnell's son right against his elbow.

"The clutch is real tight. You gotta do it just right to get it goin'," the Darnell boy said, sort of squinting at him through a beer-fog.

"I think I can manage," Mason said, easing the truck into motion.

He drove the boys into town to the Stidham boy's small, old duplex apartment. A Harley motorcycle was torn apart on the front porch. The two other boys slipped out of the truck and headed for the apartment.

Mason told young Darnell where his own place was. "You can come for your truck any time after nine."

When the boy glared at him, Mason said, "It's better than goin' to jail and havin' your mother and father find out, isn't it?"

The boy gazed long at him, and Mason gazed back; without words the boy asked why, and Mason refused an answer.

The kid slammed the door, then called through the window, "Don't scratch my truck."

Mason laughed, a pleasure he recognized as rare washing over him.

He managed the clutch and drove off down the street to the stop sign. He lingered there, revving the engine and working his hand over the round gearshift knob and rushing back in time to his twenties again, when he believed there wasn't anything in the world he could not do.

Overtaken by the youthful sensation, he gave in and turned right, heading out of town and along the road past Charlene Darnell's house.

It sat well back from the road, the Darnell house. No one would hear him. He let up off the gas and cruised by slowly, seeing the house under the trees. Light from the pole lamp filtered down on the roof. The windows were dark, but he knew Charlene was in there. Likely lying in bed.

He could have answered the boy's silent question. He would have had to say, "Because I have loved your mother since the first day I laid eyes on her ten years ago."

The City Hall thermometer reads 83°

She awoke abruptly, coming out of a dream about cars. Cars chasing her. At first she didn't know where she was. Her heart was beating like a hammer...the television was on...oh, yes, she'd fallen asleep on the couch. There were cars racing all over the screen. *The Dukes of Hazzard* was on.

She was wringing wet. She was so wet, her Goofy sleep shirt was soaked through. Goodness gracious. She wiped her fingers over her chest, and they came away wet. Had the air conditioner given out again?

Taking up the remote, she pressed the button, and the time came on the television screen: 5:00 a.m. My heavens, she had slept the night through. It was the first time in a week. She'd been waiting up for Larry Joe to come in. Wouldn't you know she would go and fall into a sound sleep on the night she wanted to stay awake.

She got up and peered out the window to make certain

Larry Joe's truck was there. It was strange that she had not heard it.

The truck wasn't there.

She jerked open the front door and padded barefoot on the still warm concrete walk, looking for the truck. Maybe he'd parked somewhere different. But all that was there was the old Suburban.

Racing back inside, she hurried down the hall and peered into Larry Joe's room. There was enough moonlight to see that his bed was perfectly made.

Larry Joe had not come home. It was 5:00 a.m., and her son had not come home and had not called. *Oh, Lord. Oh, Lord.*

She grabbed the cordless phone and carried it into the kitchen, dialing Larry Joe's pager number as she went. Her fingers were shaking, and she mis-dialed and had to punch in the numbers again.

She set the phone on the table and stared at it.

Now just calm down, Charlene. There's no need to think the worst. Don't go screaming in there to Rainey. She needs her rest, and there's no need to get the entire house in an uproar.

She kept staring at the phone, waiting for it to ring.

Then she made herself move and set the coffeemaker to brewing.

Ten minutes later, she dialed his pager number again. Maybe he was out of range or had it turned off.

Or maybe he was dead. Killed in an accident.

That was the kind of thought a mother tended to have when a son didn't come home all night. But the truth was that it was a small county, and everyone knew her and knew Larry Joe was her son, and if he'd been in a wreck, someone would have called her. He was eighteen and out all night, that was all.

Eighteen! That was enough reason to think the very worst. Maybe he'd gone wild and crashed his truck somewhere no one would see. Or maybe he was knocked out, attacked by someone he picked up. An eighteen-year-old didn't know fear. Maybe someone had led him astray or had slipped him drugs. Joey should be home with her. Maybe she should call him and tell him to come right home. Maybe she should call him and tell him to get out there and find their son.

She reached for the telephone, and at that very moment it rang, scaring her so badly she almost dropped it. She said hello before she got the button pushed.

"What is it, Mom?" Her son's voice was groggy.

"Where are you?" She was just below screaming, and she didn't wait for an answer but jumped in, demanding to know why he wasn't home and what did he think he was doing and he could have at least called.

"Mom…"

"I've been so worried. How could you do this to me now, Larry Joe? This is no way to behave."

"Mom…"

"You could have called. I don't have to know what you're doin'. I'm not tryin' to butt into your business, but you could have called, Larry Joe." She was in tears now and shaking all over.

"I did call, Mom."

"What?"

"I called and left a message. Didn't you check the recorder?"

"No…" She sniffed and wiped beneath her nose with her fingers. "No, I didn't."

"I guess you and Aunt Rainey were still out. I called you a little bit after you came by the station, and I left a message that I was going to stay with Randy tonight. Or last night.''

She walked into the dining room where the recorder sat on the sideboard. The green message light was blinking.

With a great sigh, she apologized the best she possibly could. In his normally patient way, he said it was okay. She saw him in her mind's eye, stretching and grinning at her foolishness. He said he was going back to sleep and would be home late in the morning.

After breaking the connection, Charlene pressed the button on the recorder and listened to her son's voice. *Well, thank you, God, that he's okay.*

She poured a cup of coffee and stepped out the back door and sat on the concrete step, where she watched the golden sun come up on another day of her messed up life. It was Sunday. For a moment she had a panic, thinking about having to make dinner, but then she remembered it wasn't her Sunday. She thanked God quite literally.

Eight

The City Hall thermometer reads 82°

At breakfast Rainey suggested horseback riding before the day got any hotter. Charlene didn't bring up the matter of church; she wasn't certain she would ever again be able to leave the house. It was all she could do to drum up enough gumption to go out and face the barn and help her children get mounted. Needing to be with them and be a part of what they were doing prodded her into this action. Once there, she was relieved to find that she could face the barn, knowing Joey wasn't there, and not have a heart attack.

"Up you go," she said, boosting Jojo into the saddle. Then she made certain Jojo's little feet got tucked into each stirrup. The paint pony had become quite stout, so that Jojo's short nine-year-old legs sort of stuck out like sticks on each side.

Charlene's hand was lingering on Jojo's small leg when Jojo whopped the pony's sides and took off, galloping away.

A caution leaped to Charlene's tongue, but she bit her bottom lip, holding herself and her breath as she watched her daughter race to the pasture, where Danny J. had gone already and was struggling to put the red barrels into their triangle pattern.

"Rainey, don't you dare go galloping. I don't care what you say, you'll give me heart failure."

Rainey sort of jumped, as if attacked. Then she said, "I have not come off a horse in fifteen years." At Charlene's look, she added, "I'll be careful, I promise."

Rainey rode her horse slowly out to join the children, leaving Charlene at the barn opening, squinting in the bright morning, the warming breeze tugging her hair.

She stood there a long time, arm raised against the sun, and watched her children and her sister exercise their horses in circles. Coming out of a circle, Jojo directed her pony toward the barrels, pounding her little legs and showing daylight between her little fanny and the saddle. Danny J. gave a whoop and took off after her, the both of them riding wild and free as only children devoid of fear and sense can…and then there went pregnant Rainey doing the same.

In the bright light, Charlene's eyes started watering. She had ridden as a girl; she and Rainey would ride just like that. What had happened to her?

She was fairly certain it had begun the day she had Larry Joe. When a woman has a child, she is never again fearless. Her heart is walking around outside her body, at the mercy of every threat in the world.

Turning, she strode across the dried-up yard to the house, up the stairs and into the shade of the kitchen.

The phone rang just as she entered. *Joey?* She raced to pick up the receiver and say a breathless hello.

"Hello, Daughter."

It was her father. He asked if she and Rainey and the kids might want to drive up to Oklahoma City for Sunday dinner.

"Oklahoma City? Daddy, isn't that a long way to go just for dinner?"

"We could shop," he said.

"Oh, Daddy, I really need to rest around the house today. Do you want to drive that far?" She was thinking that she would have to run out there and get Rainey to drive their father.

But he said he and Mildred and Ruthanne would go on the senior bus that was going up to the City.

"Well, good. You all have a good time, Daddy. And thanks for thinkin' of me."

Hanging up, she wondered what in the world she was going to feed Rainey and the kids later for dinner.

She began to clear the breakfast dishes from the table, stacking plates along her arm and depositing them into the sink. The picture and low sound on the tiny television on the counter caught her eye. Reba MacIntire on the Country Music Television channel. Rainey watched a lot of CMT now that she had quit work to be full-time pregnant.

Charlene picked up the remote to punch up the volume. She loved to hear Reba's songs. They seemed to tell little stories about women. Well, goodness, Reba had gone and cut her beautiful red hair. Wonder what shade of hair color that is?

Reba faded, and another woman took her place. A really pretty young woman with short bouncy hair and a slim, sexy body, singing dynamically about John Wayne walking away. All the female country music singers these days looked young and beautiful, even those like Reba who weren't all that young didn't look over thirty years old, year after year, all of them with bright hair and perfect bodies and knockout glamour. Not like Patsy or Tammy or Loretta, who in their day had all been beautiful, but in a normal manner that was not so different than any average woman in America dressing up for a Friday night. How could any average woman these days keep up?

Flipping channels, Charlene stopped when the picture

came on black and white. It was *Father Knows Best,* just coming on.

The introduction faded, and there was Margaret vacuuming her living room. Margaret had never had gray hair, although the show was in black and white, so you couldn't know exactly what color her hair was. Right now she had a scarf tied around her head, but Charlene recalled how her hair was short and sort of sophisticated looking. She wore a dress while cleaning because only her daughters Betty and Kathy could wear jeans in those days, although Charlene seemed to recall seeing Margaret in slacks. And there came Father, sneaking up behind Margaret to grab her and give her a kiss. Margaret gave a little cry; then she smiled, slipped the scarf from her hair and melted right at him, both of them smiling as if they'd just made love.

The scene cut to a commercial for paper towels, and Charlene poured the last of the steamy coffee into her cup. Pulling a chair over in front of the television, she sat to watch the rest of the show.

After it was over and all the Andersons were perfect and happy, Charlene went to the laundry room, dug a red bandana out of a drawer and tied it around her hair, fastening it at the back of her neck. It did keep the hair out of her face while she washed dishes and wiped every inch of counter space and every appliance with vinegar water spritzed from a spray bottle, so everything sparkled and shined and was fit for a television commercial. From there she moved on through the house, working over the lamps and television screens and mirrors until they all about knocked the eyes out. She thought that Sheila Arnett probably didn't know anything about the uses of vinegar. And probably Margaret Anderson would shine her stuff to perfection like this, and Father never left her.

It was in her own bathroom, shining the mirror that

stretched across the double sinks, that Charlene paused and looked at herself. Her complexion was flushed, her eyes shimmered spring green. She looked pretty, or on the edge of insanity.

Slowly she slipped the bandana from her head and shook out her hair. It fell softly, longer on her shoulders than she had realized.

Opening a drawer, she pulled out hair-clipping scissors.

She looked at herself again in the mirror. Then she took a breath, combed up a section of hair and proceeded to cut it off, at first slowly, but then faster and faster, chopping and whacking with great abandon and tossing the tresses heedlessly to the floor.

"Hey, Mace!"

With some surprise, Mason saw his brother wave at him from his own back porch.

"Hey!" He gave a wave from out at the back fence, where he was feeding his old gelding and mule. He watched his brother, his tie blowing in the wind, come striding across the sun-browned yard in the purposeful manner in which he always walked. Even with his eyes shaded by his beat-up old Stetson, Mason squinted not only from the sunlight, but from the brightness of Adam's crisp white shirt and pale blue summer slacks.

"Good mornin'," Mason said and reached over to flip on the spigot above the water tank.

Adam mopped his balding head with a handkerchief, then gestured with it. "Why do you keep these old critters? That gelding doesn't even have any teeth left. Cost you an arm and a leg in feed. You could get five hundred or better for both of them over at the sale barn," he added, stuffing his handkerchief into his back pocket.

"I imagine I could. But this gelding was a damn good

roping horse for me, and I'm not turnin' him into dog food now. Especially not when I own a share in a feed store.''

Adam frowned, just as he always did when Mason mentioned his partnership in the store. Then he said, ''Iris and I are on our way to church, and I thought I'd drop these papers by. Before you jump the gun in turnin' this deal down, I want you to see what they're offerin' for this place. I want you to see it written out—twice what it is worth, Mace. Twice.''

For the first time Mason noticed the papers in his brother's hand; Adam unrolled them and held them up, tapping a figure in black ink with his finger. Mason couldn't quite read the figure, although he knew what it was, since Adam had kept hammering it home to him yesterday evening on the phone.

''They didn't have to make such a generous offer,'' Adam said. ''They can get a good piece of land Freddy Valentine owns north of town a lot cheaper. The thing that's held them up there is Freddy being in the nuthouse. But his wife can and will sell it, if we don't snatch up their offer pretty quick.''

''I told you I don't want to sell, Adam. I haven't changed my mind.''

Adam put his hand on his belt, and his expensive watch and big pinky ring glimmered in the sunlight. ''Here is a good deal, Mace.'' Adam paused for emphasis. ''Now, I want you to take a look at this. This came out of the blue to you—and to me. It isn't only you in this, you know. I could make enough from my share of the sale to send Ellie to two years of college.''

''You already can send Ellie to two years of college and more.''

Adam snorted. ''You don't know the prices these days. Gonna cost two arms and a leg by the time she's done. She wants to be a dadgum doctor. And furthermore, this community could use the jobs a juvenile detention center built right here would bring. Seventy jobs right off the bat... seventy people won't have to go up to Lawton to work. They can work right here where they live."

"Half of that forty will be people movin' in here from outside," Mason said, turning off the spigot.

"So? So twenty people here get jobs. That's progress. You're standin' in the way of progress. And those juveniles—they're gonna be buyin' for those kids right here in Valentine. It's a good deal all the way around."

Mason started toward the house, thinking that they might as well argue out of the sun. Adam's face was getting awfully red. "A lot of people in this town may not want a juvenile detention center here, Adam. What if we sell this place, and the people veto the idea?"

"That won't happen," Adam said in the manner of a man who was set to arrange life as he saw it.

They stepped up on the porch. Mason looked at Adam. "I don't want to sell this place."

"Why don't you want to sell? Because this place was Grandaddy's? It's just an old house and an old barn, that's all. Grandaddy never was what you thought he was. I never knew what you saw in him, but he is gone. Stayin' here doesn't bring him back, and you could get a really nice place anywhere you want. A new brick ranch with central air, big fireplace instead of some old stove. Room for those old critters, too, if that's what's botherin' you."

"Grandpap," Mason said. "His name was Grandpap. And I am not tryin' to bring him back. All I want is to live here. I like it here. I like the big apple tree in the front yard, and I know all the creaks in the house. I'm perfectly content here, and I don't see the need to move off."

"Why do you always have to be so dadgum difficult

about everything?'' The veins stuck out in Adam's neck. ''Tell me. I want to hear it.

''You always have to take the hard way. And you act like you just don't want to touch money. Like it is contaminated. You've always acted like Daddy and me makin' money was just too low for you, and that Grand-*pap* was some special god. What did that old man ever do but run a car around a dirt track some? He had to have his daughter's husband dole out to him. Now, those are the facts of the case, and I'll tell you somethin' else—it was me and Daddy buildin' that feed store up that gave you a place to work when you come out of the pen. Now, isn't that true? You wouldn't have had anything. Ex-cons don't get to be made partners of businesses when they come out. They don't hardly make it, but you had a partnership just waitin', so don't go lookin' down your nose at me wantin' to do business. No, sir.''

That last set Mason on fire. Adam always had to bring up the penitentiary. ''Why am I the one who's difficult, just because I don't want to sell? Maybe you are the one who's difficult.''

Adam shook his head in clear aggravation.

Just then there came the insistent beep of a car horn from the front yard.

''I want you to think about this,'' Adam said, holding up the rolled sheaf of papers. ''I want you to think about the fact that you'll keep a lot of people from jobs and me from sellin' and makin' some money. They don't want just my side. It's got to be all of it.''

It struck Mason that the old man Adam claimed hadn't achieved anything had managed to leave Adam something he valued highly. He was about to say this, but the car horn sounded again.

Adam jerked open the screen door. "Think about it, Mason. That's all. Just think it over."

Adam entered the house, tossed the papers on the kitchen table as he passed on through the room, down the hall and out the front screen door, letting it slam behind him. Gazing down the long, dim hallway, Mason caught sight of the red Cadillac through the front screen before it drove away toward town.

He looked over at the papers lying in a loose curl on the vinyl tablecloth beside the well-worn copy of *The Screwtape Letters* that he'd propped open with a little tack hammer.

Larry Joe looked up and saw the big red Cadillac pulling out from the yard up ahead. Recognizing it and knowing how Adam MacCoy drove, he stepped off the rough blacktop onto the grassy shoulder. He wished he hadn't been so stubborn about walking it, because he felt foolish walking along the side of the road, the way a teenager who is used to driving everywhere in his own vehicle usually does.

The Cadillac came flying past him, and he saw Iris MacCoy on the passenger side staring at him. He quickly looked back down at the ground. That woman looked at him when she came into the Texaco, too. At first he'd thought it was his imagination, but Randy had mentioned noticing it, and teased him about it. Larry Joe finally admitted to himself that Iris MacCoy looked at him pretty boldly, and so did a number of other older women who came into the Texaco. Ignoring the looks seemed the safest course.

Joey, driving along the same road, looked ahead and saw a figure walking on the shoulder. He wondered who it could be, but then he had to jerk his attention back to the road as a red Cadillac came rolling at him. Adam MacCoy.

Adam always drove like he owned the road, and right then he had aimed that car at Joey in his big Dodge towing a twenty-five-foot horse trailer like the rig could just get out of the way. Joey downshifted and moved over to the edge of the one-lane road as far as possible. He saw Iris MacCoy's wide eyes on him as they passed.

The Cadillac passed, and Joey got back in the middle of the road. The figure was still walking along the side of the road up ahead. A young man.

Recognition of the stride and shape of the shoulders dawned on him with great surprise. Larry Joe. *His own son.* And then, *What was Larry Joe doing out here?*

His son didn't seem to hear the truck, had his head bent and walked along determinedly.

Joey pushed the button to lower the tinted passenger window. As his gaze lit on Larry Joe's bare upper arms, it came hard to him that his son had grown up.

Larry Joe's head came up, and his eyes widened. He and Joey gazed at each other for long seconds, while the truck engine idled and a horse banged on the floor of the trailer.

Then Joey said, "Do you want a ride?"

Larry Joe, who had set himself not to take anything from Joey for a long time, shook his head.

Joey saw red.

But then Larry Joe offered quickly, "I'm just goin' down the road...to that house. My truck's there," he added, stuffing his hands in his pockets and averting his gaze. This was as weird a situation as he'd ever been in.

Joey peered out the windshield and saw the truck in the yard—Mason MacCoy's front yard, which added to his surprise at finding Larry Joe out here.

Then he told Larry Joe, "Get in. I'll save you the rest."

Larry Joe gazed at him a second, but then he got in and Joey started off. Larry Joe sat up close to the door and poked his arm out the open window, even though the air-conditioning was going. Joey wondered what he should say, had things all jamming up in his chest. *Why was it like this with his own son?*

He stole a glance at the boy, seeing his handsome profile. Not a boy anymore. But still, he looked so much like Charlene. He was Charlene's child.

"What's your truck doin' down here at Mason Mac-Coy's?" he finally asked, mostly because it seemed so stupid to be afraid to speak to his own son.

Larry Joe looked straight out the windshield. "He borrowed it."

"He borrowed it?"

"Yeah." Larry Joe kept his gaze out the windshield and his hands pressed flat on his thighs.

"And you had to walk out here to get it?"

"It just sort of worked out that way."

"Oh."

Larry Joe cast him a hot accusing look, as if he could ask a few questions of his own. Joey immediately averted his gaze straight ahead out the windshield.

Then they were at Mason's, and even as Joey brought the truck to a stop, Larry Joe was taking hold of the door handle, saying, "You don't need to pull in, you can just stop right here. Thanks for the ride." And he was out of the truck.

"Larry Joe."

"Yeah?"

"Anytime you need a ride, I can give you one."

"Yeah…well, thanks." Larry Joe slammed the door and jogged off across the dry, shallow ditch and up the yard toward the house.

Joey watched a minute, feeling a confused ache and wondering what was going on with his son. Why did MacCoy have his son's truck? What did Mason MacCoy have to do with *his* son?

Then he thought that Larry Joe had definitely not invited him into the business, and he had horses to get unloaded before it got any hotter, so he shifted into gear and headed on down the road.

Mason had heard the truck and gone to the door. Through the screen, he saw the kid coming toward the house and Joey Darnell driving away with a trailer of horses.

The kid stepped up on the porch, and Mason said, "Good mornin'."

"Hello." The kid looked at him straight, and Mason liked that.

The scent of dust and sweat came in with the kid. He wore a denim shirt with the sleeves torn out of it—popular with the teens these days, who didn't know Mason's generation had done the same thing—revealing the tanned, wiry arms of a young man. Sweat ran down his temples and caused his skin to glisten.

Mason said, "That's a heck of a truck you've built yourself."

The kid blinked. "How'd you know I built it?"

"I can figure things," Mason said with some amusement. He moved to the mahogany slant top desk and picked up the keys.

When he turned back to the kid, he saw him glancing curiously around the room. People always did that. The room was an unusual sight, with solid oak bookcases filled with books lining the small walls, and that mahogany desk. People were always struck by the room, and bowled over when they saw the other small rooms, with more books stacked here and there. Many people were surprised that hicks such as his Grandpap and himself would actually read.

"Here's your keys."

The kid nodded and started out the door. Mason followed.

On the porch the kid paused. "Uh...thanks. For last night. We appreciate it."

"You're welcome. Us old folks didn't just sprout out forty years old, you know." He could grin then.

The kid gave a shy, sheepish grin in return, his eyes averted downward as he bobbed his head again. Peering upward, trying hard to be cool, he nodded. "Later..."

Mason followed him out the door and stood on the porch watching him walk away, watching the youthful stride and movement, while something swelled and twisted in his chest.

"Hey, kid!" he called.

The kid stopped like Mason had shot him, then slowly turned.

"I got somethin' you might like to see. In the barn." He wouldn't sound eager, wouldn't sound like it mattered.

The kid didn't move. "What is it?"

"An elephant," Mason said dryly and stepped off the porch into the hot sunshine, counting on the kid to follow.

He crossed the yard and the wide graveled drive to the barn. He unlatched the big double doors. They were bright and burning hot in the sun as he took hold of one to push it open. Suddenly the kid was there, pushing open the opposite door.

The barn was blinding black after the brightness of the sun, and hot as an oven. Perspiration instantly started running down Mason's back as he walked deep into the barn, over to the far wall, and shoved open the tin windows. The kid remained at the doorway, a silhouette against dusty golden light.

Going to a large object covered by a dusty old tarp, Mason rolled back the tarp, revealing the still shiny chrome of a much dented front bumper, and further, a bright blue hood with lettering and dented fenders of an old stock car. He kept folding back the tarp, and the kid came forward as if drawn by a magnet.

"My Grandpap's," Mason said, when the old '56 Chevy was revealed.

"You're kiddin'?"

Mason chuckled. He enjoyed the kid's expression, as, arms folded and hands tucked up under his armpits, he walked around and around the vehicle.

"When was it last driven?" the kid asked.

"Oh, a couple of years ago now. I took it out to see how it was, but I never got around to doin' anything else, and then it needed tires."

Mason told him how his grandfather had parked the car in here and covered it up when diabetes began taking his eyesight back in the early seventies. "Except for a few times I rode him around in it, it's been sittin' in here like this. I've kept mouse poison under the seats to keep them from eatin' it up."

He popped the hood, and they both peered at the engine. The kid noted the cracked hoses and corroded battery, then the kid squinted an eye at him and mentioned that the engine could be frozen up. The battery was corroded.

The kid squinted an eye at him. "You could get some good money for this machine."

"Yeah…I've thought about it. But sometimes there's things worth more than money. Maybe I'll get her goin'."

The kid helped Mason cover it once again with the tarp

and close the barn doors. Then together they walked toward the kid's truck.

"Well, thanks again," the kid said.

"You bet." Mason stuck out his hand, and the kid took Mason's hand in a firm shake. It was easy between them now.

"You've made a smooth vehicle here." Mason said, as the kid got into his truck. "She gets up and goes real easy."

"I like workin' with cars."

"You have real talent with it."

The boy cocked an eye at him.

"That's somethin' to remember, you know," Mason told him. "Think how much you like doin' something, and you'll also think about how you'd miss doin' it, if you drive drunk and get yourself or someone else killed."

The kid gazed at him, and a flush came over his face.

"Too much alcohol messes up your mind, and so does hangin' out with people who aren't worth your time." He held the kid's gaze, and he saw the blue-green eyes jump when he said, "One time I got drunk and I killed someone. It's with you every day, and it's a hard mountain to get over. I'd hate to see that happen to you, kid."

The kid stared at him, then looked away. After a moment his eyes returned to Mason's. "My name ain't kid. It's Larry Joe. I'm Charlene Darnell's son—the woman you were talkin' to at your feed store the other day."

Mason looked into those blue-green eyes and felt as if the kid understood every bit of the real truth of what was going on, much more than Mason did.

"I know that, son," Mason told him and stepped back. The kid hit the pedal and drove off in a roar of powerful engine.

Nine

The City Hall thermometer reads 99°

They were swarming around the kitchen, laughing and chattering, washing their hands and faces, jerking open the refrigerator and slamming it again, finding drinks to cool them down and snacks to fill them up.

Charlene stepped into their midst and asked, "What do you think?"

The three stopped and stared at her head.

"I just did it. I haven't fixed it. It'll curl more when I wash it."

Rainey started forward. "You cut your hair," as if Charlene hadn't known what she'd done.

"What'd you do that for?" Danny J. erupted like a furious volcano. "You're crazy, you know that? You and him...you're both crazy!"

He yelled this at the top of his lungs, and then he slammed the refrigerator door shut so hard the refrigerator swayed and the decorative tins on top of it clanged. With a glare hot enough to melt metal, he pushed past Charlene and raced out of the room.

Stunned, Charlene looked at Rainey and Jojo, who were standing there looking back at her in much the same way. The sound of Danny J. slamming his bedroom door reverberated, causing Charlene to jump. The door must have bounced open, or else Danny J. opened it and slammed it again for good measure.

In the silence that followed, Rainey said, "Honey, you've just chopped it all off."

Charlene turned and hurried through the house and down the hall.

All manner of sounds came from Danny J.'s room. It sounded as if he were tearing the room apart, slamming the closet door, breaking things, pounding the wall. She thought of his violence with the Coke machine up at the IGA, and the sound of this now scared her to death.

"Danny J." She knocked on the door. There came a crash. "Danny J.," she said more ardently and tried the door handle, but found it locked. "Danny J., please let me in."

There came more thudding. Rainey and Jojo, who clung to Rainey's leg, came to the hall and gazed at her.

"Danny J., let me in now."

"Go away!" Something else broke, and then music blared.

Charlene pounded on the door. "Daniel Joseph, let me in!"

Distorted visions of her son slitting his wrists or choking himself with his bedsheet and the headlines in the newspaper: Preoccupied Mother Allows Son's Injury, played across her mind.

She threw herself against the door. *"Open the damn door now!"*

The music stopped. The door handle rattled, and then the door came whipping open with such force that it smacked the wall behind it and swung back at her. Already entering, Charlene caught it before it hit her nose.

Danny J. was jerking clothes up from the floor and

throwing them in an empty drawer. All his dresser drawers were empty and cockeyed. One lay on the floor. It looked like he had jerked everything out and thrown it all around the room. He'd torn things from the wall, wiped stuff from the shelves, and even made an attempt to tear off his bed-covers.

Charlene closed the door and then stood there. She wasn't certain she could cope with this. *Oh, Lord, tell me what to say to make it okay.* Remembering her hair, she ran a hand regretfully over it.

Then she stepped forward to begin what she knew best. She picked up boots and a pillow directly at her feet. She set the boots neatly together and put the pillow on the bed. She saw he had swept his FFA awards off the shelf. The ones he'd won for his sheep and the two fillies he'd raised.

"Oh, Danny J."

She sank to her knees and reached for the trophies. They were bent and broken. With a small shock, she found one of Joey's old rodeo buckles peeking out from beneath a shirt. She picked it up and ran her finger over it. Usually it sat with Joey's other buckles in the glass case in the living room. Danny J. must have gotten it...and he'd stomped on it pretty good. The loop where a belt went was terribly bent.

She wished she'd pretended not to see it. She wanted to slip it back beneath the shirt, but she had it in her hand, so she stood up and put it on his bedside table.

He was looking at her, but when she looked at him, he turned his head.

Reaching for him, she tried to hug him to her, because that was what she had always done and the best she knew to do. But he jerked away and threw himself on the bed, pulling a pillow to his chest, as if for protection.

She would not cry, please God. She put the trophies,

broken though they were, back on the shelf. Then she gazed at her son, trying to figure out what to say.

"I'm sorry I upset you by cutting my hair," she said finally. "You're right...I am a little crazy right now." She felt her hair, the shortness of it sticking out all over. It must have been a shock to him. She had never in her life had her hair so short.

"It'll look better when I wash it and mousse it up," she said, trying to sound positive.

He shrugged. "It's *your* hair."

She lowered herself to the bed and sat there for a minute. Finally she told him that she was sorry, that she knew what had happened between herself and his daddy was causing him pain, and that she knew she had let him down lately in regards to providing a stable home environment.

"Honey, I wish it didn't have to be this way," she said. "But it *is* this way. That's just how things are. I'm doin' the best I can, Danny J."

He looked at her. "Are you and Dad gonna get a divorce?"

The question sort of hit her in the face. "I don't know yet."

"You could make him come home—if you wanted."

There it was, the truth in his angry eyes. He knew her and Joey better than she'd had any idea he did.

"No, I can't," she said. "Oh, I might be able to get him back here, but I can't make him come home, and there's a difference."

Confusion flickered across his face.

"Honey...your father left by his own decision for his own reasons. If I was to make him come back, things still wouldn't be right, not how you want them to be. He wouldn't be happy, Danny J., and if your daddy isn't happy, none of us around him will be happy. And your daddy hasn't been happy for some time.''

He flung his pillow aside and sat up.

''It doesn't have to do with you. Your daddy loves you. He's sort of mad at me, but it isn't really something I can explain. I don't have any easy answers for you. It would be wonderful if people fell in love and got married and always lived happily ever after, but I guess that isn't true for everyone. People grow and change, and their needs change. There is a happily-ever-after—but it isn't like people want to think it is. Happily-ever-after sort of comes one day at a time, coming through all the good and the bad parts of life.

''What you have to do is think about the good times and trust that everything will work out and come around to the good times again.''

She was reaching for a lot with that last part. She wasn't certain it was true, but sometimes mothers had to pretend to trust, in hope that it would eventually take hold.

Frowning, he said, ''He was gonna get me a buckin' horse, so I could start learnin' to ride broncs. He said he was gonna talk to you and get me that horse. But now he ain't gonna talk to you. You two fight every time you talk, and he's just gone and forgotten all about it.'' He pushed himself to his feet and stood gazing out the window.

''And now, because of your daddy and I, what you want gets pushed aside,'' Charlene said. *Why, he's turning into a man. Isn't that sideburns beginning to grow?*

''It doesn't matter.'' His voice was thick.

''Yes, it does matter. Every person's desires matter, and what one of my children desires matters most of all.''

Reaching out, she took his hand in hers. After several seconds, he squeezed her hand in return.

''Oh, Danny J....bronc ridin'?''

"I'll be okay, Mom. It's not like it's ridin' bulls."

"Oh, right. Horses aren't like bulls, even though they buck just as hard and have these hooves that can stomp you to pieces." She smiled like mothers do, when they really want to cry and scream. "Saddle broncs or bareback?"

"Saddle broncs. Like Dad did," he said at first eagerly, and then dropping off, as if saying something he shouldn't.

"I know," she said. Joey had been a high-school champion and won money to buy his first good horse for training.

"If I can get a bronc, Rick Butler will come give me and Curt lessons. Curt wants to bronc ride, too, but they can't keep a horse over there."

"I see." She saw the gold flecks in his eyes.

"All the big ones started young, and I'm goin' on fourteen, Mama."

Mama. Her heart sort of ripped right in two at the name from his lips. She gazed into his face, so eager. Never had she felt less adequate to be what he needed her to be.

"I got to make a start," he said, "so I can get into the finals at the end of next summer."

Already he was thinking way ahead to next summer. She wanted to tell him not to hurry. That his future was coming toward him fast enough, that it would just zoom right past, like a car on an interstate, there and gone before you hardly knew it, leaving you wondering what your life was really about.

"We'll get a hold of your daddy and talk to him about a bucking horse," she told him. "Now clean up this mess."

The City Hall thermometer reads 86°

Late that night Charlene sat at the kitchen table and glued the broken parts of Danny J.'s trophies.

"Can't even tell it was broken," Rainey said, admiring Charlene's work with proper appreciation.

"Super Glue can fix just about anything, I guess," Charlene said, polishing a silver nameplate. "Except broken hearts. It's useless there."

"That's God's department. He binds up the broken-hearted," Rainey said, and stuck her head in the refrigerator. "Do you have any chocolate? I think I'll make some pudding. Chocolate pudding also helps the broken-hearted...and the pregnant."

Ten

The City Hall thermometer reads 93°

Rainey had to leave. She kept telling Charlene she was sorry, but she really had to go home to Harry, as if Charlene were too dim to understand this.

"I know you have to go, hon. You cannot stay here with me forever. Even if you could, we'd drive each other nuts, or end up shootin' each other or something."

Charlene acted like she was putting up a brave front, to make Rainey feel good, but the truth was she was past ready for Rainey to leave and on the brink of shoving her sister out the door and tossing her clothes after her.

Rainey kept telling Charlene things like, "This time will pass," and "You just have to be strong, hon," and "Don't let it get you down, Charlene." As if Charlene being down was totally unacceptable. Whenever Charlene started crying, Rainey would look stricken. Upsetting Rainey made Charlene feel doubly guilty and overwhelmed. And she was getting awfully tired of Rainey observing her as if looking for the first signs of a crack-up.

With observation like that, Charlene herself was waiting for the crack-up, and she felt she could handle it better if she was alone with the children when it came. The children, being naturally focused on themselves as children tended to be, weren't likely to notice or make too big a deal out of their mother cracking up. They assumed their mother was not in any way a woman; she was a mother, put on earth to provide answers and food and to pick up dirty socks. If she happened to appear a little unreasonable or unfathomable while doing these things, her children would just put it down to normal motherhood.

Another thing Charlene made up her mind had to leave along with her sister were all the maternity and baby clothes she had been saving in her hopes for another baby. The very thought of the things in the house had become intolerable.

She went to the garage and found the boxes, all neatly labeled, everything inside protected with plastic and cedar shavings. There were the wicker bassinet and little cushion for it, and all the eyelet lace that went around it, too.

"Might as well not let it set around and rot," Charlene said. "I'm certainly not going to be using any of this."

"Honey, you don't know that," Rainey said, because she thought she should say something of the sort, rather than agree with her sister, but already she was opening the boxes and pulling things out. Charlene had always bought really nice things and taken care of them, too, so even second-hand, most all of it was like new. Rainey admired the bassinet and lace and then went through the clothes, holding them up in front of her and swishing over to the mirror to get an idea of how she was going to look. But then she glanced at Charlene's face and tried to hold herself in.

"Don't bother to try any of it on," Charlene told her, throwing things back in the boxes. "Just take it all, and what you don't want, give away to one of those thrift shops."

"Charlene, hon…"

"It's okay, Rainey. I'm fine. Really. I'm forty-six, for

heaven sake, and not one of those Hollywood movie stars who can get away with having a baby at that age. I have three wonderful children. No need to be greedy."

She could not stand to look at any of it.

At last they had the little red Mustang packed. The bassinet and stand it went on took up almost all the back seat. Larry Joe had to tie the trunk closed with a cord. He said that would be perfectly fine to get Rainey up to Oklahoma City. He had also gotten the car gassed up, checked the oil and tires, and tightened a few loose screws in the door panel. Now he started the engine to get the air conditioner going so it would be cool when Rainey got inside.

Rainey told him as she hugged his neck, "The family has a doctor and an auto mechanic, so we have all the bases covered." Then she hugged Danny J. and Jojo.

"I'll call," she said, sweeping them all with an earnest look. "And I'll get back here in about three weeks."

It sounded like a threat to Charlene, but she told herself it was three weeks away.

Rainey wrapped her arms around Charlene's neck, and Charlene felt herself melt all over, and then she was hugging back.

"Thank you for stayin' all this time, Rainey," she said, her voice thick.

Breaking away, Rainey took Charlene's cheeks between her hands and looked deeply into her eyes. "A year ago, when I was so confused about my life, you said something that helped me, Charlene. You said, 'Don't be afraid of yourself.' Now I'm tellin' you the same thing, honey. Don't be afraid. Trust yourself. Trust the Spirit that is God inside you."

Charlene really wished Rainey wouldn't expect so much of her.

She said, wiping her brow, "It's gettin' hot out here.

You better get goin' in the air-conditioning. And don't speed. You have to think about a baby now."

Tucking Rainey into the seat of the little car about the same way she would tuck Jojo into bed at night, she closed the car door, then tested it to make certain it was shut tight.

Rainey started down the drive and thought of Harry and pressed the accelerator so hard she slung gravel. Immediately, imagining Charlene's frown, she let up on the pedal and cast a wave out the window. When she glanced in the rearview mirror, she saw dust billowing and blowing away, and the children already going in the front door, while Charlene stood there, her hand still raised in a wave.

Her sister looked so small and sad.

Rainey felt really sorry for Charlene, but she felt the need to get home to Harry and make certain he was still her husband even more strongly. Turning onto the blacktopped highway, she hit the gas for home.

Charlene stood there staring at the rear of the red Mustang as it disappeared down the highway. She didn't realize she was standing there alone and staring at nothing until a good gust of wind hit her.

The wind had come up hard. She blinked, dust getting into her eyes. The wind sent the three horses thundering from the big west pasture to the big east pasture. She looked upward, but the sky was still bright, so bright her eyes hurt. She shaded them and saw the wind sending dirt devils across the empty corrals and creaking the training pen gate that was still hanging open and crooked.

She heard Rainey's voice: *Don't be afraid.*

She braced herself and put her face to the wind. It came hot and dry on her cheeks, sucking her breath and all traces of moisture from her skin. It was so strong that when she finally turned for the house, she was practically sent running in order to keep on her feet.

She slammed the door closed and leaned against it for a few seconds, breathing rapidly, hearing the wind buffeting against the door, as if it was trying to get inside and suck her dry some more.

Pushing away from the door, she went to the kitchen, where she poured herself a glass of ice tea and rubbed lotion on her face and hands. She turned on the television, flipping through the channels, looking for an episode of *Father Knows Best*. She caught the last ten minutes of one and watched about a time when life was easier and everything could be made right in a half hour. After that, she flipped over to CMT to get country music, because she didn't have a radio in the kitchen.

She watched a minute, then turned the little television set to face the wall.

Larry Joe was getting a glass of orange juice from the refrigerator and asked, "What'd you do that for?"

"I just want to listen. I don't want to see any of it."

She did not need to see all of those trim, unlined twenty-five-year-old women swaying and thumping all over the place and attracting men like flies.

"I don't know why they can't have real women in any of those videos," she said.

Larry Joe said, "No one would watch, I guess."

When in good spirits, Charlene recalled her early childhood, until the age of eleven, in pleasant scenes like those out of a Bessie Pease painting, all sweet and rosy-cheeked. She recalled lovely times of walking along the tree-lined sidewalk with her hand in her mother's on their way to church, of sitting between her parents when they drove to visit her father's family. She recalled the easy way her father drove, and that he let her have a Popsicle in the car.

There were scenes of racing around on horseback with her mother, while her father watched from the fence.

Her brother Freddy only flitted briefly in and out of these pleasant scenes. Freddy was five years older than Charlene, in the throes of adolescence by the time Charlene was turning eleven, and had never had much to do with her. Early on he had taught her things: to be firm on a horse, to ride a bike, and to tie her shoes. Then he grew up and became the big brother who existed on the fringe of her life, hardly there at all, really.

Charlene's life was running home from school to show her mother her papers and then helping her mother prepare supper. Many times it was just Charlene and her mother having supper, but these times seemed special and cozy. And when her father was home, after supper he'd sit in the living room and read the paper, and she would sit on the floor and play with something and smell the scent of his Camels. He had always smelled of Old Spice and crisp shirts and Camels, and her mother of flowery bath powder and Chanel No.5. Sometimes her father called her Princess.

All this seemed to change one summer. The year she turned eleven, when her mother had become pregnant with Rainey. Her memories of this time were blurry and dim, like shadowy out-of-focus shots from a camera. She had not been told outright about her mother being pregnant. Just one day she knew, and that her father was very mad about it. Before this she had never seen her parents fighting, and then suddenly they were, terribly, and all the time.

She would be awakened by angry voices and would creep to the stairs and crouch there on a cold step, holding on to the enameled posts, and listen to the sharp tones coming from the living room. She wished a number of times for Freddy to come home, because her parents would restrain themselves then. But Freddy seemed gone most of the time.

"I don't need this!" her father often shouted, and she would catch a glimpse of his khaki trousers as he strode to the front door. He slammed the door behind him.

Once Charlene raced down the steps to find her mother crying on the couch. "Oh, Mama…what's wrong? Why are you and Daddy fighting? Where did Daddy go?"

Her mother straightened and wiped hastily at her eyes. "Nothing is wrong, darlin'. Nothing for you to worry over. Your daddy and I were only havin' a discussion. He's gone down to the store for a pack of cigarettes. Now, you need to be in bed. Go on…"

Charlene was confused by what she saw in contrast to her mother's explanation. She would lie in bed and listen to sounds from the kitchen: water running in the sink, a pan hitting the stove, the clink of a dish. Soon aromas of coffee and frying meat or baking breads would waft up. Sometimes she would hear the radio playing low. She would listen very hard for her father's return. Sometimes he would be home by morning, in which case they would all have a big breakfast that their mother had cooked in the night. Sometimes he was gone long enough to return not only to breakfast, but a full meal of chicken pot pie, gelatin salad and tomato pudding, and if he was gone for days, there would also be pecan pie and peanut patties and maybe chocolate cake that her mother had whipped up during frenetic hours in the kitchen.

The air in the house was perpetually thick with aromas and anger. The more anger, the more aroma, neither visible, but both so thick that sometimes Charlene felt she had to stay outside to play in order just to breathe. And after many nighttime arguments, she got to where instead of remaining in bed listening, she would creep back to the living room and switch the television on low. *Bonanza,* with Little Joe and handsome Adam, became her favorite show. There were also *Father Knows Best* and *Leave It to Beaver* and *The Beverly Hillbillies.* All stories of families with people who ended up happy with each other. When she came home from school, she took up watching game shows, like *The Price Is Right* and *Password.* She would sit close, so close as to be absorbed by the television. At times it seemed that she *had* been absorbed by it and was looking out, watching people walk past her but never seeing her. Her parents didn't seem to see her at all. When she volunteered to help her mother with supper, her mother would only nod absently, and more and more her father would walk off down the street, and if she followed, he would tell her to go home.

Then Rainey was born, and her parents seemed to get a lot happier. Her father and mother both smiled a lot at the new little baby girl and showed her to all the people who came to see her. Then the only one who seemed to be mad all the time was Freddy, but he still wasn't around much, so this didn't affect the returning harmony in the house.

Rainey became "Little Bit," and Charlene went from "Princess" to "Daughter." The big sister all grown-up, her parents said, as if looking at her for the first time in two years. By then Charlene was achieving A's in spelling from all the *Password* watching, but her eyesight suffered and she had to get glasses for reading, and she was some fifteen pounds overweight.

What she learned from these years was that people you loved could forget you.

The City Hall thermometer reads 101°

Joey called and spoke at length to Danny J. about the bronc riding business. Charlene, making banana pudding, lingered in the kitchen, watching her son's face light up with anticipation as he spoke of it, of this bronc rider and that one, and all his hopes and dreams of glory on the backs of wildly bucking horses. She caught mention of his already beginning to practice, incidents that she had no idea had taken place, and which he told of in a low voice, cupping the receiver.

Then he said clearly, "Mama really says it's okay, Dad. Here, she'll tell you. Tell him you said it was okay, Mom."

Charlene took the receiver. "I said it was okay with me, Joey, if it was okay with you."

"Well, okay then."

Joey's low, soft voice brought a jumble of yearnings roiling over her. She squeezed her eyes closed. But then Danny J. was reaching for the phone.

"I have a few more things to tell him, Mom."

Charlene was having trouble letting go of the receiver. "Danny J. has some more to say," she got out before the receiver was pulled from her hands.

She had more to say, too, she thought. *We need to talk, Joey, not yell at each other. Can't we do that? Can you come home, Joey?*

She waited with her ear cocked and her breath held, but Joey didn't request to speak with her.

Danny J. plopped the receiver on the hook and said, "Dad's gonna look for a buckin' horse."

After her son left the kitchen, Charlene gazed for a long minute at the phone. Then she strode out of the room and went to lie in her bed with a cool rag over her eyes.

The City Hall thermometer reads 86°

She would write Joey a letter. She got her favorite blue ink pen and linen stationery and sat at the kitchen table, with CMT playing on the television with its screen turned to the wall. Then she sat gazing at the night-black window reflecting the kitchen, seeing in her mind's eye Joey's blue truck arriving in a hurried dust ball and herself running out there to hear him say, ''I've come home. You won't be a divorced woman.''

What she truly wanted was to wake up and find him riding a horse around the training pen and that all of it had been some horrible nightmare that she could forget. She so wished everything to be like it used to be between them, in the good times, before it all fell apart.

Remember that first kiss? *Oh, Lord, what a kiss.*

It had been their third date before Joey kissed her. They'd been driving home from a movie in Lawton, and she'd been sitting beside him, imagining what it was going to be like to kiss him, imagining turning into his arms when he pulled up in front of her house, tingling from the sweet anticipation of every bit of it, when all of a sudden, Joey ripped the truck off the road, jammed on the brakes and looked at her with his chest heaving. Then he grabbed her and kissed her socks right off.

She blinked, coming out of memory and seeing the blank paper in front of her. She smoothed the paper and then wrote: *Dear Joey, I...*

And where was she going to mail this letter? To Sheila Arnett's?

She got the telephone book and ran her finger down the listings. Arnett...Sheila A. Address listed simply as ''East of City.''

She stared at the phone number for long minutes, imagining the sound of Sheila Arnett's voice answering on the other end.

Sitting herself down once more, Charlene again took up the pen. All she had to put on the envelope was Joey Darnell, the Arnett farm, and the letter would be delivered. That was how things were in Valentine.

Yes, and before the afternoon was up, word would be whispered from one end of town to the other that Charlene had sent a letter to her husband out at the Arnett farm. And it would be black-haired Sheila Arnett walking to her mailbox and pulling out the letter meant for Joey. Charlene saw it all clearly in her mind.

Throwing down the pen, she shot up from the chair, and before she knew it, she had walked out to the Suburban parked beneath the swaying limbs of the elm.

Opening the door, she got in behind the wheel. The keys were in it; they were always in it. Larry Joe would say, "Mom, really, who's gonna steal it?"

She sat with both hands gripping the steering wheel. Even if she could manage to drive herself over there to Sheila Arnett's, she couldn't go there. She couldn't risk seeing Joey with that black-haired woman who could be one of those perfect women dancing around in a CMT video.

She was sweating, she realized. Great heaps of sweat, and she was so hot she couldn't stand it. She got out of the Suburban and gulped in air.

Eleven

The City Hall thermometer reads 81°

Just before dawn, after her husband Perry took himself off to the drugstore and while Belinda was still in bed, Vella Blaine went outside to tend her rosebushes while it was as cool as possible. She wore a wide, leaf-green straw hat decorated with cloth ivy, and a green apron with deep pockets for her hand tools. She was inspecting her Mr. Lincoln for aphids when she saw Winston Valentine come out on his porch.

Quickly, she stepped behind the big lilac and pulled her binoculars from her apron pocket. She peered through the leafy branches, moving the binoculars over to Everett Northrupt and back to Winston, the two old coots and their silly flag business. Winston had a time getting his set in place today, and when it unfurled, Vella saw why he'd been struggling—it was a much bigger flag. So that was what the UPS man had delivered to him yesterday. It draped clear down into his boxwoods.

Winston looked down and saw the edges of his flag snagging in the bushes, and his stomach about hit his shoes. He'd known that he needed to try out the flag first, to see what he was going to do about the hanger. He'd been too dang impatient, and this self-knowledge was not helped when Everett called over, "Winston, it's hittin' your bushes."

"I see that, Everett."

"You can't let it stay like that," Everett called. "You'd better take it down."

Winston looked over his shoulder at his neighbor, who turned from him to his own flag, fluttering nicely, and smiled with appreciation. The Northrupts didn't have anything but little pansies at the edge of their porch.

Winston wasn't about to take his flag down. It had taken him nearly a week to get it. He started off purposefully for the toolshed at the back of the house.

Just as he passed by the roses, here came Ruthanne, wearing nothing but a slip. Thank heaven it was a full slip that at least partially covered her breasts that were swaying back and forth as she carried a dishpan of soapy water.

Winston took note of her surprising appearance but kept right on walking, saying only, "Ruthanne, do you know you're only wearin' a slip?"

Already past, behind him Winston heard, "Oh! Oh, my goodness!" and then the sound of a splash, footsteps scurrying up the steps and the banging of the porch screen door.

In the toolshed, Winston looked at the electric trimmers but then grabbed the large loppers from their hook.

Vella was about to leave her position behind the lilac when she caught sight of Winston coming back from the rear of the house, striding with loppers in his hand. She had a rising panic for a moment in which it crossed her mind that maybe he was going to attack Everett Northrupt. She was just about to run for the phone to call the police, but then Winston was at the boxwoods, and of course he was attacking them.

Vella watched until there didn't seem to be much left of those boxwoods, and the big Confederate flag flew free. In fact, it started fluttering high above where the bushes had been because the wind began to pick up.

"Minnie, I just saw Ruthanne come out of the house half-naked," she reported to her friend on the phone. "Lord knows, she must walk around like that inside. Poor thing doesn't have but half her mind, and no tellin' what Winston encourages her to do."

"What was she doin' outside?" Minnie wanted to know. "Just walkin' around? In her slip?"

"No, she came out and threw something on the rose-bushes, and Winston whacked down his boxwoods. All the way down."

Minnie was a little confused about this, and Vella had to back up and tell it all. Then Minnie said she remembered when those boxwoods were planted, but Vella wasn't paying too much attention to that. She wondered about what Ruthanne had thrown on that rosebush. Looked like wash water. Maybe she should find out what dish soap they used. Maybe that was why Winston's roses were blooming so abundantly.

The City Hall thermometer reads 88°

The two things Joey liked best in the entire world were the gentle creak of saddle leather and the jingle of spurs. He listened to the mingled sounds and the thud of hooves as he rode the sorrel colt down the valley beneath the tall elms and around the mesquite, a rare treat for both man and horse, who both seemed to need the break from the confines of fences and people.

Joey's father had put him on his first horse at the age of three, given him his first spurs at four, just as he had Joey's brothers—Bull, who died in Vietnam, Theo, who went to

Mexico, and Purvis, who went off in the army and had never been heard from again.

Their father had been a horse-trainer. He'd kept them moving all over, from Texas to Colorado. His father had always spoken of having his own place, but he hadn't settled down until he got stomped really badly and couldn't ride enough to train. They'd had to move to a cotton farm one of their mother's relatives owned. No matter that his father had had a massive heart attack at the age of fifty, Joey believed what had really killed him were the confines of plowed fields and mounting debts and faded dreams. Bull, who had witnessed it, said their father rose up from where he was patching over patches on the roof of their shotgun house, looked off in the far distance, then collapsed like a balloon with the air going out of it and rolled off the roof easy as a child's rubber ball. It was figured he was dead before he ever hit the ground.

The image of his father lying like a discarded rag on the ground that day filled his mind, until Joey blinked and realized he and the horse were approaching the gate to the long barn. He dismounted and led the colt through the gate and into the barn. The alley with stalls lining either side stretched ahead, a barn such as he'd always wanted. He looked at it with a mixture of excitement and shame, the thought coming, *Did you leave your family for a barn?*

Then here came Primo. "Mr. MacCoy has come with the feed delivery," Primo told him. "He has asked for you."

"Oh…thanks," he said when Primo took the horse's reins. "He's not too hot. You can just rinse him off, but leave him tied for at least thirty minutes. Watch him, now…he's knowin' he's a colt these days."

The next instant a figure came wheeling a dolly of feed sacks in the walk-through door.

It was Mason MacCoy, and at the sight of the man annoyance crawled over Joey. He resented the man for drawing him away from the horses. And that MacCoy had witnessed an embarrassing moment in Joey's life still nagged at him.

"I have that order," MacCoy said. "Got some cow feed in it. That correct?"

"Yes," Joey said, nodding and remembering Larry Joe's truck being at MacCoy's house. "We got in twenty head of calves for practicing cutting. The feed doesn't go in here. We'll put it in the shed near the pasture."

"Okay...right here I have the pelletted horse feed. I had to substitute with a brand that has fourteen percent protein but two percent less fat. Do you still want it?"

"Let me have a look," Joey said. He was particular about feed. These high-bred horses could up and colic on the least change.

He turned the top sack over to read the listing of ingredients. The print was somewhat blurry.

"Here." MacCoy offered a pair of reading glasses.

"That's okay. This looks fine." He was not about to use the reading glasses. Old man glasses.

He turned and walked ahead, opening the door to the feed room. MacCoy wheeled the sacks inside and began to unloaded them. Joey noted the man didn't look so old, and he had thick shoulders, thick arms. Joey jumped in to help with the sacks. He could toss fifty-pound sacks as easily as MacCoy.

He remembered how MacCoy had often delivered feed to Joey at his and Charlene's place, too. He thought of dropping Larry Joe at MacCoy's yard.

Then they were straight and looking at each other again.

MacCoy said, "You want to show me where to put that cattle feed?"

They walked out to the delivery truck. Joey heard his

spurs jingle with each step. They made him feel good. He slid into the truck seat and directed MacCoy to the small building near the pasture where they fed the calves. The wind had picked up.

"May get rain," MacCoy said.

They both looked up to see a plane buzzing in and out of billowing clouds.

"It'd be helpful," Joey said.

He pitched in to help MacCoy unload the sacks of grain. The memory of his son's truck in MacCoy's front yard tugged at him.

Finally he said, "My boy's truck was out at your place on Sunday."

MacCoy squinted at him. "Yep, it was."

Joey tossed a sack in the shed and straightened. MacCoy tossed his and got another.

"What was it doin' there?" Joey asked.

Mason paused and squinted at him. "Why don't you ask your son?"

"'Cause I'm askin' you."

MacCoy threw another sack in the shed, and Joey waited.

"Well," MacCoy finally said, "he needed a place to park it Saturday night."

Joey figured things in his mind as he unloaded another sack. "Where'd you and Neville pick him up?"

"Out on Cemetery Road. He wasn't causing any trouble, just havin' a good time with a couple of buddies and some beer. He's a good kid."

"I know that. He's my son."

Mason inclined his head. "Just thought I should say it."

Joey thought he probably should have said thanks, but he couldn't. Then he said, "I think if it happens again, you'd better call me or his mother."

"I can do that," MacCoy said, "but the boy is eighteen.

Anyone else catches him, calling his parents isn't required.''

Joey looked at him, and MacCoy looked back, then finished unloading the last two sacks. Handling them both, as if he just had to show that he could do it easy.

They got back into the truck, and MacCoy drove to the barnyard. As he pulled to a stop, Sheila came walking across from the house. The wind was blowing her black hair back from her face and plastering her thin shirt to her body. She had that stride about her that drew a man's eye. Joey noted that MacCoy looked.

He wished deeply that she hadn't come out. Somehow he didn't want to be seen with her. He sure wished she wouldn't wait there for him to get out of the truck. And then he sure as hell wished she hadn't slipped her arm through his as she turned him to the house, all right in front of Mason MacCoy.

Mason, leaning a bit, watched the two in the rearview mirror, the black head very close to Darnell's shoulder and the dust swirling up around them.

So that was the true fact of the case, Mason thought with a good deal of satisfaction.

Mason could still recall the day he had first seen her. Oh, he had seen Charlene before that day, of course. He knew her as Charlene Valentine, one of those Valentine girls. They had gone to the same school, and he wasn't but two grades ahead of her. But back then she had been just one of many schoolgirls and nothing to interest him. He had been wild and chasing girls equally wild. Then, fleeing his daddy more than growing up, he had gone out into the world, a tough guy working tough jobs roughnecking on oil rigs all over the country, getting wilder and wilder until he landed himself in prison. He had not returned to Valentine until he was thirty-five, and then, with wounds freshly patched and tender, he had kept to himself and his Grandpap for a number of years.

Eventually he had gone to work in the feed store warehouse, and one day he had come to deliver feed to Joey Darnell. There she was, walking out from her house, the prettiest woman Mason had ever seen. His eyes had landed first on her coppery hair shining in the sun, and then her smiling face, her skin like fresh-from-the-warm-cow cream.

He tried not to stare at her.

"Hello," she said to him in the voice of an angel. "Do you know where to put the feed?"

He didn't, since it was his first trip. She showed him the shed, and he watched her graceful stride as she went on ahead of him. She had a walk that was more of a glide, as natural as the breeze that fluttered her hair.

When she turned slightly to say something over her shoulder, he realized that she was pregnant. He was hit with the full realization that she was Joey Darnell's wife, when she said, "My husband just went to town for a few minutes. I bet you two passed on the road."

That day love at first sight happened to him. The kind of love no one believes can happen but that poets and novelists write of with regularity. And no matter that she was married, and that he would never have anything with her, Mason could not stop loving Charlene Darnell.

It was a pure love, and, as such, strong as a love can be. For ten years he had enjoyed seeing her, usually from far away. His eye would follow her walking down the street, or maybe into a store, or even out to greet him from her house when he brought grain, which he always did with a mixture of eagerness and fear of his feelings being discovered. He made a point of not ever approaching her. That would not be right and might tarnish his shining love.

Although, sometimes when he delivered feed to the Darnell place or he met her in passing, when she would invariably smile at him, he would exchange a greeting with her, in the manner of two casual people who lived in the same town. And he had made himself be content with that.

Until now. Now he began to have fantasies that kept him awake at night, tossing and turning with sweat. Fantasies that made his heart swell with so much yearning he thought he could not stand it.

Now, whenever he went into town, he looked hard to see her. Now he carried on entire conversations with her in his mind, in which he got around to telling her how he felt, and she replied that she felt the same. Now hope that he could actually experience these fantasies had risen, and he couldn't seem to snuff it out.

Twelve

The City Hall thermometer reads 103°

The clouds billowed, giving hope for rain. A couple of times airplanes darted and swooped around, as if to ascertain the wisdom of cloud seeding. Nothing ever came of it. The wind got harder and blew the clouds right away. It also blew down some of the cable company's tower equipment, so that Charlene lost a number of her favorite stations. After a day of this, she disconnected the cable and had Larry Joe help her to climb around on the roof and get hooked up to their old antenna on the chimney. She could get a Wichita Falls station with it, and they had a few good old shows.

Father Knows Best was just coming on and Charlene settling at the kitchen table with a glass of ice tea when Larry Joe and Danny J. came in to tell her that they were leaving. Larry Joe was going to meet Randy Stidham and do whatever they did to engines, and he would give Danny J. a ride over to Curt Butler's house. Mr. Butler would bring Danny J. home. Charlene kissed both her sons and sent them on their way, returning to find she could still get the gist of the story on *Father Knows Best*.

Later, while watching *Lassie* with Jojo, they had a call from Mary Lynn Macomb, who asked if Jojo could come spend the night with her Sarah, to keep her entertained while Mary Lynn and her husband wallpapered the dining room.

With a hand over the receiver, Charlene discussed the matter with Jojo.

"Can I come home whenever I want?" Jojo asked.

"Of course."

"Even in the middle of the night?" Jojo was a detail person.

"Yes. I'm sure Mary Lynn would bring you, or if Larry Joe is home, he will come get you, if you want to come home."

Jojo said she wanted to go stay.

Mary Lynn offered to drive down to get Jojo, but Charlene said quickly and firmly that they would walk.

It was a half mile along the blacktopped highway to the Macombs' house, and the wind blew them most of the way. Charlene carried an umbrella to shade them, which turned out to be a mistake because the wind tried to snatch it out of her hand and finally succeeded in turning it inside out.

She kissed Jojo and watched her daughter cross the road and, with her little blue suitcase bumping her leg, run up the manicured, if sunburned, yard. The house looked like something out of *Southern Living* magazine, with ceramic ducks sitting at the edge of the porch stairs and a green wooden bench on the green-railed porch, which Jerry Macomb was that minute painting. He was wearing painter's overalls and no shirt. He had the muscles of a thirty-five-year-old man, which he was.

Charlene jerked her gaze away from his bulging shoulders and saw Mary Lynn Macomb poke her head out the door. Mary Lynn motioned and hollered something the wind snatched right away.

Charlene acted like Mary Lynn's motion was a friendly

wave and waved in return, then headed back the way she had come, her face turned to the hot wind.

When she went into the house, she stood a minute, listening to the quiet. She was alone. She could let her shoulders sag all she wished.

Rainey telephoned. "What are you doing?"

"Watching television. *I Love Lucy.* The one where she's learnin' to drive."

"You need to get out of the house. Have you been out of the house?"

"I was on the roof this morning." Charlene explained about the television crisis.

"I was thinking more in the direction of going to the beauty shop and gettin' your hair done," Rainey said. "It'll give you a real lift."

"Yes. That is a good idea." It *was* a good idea, only the thought of going to the beauty salon didn't appeal to Charlene. She didn't see a need to upset Rainey with that information, though.

"Well, have you spoken to Joey?"

"Yes."

"Good…so what have you two decided?"

"I told him I had agreed that Danny J. could pursue bronc riding," Charlene said. "We decided that."

"I meant what have you two decided to do about your marriage? Are you two discussing things?"

"No…" Charlene spoke low into the receiver. "We haven't discussed anything. I thought to write him a letter, but I didn't want to mail it and have Sheila see it. I really don't know how to start talking to him. I'm afraid we'll get in another fight. I don't want the kids to see us fighting anymore."

"You both need to get away to a neutral place. Why don't you meet out at the lake?"

Charlene sat up straighter. "Yes...we could do that, I suppose."

She pictured it: the lake sparkling in the red light of a setting sun and her wearing her sundress, with no panties. He would turn to her and say, *"I made a terrible mistake, and I want you and won't leave you a divorced woman."*

The idea of the lake seemed promising, although by the time she and Rainey finished their conversation and hung up, all sorts of doubts had crept into the picture. She would have to have Joey come pick her up, and what if they got into a fight on the drive over there? And the lake was about to go dry, so the setting sun would be shining on mud, which dulled the picture quite a bit. And it was really hot, and the heat and sweat led to tempers, and she would have to wear panties, because there were chiggers at the lake.

And she just didn't think she could call and ask him to do it. What if he said no?

The City Hall thermometer reads 82°

Just after midnight Mary Lynn called to say that Jojo had had a bad dream. "She wants to come home," Mary Lynn said. "I'll drive her down."

Charlene smacked down the receiver and raced immediately out the front door and stood beneath the elms swaying violently in the wind, peering at the road for headlights. She saw the minivan come slowly down the drive, and when it stopped, she jumped forward, snatched open the passenger door, and Jojo fell crying into her arms.

"She woke up screaming and hasn't stopped crying," Mary Lynn said, coming around the minivan and raising her voice over the wind. "She said she's had this dream all week." Her tone had questions and suppositions vibrating in it.

Charlene cuddled Jojo close. "Thank you for bringin' her, Mary Lynn," she said, and carried Jojo to the house without a backward glance.

Larry Joe came down the hallway, wearing only boxer shorts and scratching his head. Jojo reached out for him, while still holding on to Charlene's neck. She hugged them both, and then Larry Joe managed to take her so Charlene could get her a glass of warm milk. Jojo insisted that the three of them settle together on the couch. Jojo curled in her lap, and Larry Joe ended up reclining on Charlene's one outstretched leg. Long after her two children fell asleep, Charlene lay awake, feeling the beat of their pulses against her. She might have gotten up and gone to get Danny J. to be with them, if she hadn't been afraid of rousing everyone.

The City Hall thermometer reads 103°

Her father came to see her. Charlene didn't hear him arrive, because she was out back watering her garden. He came through the house and out the back door and said, "Here you are."

"Yes, here I am," she said.

"What are you doin'?"

"I'm waterin' the garden."

After a moment, her father said, "Honey, those plants are dead. I don't think a little water is gonna bring them back."

"Maybe it will. Then, when it's cooler, the tomato plants will produce a bit before winter."

Her father stood there looking at her, so after a few

minutes Charlene shut the water off, and they went into the kitchen to have ice tea.

"Where are Mildred and Ruthanne today?" It was rare these days to see him without the two women. It struck her suddenly that her father enjoyed feminine company and always had. Losing their mother had been very hard on him. He had hardly spoken for weeks after she'd died, until that Mildred had started going over and visiting him.

"They went off to a Country Home party down at the Senior Center."

"That's a decorator party. People buy pictures and things to decorate their houses. Where will they put anything they buy?" The idea of the two women decorating her mother's home was disconcerting to Charlene, but her sister-in-law Helen was likely to go into a tizzy.

"Naw...soon as Mildred heard they were havin' it catered from an outfit up in Lawton that serves a double chocolate fudge cake, she was hot to go. Where are my grandkids?"

"Larry Joe went to Lawton for a car part, Danny J.'s over at Curt's again, and Jojo is sleeping. She was awake a lot last night."

She spoke as she reached for the television remote; it was about time for *Father Knows Best* to come on. She hoped her father wouldn't stay long enough to make her miss the program.

"I went up to see your brother Freddy yesterd'y." He always said *your brother Freddy*, as if they didn't know which Freddy he spoke of.

"How's he doin'?" She told herself to pay attention. She had been neglectful about her brother.

"He's about the same. Paintin' some of those paint-by-number pictures most of the time. The nurse said he started watchin' a baseball game the other afternoon, but he switched it off in the middle, got a bunch of fellas mad at him.

"Mainly he don't want to come out of there. And he says Helen's probably gonna divorce him."

"Oh." Charlene felt a pain in her chest. Everyone had halfway waited for years for Helen to divorce Freddy, but now it seemed too cruel. "Do you think she means it? I mean, she didn't divorce him when he had his girlfriend."

"Helen's tryin' to shake him up, she told me. Thing is, I'm not sure anything can shake Freddy up. He's hidin' in a hole, like."

Winston gazed at his ice tea glass, running his finger up and down the beads of sweat, seeming a little lost.

"I should go to see him," Charlene offered. She had gone several times weeks ago when he first went in the hospital, but she and Freddy barely knew each other. Freddy was not a man to have close friends, which made all the more reason why she should make an effort, she thought.

"He'd appreciate that, I imagine," her father said.

Charlene had doubts about her brother caring one way or another, but that was no reason not to try. For long seconds memories of their youth flitted across her mind, and in each one of them was her mother.

"It's sort of like we all went to pieces when Mama went to heaven, isn't it, Daddy?"

His eyebrows rose, and a pained look shot across his eyes, and then he nodded sadly.

Charlene remembered them, her mother and father together, how her father would put his hand on the back of her mother's neck, and they would gaze at each other with a certain look that blocked everyone else out. The look that had made her feel all lonely.

"What did Mama do to make you stay with her, Daddy?"

He looked startled. "What did she do?" he repeated.

"Yes...what was it that kept you comin' back after you stomped out? What did she do that made you want to stay married to her, even though she had an affair and a baby?"

The question gripped Charlene. She had long wondered it, deep inside, and now that she had at last given the question voice, hope pushed her to sit a little forward and to hold her breath so she wouldn't miss anything he might say.

"Oh, I don't know, Daughter." Her father dropped his gaze to his glass. "That was a long time ago. People didn't get divorced as easily then as now."

Disappointment washed over her. He was hiding from her. Unavailable to her, just as he'd been all those years ago when he and her mother had left her to make her way through their arguing as best she could.

She blinked and tried to breathe.

Then he said quite firmly, "I never thought of Rainey as another man's baby."

"I know that, Daddy. And Rainey knows it."

Charlene got up and took a pitcher of tea from the refrigerator and refreshed their glasses.

"It wasn't really what your mother did," her father said quite suddenly.

She looked down to see his eyes all pale and pained on her.

"It wasn't a matter of her knowin' some special secret, like her chicken pot pie, or the way she always smelled of Chanel. It wasn't some special trick she had that made me stay."

He nervously broke the gaze and fiddled with his glass. Charlene lowered herself into her chair.

"Honey, I wish I could tell you exactly what it was, how we did it, but there's so much I myself don't understand about what happened." He sighed deeply and stretched one of his legs, saying, "We just sort of kept on goin', each of us. Sometimes I'd get mad and quit, and sometimes your mama would get mad and quit, but it just worked out that neither of us quit at the same time. Maybe that was because neither of us wanted to lose each other, but consciously there didn't seem to be any design in it, not on our part, except to ask God for help.

"Oh, your mama wanted to drag me to church, and she got pretty aggravated that I mostly wouldn't go, but that wasn't my way then. It didn't mean I didn't talk to Him, though. I did."

She was staring at him, trying to find hope but not quite doing so.

He cleared his throat. "I guess what it amounted to mostly was that I finally came to terms with myself and what I wanted. That was it mostly…I got where I trusted my own self so that I could trust myself with your mama. What you have to come to is that you know people are always gonna let you down because they're only as human as you are, but that all of that is okay. You'll be okay because you trust the God inside you and them."

Charlene gazed into his glistening eyes. Then she looked long at her own glass of amber ice tea.

"I don't feel like I'm going to be okay," she said, feeling tears trying to come. "I just don't know what I'm goin' to do, Daddy."

"You're doin' it, Daughter. All you need to do is take it a day at a time. And pray for strength to keep goin' on."

"Well, I can't hardly pray, Daddy. I feel all stopped up."

"That's okay. God knows it all anyway. Prayer doesn't have to be much."

Again the silence came over them. She glanced at her father, and he looked helpless.

Charlene put her hand over his on the table. "Thank you, Daddy."

He looked a little anxious. "Can I do anything to help you, Daughter?" he asked, pushing forth the question.

Charlene didn't think she should say, "Hold me, Daddy. Make it all go away." He couldn't make it go away, and her crumpling like that would be hard on him.

"Well, Daddy...you might see if you can get the cable connected back correctly to the hook-up. I got aggravated and pulled it out too hard yesterday, and the reception's been poor ever since."

Thirteen

The City Hall thermometer reads 125°

The digital thermometer on the City Hall building was responsible for a four-car pile up on Main Street, when it went crazy and not only reported an abnormally high temperature, but it began blinking on and off like an emergency announcement. Vella Blaine and Minnie Oakes, coming out of the drugstore, eating ice-cream cones, saw the accident happen before their eyes and gave a thorough report for the *Valentine Voice*.

"Everett Northrupt caused it," Minnie said. "He slammed on his brakes right there in the street so hard he squealed the tires and liked to have scared me to death."

"That's right," Vella agreed promptly. "We had just come out the door, and I was trying to open a napkin for Minnie to catch the drips from her ice-cream cone. She'd already got a drop on her dress—it was chocolate, but I told her I had this stuff that would get it out. It's called Zip, best stuff. Then Everett squealed his tires, and Minnie jumped, and I almost smacked her ice-cream cone, and then that green little van of colored…of people of color slammed into Everett. Minnie screamed, too."

Everett's story was that his wife Doris, an excitable woman, had looked up and seen the thermometer and given out an exclamation. Everett, vigilant because his wife had had a poor heart for twenty years, looked over and saw her mouth open and her hand on her chest, and slammed on the brakes.

The car behind him, a family in a green minivan—turned out they were an army family checking out the town to settle in, so they were really looking around—slammed into the Northrupts' Mercedes hard enough to throw Everett and Doris against their seat belts but not really give them whiplash. That came when Iris MacCoy in her red Cadillac, driving fast and dreaming dreams as usual, couldn't get stopped in time and hit the minivan, shoving it up a second time very unexpectedly into the Mercedes.

Coming behind Iris were Odessa Collier and Lila Hicks in Odessa's big black Lincoln. Odessa, flat out honest about being a little careless in driving, said that she was not going especially fast but that she and Lila were discussing the necessary evils of mammograms, and that she saw the Cadillac stopped in the road at about the same instant that she hit it. She hit it hard enough to move all the other cars up another inch and spilled her cup of Hardee's coffee all over her lap.

"The next thing I knew," Vella said, "is that people were yelling all over the place. They were just coming out of ever'where."

"Iris's Cadillac was honking," Minnie said. "I think that's why nobody could hear Neville hollering for people to be quiet and calm down. He was right there first thing. He's always first one there."

"Everett and Doris were really goin' at it," Vella put in.

Everett Northrupt was getting out of his Mercedes and holding his neck and yelling at his wife, who he had discovered was not having a heart attack after all. And then came Mason MacCoy and Deputy Midgett to Doris's door to see if she was okay. Neville Oakes, Minnie's grandson, passed them and went on to the minivan, where the mother was getting out, a foreign-looking woman, heavy but really pretty. She obviously wasn't hurt, but she was angry.

"She looked like she could spit nails, and she was jerking her kids up out of the van," Vella reported.

Then there was Winston Valentine getting Iris MacCoy out of her Cadillac. Minnie said she saw him come bursting out of the cafe, and he went right to Iris.

"I didn't think you were supposed to move people who've been in an accident," Minnie said. "But Winston got her out, and she was slumped over him, and he had his hands all over her."

Then Neville got there to help him. They got Iris lying down on the sidewalk beside where Mildred had come out and ended up sitting down. They put Mildred's purse under Iris's head.

"That Odessa was a sight," Vella said. "She was still in a bathrobe, just like she always is half the day. Polyester. I doubt that coffee stain'll come out."

"Winston went to help *her,* too," Minnie observed.

Everybody kept remarking on the thermometer, and Neville Oakes sent Deputy Midgett to go into City Hall and pull the plug. Told him to use his gun for authority if the mayor's nutty secretary stood in the way.

Traffic was piling up, and Larry Joe went running up to the west end of the street to divert traffic around town. Danny J. followed and took up a position right beside his older brother, watching his hand motions and doing the same.

The next vehicle to come along was their father, towing a horse trailer, and with Sheila Arnett sitting beside him. He stopped and stared, and Larry Joe waved him on like

everyone else, like he was a stranger. He was embarrassed
to have his little brother see his father with that woman and
really glad his mother had not seen.

Joey went on and pulled off the road at the first available
place. Leaving Sheila, with the engine going and air-
conditioning blowing, he jogged over to Main Street, where
he joined in to push Odessa's car out of the way so the
ambulance could come up closer. He found himself pushing
on a fender right beside Larry Joe, and across from him
was Mason MacCoy. Larry Joe would not look at him,
acted like he didn't even exist.

The ambulance took Iris and Everett and Doris off to the
hospital. Iris had come to as much of her senses as she ever
possessed, and her only wound was a broken fingernail, but
the medic wanted her head examined. Everett thought his
neck should be looked at for insurance purposes, and Doris
had started crying hysterically. Everett, who was now horribly embarrassed about their public row, was beginning to
worry that she might be so upset as to precipitate a true
heart attack.

The commotion had pretty much emptied the cafe, leaving only Ruthanne and Charlene and Jojo in the corner
booth. Having heard the all too familiar screeching and
banging sounds, Charlene had grabbed her daughter from
racing out the door after Fayrene, the waitress. "You are
not goin' out there. You are liable to get run over yourself." She did let Jojo go stand at the window.

"Are you all right, sugar?" Ruthanne asked her. "You
look so white. Here, drink a few sips of water."

Charlene said she was okay. She did drink the water,
though.

"There wasn't anyone seriously injured," Fayrene reported when she came striding back inside. "But it's horribly hot. People need water." She got a pitcher of ice

water and a stack of white foam cups, and Charlene let Jojo go to help pass out the water.

"You and I should just sit here," Charlene told Ruthanne. "There's no need for you to get overheated." She felt a little guilty that she herself didn't go, but she just couldn't stand to see the wreck.

When everything was finally calming down and people straggling back into the cafe, the army family—the dad was a really big man in camouflage—came in to sit down and gather themselves together. Charlene watched Fayrene bring them all drinks on the house. Their littlest boy was crying. Jojo came in and said the boy had lost a tooth—a baby one set to come out—during the accident. They had searched the van but hadn't found it. The mother told him that he should have been in his seat belt. The mother was scared of what could have happened, Charlene knew, but she wished the woman would hug the boy, who kept crying about not having his tooth for the tooth fairy. His little dark face was just awash with tears.

Charlene reached into her purse and pulled out a tiny gold pill box, a precious memento she kept with her at all times, in case the house caught fire; it contained several of each of her children's baby teeth.

She took out a tooth and pressed it into Jojo's hand. "You go tell him you found it in the road."

"Oh, Mama...it'll be a lie," Jojo whispered, turning red.

"Go on. It'll just take a minute."

Jojo, scuffing her shoes, went over to the table, quickly and shyly handed over the tooth, then hurried back to Charlene, pushing her little body close.

Charlene saw the boy examine the tooth, and the mother smiled at last, really big, and hugged him. Charlene knew just how that mother felt; it made a mother cross when she wasn't able to make everything right for her child.

Later they all sat around on Winston's front porch, grandfather and grandsons swapping tales about the incident. Laughing now about it. Leo, the boy who delivered the *Valentine Voice,* came riding up on his bicycle and said he had been sent to get names of people who had taken part in helping. Charlene heard Joey's name given as one who pushed Odessa's car out of the way.

When the boy pedaled away, Mildred said she hoped no mention of the big fight Everett and Doris had had got in the paper. "Everybody's gonna be talkin' about it anyway."

They were all still sitting there when Neville Oakes brought the Northrups home. They all waved warmly at the couple, and Winston called that he was sure glad they were okay.

Northrup waved in return. About fifteen minutes later he came out to get his flag down because dusk had come. Everyone was quiet as Winston rose and did the same.

Fourteen

Saturday morning, Joey was riding a mare—Sheila's top mare—hard on a steer when Sheila came running into the arena and called out to him.

"Joey!"

He heard Sheila's call, but he ignored her. He couldn't afford to be distracted. It was never a good idea to stop a horse right when it was finally beginning to get the gist of the idea. Focus was key in training.

The steer turned, and...*whoo-ee*...that mare turned right with him. Joey jabbed with his spur, once, hard enough that the horse backed off. "Don't you crowd that cow," he whispered. Just the right distance, the horse had to learn.

Joey felt the mare lean into her strong hips; her ears went back, and she lowered her head toward the doe-brown Brahman. The steer moved, the horse moved. The steer stopped, the horse stopped.

Joey pushed himself deeper in the saddle and thought that cutting didn't get much better.

But Sheila was there, so reluctantly he lifted the reins to pull the mare off. It was always best to end on an up note, and the mare was tired. For himself, though, Joey would rather have remained riding on the cows. It was always a little annoying when people dragged him back into the real world.

Sheila had climbed up on the arena fence. "She's lookin' real good," she said.

"Yep, Peggy Sue here is gettin' the idea." Beneath him, the mare was foamy wet and breathing hard.

Joey was pleased with the horse's growing ability. This was the best horse he'd ever had, and she was going to give him a crack at going to the World Show. He wanted to go there, and he knew he had to bring it about for Sheila, who was counting on him to give her a winner.

He watched Sheila reach out to touch the mare's forehead, about the only place not all wet with sweat. Just then Joey noticed the way Sheila was dressed, in tight jeans and a silky shirt, unbuttoned low. There was something about the way Sheila dressed that seemed to draw attention and always made Joey a little surprised he hadn't noticed before.

Then he saw that her eyes were glowing with excitement and moving from him to the horse and back to him again, as if she were already imagining fame and fortune.

Joey felt called on to say, "We'll take her to the World Show, but winnin' is another matter. I can't guarantee a win. There's all the top horses there."

Still, Sheila was looking at him like she was just bursting. "I just talked to Clem Shackleford," she said. "He's finally come around to being willin' to discuss sellin' Peggy Sue's half brother."

"That Boon Bar horse?"

"Yes. I told him we would drive down this afternoon. He's not feelin' well and is talkin' about sellin' out again. We have to get down there and see him before he changes his mind—or before he dies, because that son of his won't sell that colt." She was speaking fast and already climbing down from the fence.

"I need to walk the mare out," Joey told her. "Twenty minutes."

"Let Primo cool her off. You go shower and get ready. I told Clem we'd be down there by noon for lunch, and afterward we can celebrate by goin' on down to Dallas and stayin' at the Adolphus."

Joey was halfway out of the saddle when she got to the last part and was so startled that he slipped and had to jerk his foot out of the stirrup or he would have fallen.

"Dallas?"

"Yes. Saturday night in the big town. Won't that be fun?"

Her gaze was intense on him. He looked back at her, not knowing what to say.

"I want to buy a new saddle over in Fort Worth," she said, "and I'll need you to help me pick it out, Joey, so it's my treat all the way. We'll have us a real good time. And just think if we get that Boon Bar colt."

He *was* thinking of it, and of what Sheila was requiring of him, and when he got to that, his mind got all confused.

He was shirtless, standing in the small trailer bathroom and combing his wet hair, when he heard the door open and Sheila call out. He stepped into the bedroom and snatched a fresh starched shirt from a hanger, jerking it on as fast as he could as he heard her coming down the little hallway.

Then she was there, her eyes on him and running up and down him in a manner that caused all sorts of commotion inside of him.

"Hurry up and come on. We'll take my car," she said and tossed him the keys to her Lexus. "You drive."

He buttoned his shirt and grabbed his hat on his way through the trailer. At the door he had to stop to tuck in his shirt. Sheila went on out and got into the passenger seat.

As he followed and slipped himself behind the wheel of the fancy automobile, he felt a great weight of guilt fall over his shoulders.

What if Charlene needed him for something? What if Charlene found out?

They would only be gone overnight, he reasoned. Really no more than if they drove over and saw about the horse and came home and went about their normal business. And maybe nothing at all was going to happen in Dallas, he was jumping the gun about that, and besides, they would get down there and get back, and no one needed to know about it.

He made certain to take the back road away from Valentine, and it occurred to him that sometimes a man just got drawn along by things he did not understand at all but could not stop.

Mason was driving past and saw the Darnell Suburban swinging into a space in the IGA parking lot. Instantly he tapped his brake, taking a second look.

Someone in the passenger seat. Could be Charlene, even though the figure wore a ball cap. Maybe one of Larry Joe's girlfriends.

The next thing Mason knew, he was turning around at the post office and driving back to the IGA, all on a chance that it could be Charlene. As he pulled his pickup into the IGA lot, Larry Joe and Charlene were entering the grocery store. It was her—he recognized her curvy shape and flowing stride.

Mason whipped into a space, stopped, and his hand hovered over the key in the ignition. He wondered if he was going a little crazy running after her. What would he say when he caught up?

He did need a few things, he told himself, shutting down

the engine. He jerked off his ball cap, raked his hands through his hair and checked the mirror. Outside his truck, he paused to rub the toes of his snakeskin boots on the backs of his pants legs.

Walking with quick strides, he went inside, got a shopping cart and cruised along the front of the store, looking down each aisle as he went. At an end-cap stack of coffee, he paused to grab a can and throw it in his cart. He didn't want his cart to be plumb empty when he came on them.

He found Charlene and Larry Joe at the far end of the store in the produce section. When he saw them, he stopped and pretended to consider the stuff in a display on his right.

She was choosing a cantaloupe, picking one up and sniffing it. Larry Joe was getting bananas. Where was Charlene's hair? Maybe it was put up under the cap. No...it was plumb cut off.

Mason considered how he should approach them. He couldn't just race over there and scare them to death. He would ease over, like he was after cantaloupe, too. He could say hello and ask Larry Joe about his truck.

Before he could take action, however, the two were moving on.

Keep cool, Mason told himself, as he cruised along the bread racks, picking up a loaf, and proceeded slowly, counting on just the right moment opening up. He rounded the corner and saw Charlene and Larry Joe heading down the coffee aisle. With what he took as inspiration, he rolled his cart on down to the meat case. When Charlene and Larry Joe came back down the next aisle, they would be getting really close to the meat case. He had been told once that the meat section was the best place to meet women.

This thought took a downturn, though, when he saw Lila Hicks pushing her cart along the meat case. She looked up at him and instantly smiled.

Lila liked to talk, and she liked to flirt. She didn't mean anything by it, did it as naturally as breathing, never mind that she would never see fifty again and was twenty pounds overweight.

"Well, hello, Mason." She had bright blue eyeshadow. She would have been rather pretty, was nice-looking even with the shadow, but it was quite disconcerting. It sort of gave the impression of constant winking as her eyes blinked.

"Hello, Lila."

"That was quite a mess in town yesterday, wasn't it?" she said and started in talking about the big wreck. It was what everybody he had come upon all day talked about.

He thought to cut her off a bit by saying, "Well, it's good to see you are doin' okay after it. Odessa's front end was pretty smashed up." He meant Odessa's car but suddenly realized how it had come out.

Lila didn't notice. "Oh, no, I didn't get hurt. I'm better than I have any business bein'," she said, giving her tinkling girl laugh.

Lila had a really pretty smile. She also liked to touch people, and her hand came out and squeezed his arm in an intimate manner at the same moment that Larry Joe appeared from the aisle, with Charlene coming up right behind him.

Charlene looked at Lila's hand on him. Mason saw her eyes go right there. No telling what she thought.

He shifted from Lila's touch, thinking desperately that he had to get away from her to strike up a conversation with Charlene and Larry Joe.

But then Lila was saying, "Well, hello, Larry Joe... Charlene. How are you two doin'? Y'all know Mason MacCoy, don't you? We were just talkin' about the big wreck yesterday. It sure was somethin'."

Mason was looking at Charlene, and she was smiling shyly at him.

"Yes, we know Mason. Hello," she said. She looked really cute in the ball cap. Her eyes were blue-green.

"Hello," he said. He looked at her, and she looked at him, then away.

When he looked over at Larry Joe, he saw the boy watching him and his mother.

"How are you doin', Larry Joe?" Mason said.

"Okay."

"How's that hot rod of yours?"

"Runnin'."

"I see you just cuttin' around with the girls in that truck, Larry Joe," Lila said. "I can hardly believe it. Seems it was only yesterday your mama would bring you to town to ride your tricycle up and down the sidewalks. Remember that, Charlene?"

Charlene said she remembered and that Larry Joe had been driving something since he was two years old. Her eyes were warm and proud when she gazed at her son. Mason knew he was staring at her, but he could not stop himself.

They talked about the thermometer no longer being there and how the temperature seemed a little cooler, and Mason spoke of all he knew on the subject and then started making things up about hearing there was rain coming. He was determined to stand there talking to Charlene until Lila Hicks left, and was grateful when Lila finally said she had to go give a piano lesson.

"Lila's quite a fine pianist," Charlene said, her eyes back on him.

He nodded in agreement. "I've heard her at church."

"Oh?" She cocked her head, peering at him.

"I get myself there from time to time," he said, enjoying

gazing into her eyes. Saying just whatever came to mind, he added, "She's got a good touch." Immediately he felt the red creeping over his face.

Larry Joe grinned knowingly, then he said, "Mom, I really need to get goin'."

"Oh, yes...nice to see you, Mason."

He nodded at her.

She smiled at him and turned away with her son.

Mason just stood there watching her walk away, seeing her graceful neck and the slope of her back and gliding hips.

Then she paused, casting a glance back at him, before disappearing down the paper products aisle.

Mason took hold of his shopping cart and began to push it back the way he had come, not really even knowing what he was doing. It was amazing. Here he had been in prison, had seen the toughest things a man could see, and his heart was beating like crazy over a simple encounter with a woman.

He'd been in prison. He found himself staring at his hands on the grocery cart handle. They were thick and rough and callused. They had touched and done things, ungodly things.

It had been years since Charlene had seen a man look at her. A pair of blinders suddenly went over a woman's eyes when a wedding ring was put on her finger. Or they were supposed to; she guessed for some women the blinders didn't take. They had for her, though, and she had not looked at a man or noticed any man look at her since the day she had married Joey.

Mason MacCoy had looked at her.

Charlene told herself this was impossible. He had been standing there with Lila Hicks's hand on his arm. Lila, who was friendly with every man, and who had a good touch. Wonder how far that went?

She was being really silly. Mason's relationship with Lila was none of her business, and furthermore, why would Mason possibly look at herself—a woman of forty-six, bare-faced and wearing a ball cap?

Slipping off the cap, she flipped down the visor and peered in the mirror. She hadn't cared what she'd looked like when she left the house. Her lips were colorless as a corpse, and she had hat-hair, too, just flat all over.

She really needed to drum up some pride in her appearance. She might have run into Joey. The way she looked now certainly wasn't going to attract him. Like she was now, people would say it was no wonder Joey had left her, more so than they probably already were saying it.

They were well down Main Street by the time Charlene made up her mind about going to the beauty shop and Larry Joe had to drive around the block to go back.

Fifteen

A bell tinkled as she opened the door with the lettering Cut and Curl in white script on the glass. Then the sweet-acrid scents of beauty products enveloped her. So did the color blue. The light seemed hazy blue, shining as it did through blue blinds at the window and bouncing off the blue walls and all the blue decor. Even the woman coming toward her wore blue neck to toe.

"Hello, Charlene. So nice to see you."

It was Dixie Love, owner of the shop, who had once lived in California. A flamboyant streak of pure white ran through her dark hair, which was swept back from her face. Bold earrings with blue stones dangled from her ears. She wore a light blue smock over a blue knit top and a long, filmy blue print skirt that flowed and swirled with her strides. Her lips didn't really smile, but it was as if her entire face beamed. "What can I do for you today?"

"My goodness, Charlene...Charlene!"

Oh, Lord. It was Mildred, waving and struggling to get herself and her big rollers out from underneath a hair dryer. One of the rollers caught the hood, causing her to lose her balance and propelling Charlene to sprint forward and try to catch her and the dryer, both tipping toward the floor. Thankfully Dixie Love was equally quick, because Mildred's bulk and the dryer chair were too much for Charlene alone.

"Well, my goodness," Mildred said, when she got straight and fixed an eye on Charlene. "I wouldn't have known you, Charlene. What did you do to your hair?"

"I cut it."

"Yes, you did." Mildred blinked, then she called to Ruthanne, "Look who's here, Ruthy."

Charlene saw Ruthanne sitting in the second beautician's chair where a tall, skinny somber-faced woman worked on her hair. Next to her, in the front chair, another woman spun around—Kaye Upchurch, the mayor's wife and deacon of Charlene's own Baptist church.

Kaye waved, and Charlene nodded.

Ruthanne looked at Charlene and blinked. "Hello."

"It's Charlene, Ruthanne," Mildred said in a raised voice, as if Ruthanne was deaf rather than confused.

"Hello, Charlene," Ruthanne said with a smile of genuine recognition. She appeared to be afraid to move the least iota beneath the beautician's hands.

Charlene returned the hello, her gaze moving from Ruthanne to Kaye Upchurch, and a quivering flitting across her stomach.

Ruthanne said sweetly, "I'm fine," although no one had asked.

Dixie Love took hold of Mildred and told her, "Now, hon, you are not quite done. You just get back under here and finish cookin'."

Charlene began to edge backward toward the door. "I see y'all are busy. I'll call for an appointment...I just wasn't thinking."

She had gotten foolishly carried away. She could not possibly sit in here and get her hair done, with That Mildred and Ruthanne and Kaye Upchurch and heaven only knew who else might come through the door.

"Oh, nonsense." Dixie Love captured her by the shoulders. "We take walk-ins. We're just about done with these ladies and can fit you right in."

She escorted Charlene to a chair, eased her down and swirled a cape around her shoulders, and introduced her to the tall, skinny woman, whose name was Oralee. Then, seemingly from out of nowhere, she produced a tumbler of sweet ice tea, which she tucked into Charlene's hand, while chatting on about remembering that Charlene herself had been a beautician and saying that she thought the short haircut was "just the thing for Charlene's features," but maybe they could give it some lift.

"What do you think, Oralee?" Dixie Love asked. "Maybe we should cut more back here and encourage it up on top."

Oralee's ebony eyes gave Charlene a quick, penetrating survey. "Uh-huh, and a rinse. That new red highlight rinse that just come in. Not a dye," she said to Charlene. "You don't want to dye."

"No, I don't want to dye," Charlene said.

"What you ought to do, Charlene, is give Joe a lesson. Show him what a mistake he has made," Kaye Upchurch said.

"Yes…get another man and make him jealous, and Joey'll come runnin' home," Mildred said, her lips forming a firm line.

"Where'd Joey go?" asked Ruthanne, who now had her hair all fixed and was sitting primly in a chair near the door.

"He ran off with a girlfriend, Ruthanne," Mildred said loudly.

Charlene, having abandoned herself to the fate of being openly discussed, sat there occasionally sipping her ice tea and watching the tall, skinny woman's dark hands tease up

Mildred's bright gold hair and Dixie Love's pale ones pile Kaye Upchurch's brown curls on top of her head.

"I am not talking about bringing him home," Kaye said. "She doesn't need him to come home, not after this sort of thing. You won't be able to trust him ever again. He just needs to get a lesson. You make sure he knows what he's missing out on, and when he realizes that and tries to come home, just shut the door in his face."

Charlene didn't know what to say to that, but apparently no reply was required. Quite quickly the tall Oralee said, "A man's nothin' but trouble anyway. A woman's better off without. I've had three, and none of them gave me nothin' but trouble."

"Then why are you always lookin' around for another one?" Dixie Love asked, amusement ringing in her voice.

"Well, they are trouble, but they are good for one thing," Mildred said in a knowing fashion.

Charlene's eyes popped wide at the statement that instantly caused her to think of Mildred and her daddy— together. She ran her gaze over Mildred, thinking of it.

"Oh, *that* is not worth having a man hangin' around your neck," Kaye Upchurch said in a matter-of-fact fashion that further surprised Charlene. "That is not what makes up life, anyway. Not worth the annoyance."

It was very hard to imagine Kaye Upchurch, a deacon in polyester, saying such a thing.

Oralee said, "I think she ought to chase him down and scratch his eyes out. A woman needs to stick up for herself."

Charlene looked at her and thought: Oralee. A pretty name. Her voice sure is deep for such a skinny woman. Probably she could do Ruthanne's hair well because it was so kinky. Oralee's own hair was in a million braids, what

that was called Charlene couldn't remember, but it looked
so artsy on the young woman.

"Look at her fingernails," Oralee said, jumping over and
snatching up one of Charlene's hands to display to everyone. "You could mark him good with those. Do you do
them yourself?"

"Yes." Charlene looked at her hand in the same manner
as everyone else.

"Well, you ought to give him a scratch, just to pick your
pride up, and then take all his money," Oralee said, dropping Charlene's hand and returning to Mildred's hair.

"Oralee, you do not mean that," Dixie Love said. "She
doesn't mean that, Charlene. She is pullin' your leg. And
all bitterness does for a woman is give her wrinkles."

Dixie Love herself had a face right out of an Ivory soap
commercial, pale and creamy and absolutely smooth. Charlene did quick calculations and came up with near sixty
years for the woman, which was amazing. She wondered
if Dixie Love had had plastic surgery. Maybe it was the
woman's last name of Love; maybe she was just filled up
with it.

"I did not say anything about being bitter," Oralee said.
She was quick as a wink putting Mildred's hair in place.
"No...bitterness only eats up the soul. You have to forgive
like the Good Book says, but you can forgive at the same
time that you give him the smack he needs. You give him
the smack because he deserves it. You can't respect yourself if you just let them men walk all over you, and they
don't respect you, either. You can't give forgiveness if it
isn't asked for," she added practically.

Was that what Joey had done? Walked all over her? He
had walked out, that was certain.

"Oralee is right about getting what money you can,"
Kaye said pointedly to Charlene. Then she returned her face

to the mirror and expounded at some length on how forgiveness did not mean one should be foolish and how a woman needed to look after her future.

"A woman is the one in charge of the home, and she needs to be capable to support it," she said. "She needs to understand the finances involved. I pay all the bills and manage all the money. If it was left to Walter, we'd be in the poorhouse. And then you never know when a husband is going to die or run off, like yours has done. That's why I started my own business sellin' Country Home decor. You might want to consider that, Charlene. I can get you started." She was looking at Charlene in the mirror.

"I...I'm not sure."

Mildred said, "You do need to think about your finances, dear." She was digging into her purse, pulling out her wiping cloth and packets of mustard. "You mostly need to think about retirement income. Too many women...like Ruthanne..." she whispered, "...never thought of it. Just left it to their husbands or daddies, and then you get to a certain age, and there's nothing but Social Security, and a person would starve on Social Security alone."

Charlene knew that Mildred herself had only a small bit of income from the sale of her home.

"You could go to work as a nail tech," Oralee said to her. "Around here that brings you about two hundred a day on average, which may not be a fortune but sure isn't starvin', and a lot of it is in cash."

Charlene was amazed at the figure. "For doin' fingernails?" She had not been a manicurist when she had worked as a beautician.

"Oh, yeah, honey, fingernails are big business. You got manicures and artificials and wraps. And then there's sellin' products, too. You can make upwards of three hundred a day at one of those salons up in Lawton. I'm fixin' to go up there myself, where I'm not overwhelmed with all these white people's hair.''

Oralee cast Dixie Love a pointed expression, and Dixie Love only gave her a serene smile in return.

"I don't have a license anymore," Charlene said. "I'd have to go back to school and all."

"Not necessarily. I'm a licensed teacher," Dixie Love put in quietly. "You could work under my supervision. I have an opening, if you're interested."

Charlene gazed at her. "I really don't know what I'm going to do." The idea unnerved her. She didn't want to commit to anything that might interfere with Joey coming back home.

Mildred had succeeded in finding her checkbook and wrote a check for services rendered. Before she left, she asked, "Are we still havin' Sunday supper at your house this week?"

"Oh…yes," Charlene said, because she couldn't think of a reason why not.

The next instant Oralee was laying her back and spraying warm water over her head. Oralee's ebony eyes hovered over her and shone with unexpected warmth.

Then suddenly there was Kaye Upchurch's face jutting in beside Oralee's above her. "Here's my card. You call me, if you want to become your own boss selling Country Home decor." She dropped the card in Charlene's lap and was gone.

Oralee said, "Whew, that woman can wear you out with her righteousness. Now, sweetie, you just close your eyes and enjoy this. You'll feel a whole lot better when I get done. We're gonna put some starch back into you."

Charlene closed her eyes and imagined the sultry Oralee pouring starch from the shampoo bottle and working it into her head with her massaging hands. Then she thought how sad a woman she must appear, needing starch.

Dixie swung the chair around, and Charlene saw herself in the plate glass mirror.

"Oh..."

Tentatively she reached up to touch her hair. It was soft. She moved her head this way and that. She had not imagined simply cutting and curling her hair could do this, make her look so much more alive. Her hair had come alive. Big, bold curls that set off the coppery color. And she'd had her eyebrows waxed and a facial and new makeup applied, too.

"Here's an extra." Oralee dabbed perfume on Charlene's neck and wrists, a very sweet, sultry scent.

As Charlene rose from the chair and paid Dixie Love, she kept glancing in the mirrors all around. An emotion she could not name began to rise in her. It made her heart beat faster, made her feel as if she could feel her blood pumping through all her cells.

A last look in the mirror and she said to the two women, "Oh, thank you both so much!"

Oralee's lips formed a rare grin, "Honey, we didn't make the material. God did that, and it is *fine*. Just worn and needin' a little starch to make it seem like brand-new."

Charlene did feel brand-new. All along the sidewalk on her way to the cafe, where Larry Joe was supposed to pick her up, she caught her reflection in window after plate glass window. The sense of newness, boldness, just grew and grew. She felt like a woman who would go without her panties and not worry a bit.

As she passed the saddle shop, a man came out—a very handsome man—and he smiled at her. She smiled back before she knew.

Then she quickly averted her eyes, walking on and marveling at the feelings whirling inside. She felt so good, and she wanted to share it all around. It was a feeling of strength, she thought, like a starched shirt had. It was a feeling she knew as vaguely familiar, from a long time ago, when she'd been young and fresh and without the scars of twenty-plus years of daily living.

She began to wish very much to run into Joey. At that moment anything seemed possible, and a surge of eagerness went through her. She looked up and down the street for his blue truck; he often had lunch at the cafe because he liked their country fried steak.

That she didn't see his truck was a little disappointing, and when she got to the door of the cafe, she had a moment of uncertainty about going inside all alone. She wished she'd told Larry Joe to pick her up at the drugstore, and then she could have perused the magazines until he came.

But, catching sight of her reflection in the glass door, she thought that a starched shirt was ready to go anywhere, so she pushed right on through the door, telling herself that if Joey happened to be inside after all and Sheila were with him, she would go right over and shove the slut out of the booth.

She very quickly, and with some disappointment, saw that Joey was not there. She went to sit at the counter—she had read in one of those magazines that the comfortable way for a woman to eat alone was to sit at the counter—and while waiting for Larry Joe, she enjoyed a glass of ice tea, a bacon, lettuce and tomato sandwich, and Fayrene Gardner going on and on about how great her hair looked.

"It just suits you to a *t*," Fayrene said. "To a capital *T*. You know, it looks like Marilyn Monroe's hair…only yours is red, of course. But just like hers in *Some Like It Hot*. Don't you think it does, Judy?" she asked the waitress working with her.

"Does what?"

"Look like Marilyn Monroe's hair in *Some Like It Hot*."

Charlene was getting embarrassed. A man sitting several stools away was looking at her hair, and she didn't even know him.

"That was before my time, Fayrene," Judy said. She couldn't have been but thirty. "But your hair does look great," she offered to Charlene.

Then, the next thing, Ray Horn, the agricultural teacher from school and a longtime customer of Joey's, came over to her. Charlene didn't see him until he was slipping right onto the stool beside her and saying, "Well, hello, Charlene." He sat loosely with one foot stretched to the floor.

Charlene quickly wiped her mouth in case she had mayonnaise on it. "Hello, Ray." She felt uncertain. She had never said much to him beyond commenting on how pretty his horse was or questioning Danny J.'s performance in class.

Ray tossed his restaurant check and money on the counter for Fayrene; apparently he'd already had his lunch and wasn't going to sit there and eat with Charlene, thank goodness. She had always thought he had the most beautiful head of hair, but his face and neck were way too thick for her taste.

"How's Danny J. doin'?" he asked. "Am I gonna have him in FFA this year?"

"I don't know. He hasn't said."

The number of weeks until school began and thoughts of all the clothes she would need to buy were going around in Charlene's head, when Ray said, "I was sorry to hear about you and Joey."

"Thank you," she said and smoothed her folded napkin.

"Me and Susie broke up, too."

"You did?" She had seen his wife, a petite woman with frosted hair, but had not known her name.

He nodded and twisted his stool back and forth. "It wasn't a surprise. It'd been comin' for some time. We saw a counselor and everything. We tried, but...you know."

He had dropped his gaze.

Charlene thought frantically for something to say and came up with, "I'm sorry for you and Susie."

He nodded again and then cocked his head. "Maybe you'd like to go out, have dinner or somethin'."

"Joey and I aren't divorced. We're separated, but we aren't divorced."

"Susie and I are just separated right now, too, but the divorce is pending. It might be nice for you and me to have dinner...to commiserate with each other."

Charlene's gaze slid from his hopeful face to his neck so thick it didn't look like he had one. "I'm pretty busy with the kids right now."

Surely he wouldn't press it. But she saw that he was going to.

Then here came Larry Joe—thank you, God—through the door. "Here's my son now. He's giving me a ride home, and he has to get back to work."

She was off that stool and out of the restaurant, tugging Larry Joe along with her.

When Larry Joe let her out in front of the house, she went straight in the front door and strode through to the kitchen, pausing for a minute to check her reflection in the mirror over the buffet, and then threw her purse on the table and picked up the telephone to dial Joey's pager number.

We need to talk, Joey. How about if we go out to the lake?

After punching in his number, she hung up and stood there, gazing at the phone and waiting for it to instantly ring. When it did not, she made herself get busy making a pitcher of ice tea. *Lord, please give me the words.*

When Joey had still not called by the time she had poured a glass of tea, she picked up the phone and dialed his pager number again.

Then she sat at the kitchen table and stared at the telephone, having no way of knowing that Joey's little black pager was beeping like crazy where Joey had left it—lying on top of the fake wood dresser in the small camper trailer.

It took some time for her father to come to the phone. Mildred had to go look for him, and she made a point of saying, "I move slow since my stroke, you know."

Charlene sat at the kitchen table, gripping the receiver and pressing it tight to her ear.

"Charlene, are you still on here?" Her father's voice came across the line.

"Yes, Daddy."

"I'm sorry I took so long. I was just outside at the rosebushes with Vella Blaine—she came down here chasin' after an armadillo with her shotgun, and I was tryin' to help her. I guess it was too dark for Mildred to see me through the window. She could have just hollered at me, if she would have opened the window."

"That's okay." She got up and moved to the counter, speaking low into the receiver. "Daddy, I need you to do something for me."

"What's that, honey?"

"I need you to go out to Sheila Arnett's and tell Joey I want to speak to him. I've been paging him all afternoon and evening, and he hasn't answered. Maybe he has it off or something, but he doesn't usually do that. Maybe he's gotten hurt."

"Okay, Daughter," her father said slowly. "Do you want me to go right now?"

"If you can."

"Well, sure. I'll drive out there right now."

"Thank you, Daddy. Now, don't hurry. You be careful."

She sat and waited and worried about asking her father to drive in the night. What if, because of her selfish need, he had an accident. She prayed for God to keep him safe and promised to get a better grip on herself. She switched on the television, turned to the bluegrass music station that she had recently discovered, and poured another cup of coffee, holding it in both hands while her gaze went again and again to the clock on the wall. She walked over and looked out the window. The moon was bright.

And then she saw the flicker of headlights. She looked, her mind going automatically to hopes and visions of Joey coming, but then she saw her father's big sedan pull up beneath the tall pole lamp. She went out the front door, hearing as she opened it Danny J.'s. radio going in his room.

"Honey, Joey isn't at the Arnett ranch tonight," her father told her.

"He isn't?"

"No. He and Sheila went down to Dallas this mornin' and aren't expected back until tomorrow evening."

She searched her father's face. "He went to Dallas with her?"

"Yes."

She hugged her father's neck and told him she was okay, and then she went back into the house. She unplugged the coffeemaker, turned off the television and turned out the kitchen light. Passing Larry Joe's closed door, she pressed her palm against it, then moved on to Danny J.'s room. His door was open, and he was sprawled atop his bed, one bare foot hanging off. She turned off his radio, and bent and kissed his head. She stood for a moment in Jojo's doorway, then went on to her own room and bathroom, where she stripped off her clothes, got in the shower, put her face into the spray, and cried and cried. When she got out and wrapped herself in a towel, she slipped to the floor in a heap and cried some more because her husband had gone off to Dallas with another woman.

Sixteen

Winston came awake earlier than usual. He couldn't stretch out his legs because there was something on the end of his bed. He rose up and looked, blinking to clear his sleepy vision.

It was Ruthanne. She lay sideways at the end of the bed, snoring gently.

Winston was not terribly surprised; he'd reached the age where little could surprise him. He thought it was good he had taken to sleeping in pajamas. He sat up and let his feet rest on the floor for a full minute, letting his blood even itself out. Old people shouldn't go jumping up, his doctor had told him. Old people *couldn't* go jumping up, he thought.

He considered waking Ruthanne, but only for half a minute, before getting up and stiffly going into the bathroom. Now that he was old, he had to get to the bathroom first thing, and that was a real irritation.

The loud flushing toilet did not disturb Ruthanne. He found his slippers, noticing as he put them on that his toenails needed trimming. He went down to Dixie Love's for that.

It was the first bare light of day, enabling him to go through the shadowy house without turning on lights. He began to anticipate a full cup of coffee this morning before getting out the flag. As he passed through the dining room, something outside the window caught his eye.

Why, it was somebody out there. Unless his vision was failing him like his bladder.

He went over to the window.

It *was* somebody. It was a woman.

Vella Blaine? Naw, couldn't be.

Yes, it was. What in the world was Vella Blaine doing out there? Maybe she was walking in her sleep. She could hurt herself. He needed to do something.

She wasn't asleep. She was stealing his roses? Why would she do such a thing?

That's what she was doing, though. She had snippers and was snipping.

Maybe I'll holler at her out the window, see what she does. No, don't think so. I want to see what else she does. What's that she's picking up? Looks like a jar of something. Well, I'll be doggone. People are forever a source, aren't they?

He watched his neighbor slip through the old fence and hurry off across the pasture toward her own home. He hadn't known she could move so fast. She was just a young thing yet, though. Not yet sixty-five, he didn't think. He hoped she didn't step in a gopher hole and break her leg.

Charlene's eyes were nearly swollen shut from her crying most of the night. She peered at herself in the mirror and then went to the kitchen for some ice to wrap in a cloth. Jojo was at the table, eating a bowl of cereal.

"Mama, are you sick?"

"No, honey. I just have a bit of a headache."

Charlene took three aspirins, then got the ice from the freezer, wrapped it in a wet washcloth, went back to bed and placed the cold cloth over her eyes. She lay there, try-

ing not to imagine Joey in bed with Sheila in Dallas but,
the thought had lodged like a giant splinter.

She checked the clock and realized she had dozed at last.
Thirty minutes had passed. She got up and checked her eyes
in the mirror and found they looked a little better. She saw
her hair this time. She raked it back from her face. It looked
odd to her, so bold and vibrant, when she felt limper than
a wet shirt that hadn't seen starch in a month.

Jojo appeared at the bathroom door. "Mama, are we
goin' to church?"

Only then did Charlene remember it was Sunday. She
gazed at Jojo a moment. "Yes, we are. You come on in
here and get a bath, so that your brothers can get showered."

She went in and woke Danny J. and Larry Joe, who
protested that he was way too tired to go to church. She
told him to think of the girls who would be eager to see
him. Then she went in to make a pot of strong coffee. She
had to get herself together. She would never forgive herself
if, because she fell apart, her children were allowed to lose
their way in life.

Joey opened his eyes and found himself staring at black
hair. He lay very still, trying to figure out where he was,
and just whose naked body he was lying against.

Memory came rushing all over him, and he jerked back
from Sheila. Her arm flopped over, but, to his great relief,
she didn't wake up. He scooted out of the bed as quickly
but quietly as possible.

Breathing deeply, he stood looking at Sheila a minute,
then padded into the bathroom and closed the door. He
locked it.

The room was cold, with lots of gleaming marble and
shiny chrome and a plate glass mirror. He stepped in front

of the sink and peered at his reflection. He leaned closer to look at his face. He had the distinct and unsettling sensation of looking at a stranger.

The pastor raised his hands. "Every head bowed, every heart humble."

It was the prayer session. Lila Hicks's soft organ music floated around the sanctuary, rising to the tall ceiling. Neville Oakes's guitar music joined it. This was a new addition. The young pastor had gone off to retreat and returned with a number of ideas, and that always made people nervous. Charlene didn't much care for his idea of people feeling free to dance around in the aisles during some of the more stirring hymns; children and older people could get trampled. But she really liked Neville's guitar and people singing along if they wanted.

"Just as I am, without one plea..." Eyes closed, Charlene silently sang the familiar song and tried to settle her disturbing emotions. She was desperate to settle her emotions.

She sat on the pew between Larry Joe and Danny J. and felt awfully warm. The stained glass windows filtered the strong light, yet still the room seemed to be getting hot. The church was quite full, people squeezing the pews. A cough here and a sneeze there, someone mumbling and a baby crying.

Charlene began to feel like everyone was sucking up all the available air. She picked up the bulletin and fanned her face. *Oh, Lord, I really do want to pray, but I feel so far away.*

Then, just as the minister was ending the prayer session, she was on her feet. "Excuse me," she whispered to Larry Joe as she edged in front of him out of the pew and into the side aisle. She stuffed down the urge to run, to scream, and made herself walk to the door that led out to the covered veranda and the Sunday school rooms.

She burst outside and fairly held her breath until the door closed behind her.

"Whew!" She fanned her legs with her dress and thought maybe if she'd gone without panties, she would be cooler. Sweat was fairly soaking her bra. At least she hadn't worn hose.

Breathing deeply, as if she had just escaped drowning, she walked the length of the veranda, past the solid Sunday school doors, to a white painted bench at the end. She had never noticed the bench. She wasn't usually out here with time to sit. Why, it was a lovely place to sit, in the shade of both the porch and a giant elm, and with rosebushes edging the walk.

She settled herself, fanning her skirt some more. Maybe the temperature was high, but at least there was a breeze. It was almost as if God had led her out here, where she could breathe. Too bad the bench wasn't a swing. She really would like to have a porch swing like the one at her parents' house. Maybe if she went over there and sat on her mother's old porch swing, she could get herself back together.

The congregation was singing now. It sounded lovely from outside.

"Rock of ages, cleft for me...dum-de-dum...let me hide..."

Charlene, having closed her eyes, popped them wide open at the sound of a woman's voice singing.

Coming around the corner of the Sunday school building was a woman. In a filmy pale rose-colored dress and apron, and with a big straw hat. Why, it was the lovely white-haired woman from the other day in town, Charlene realized with some amazement.

"Hello, hon," the woman said cheerfully. She had a pink rose on her hat and carried several in her hand, along with garden snippers. "I was just clippin' a few of these Briar's Hedge roses, but you won't tell anyone, will you?"

"No," Charlene said. She glanced around uneasily to see if some usher might have stepped out to catch a smoke and would see. Then she would have to explain being out of the sanctuary, and about the woman clipping church roses.

With a stride that made her filmy skirt swirl, the woman came around and up onto the veranda, holding one of the roses out for Charlene.

"Thank you."

"You're more than welcome. You've found a nice spot."

"Oh...have a seat. This may sound crazy in this heat, but it seems cooler here than in the church. I was havin' trouble breathing in there. Maybe the air-conditioning isn't working right."

"It is a full crowd today. Everyone's praying for rain."

"Yes, yes they are," Charlene said, ashamed because she hadn't been praying at all.

"People should expect their prayers to be answered," the woman said. "When you pray for rain, you must *think* of rain, not the drought. Quit moanin' and get out the umbrellas, because you've prayed and know it is now going to rain."

"I guess I was more thinkin' about smacking my husband with a two-by-four," Charlene said, and, startled by her own admission, she looked at the woman to see her reaction.

The woman chuckled. And Charlene sort of did, too.

"I imagine you have good reason to want to smack your husband," the woman said, cocking her head.

"He left me." Charlene let that hang in the air. "I

thought he would come home, if I just gave him a chance and waited. But I know now he isn't going to.'' The truth rippled through her, causing her to suck in a ragged breath.

"Sometimes people do very foolish things, and we do want to smack them. Sometimes it helps to give them a good smack."

Charlene said sadly, "I don't think smacking him will change anything."

"Well, likely not, since he's gone."

"I'm not even mad anymore. Not really. He didn't set out to hurt me, and he's hurting himself terribly. I just don't know what I'm going to do."

"About what?"

Charlene, a little surprised by the question, said, "About him leaving."

"It seems he's already done it. What's there left for you to do about that? You can do a lot about other things, but not about that."

"That's just it, I guess. I don't know where to begin about anything," Charlene said. "I just feel so confused. I can hardly think. My mind just jumps around...and a few minutes ago I really thought I was going to fly all to pieces."

She had to tell someone about it; she thought maybe she was going crazy. "I have these times when I feel like that all of a sudden. I get so hot, and I feel like I'm going to lose my mind. Or that my heart is really going to stop beating because of the pain."

Averting her eyes, she lifted the rose to her nose and inhaled the scent. She guessed she'd cried herself out, thank heaven.

"Oh, honey, a lot of that is from the change. You can't help any of that."

Charlene looked at her and felt her breath leaving again.

"It's natural, honey, at your age." The woman patted her leg. "You are changing and growing in your body and your spirit. You're comin' into your new life as a full-fledged woman. Sometimes it's a little hard. It is just like being born, you know. And this stress in not helpin' your body at all."

"Oh God."

"Yes, you need to pray…call on God for His help, which is always there," the woman said. "And go get some books and read about menopause. If you understand it, it won't be so frightening. And get yourself some calming teas—some chamomile or saffron, or ginseng. And try some of that tofu that's in all the health magazines. It's supposed to be real good for a woman's hormones."

Charlene raked her hand up into her hair and fanned her face with the bulletin. The woman kept on talking.

"Don't look like that, honey. It isn't anything to be afraid of. Why, when I got through it, I came into the best part of my life. Getting through it takes years, too. You are young, yet—just startin'. It'll come and go for a number of years. I'm pretty certain it took me twelve years. Any change takes time—the world wasn't built in a day, you know."

Charlene wished the woman would shut up.

"And like when they're workin' to change a street, to make it wider and better, you'll have some inconvenience. You'll feel hot sometimes, and like you want to scream your head off. And then sometimes you'll want sex so bad," the woman said, laughing.

Charlene's face burned. She wasn't certain she should think about sex at church.

The woman took her hand. "Honey, these things are normal for a woman, and nothing to be ashamed of. Our good Lord made us, our bodies and our emotions. You are made in the image and likeness of God. There's not a thing wrong with you.''

''I don't feel like that,'' Charlene said.

''That's because you listen to the world around you. You have to get quiet and listen to *you,* and that's God speakin' inside you.''

Charlene said, ''I can't hear anything. And I've messed up so horribly.''

''I'm sure you've made some mistakes. You are human, and that means imperfect, but it certainly doesn't mean bad. God made you. Now, honey, look over there. See that car turnin' the corner? What if he finds out that he turned on the wrong street?''

Seeing a response was expected, Charlene said, ''Well, he can turn around in a driveway.''

''That's right. He's in charge of that steering wheel. He can turn around and go back the way he came, or maybe he can go around the block, or even a couple of blocks, or maybe all the way out in the country and back, until he finally finds the right road to get where he's going.

''The thing that won't help him is to stop right in the middle of the road and just sit there, afraid of making a wrong turn. These are the ones who cause wrecks when everyone smashes into them, like what happened to Everett last week.''

''Well, sometimes you need a rest from making so many mistakes,'' Charlene said, feeling called on to defend someone who stops.

''The main mistake people so often make is assuming that because they make mistakes, *they* are a mistake.

Charlene stared at the woman, who was rising to her feet.

''When you make a mistake, honey, it is nothin' more than a mistake. You learn from it and know you profit from it. You don't get better—you're already perfect from God—but you understand more. The one thing to keep in mind is that you can't steer a stopped car. You know how hard it is to turn the steering wheel of a stopped car?''

Charlene nodded. She could see it was expected.

"Well, even God has trouble with that, but a moving vehicle steers so easily. You can turn it any which way. And if you keep on going, you will eventually get where you want to go, no matter how many wrong roads you go down, roads with curves and potholes and all sorts of detours. You will get there eventually. And usually you had a mighty interesting trip,'' she added with a smile and a wink.

"I have to go, honey.'' She inserted one of the roses into her hat and then handed the rest to Charlene. "Here, you take these. I wouldn't wave them around, though. There's some who get all tight about the church roses. They don't understand that the more you share them, the more they grow, just like love.''

She stepped off the veranda, and at that same moment people began streaming out of the sanctuary.

"Wait!'' Charlene called to the woman. "What's your name?''

As she disappeared around the corner of the building, the woman tossed a wave and a name back over her shoulder, but Charlene didn't quite catch it.

Charlene jumped up and ran after her, but the woman was gone when she rounded the corner. She hurried on, and when she came around the south corner there was a crowd of people streaming out the rear sanctuary doors, heading across the parking lot to their vehicles. She looked for a straw hat and pale rose dress, but she had lost the woman again.

* * *

Larry Joe and Danny J. stood at the top of the church steps and looked around for their mother.

"She could be talkin' to somebody around the back," Danny J. said.

"You go look around. I'll wait here for her." Larry Joe was a little worried. His mother had looked pretty wild when she'd gotten up. He was thinking he should get Jojo or maybe Mildred to go into the bathroom to see if she was sick. Jojo had gone off with their grandfather and the old women. He looked around for them.

His gaze landed on Mason MacCoy, wearing a white shirt and with his hair all neatly combed, standing a few yards away in the shade of the cedar tree. Mason saw him at the same time.

He went lightly down the stairs and over to Mason, who stuck out his hand and said, "Hey, man." The way Mason shook his hand made him feel really good.

"I don't think I've seen you here before," Larry Joe said.

"I've come from time to time."

Larry Joe nodded, not sure what else to say. "Uh...have you seen my mother?"

"I saw her get up in church."

"Yeah. She wasn't feelin' too good." He glanced around the church yard. The crowd was thinning fast now.

Then he saw Mason looking at him intensely. "Did you check the ladies' room?"

"I was goin' to find Jojo to go in there."

Mason's gaze lifted, looking at someone over Larry Joe's shoulder. Larry Joe, thinking it must be his mother, whirled around.

"Hello, Larry Joe. I hardly recognized you away from the station." It was Iris MacCoy, smiling at him.

Larry Joe nodded and stuck his hands in his pants pockets. "Hello, ma'am."

"You don't have to ma'am me, Larry Joe. You aren't at work now." She seemed to get a kick out of saying his name. "I don't think I'm old enough to be your mother." She was looking at him in the way she had of making him feel self-conscious.

Larry Joe glanced at Mason, to see the man was amused. He felt his face heating up.

Mason said, "Iris, did you see Larry Joe's mother anywhere back around the rest rooms and fellowship hall?"

"Why, no. I wasn't in the rest room. I just left Adam and the other deacons in the fellowship hall, havin' their few words." She lifted her foot to adjust the strap of her sandal, reaching out to hold on to Larry Joe for balance.

"Would you mind going to check the ladies' room to see if she's there?" Mason asked. "She wasn't feeling very well."

"Well..." she cast a curious look at Larry Joe "...sure I will. It's probably the heat, and the ladies' room is the coolest place in that whole building. Here, Mace, will you hold my Bible and purse?" She thrust the things at Mason and turned and left.

Larry Joe watched her go, her bottom swinging in her tight pink skirt and her high-heeled sandals clicking on the concrete walk and up the stairs.

Then he looked over at Mason, and Mason, with a knowing grin, looked back at him.

"Why don't you hold the purse?" Mason said.

Larry Joe kept his hands in his pocket. "You've got two hands."

"You're a smart aleck," Mason said, "but I like you, and I've decided to work on that Chevy. Maybe I'll take it to some shows. Want a job?"

"What are you payin'?"

Just then, here came his mother with Danny J. from around the parking lot side of the building. Quite suddenly, watching her come down the walkway, with her hair bright and shiny in the sun, he was struck by how pretty his mother was. Every bit as pretty as Iris MacCoy, he thought, but in a different way. In a classy way...the way she walked and held herself straight. She smiled first at him and then at Mason, which sort of made Larry Joe mad.

"We've been lookin' all over for you," Larry Joe said, just then realizing he had been very worried. His father going nutty, he could understand, but he sure expected his mother to at least mostly stay stable. She'd always been there for them.

"I didn't mean to worry you," she said. "I got a horrible headache, and I needed some fresh air. I sat out on the bench over by the Sunday school rooms." He saw then that she had roses in her hand. "I picked these. Don't tell anyone." She blushed.

"I don't think pickin' the roses is an arresting offense," Mason said, and his voice was warm as melted butter.

And then she was looking at Mason and Mason was staring at her. Larry Joe watched them, feeling all sorts of confusion.

"Oh...you found her!" It was Iris MacCoy coming down the stairs. "Larry Joe said you weren't feelin' too good and sent me to see if you were in the ladies' room," she said, and as friendly as anything, she came close and slipped her hand right through Larry Joe's arm, giving a sort of laugh.

"It was too stuffy in the church for me, but I feel fine now," his mother said, her eyes straight on Iris. "I'd like to get out of this heat, though, so I'll claim my son to drive us home."

His mother's voice was every bit as bright as Iris's, and she slipped right in between Iris and him and took his arm. "It was so nice to see you all," she said, then grabbed hold of Danny J.'s hand and walked them both off toward the Suburban.

"Mom?" Larry Joe said.

"Yes, sugar?"

"You're squeezin' my arm."

"You said last week at Dixie's that you planned to have Sunday dinner," Mildred reminded her with an accusing eye.

"We are," Charlene said. "It's just that I forgot, and I really don't feel like cookin', so I sent Larry Joe and Danny J. to get pizza at Mazzio's. They'll be right back."

"I'd have been glad to take everyone out," her father said, looking a little uncertain.

Ruthanne was pulling out her chair and sitting at the table, just like always. Mildred looked like she was going to faint. She sank down into a chair. "Pizza just doesn't agree with my stomach," she said faintly.

Charlene went over and crouched in front of the older woman and took one of her hands. "I'll be glad to heat you up some canned soup. And then we can have the family meal right here, no trouble for anyone."

"I guess so," Mildred said, clearly disappointed. Then she pulled open her purse. "I have a packet of instant chicken noodle in here. I like it real well. You just add water and heat. Do you have oyster crackers? I just love oyster crackers."

Charlene was sitting on the back stoop, sipping coffee, when the door opened. It was Larry Joe. She asked him to turn off the porch light so she could see the stars better.

He did so, and then came and sat beside her on the middle step. They were both barefoot, and they put their feet hard and flat on the concrete, experiencing the amazing heat it held from the day.

"Weather report just said there's a hurricane comin' in the Gulf," Larry Joe said, "and maybe we'll get rain."

"We have to pray for rain and think rain," Charlene said. "There—Orion. See his belt."

"What is Orion?"

"A constellation. That's all I know. There's legends with each constellation. I used to know that stuff. Grama and I would sit out at the edge of the orchard and look at the stars. She knew all about them."

They saw a shooting star, and what Larry Joe told her was a satellite. They watched a frog hop across the walkway. His nighttime feeding of bugs had been interrupted when the light had been turned off. Out in the pasture the horses came running around, dark shadows with pounding hoof sounds. Larry Joe could make out each horse, but Charlene's eyes would not. She could do it by instinct, though. There was rustling out near the half-dead forsythia bush. They speculated that it was a possum, but then they saw it was a skunk. They almost jumped up to run inside, but then sat very still, watching it dig for grubs until it disappeared in the deep dark. They did all this while Charlene waited for Larry Joe to get around to telling her what he had to say.

"Mom," he said at last, in that hesitant tone of uncertainty.

"Yes?"

"You like Mason MacCoy, don't you?"

That was not what she had expected. "Well, yes. I think he's a nice man. What I know of him."

"You look at him, and he sure looks at you."

"Oh, we do not." She buried her nose in her cup, drinking the last of her coffee.

"Yes, you do. It's okay. He seems like a pretty good guy."

"There's nothing there, Larry Joe. He's just a polite, nice man." If Larry Joe saw it, then it wasn't her imagination.

"Whatever."

"What does that mean, anyway?"

He shrugged and played with his toes. "I guess it means whatever you want it to mean."

A few seconds of watching him, and Charlene leaned over and kissed his ear. "I'm so glad you're my son."

He gave her that charming grin, but she didn't think it was in his eyes. He wiggled his toes and then said, "I have somethin' to tell you, Mom."

"Oh?" She thought he'd told her what it was he had to say, but now she sensed there was something much more serious. "Well, go ahead."

"Dad went to Dallas with Sheila Arnett. For the weekend."

She let out a breath. "I know, honey." She wasn't certain what else she should say, but she felt Larry Joe needed her to speak to this. "How do you know?"

"I went over there yesterday. I was gonna talk to him. I...I just thought we should talk. One of the guys over there told me. Told me what hotel they were at, even."

"That must have taken a lot of courage for you to go over there," she said, feeling at a loss and so angry at Joey for missing the opportunity with his son because he was being a fool with that slut. "I'm sorry you missed him. But you can go again. I think you should plan on it. It's a good idea, honey. Your daddy would love to talk with you."

He gave that I-don't-care shrug that was filled with hurt.

"Larry Joe, your father loves you. He does. He just doesn't know how to show you."

"I'm not a cowboy. He wants a cowboy, like Danny J."

"Oh, honey, it's just that you frighten him a little." She laid her hand at the back of his neck, feeling his silky hair. "Sometimes it is like this between fathers and sons. He wants to be able to help you with things and share things with you, but what you are interested in, he doesn't know about. And it frightens your dad a little, you growing into a man. He hopes he's done right as a father. He so wants you to be happy, and he worries that he can't help you, so he backs away. I really think your father thinks you don't need him. You are awfully self-sufficient, Larry Joe."

He sort of shrugged. Then he said, "Are you still wantin' him to come back?"

She thought. "I haven't decided. These things can't be decided quickly, Larry Joe. They just sort of have to evolve. You have to go down the road, and see where it takes you, I guess."

He folded his arms across his knees and rested his chin there.

"That your father and I have our differences has nothing to do with you and Danny J. and Jojo. You are his children, and he is your father. He wants to be your father, and he needs you all."

He did not answer this. Her gaze flowed over his profile, his features dim but his handsomeness clearly visible. A proud ache filled her heart. The memory of Iris MacCoy flirting with him flickered across her mind.

"Have you made up your mind about junior college this semester?" she asked.

"I think so. I'm gonna go. Mr. Stidham said he would work my hours around my class hours. And I can pick up extra work around, too." He looked around at her. She couldn't fully read his eyes in the dimness, but his voice was certain. "I want to save my money and see if I can get enough to go up to Michigan, to a school there."

Charlene stared at him. "Michigan?"

He nodded. "There's a really good school there for car design. I think I want to give it a try."

"Well."

"I know it'll take a lot of money, but there's scholarships. 'Course, I probably can't qualify with my grades, but they have student aid. And I can work. I can always get work."

"Michigan, Larry Joe? What's wrong with University of Oklahoma or even up at Oklahoma State?" She felt hysteria edging in.

"They don't have this sort of program."

"But you could start out at one of them. You don't have to go all the way up to Michigan right away."

"I told you, I'm gonna start here at junior college. My grades aren't good enough to get right in up there."

She swallowed, and he sat there with his chin on his arms.

She found her breath and some patches of sanity and told him not to worry over the money. "We'll work it somehow, if you want to go. God will show the way. Now tell me about the school."

Later, as she lay in bed, unable to sleep, she thought that her son surely had had a few things to tell her. He'd kept them all bottled up. That wasn't good for a person.

Reaching over, she picked up the phone and dialed Joey's pager. She held the phone, waiting to see if he called back quickly. Or at all.

The phone rang five minutes later, and she jumped.

"Are you alone?" she asked immediately.

"Well, yeah," he said, clearly surprised.

"There's some things you should know. Your eldest son found out you went to Dallas with Sheila. He found out when he went over there to talk to you, but you weren't there, so some stranger told him his father had gone off to Dallas with his girlfriend. Also, the school year starts in two weeks, and I'm gonna be spending most of what's in the checking account to take care of the kids' school clothes. Good night."

She hung up the phone, then took it off the receiver and rolled over. She could not believe she had spoken to him like that.

She wished there was someone she could run off with to Dallas, and she briefly imagined running off with Mason. But then she told herself to quit being ludicrous. For one thing, she was a mother and would not behave in such a manner.

Seventeen

Winston got his Confederate flag put out about the same time as Northrupt across the street got out his Stars and Bars. He was a little surprised to find himself breathless with the effort, but nevertheless, as he went down the steps to get the day's edition of the *Valentine Voice,* he felt satisfied that another morning had gotten off on the right foot.

Just as he bent for the paper, music filled the air. The sound so startled him that he like to have lost his balance and fallen over. "The Star-Spangled Banner." It came from across the street, from a long black box—one of those boom boxes—that his neighbor was that minute setting on the edge of his front porch. Northrupt fiddled with the machine, and the music got louder.

Then Northrupt straightened, saluted his flag and grinned at Winston, and saluted him, too. Doing a sharp pivot, the man went in his front door, leaving the flags waving 'neath the rockets' red glare.

Winston strode on off to his roses, with the music floating after him, like stink on a skunk.

Vella, stuck behind her lilac bush where she caught the strains of the music, lowered her binoculars and shook her head, saying, "My land."

An hour later she drove herself over to the county agent's office and plunked the jar of dirt she'd gotten from around

Winston's roses on the clerk's government-gunmetal desk. "I'd like this analyzed, please."

Charlene was alone in the house, her children gone off to friends. The house seemed to echo.

Before leaving with Larry Joe, Danny J. had reminded her that the horses needed grain. She would call MacCoy to have them bring it out, of course. Likely Mason would bring it. She hoped he would bring it.

Charlene thought of this as she dialed the feed store. Bennie answered and said, "How are you today, Miz Darnell?" and she said, "Fine, thank you."

She gave him the order, adding, "Oh, and I need four bags of water softener salt, too." She felt a little guilty at them delivering her small horse feed order and wanted to improve it as best she could.

"Okay. We'll get that out to you this mornin'," Bennie said.

She almost asked if Mason would bring it, but, of course, she couldn't ask that. Likely he would, though, she thought with anticipation as she hung up.

She was anticipating too much, she told herself. But Mason was a handsome man, and thinking of speaking to him did give her something to occupy her mind in the empty day ahead, and that was the truth of it.

She went to comb her hair and put on some lipstick. She did not have energy for a full makeup job, which would have been too silly anyway.

Mason strode in the front door of MacCoy's Feed and Seed, passed Bennie at the front desk without a glance and went straight into Adam's office. "Why were there surveyors at my place when I left?"

"They're surveying," Adam said, rising up from his chair.

"I told you I don't want to sell."

"Did you look at those papers good? At that offer?"

"Yes, I did, and I still don't want to sell."

"Okay, fine." Adam held up both his hands, then leaned forward, jutting his face determinedly. "But I'm gettin' the place surveyed. It won't hurt to have that done. Might be I can find a buyer for my half. I do own half, by God."

"Suit yourself." Mason turned and left.

"You're pigheaded, you know that!" Adam yelled after him. He strode to the doorway, yelling out, "You don't want to sell just to mess me up on this deal! You just got a dad-gum problem with your older brother, that's what."

Mason, who had stopped at the front desk to get the order invoices from Bennie, said, "You got that right. My older brother is my problem."

With that, Adam got so wrought up that he half jumped off the floor, yelling, "I'll kick your ass out of here, and then where will you be?"

"You can't do that," Mason said with a deliberate calm he knew drove Adam crazy. He snatched up a Tootsie Pop from the cup on Bennie's desk, and left Bennie, who was used to the occasional confrontation, shaking his head, and walked out the door thinking of how their mother, after forty years with her husband, had been ahead of them and fixed it so Mason couldn't be cut out of the business.

Adam came shooting his head out the door to yell, "I'll buy you out. That's what. You just name your price."

"Don't want to sell," Mason called back, not looking around. He stuck the Tootsie Pop in his mouth and thought that he should be ashamed of himself for enjoying the moment so much at his brother's expense.

He strode across the concrete lot in the hazy sunlight to

the warehouse, adjusting his ball cap against the brightness, shifting the sucker from one side of his mouth to the other. *Lord, send us rain, and thank you for it comin'.*

Out front of the warehouse was a flatbed truck and in it a farmer he knew simply as Hoover. Mason said he would fill the man's order directly.

"No hurry. I gave up hurryin' in this heat," the man said.

Mason let himself in the small door and went over to press the button to raise the loading door. As it rolled up, he pulled his reading glasses from his shirt pocket and went through the invoices looking for the man's order.

Charlene Darnell. His eyes lit on her name and stuck. He shifted the sucker around in his mouth and read her name again, just to make sure, and all sorts of stirrings happened inside him. The invoice was for eight sacks of pelletted horse feed, three mineral blocks and four sacks water softener salt.

Another truck pulled up at the loading dock, bringing him back to the present. He found Hoover's invoice, stuck the rest in the clip on the little desk, and went back to fill the man's order. He threw away the mostly eaten sucker and started whistling.

In the weeks Joey had been at the ranch, it had become his habit to begin riding before daylight and then have breakfast with Sheila. Somehow he always felt he could take Sheila on after he had gotten in some good riding, although this thought was not clear in his mind. Sheila had breakfast on the rear patio of the big house. This was the time he would report on the condition and progress of her horses. Breakfast usually consisted of sweet rolls and coffee so strong it made a person's eyes fly open. Sheila made that herself. She added chicory, and Joey really liked her coffee.

He had just taken his second sweet roll when she brought up the subject of him moving into the big house with her.

"You'd be a lot more comfortable," she told him, a promising light in her eyes that made him squirm in his seat.

That Larry Joe knew about their weekend in Dallas kept going through his mind.

He had been so bothered by this that he had mentioned it to Sheila. She had laughed and said, "Larry Joe is eighteen. He knows about what goes on."

That was what disturbed Joey most.

"And now that your children know about things, you might just as well move up to the house and be comfortable."

Joey shook his head and laid the sweet roll on the plate. He looked at his coffee but didn't take it up. He had the feeling that if he touched her food, he was accepting her offer. "I'd rather stay in the trailer."

"You can have your own room and private bath," she said. "Daddy's room. His bath has a nice whirlpool tub."

"I really do like the trailer just fine." He wasn't touching her father's room.

"Oh, Joey, don't be silly. We'd both be so much more comfortable with you up here in the house. I don't care what anyone thinks." With an irritated expression, she threw down her cloth napkin and fixed him with a gaze. "What is it? If you don't want Daddy's old room, you can have the guest room."

"Thank you all the same." He stood and reached for his hat.

"Well, I'm not comin' out there. You know that. You know you'll have to come up to my room anyway."

He stared at her. He didn't think he should say that he didn't plan to come up to her room.

They gazed at each other. He thought that he was not moving into the house with her. He wasn't doing that, even if he had to walk away from this entire place.

Sheila broke the gaze. "Okay," she said, unfolding from the chair with a coy smile. She wrapped her arms around his neck. "The offer is there, when you're ready."

She kissed him, and he broke away, saying he had five more head to ride before the heat got worse. He walked quickly down the stone path, and he heard his spurs jingling, but somehow they didn't help him much this morning.

Charlene watched a tape of yesterday's *All My Children* while she did the breakfast dishes and repeatedly glanced out the window, halfway looking for someone to drive up, but mostly looking at the Suburban parked beneath the elm tree. It was like the Suburban was sitting out there honking at her.

The phone rang, and she let the answering machine get it, while she stood there and listened to see if it was one of her children. She always answered her children, but she sure didn't want to speak to Joey. She really wished it would be Joey, so she could not talk to him.

It was somebody selling funerals. She erased the message and went back into the kitchen, tuned the television to CMT and watched the latest fifteen-year-old star dolled up to look a seductive twenty-five singing about lost love. Charlene wondered about the world in general, and about women in particular. Why would a mother let her child do such a thing? Why would women still keep using their sex? Maybe because they had to use everything they had to get along in this world, and sex worked so well. She sure hoped she could teach Jojo better.

She switched off the television and walked out to the Suburban and slipped in behind the wheel, leaving the door open for air in the hot truck.

She needed groceries. She could just start the truck and drive down to the IGA. She'd kept her license current. People said you didn't forget how to drive.

The squeal of tires and the loud crash sounded in memory, and then Rainey sitting there slumped over.

Charlene took a deep breath. It probably wasn't a good idea to go anywhere near traffic the first thing. Maybe she would simply drive to the road, turn around and come back. She had to start slow and build her courage.

She started the Suburban and sat there a minute with it rumbling smoothly, telling herself there were no other vehicles on her own driveway. She would be fine to drive to the road. She put it in reverse and hit the brake, remembering just then to shut the door. This shook her a little. If she couldn't remember to shut the door, no telling what she might forget, she thought as she rolled down the window.

She backed the truck a few feet and then put the stick in drive and turned around on the front lawn and headed up onto the gravel driveway.

At that particular moment she saw a big truck coming at her. The MacCoy delivery truck!

She veered over to the barn, turning in a swoop and stopping near the south entry, hitting the brakes a little harder than necessary because she wasn't used to them. The big truck rumbled past, leaving a trail of dust, and disappeared behind the barn.

Oh, my. She checked her image in the rearview mirror, raking her fingers through her hair to fluff it up, seeing that she still had traces of lipstick, thank heaven. She suddenly wished she had done the full makeup job, and why in the world had she not put on something besides her old clothes? And why in the world was she having such ridiculous thoughts?

Maybe it wasn't even Mason.

It *was* Mason. He was out of the truck and walking toward her when she rounded the corner of the barn. Like always, he wore jeans and a short-sleeved shirt that showed his muscles, and a ball cap.

When she got close enough, she saw his blue eyes shone out from his face, just like she remembered.

"Hello," he said. "If you were goin' somewhere, I can put the feed in the barn. You don't need to wait."

"Oh, no...I was just moving the truck over here." It seemed like his gaze lingered on her hair, and she raked her hand through it in reaction, then stuck her hand in her back pocket.

He slipped on cotton gloves, lifted the dolly to the ground and began stacking the bags of feed on it. "Eight bags Golden Choice pellets, right?"

She nodded. "Yes...right in here. Since there aren't any horses in the stalls, we're just putting it here in the alley. It's easier for the kids to get to."

He unloaded the sacks with strong arms and the rhythmic movements of a man in good shape. He was a thick man in the shoulders. She took in his hard arm muscles showing below the short sleeves of his shirt. He glanced at her with his blue eyes. How did anyone have eyes that blue?

She looked away, caught by the ingrained habit of a discreet married woman, as well as embarrassing stirrings inside herself. *Well, my golly, Charlene, you cannot just throw him down and have your way with him.*

He wheeled the mineral blocks all the way out to the pasture for her, while she walked along beside him and told him the horses' names and ages, which one belonged to who, and every one of their habits. She was chattering, so on the way back to the truck, she abruptly stopped.

He got the water softener salt, which he not only wheeled into the house and to the utility room, but he emptied two of the bags right into the water softener.

"Could I offer you a glass of tea for all your trouble?" she asked. "I just made it. It's brewed tea, with lemon and a little sugar." It seemed the polite thing to offer. And oh, the house was so empty.

"I'd like that a lot. Thanks." Those blue eyes shone. She turned quickly away to open the refrigerator.

"Maybe you'd rather have a cold drink. I have Coke."

"Ice tea is fine." He sat at her kitchen table and removed his ball cap, laying it on his knee.

While Charlene got their glasses and ice and the pitcher of tea, she chattered again, about the weather and how it was hot enough to make tea in fifteen minutes in the pitcher out in the sun, and how the trees were beginning to lose leaves, some trees to outright die, and about everyone's prayers for rain and her view that she was planning for it.

She said all these things while her mind carried on an entirely different conversation. Her mind asked him if he had been married. If he had, what had happened between him and his wife? Or maybe wives. Was he a man who ran off? Or maybe he had never found the right woman, though she couldn't quite believe this. A man with those blue eyes and that body, and part owner in his own business? Some woman would have snatched him right up. Did he have filthy habits that were not readily apparent? Was he seeing someone now? And what was this rumor of prison?

Of course she could not say any of that, and so for fifteen minutes, while she watched Mason's rough fingers play up and down his glass on the table and his blue eyes flicker to hers and away, she held her glass with both hands and pressed her legs tightly together and engaged him in conversation about the weather.

Then Mason rose to go. "Thank you for the tea."

"You are most welcome. Thank you for...delivering."

Charlene held the kitchen door. At the bottom of the steps, he cast her a wave, and then he disappeared around the corner of the house. She closed the door and went to the table, gazing long at the empty glasses there. She picked them up and carried them to the sink.

A knock at the back door made her about jump out of her skin. She hurried to open it, but then peeked around it instead. When she saw it was Mason, she flung it wide and opened the storm door.

He swept his ball cap off his head and cleared his throat. "I was wondering if I might call on you sometime." He cleared his throat again. "If you would mind if I came to visit, or maybe we could go out to dinner."

Shocked, Charlene stared at him. Finally she managed to say, "I enjoy visiting with you." She couldn't speak to having dinner, and she felt obligated to inform him, "Joey and I aren't divorced."

He nodded, a shadow coming over his features.

"But I'd like you to come to visit," she said firmly. "I'd really enjoy it."

He smiled then. "Good. I'd like to do that," he said, his smile widening as he backed up. "Well, I have to get back to work. I have more deliveries. But I'll call you."

Charlene watched him disappear around the side of the house; then she closed the door and leaned against it for a second, realizing she was smiling for all she was worth.

The phone rang. Charlene, with her hair wrapped in a bandana, was dusting in the living room. She raced to the dining room buffet and stared at the answering machine. When the answering machine picked up, whoever was on the other end hung up.

Well, if it had been one of the children, they would have spoken into the machine, she assured herself as she went back to the living room to continue dusting. So would Rainey or her daddy, and if it had been Mason, he should have spoken. Maybe it had been Joey. He did not like the answering machine, had hardly ever used it. It had probably been a salesman. She thought of Mason again, which was the silliest thing ever.

Ten minutes later, the phone rang again. Charlene hurried into the answering machine and waited.

"Uh, Charlene?"

It was Joey. She looked at the phone, raised her hand, but did not answer.

"I wanted to let you know that I deposited money into the account today. It was all I had, but I'll have more next week when a guy pays me for a horse. That's all, I guess."

The line clicked.

Charlene was very glad for the opportunity to not talk to him.

Rain came that evening. Charlene and Danny J. and Jojo were eating a late supper when the wind began to gust. There came the sound of the horses' hooves pounding as they galloped from the west pasture to the east, instinct compelling them closer to the house and their owners.

Danny J. got to his feet, saying, "I'm gonna go open the gate so the horses can come up to the barn if it hails," and rushed out the door.

Charlene motioned to Jojo. "Turn on the TV and flip over to the local channel. Let's see what the weatherman says."

She looked out the window and realized she didn't have to move the Suburban from underneath the tree. It still sat over by the barn. On the local television channel, a few strong storm cells were indicated west and north, but nothing right near them, and no tornado activity. Still, Charlene went out back and made certain the tornado shelter door was ready to open. She called Larry Joe at the Texaco, to hear his voice and remind him not to hesitate to get down in the hole for the lift, not that he would pay her advice one bit of attention, but giving it made her feel better. He said in an excited and wondering voice that the Texaco sign was making a great deal of noise and sand was blowing down the street.

All over town, people stopped what they were doing. They got up from in front of televisions and left supper tables and business counters and went outside to stand and watch the sky with wonder and hope and a little worry. Winston and his neighbor brought in their flags; it was near sundown anyway. Ruthanne sat beside the open window in her bedroom, sinking back in time and becoming a little girl who would do the same on the Oklahoma prairie. Mildred watched the Weather Channel for a tornado alert. Joey and Primo hurriedly shut anxious horses into corrals and brought others into their stalls. Sheila tossed hay into feeders to calm them. Mason gave up working on his grandfather's car and struggled to shut the barn doors, while over in the pasture his old horse kicked his heels and ran, and the old mule ambled into the shed.

At last darker clouds came. Standing in their front yard, Charlene announced loudly, "It is going to rain. It is going to soak the trees and flow down the gutters." Hearing a rumble of thunder, she urged her children inside, safe from any evil bolt of lightning looking for a path to the ground. They stood at the glass front door, anticipating.

The rain came first as big drops splatting on the hot concrete and dusty dirt. It made a sweet, musty smell even through the window glass. The drops got bigger and hit harder. Tiny hail mixed in. And then rain came in a flood from the sky. Oddly, with almost no thunder, no visible lightning, just a solid sheet of rain pouring down, pounding the roof, rushing down the gutters and flowing over the concrete walk.

"Hallelujah!" Charlene said, grinning at her children, who grinned back.

Five minutes later it stopped. Completely, as surely as if someone had turned off the faucet. The clouds lifted and broke apart. Orange sunlight filtered from the western setting sun.

"Is that all?" Jojo said quite righteously.

"I guess so," Charlene said, shaking her head and looking sadly at the sky. "I'm sure the Lord knows best. It's enough for now."

Three times while the children were gone, once one afternoon and twice the next, Charlene drove the Suburban up the drive to the highway and back. She turned around on the grass, not daring to go out on the road. When she would pull the Suburban to a stop under the elm and lift her hands from the wheel, they would be wet with sweat. The first time she had to sit there for a full minute to quit shaking.

She told herself it was silly, but she could not seem to get control over the fear. Would it never go away?

She put off going shopping for the children's school clothes. Larry Joe was working more hours, and she hated to inconvenience him to take her, and besides, she didn't feel up to shopping. Rather than admit this, she threw herself into cleaning out closets. "We have to make room for your new clothes before we buy them," she told her children.

She told each of them what time she would clean their closet, in order that they could remove anything they didn't want her to see. Still, she found surprising things, such as a lacy bra in Danny J.'s closet, which he said was Curt's sister's, and what looked like part of a carburetor in Larry Joe's.

Late at night, when she could not sleep, her fingernails were perfection and she had seen all the old movies on television, she cleaned out hers and Joey's dresser drawers. She sat on the floor and looked at things such as a birthday card he had given her and a picture of them at one of his horse shows, and a T-shirt that she had given him years ago that said No. 1 Dad. He had left that behind. When she got up, she had a wet face and a bulging plastic bag that she took out the back door and plopped into the trash can.

She would not answer the telephone, but when home alone, she raced to listen to hear who spoke over the answering machine. She avoided three calls from carpet cleaners that way.

Joey called twice. Charlene hovered over the machine, listening breathlessly to his voice.

"Charlene, uh…I put some more money in the account this mornin'. Uh, that's all, I guess. Bye."

The next time: "Charlene? Can you give me a call. Call my pager when you get time. Okay?"

She took up the phone, and then she put it back down. She couldn't call him. She didn't know what to say to him. The pain was too much for her.

She wanted to run away. She tried to hide in the house, to not answer the phone and to watch television to distract her troubled emotions. One afternoon, upon passing the

bed, she lay down and was there for three hours, until
Danny J. came in, calling he was hungry.

"Mom? Are you okay?" he asked, his face worried.

"Yes, I'm fine. I'll make hamburgers for supper. How
'bout that?"

She dragged herself off the bed. She wanted to please
him. She wanted to be what she used to be. Or what she'd
hoped to be, only she didn't know what had happened to
that woman. She sensed that she was on the wrong road,
but she could not turn around and go back, and she didn't
know which way to go, anyway.

Then Rainey called to say that she had been confined to
bed for the duration of her pregnancy.

"I almost lost him," Rainey told her, and there were
tears in her voice. "It is a him. And he's goin' to be okay,
but I have to stay in bed. Stay off my feet. If I get stronger,
they'll let me up, but right now, the only time I can get up
is to go to the bathroom."

"I'll come right away," Charlene said, her mind already
racing with preparations.

"Oh, Charlene, honey. I'm okay. Next week Harry will
be able to get some time off, and he'll take care of me.
Harry takes good care of me," she said, speaking warmly
with sniffs. "And until then my neighbor is goin' to come
over to help. She's really a nice lady."

Charlene knew she did not mistake the hesitancy in Rainey's voice. Rainey and their mother had always been the
nurses of the family, not Charlene. It was a family joke
how Charlene ran from illness.

She said now very sincerely, "Let me come, Rainey. I
want to help. Really. This will be very good practice for
me. I have to learn to tend now, with Mama gone. Jojo will
come up with me. She can sleep on a pallet on the floor. I
need to help you, and I really need to get away from here."

"You come on, honey. I can't wait to have you," Rainey said, and when Charlene hung up she cried a little from happiness at being blessed with a sister like Rainey.

It occurred to Charlene that there would be a problem with traveling up to Rainey. Larry Joe would have to take off work to drive them, and she could hear the frustration in his voice. He was trying so hard to save his money. Her father wanted to take them, but Charlene wasn't going for that idea at all. She considered it too long a trip for her father, although she didn't want to say this and hurt his feelings by making him feel infirm.

She said, "Jojo's never been on a bus, Daddy. She should have the experience."

She telephoned the cafe and got Fayrene, who told her that the daily bus came through at six in the evening, up from Fort Worth. Charlene went around like a madwoman and had herself and Jojo and everyone else waiting in front of the cafe on the still hot concrete when the bus rolled up.

"Y'all look out for each other now." She kissed and hugged her father and sons. "If anything happens to either one of you, I'll kill you," she told her sons, kissing them yet a second time. Everyone kept assuring her that Danny J. was old enough to stay at home with his brother, but Charlene suddenly felt very uncertain.

"Mom," Larry Joe said with his wonderful grin, "you're goin' two hours away for maybe a week. I think we can handle it."

She hugged him again, and then Mildred and Ruthanne, who were there, too. With one more wave to them all and instructions to take care, she followed Jojo onto the bus, where they both settled in seats much more plush than she had expected. They waved out the darkly tinted windows, and then with a whoosh and the smell of diesel exhaust, they were away, town buildings giving way to countryside trees and pastures as the bus sped along.

Charlene settled back in the seat and closed her eyes. Oh, she liked the gentle rhythm of the bus rolling down the road. She was away…away…*oh, thank you, God.*

The next instant her eyes popped open as she realized that she had not thought to call Joey and tell him she was leaving. She hadn't thought of him at all.

Eighteen

The City Hall thermometer reads 90°

It would not be enough to get a boom box and recording of "Dixie" to play in response to Everett Northrupt's "Star-Spangled Banner." Northrupt had declared war by doing that, and no war was won by simply matching the aggressor. The Confederates had learned that the hard way. Winston had to better Northrupt. He was going to get music and *more,* which he had been patiently considering for some days.

He walked down his front porch steps and out into the yard, where he stood and looked back at the house. The windows glowed with light. In the living room, he could see Mildred sitting on the couch. Her head bobbed; she was watching *Hawaii Five-O* and eating microwave popcorn she'd gotten as free sample packets at Wal-Mart.

He sized up the situation and paced off distances in an arc around the porch. He continued on around the side of the house, into the deep shadows of the roses and trees. He had to maneuver between a couple of rosebushes. A couple of thorns snagged his clothes, and then he felt a little dizzy. He blinked, straining to focus on finding what he sought.

Okay, he found it. He got out from the rosebushes and

stood still to catch his breath. There wasn't anything to hold on to, so he stood with his hands on his knees.

"You are eighty-seven years old, Winston, and should know better than to climb through rosebushes at night."

It was Coweta coming toward him out of the deep dark. At last.

"I don't know what age has to do with that. I had to find the electric outlet, and I found it." He got himself up straight. He was put out with her pointing out his age, and he was darn angry that she had been absent so long.

"You could have found it in the morning. And what do you want with it, anyway?" Her figure sort of shimmered as she bent to smell a rose blossom.

"That's my business."

"Oh, Winston." She smiled at him, and he gazed at her.

"Where have you been?" he asked. "You haven't been around here in weeks."

"I can't hang around here forever, Winston. I have to get on with my life."

He thought that was pretty funny. She was dead, and he pointed that out.

"Life goes on, Winston," she said in that graceful tone he had always loved to hear. Then she changed the subject and ordered him in a fashion he had never liked. "Winston, you need to go see our Freddy. You need to talk to him."

"I've tried talkin' to him. He just sits there at the funny farm. I told the doctors they needed to test his hearin'." He felt a failure in connection with his son, and he didn't like to think of it.

"You need to go try again," she said in a pointed manner, "and you need to be firm with him. You might suggest that if he doesn't want to go home, he can come here."

"Here?" The idea of his son in his present state—or any

state, actually—being in such close proximity was wearing. "I've got Mildred and Ruthanne."

"And you still have two empty bedrooms. You could have him for a while. Time is runnin' out, Winston."

There was something about the way she said that. He peered at her, but he didn't ask about it.

"I'll go talk to him. I was goin' to anyway. I'll make a point of it tomorrow afternoon. I'm goin' up to Lawton anyway."

She smiled in a satisfied manner, came toward him and gave him a kiss on the cheek that felt like the flutter of a butterfly and patted his chest in a way that felt the same. "Cut me a rose, Winston."

He pulled out his pocketknife and chose one.

Up in her bedroom, Vella Blaine was working lotion into her hands. She happened to glance out the window. She stopped and peered toward the Valentine home. There was that light again. Maybe it was Winston with a flashlight, like Perry said. But if it was, what was Winston doing out there at the roses in the night?

Under the light of a single bulb, Joey saddled up the red gelding. He threw on his oldest and favorite saddle, savoring the scent of the leather and the horse, his hands working quickly and his ears listening for footsteps. These days it was like Sheila was around him every minute, her dark eyes tugging on him, wanting from him. He hoped to get away before she came looking for him.

He didn't. The door opened, and boots crunched on the gritty concrete as she entered.

"Are you going for a ride?" she asked.

"Yep." He cast her a glance. "It's a good night to ride him, get him used to different situations."

He felt her gaze, sharp and wanting, raising all sorts of

confusion in him. "It is a lovely night. Maybe I'll go with you."

"I'd rather ride alone," he said, the words rushing out without thought. She stared at him with her big brown eyes. "I have to keep my mind on the trainin'," he said, took the reins and led the horse out of the barn and toward the gate. Without looking back, he knew that she had come to the door and stood there watching him.

Her angry words came out through the darkness. "I'll leave a light on for you, Joey. But not forever."

He threw himself on top the horse and rode away at a canter, calling himself all sorts of a fool.

The City Hall thermometer reads 87°

Mason had to discuss it with someone. He kept going over and over the list of possible people to talk to, and it was a sad thing to admit, but he didn't have anyone close to him. For all of his life, he had talked to his Grandpap, but Grandpap was gone now. Adam was out completely. He was so desperate that he thought of Iris, but thankfully, he didn't get that silly. That left Neville. He guessed he was closer to Neville than anyone, and that wasn't all that close.

This was weighing on his mind when he got into the patrol car with Neville for their night on duty.

"I see they fixed the thermometer," Mason observed as they went along Main Street.

"Yep. The mayor's thrilled." Neville pulled at his already open collar. "Eighty-seven degrees. I thought it was a little cooler than that. It's seemed a little cooler since the rain."

"That wasn't rain, it was a giant spit."

They drove out of town by way of Church Street. Mason

looked over at the Valentine house and thought of Charlene.

"Neville?"

"Yeah?"

Words scrambled in Mason's brain. "How would you feel if someone like me was to start dating your sister?"

"Wendy's married, Mace," Neville said with some alarm. "She's got two kids. You know that."

Mason looked at Neville. "You're enough to drive a person crazy," he said, squirming in his seat.

"What is goin' on?" Neville demanded.

"It isn't your sister. It's nothing to do with her. It's…I think I'd like to ask Charlene Darnell out."

"Oh." Giving a puzzled frown, Neville drove one-handed and pulled a butternut candy out of his breast pocket. "Well, haven't heard if her and Joey are divorced, but he's sure not with her, if that's what you're wonderin'. I saw him driving one of Sheila's trucks and trailer just this afternoon."

"No that's not it." Mason rubbed his upper lip. "I don't guess she knows about me bein' in prison."

"Oh. That was a long time ago, Mason. Nobody remembers. I forget it half the time myself. Charlene probably doesn't even know, and I doubt it would make any difference, anyway."

"You don't think so?"

"Mason, that fella's death was sort of an accident. And it isn't like you ever led some life of crime."

"Yeah, well, prison makes its mark." Sometimes, after all these years, he felt dirty. "I'd tell her, though. I'd want her to know."

"Buddy, you are a puzzlement." Neville cast him several sharp glances. "I haven't ever seen you interested in a woman, even though a few have sure been interested in you. I've sort of wondered, you know." He raised an eyebrow.

"There's a lot you don't know, Neville, and I'm not gettin' into my love life with you."

Neville looked a little disappointed. Then he said, "Charlene, huh? And you're scared of her. I'll be dawged. Mason MacCoy scared of somethin'." He shook his head. "If that don't beat all."

Mason sighed. Sometimes Neville's view of him as this tough guy got very wearing. He caught his reflection in the window glass. Would Charlene think of him as some tough that she didn't want to associate with?

Yes, he was scared, because now that hope had been raised, he couldn't seem to snuff it out.

Charlene sat cross-legged on the big king-size bed. She was doing Rainey's fingernails. She studied the color she had just applied to her sister's forefinger. "Did you know that manicurists are now called nail technicians?"

"Yes. I had heard that."

"They make pretty good money, too." Charlene went on to relate what Oralee down at Cut and Curl beauty shop had told her. "I'm thinking that maybe I could give it a try. Dixie is a certified teacher, and I could get my license while working under her."

"You're goin' to go to work?" Rainey looked surprised.

"Well, I'm going to have to, Rainey. Joey can't make enough to support himself off somewhere and us, too. Don't you think I can do it?" Charlene didn't want to let on, but she was having a bit of trouble in the confidence department.

"Of course you can. I was just surprised is all. You were wonderful when you were a beautician."

"I think they may be beauty technicians or something now."

"I don't know about that," Rainey said. After a minute she added hesitantly, "I think you are goin' to need to start driving."

"I have started," Charlene told her. "I've driven up to the highway three times."

Rainey stared at her.

Charlene bent close to her sister's hand and pushed her reading glasses up. She was going to have to get better glasses if she wanted to do nails for a living.

"Do you know what Mason was in prison for?" she asked as she applied a clear topcoat.

"No. I just heard the rumor one time. I never felt it my business to go asking people. Why?"

"Oh, I was just wondering," Charlene said, feeling Rainey's eyes on her. "He brought a load of feed to the house the other day. He's awfully nice. Prison is probably a lie thought up by somebody that was jealous."

"Maybe. He's sure got a body that won't quit."

"Oh, Rainey." Her cheeks grew warm because she was suddenly thinking about Mason's body.

Rainey laughed, and after a minute Charlene confessed that Mason had asked if he could come visit her, and she had said yes.

"Well, here's something to talk about," Rainey said with great enthusiasm.

"Not really," Charlene said. "He never did call or come by."

Nineteen

The City Hall thermometer reads 101°

Just before noon, Mason went to the phone on the warehouse wall and dialed the Darnell number. He got a busy signal, which he listened to for several seconds with his hand braced against the wall. He hung up and went to check over some invoices, then was back at the phone in five minutes. The line was still busy. Then customers came in, and he couldn't try again for twenty minutes.

When the loading dock was finally empty, he went again to the phone and dialed. Ah…ringing. Four rings, while he gripped the receiver. Then Charlene's voice came across the line. But it was her answering machine.

"Uh, this is Mason MacCoy. I'll call back later," he said and hung up. He wished he hadn't said anything. She was going to think he was nuts.

He *was* nuts.

Flopping down on the little trailer sofa, Joey took up the phone and held it between his splayed knees and dialed his old home number. He got the darn answering machine again. He pictured it at the house, on the dining room buffet. He hated speaking to an answering machine. He hung up and sat there holding the telephone between his dusty knees. He had been getting that machine for days. Where was Charlene? She was always home. She had always been home.

Winston came out of the Wal-Mart with a box containing a supposedly easy-to-carry boom box, but he thought it was pretty heavy. He set it in the back seat and drove over to the hospital, where he went up to the psychiatric wing, stopping at the cold drink machine on the way to get two Coca-Colas. In cans, which he had never after all these years grown to like. The nurse greeted him by name, which seemed a very sad thing.

He found Freddy, and they sat in a small visiting room at the end of the hall, without a television, so not too many people ever came in there. Winston had been going over and over what to say to his son, but now that the opportunity was at hand, he felt too tired. He just sat there drinking his cold drink.

When Freddy said, "Dad, you don't look too good. Are you feeling all right?" it came as a surprise.

"I'm tired, I guess. It's hotter than blazes, and I got Charlene broke up from Joey, and Rainey's in danger of losing the baby, and I got you over here in the looney house, and your mother expects me to do something about it."

Freddy blinked. Winston was surprised, too.

"Rainey's gonna lose her baby?" Freddy asked, causing Winston's eyes to widen further.

He shook his head. "She'll be okay. She's havin' a bit of a time right now and has to stay in bed."

"Oh." He went to staring straight down at his slipper again. They got Freddy dressed, all but his shoes. Winston thought he should put on shoes, too, that maybe it would help.

He sucked in a good breath. "Look, son, I'm eighty-seven. I want to see you get straightened out, and if you don't go ahead and start, I may not be here to help. I want to see you out of this hospital and happy again. Well, as happy as any human can be for any length of time." Freddy had never been terribly happy. Winston didn't want to appear to want too much.

"I don't know, Dad." Freddy was shaking his head. "I almost shot a man. I'm a little scared to come out of here," he added, his voice dropping.

"Oh, Freddy, people make mistakes. People go off half-cocked. Do you think you are the first to want to shoot an IRS agent?" He paused and wiped his brow with his handkerchief. "I know it was a shock to find out that you aren't perfect. That you could break. But put it in context. He was a mealymouthed man pushing you, and you could have shot him, but you didn't."

"I fired the gun, Dad."

"You fired it in the air well over his head. You have to forgive yourself, Freddy. Nobody can do that for you but you."

"They're gonna get me when I get out of here. The lawyer says so."

"The lawyer says they're gonna *get you?*"

"He doesn't say it exactly like that, but he says I'm not in a good position."

"Son, the sooner you come out and face it, the sooner it will be over."

"Helen's goin' to leave me if I lose the dealership, Dad. She likes bein' the wife of the owner of a Ford dealership. She likes havin' money, and we may not have it much longer."

"Helen may surprise you, son. How are you goin' to find out in here? You stay in here, she's going to leave you anyway. Now…'' it was hard for him to say "…if you want, you can come on home to your mama's and my house for a while.''

"Your house?'' The hopeful spark that lit his son's eyes made Winston feel guilty.

"If you want to come stay with me for a while, if it'll help, you come on. But you have to do something one way or the other, Freddy. You can't just sit in here idling your engines. Sooner or later you'll run out of gas and not be able to go anywhere. And your insurance is running out, too.''

The City Hall thermometer reads 105°

Mason took off early and went over to the barbershop, where everyone was commenting on the temperature. The barbershop was well within sight of the town thermometer. He got a haircut and went home, twisted up the knob on the window air conditioner and took a cool shower. He shaved and put on some high-priced aftershave Iris had given him the past Christmas. He decided on a pale yellow, long-sleeved shirt, even in the heat. He buffed his dress boots with a kitchen towel. He got his good summer Stetson and looked in the mirror when he put it on.

He kept himself moving, not giving his mind time to talk himself out of his intentions. On the drive back through town, he stopped at Grace Florist. He had a time deciding between roses and a colorful mixed bouquet. He decided on the mixed bouquet. He thought roses would be too over-whelming.

His courage was ragged but holding when he drove up to Charlene Darnell's house. He fairly threw himself out of his truck and was three strides down the walk, before he remembered the bouquet and had to go back and get it out of the seat.

Bouquet in hand, he strode up and knocked on the door, adjusted his hat and rehearsed in his mind what he was going to say.

Charlene, could we visit? Or maybe, *Hello. I hope it isn't an inconvenience that I didn't call, but I....*

The door swung open. Instead of Charlene standing there, it was her son. The middle boy, who looked just like Joey Darnell.

Mason asked, "Is your mother here?"

The boy was staring at him. He shook his head. "No. She went up to take care of my aunt Rainey." The boy was looking at the flowers, and Mason felt like a clown in full get-up.

"She's gone?"

"Yes, sir. Uh—she won't be back until next week."

"Oh. Well, you can tell her I came by."

"Okay." The boy was still staring at him.

Feeling as if he had been shot in the back, Mason walked back to his truck and slipped inside. He was still holding the dang flowers. He threw them over in the seat, thinking that buying them had really been silly. He sat there a few more long seconds, feeling a little confused. He had never considered that she wouldn't be here. She was gone until next week, the boy said.

At last he started his truck and turned it toward the road. Disappointment was on him so heavy that he almost didn't see Joey Darnell waiting to turn into the drive as he was coming out. He saw Darnell's curious look, waved a finger at the man and headed on down the road to town, wondering where he was going to go now. Going home to his empty house was almost more than he could think of.

Joey went down the drive, wondering if MacCoy had

been delivering grain. That wasn't the feed store truck, though; it was MacCoy's own. MacCoy had been wearing a cowboy hat, too.

When he stopped in front of the house, Joey felt uncertainty about whether to go in the front door or the back. Deciding on the front, he went toward it, hoping that he and Charlene didn't get in a fight. He didn't want that, but somehow he always managed to say the wrong thing.

He felt a little foolish knocking, so right after a light rap, he opened the door. "Hello? Anyone home?"

The television was on, and there were a number of cold drink cans on the coffee table.

"Hi, Dad," Danny J. said with some excitement as he came down the hallway.

Joey's heart swelled at the sight of his son's smile, and he reached out to hug his son. They both broke apart, a little self-conscious.

"Where's your mom?" Joey asked. "I've called a couple of times, but I keep gettin' that machine."

"She's not here," Danny J. said. "Her and Jojo went up to take care of Aunt Rainey for a few days."

"Take care of Rainey?" It was usually Rainey who took care of people. "What's wrong with Rainey?"

"I guess she's havin' trouble about the baby. Mom said Aunt Rainey wasn't supposed to get out of bed."

Joey felt confused. This was the first he had heard of Rainey having a baby. And how could Charlene just take off like that? It wasn't like her.

"Mom had to leave really quick to catch the bus," his son said. "I guess she didn't have time to call you."

"Yeah. Probably so." He didn't want to let on that he was totally in the dark about the situation with Rainey. "She left you here by yourself?" That definitely wasn't like Charlene.

"Aw, Dad, I'm not a kid anymore. And Larry Joe's here. He's at work now."

Joey gazed at his son, still trying to take it in. "Well, you want to go get some pizza? We can talk about a couple of buckin' horses I've located."

His son definitely wanted to get pizza and ran eagerly down the hallway to get his boots, leaving Joey standing there, a stranger in his own home, thinking of how his wife had gone away and not told him.

This fact was hard enough to take in, but then, when he was backing the truck, he happened to ask Danny J. about what Mason MacCoy had wanted at the house, and his son told him, "Uh...he asked for Mom. I guess he wanted to see her about something."

Joey, thinking of Mason in his cowboy hat and private truck, pressed the gas pedal hard enough to sling gravel. He clamped his mouth shut against further questions. He was fairly certain he didn't care to hear the answers.

They drove over to the Texaco to let Larry Joe know where Danny J. was going. The MacCoy red Cadillac was pulled up at the pumps. Larry Joe was washing the windshield. Next Joey saw that Iris MacCoy was out of the car and leaning against the driver door. Sort of displayed against the door with her body covered, though not much, in shorts and a skimpy top. Iris had a body that displayed well. And she was smiling at Larry Joe in a way that caused Joey to get out of his truck and walk over to intervene.

"Hello, Iris," he said. He felt he needed to put a halt to what was going on, even if he couldn't exactly name what that was.

"Well, hello, Joey. How are you this evenin'?" Her eyes were on him then.

"Hot, like everybody else." He kept himself from looking down her body.

She gave her tinkling laugh. "I know everyone just hates this heat, but I've always liked it," she said, including them all in her grin designed to turn the heat up another ten degrees. Joey felt a dribble of sweat go down his back.

He did not like the way she was looking at his son.

When she paid Larry Joe, she told him to keep the change for himself, gave him another one of her smiles, slipped her body back into the car and drove away.

Larry Joe's gaze met Joey's, then dropped as he turned quickly and strode into the station. Joey thought he needed to speak a bit of warning about Iris, but not in front of Danny J., so he was saved from a task he really didn't know how to handle. Charlene ought to be there to handle it, he thought.

"Dad's takin' me for pizza," Danny J. said.

"Can you get off to go along?" Joey said quickly. "We could wait." He really wished his son would come.

Larry Joe shook his head. "Randy's gone over to Ryder's for parts. I'm the only one here." Then he added, "Thanks, though. Hey, bring me back some, kid," and he playfully punched his brother.

At the restaurant, Joey and Danny J. sat in a green booth, two pizzas on the table between them. They talked about horses and bronc riding. It was easy with his son, and Joey kept thinking about Larry Joe. Why was it that he and his eldest son seemed to be facing each other with fists raised all the time? When had that happened? It seemed to start when his son had entered his teens, and had gotten worse in the past year, when Joey and Charlene had started arguing so much. But it was true they had had difficulty almost from the time Larry Joe had been born.

A little bit later, Joey and Danny J. drove back to the Texaco, bringing a small pizza and cold drinks. Larry Joe's gaze was almost welcoming, so they hung around awhile.

Standing there with his two sons and Randy Stidham, Joey suddenly felt quite old and a little lost. His two sons were almost men. One was man enough that a grown woman was flirting with him. Where did that put Joey himself?

Joey took Danny J. home and stayed to watch a couple of movies. It was the first time he had sat in his own home in weeks. For the first twenty minutes he sat on the edge of the chair that had always been his spot. Finally he took his hat off and slid back, getting comfortable.

It was almost dark outside when Charlene called. Danny J. answered and spoke to her, nodding and saying a succession of yeahs and nos. Then he said, "Dad's here with me. Want to talk to him?"

Joey got ready to take the receiver, but then Danny J. said, "Okay, bye," and hung up.

Twenty

The City Hall thermometer reads 101°

Vella Blaine walked out to her mailbox at the curb and pulled out her mail. Seeing the envelope from the county extension office, she hurried back up her walk and into the house, opening the envelope as she went. In the kitchen she pulled a paper from behind the coffee container—the analysis of her own soil—and sat at the Formica table, laying the forms side by side and smoothing them with her palms. She adjusted her bifocals and bit her bottom lip as she compared.

"Well," she said, highly annoyed.

She sat back and breathed a deep sigh. The reports were almost identical. She didn't see how that could be. *She just did not see it.* Winston had great big roses all over his bushes. She did not. She had done everything she knew, everything recommended by people and in rose-care guides. Roses, as a general rule, simply quit forming in such heat. But not Winston's.

She got up, walked around the table deep in thought, and then went out the back door, snatching her bonnet from its hook and smacking it atop her head. Taking up the hose, she wet her roses that sat in the hot sun, felt of the soil beneath the mulch, murmured to them and lovingly touched leaves here and there.

Shoulders slumping, she looked down toward the Valentine house. That was when she saw the three figures in the front yard. She went over and looked from the shelter of the lilac. One of the figures in the yard was Winston; the two others were unknown to her. Younger men. There was a beat-up van at the curb, and she strained to read the printing on it. Goode Plumbing, Heating and Electric. She'd had them over once to clean out a drain. They had been real good, too.

What was Winston doing? That one fella was unrolling wire. It looked like Winston was putting in some lights in his yard. It seemed a silly thing to be doing at his age. His house wasn't any showplace, no more than her own. Except for those roses.

Maybe it was light shining on them at night that made them bloom like that. Maybe that was why she had seen that glowing out there in the rose garden. The solar lights she had seen up at the Wal-Mart popped into her mind. Simply stick in the ground lights, she thought, turning and going back in the house, taking off her apron as she went.

The City Hall thermometer reads 104°

Mason was bent over the engine of his grandfather's car. He straightened, bringing out the alternator. Air blowing from the old industrial fan cooled the sweat running down his temples. He walked over to the entry for better light, turning the alternator over in his hands.

Just then a vehicle drove up—Larry Joe Darnell in his pickup. Mason recognized the sound of the truck before he saw it.

"You left a message for me. Said you wanted to see

me," the kid said as he strode forward, all youthful muscle and cocky assurance.

Mason nodded. "You want a job workin' over the engine of this Chevy?"

"Well, that depends." The kid stepped into the shade of the barn, tucked his hands up beneath his folded arms and rocked back on the heels of his boots. "Looks like you already got started. I don't know if I want to step into any mess you might have made." His lips twitched with a grin.

"I'm payin' hard cash. How about five hundred to rebuild?"

"I think I'm your man." The boy took the alternator out of Mason's hand and walked toward the old car. "But if you help me, I'll have to charge more."

Mason followed, grinning broadly.

When he had been Larry Joe's age, Mason had worked with his grandfather on car engines in this same barn over the long hot summers and oftentimes in the winters, when they had to wear insulated coveralls and take turns warming against a portable heater. Temperature had never seemed to bother his Grandpap. Mason could recall the patience with which the old man had taught him everything that was of any import and use in this old world. As he watched Larry Joe roll beneath the Chevy, he remembered his grandfather doing the same, and eventually it had been Mason rolling under there because his Grandpap couldn't do it as easily anymore. The memories came flooding back. The day of his grandfather's funeral, he had closed this barn and in the years since had opened it only on rare occasions.

He had closed the door on a lot of old wounds, he thought. He looked at Larry Joe's young sweat-glistening arms and thought of himself at that age, running over here to be with the grandfather who thought he mattered and getting away from the hard father whom he could never please and the fragile mother who withdrew from a world and a husband she found too harsh.

His mother had been beautiful, like a tender butterfly. Her husband's domineering personality and constant infidelities had eventually caused her to become chronically ill and withdrawn. There had been weeks on end when she did nothing but lie in bed and gaze out the window. The one thing she had done, to the great surprise of Mason and everyone else, was, at the sudden death of her husband from a heart attack, to engage a powerful Oklahoma City lawyer to bestow upon Mason the bulk of her inheritance in the feed store, a share making him equal to Adam, and to tie it so tight that not Adam, or anyone else could break it. "I learned something from Mac," she said at the time, and then closed her mouth and didn't utter another word for the rest of her life, which was only three months.

Sometime in their hour of working on the old car, in Mason's mind the young man had become firmly Larry Joe, not simply kid and not a boy at all.

"Okay, Larry Joe, time for a break to cool off."

On the way to Mason's back door, they walked over to the fence, where Mason ran cool water in the trough for the horse and mule. The curious animals came over to see the humans and to receive petting. Mason rubbed the horse's ears the way the old fellow liked.

"He doesn't look like it now, but this guy was a stellar ropin' horse," he told Larry Joe, who was petting the mule.

"I don't ride," Larry Joe said, as if defensive. "I can ride, but I don't." He let go petting the mule, and the mule bared his teeth and carefully took hold of his shirt. "Hey…"

"He likes you," Mason said, chuckling. "And that's an honor. Old Buck doesn't care much for people, as a rule. He always turns and gets set to kick my brother."

Larry Joe again petted the mule, and the mule closed his eyes with comfort. Larry Joe felt sort of taken up by the mule, who had liked him with only a little touch.

They sat on Mason's back porch, in the two rockers, with their boots propped on the porch posts, drinking small bottles of cold Coca-Cola.

"You said you got drunk and killed somebody," Larry Joe said and raised an eyebrow. "Who?"

Mason, who had felt the question coming, said, "My wife's boyfriend." He looked at the curved white letters on the cool bottle and thought that he should tell the son of the woman he wanted. "I was twenty-two, and I'd been out with the guys, drinkin' and carryin' on like I did in those days. I don't think you could call our marriage very much of one. We were both young and wild. And one night I came in—I stopped in, really, to get some cash for more drinkin'—and found her in bed with this fella. I grabbed the first thing I saw, which was one of his big boots, and swung it upside his head hard enough to knock him into the night table. The blow just right killed him. Manslaughter. A boot wasn't really considered a lethal weapon, and it was understandable that I wasn't thinking."

"Did you go to prison?"

Mason nodded. "Two years, then parole for good behavior." He looked over at the kid. "I do not recommend the method, but prison is a place that can grow you up. It sure gives you time to think, and there are times you find yourself on your knees 'cause there's nowhere else to go." He sort of grinned. "Down on my knees, I was able to look at myself."

Larry Joe's gaze met his, and there was rare understanding there.

They sat there in companionable silence for some

minutes, in which Mason felt himself drifting in and out of memory.

Then Larry Joe said, "Danny J. said you came over to the house lookin' for Mom. He said you had flowers in your hand."

Mason had been wondering when they were going to get around to that. "Yes, I did," he said, slanting the boy a glance. "Do you have any problem with that?"

"No," Larry Joe said and sort of squinted at him. "What if Mom doesn't want to go out with you? Do you still want me to work on your Chevy?"

"Absolutely. You're contracted."

"I haven't seen any money yet."

Mason pulled out his wallet and handed over a hundred dollar bill. Then he asked, "You want another Coke?"

"Yeah. You got anything to eat?"

Mason made them both ham sandwiches, and then he asked Larry Joe when Charlene was coming home.

"Four or five days," Larry Joe said around his bite of ham sandwich. "Sometime next week."

Mason sat looking at his hands holding his sandwich. "Does she know about me coming by?" He wondered what she would think of him.

Larry Joe said he hadn't told her but he didn't know about his brother Danny J. "You want me to tell him not to tell?"

"Oh, no," Mason said quickly. "It isn't a secret or anything."

But still, he fairly itched when he thought of her learning of it.

He wasn't certain he could show up at her doorstep like that again. In fact, he wasn't certain he wanted to approach her again. He had begun to think that his fantasies had been a lot easier to bear. In them, he was all the man he wished to be, and she was all the woman. By turning the fantasy into reality, he risked having to face a much less than perfect picture. He risked destroying completely his dreams of their love.

The City Hall thermometer reads 100°

Joey didn't mean to snap at Sheila, but that was how it came out when he told her that she could go pick up the young colt from Shackleford by herself.

"You don't need to snap at me, Joey," she said.

"I'm sorry. It's the heat so early in the morning. Look, Primo can go with you. That colt's easy to handle. He won't have any trouble loading him." He averted his gaze.

"I want you to go with me," she said, hand on her hip and lips pouting.

He did not intend to go with her. He thought he would suffocate if he went with her. "I have to work those two mares. If we're goin' to show them this weekend, I have to work them every day. And then I want to go get bute and some of that high protein food from MacCoy's."

He felt her searching gaze as he turned to untie the mare from the rail, and then he heard the sound of her boots crunching gravel as she turned and strode away.

Sitting atop the bay mare, he watched Sheila drive away in her truck with the gleaming trailer and felt relief flow through every muscle. He was, he thought, about to lose everything yet again. She could throw him off this place, and where would he go? He didn't know, and he didn't care right then.

He did what he always did when beset by emotions he did not understand: he rode the horses. This was what he was good at. He knew who he was and where he fit on this earth when he was training a horse. That was why his horses responded to him, because he became one with them, leaving his human life and confusion behind.

After an hour, however, Joey could no longer block from his mind the image of Mason MacCoy having come to see Charlene. Both he and the horse were wringing with sweat, and when Joey took the mare to rinse her in the washing stall, he quite suddenly turned the water on himself, holding the hose over his head and letting the cold well water pelt him, hopefully to wash the disturbing memory from his mind. He blinked with the water running in his eyes, alarmed to find he wanted to cry.

He scrubbed his head under the water and then turned the hose to his chest, over his head again and back over his shoulders, thoroughly soaking himself. The mare looked over at him as if he had lost his mind. He put a hand on her neck, feeling the sleek wet and warm coat. Then, for an instant, he laid his forehead against her neck.

With tired movements, he wiped her down and put her in her stall, and walked, his pants legs stuck to him and his boots squishing, over to his trailer, where he showered and dressed.

On his way to MacCoy's Feed and Seed, he passed the thermometer on the corner of the City Hall building; it now read 103°, and it was not yet noon. He stopped in front of the store, and when he got out of the truck, he realized he'd parked in exactly the same place he had when Charlene had come and fought with him that day. His cheeks burned all over again. He thought that memory would hound him for the rest of his life.

The bell rang out when he entered the store, causing him to wince. At the counter, Bennie made him out an invoice for five bags of the special grain mixture and got him three tubes of the inflammation medication. "Here you are, Joey.

Mason'll fix you right up with the grain over at the warehouse," Bennie said in his usual cheerful manner.

"Yeah. Thanks." Joey snatched up the small bag of medication and the invoice.

He backed his truck at a good speed over to the loading dock, stopped with a jerk and hopped out. His boots tapped the concrete, and his spurs jingled. After a minute, there came Mason, rolling the bags of grain on a dolly from the dim interior.

"Hey, Joey."

"Hey."

Chewing on words he was trying to hold in, Joey stood back and watched the man high up on the loading dock toss the bags of feed into his pickup. When Mason had finished, Joey handed up the invoice, which Mason signed, ripped off the copy and crouched to return to him.

Then they were looking at each other, Joey looking up, and Mason looking down, and Joey said, "You went to see my wife a couple days ago."

Mason nodded. "Yes, I did."

Joey looked away, then back up at the man. "Just so you know—we aren't divorced."

"I'm aware of that." Mason inclined his head, and Joey thought he had finished, but then Mason said, "The facts are that you have left Charlene and are living elsewhere and are seen regularly in the company of another woman. Your wife is on her own. Those are the facts of the case."

"Yeah, well, the main fact remains that we are not divorced," Joey said, feeling small and silly and wanting to knock the man's head right off.

Instead he got into his pickup, started it with a roar and drove off with both hands gripping the wheel.

The City Hall thermometer reads 90°

Vella was out admiring the solar lights now stuck between each rosebush when Minnie Oakes hollered from the back door.

"Yoo-hoo, Vella?"

"Yes? I'm over here." Vella waved, somewhat sorry that Minnie had come while she was trying to watch and see any difference happening with her rosebushes.

"Your bread maker is beepin'," Minnie called from the bottom step. "You need me to add anything?"

"Oh, no. I'm makin' plain." She might as well go in, she thought, but Minnie was coming toward her, walking on tiptoe across the shadowy yard.

"Perry said you were out here examinin' your lights. They sure look pretty. But how are they plugged in?" Minnie glanced around, as if looking for a cord.

"They don't need pluggin' in. They run on solar."

"On what?"

"The sunlight. They get energy from the sunlight."

"But it's dark."

"They take the energy from the sun during the day and use it at night." Minnie never understood modern things. She could not even work her VCR.

"Oh. What if it is cloudy for a few days? Will they still work?"

Vella looked at the lights. "Well, I don't know. I'll have to read the directions." That could be a problem.

"Do you think they will keep the armadillos away?"

Oh, dear, Vella thought, still not settled about the cloudy days. "No, I don't think so." She had in fact heard that the light attracted the critters.

"You will be able to see the armadillos better, I imagine," Minnie said.

Vella was looking down at the Valentine house. The rosebushes there were shrouded in darkness. Maybe the glow had to be at certain times to help the bushes bloom. That might make for a problem, because the lights she had bought came on automatically at dark and stayed on until light.

She and Minnie went back into the bright kitchen, where Vella kept glancing out the window to see the glow of her lights among the rosebushes.

"You don't think those lights will attract armadillos, do you?" she asked her husband, after Minnie had left. She had been careful not to tell him how much she had spent on the lights.

"You can probably see them better to shoot them," he said, without looking up from his magazine.

"I don't want to do that," Vella said. "I'm not the sort of person who'd attract armadillos just to shoot them." She might end up with trouble from the SPCA.

Twenty-One

Rainey's patio thermometer reads 102°

Rainey was just hanging up the phone when she heard Charlene and Jojo coming in the door, Charlene calling out frantically, "Rainey! Rainey!" Footsteps thudded on the thick carpeting, and Charlene appeared through the open bedroom door, eyes wide and hair wild.

She stared at Rainey, and Rainey stared back from where she had sat up in bed, causing her dog Roscoe to rise up and tense, as if to be ready to defend his mistress.

"What is it?" Rainey asked, alarmed, thinking first of Jojo, but then, thankfully, Jojo appeared right beneath Charlene's elbow.

"*What is it?*" Charlene repeated with high annoyance.

She dropped her shopping bags and threw herself in the big flower-print chair. "I have been phoning here for the past hour, and the line has been busy. I thought maybe some emergency had happened and you were calling a doctor, or maybe had knocked the phone off the hook when you fainted getting out of bed. You knew I would call to check on you. You shouldn't have kept the line tied up."

Roscoe, thoroughly confused and certain he might have been at fault, slinked off the bed.

"I'm sorry to let you down and not be unconscious,"

Rainey said, to which Charlene rolled her eyes, and Jojo laughed and threw herself down on the bed with Rainey, telling her, "We bought lots of stuff, Aunt Rainey."

And Rainey responded appropriately with, "Oooh, show me everything!"

She had been urging Charlene for days to go shopping at the big mall very conveniently located within a short bus ride. Since her sister and niece had been gone for over three hours—during which time Charlene had phoned Rainey on the cellular three times to check on her—Rainey thought the trip must have proved successful. And now that Charlene was calming down, Rainey could see she appeared quite perky. The shopping excursion had done her good.

"JCPenney was havin' a great sale," Charlene, queen of bargains, said, as she flipped off her sandals and slipped out of her skirt and crawled onto the big bed, too.

The bags were opened and fabrics and colors poured out. Even Roscoe wanted to see. "Oh, Roscoe…you're too hairy," Charlene said, brushing stray dog hair off a newborn sleeper.

"You've hurt his feelings," Rainey said, as the dog turned to leave the room. "Come here, boy."

The dog looked doubtfully over his shoulder and waited. Rainey looked at Charlene. "You have to apologize," she whispered. "He understands everything."

Charlene blinked and then said, "It's okay, Roscoe. We'll have to wash everything anyway. Come and see."

The dog returned and laid his head on Charlene's ankle. "Oh, you old spoiled hound, you," she said and patted his head.

They all oohed and aahed over the contents of the first bulging shopping bag, which was filled with baby clothes and various articles. Jojo had chosen for the baby a musical stuffed Curious George, one just like she had had as a baby.

Then Rainey and Charlene insisted Jojo try on and model each of her new outfits. That Charlene had gone overboard was evident. Trying to make up for a broken home, Rainey knew, watching her sister's bittersweet expression.

Jojo changed behind the bathroom door and came strolling out like a model down the runway, while Charlene did narration. "And now, from the wonderful sale at Penney's, we have Jojo in a cotton pants and blouse set for the early hot school days." This made Jojo giggle—as she had not in some time, Rainey thought, remembering how quiet Jojo had been the first days and how she would lie each night against Harry and Roscoe and watch the Disney Channel.

"And this little number is for cooler fall days. The blue brings out the pale blond of her lovely hair." Charlene shot Rainey a mother's prideful glance that said, *See how lovely she is. She how she is growing up. Thank you for letting us come. It has been good for us.*

When Jojo finished modeling all of her new clothes, she and Rainey insisted that Charlene do the same with the two dresses and blouse and skirt, and even the nightgown, that she had bought for herself. Jojo stood and pretended to narrate into her fist-microphone, while Rainey properly applauded Charlene's taste and ability to get such bargains.

Then Jojo took Roscoe off to watch television, and it was just Charlene and Rainey on the big bed. Rainey thought Charlene had never looked more lovely. The new haircut and rinse set off the graceful shape of her neck and golden green of her eyes. She appeared much more relaxed than when she had arrived the previous week. Rainey was certain of it.

"I was talking to Danny J. all that time you were phoning me," Rainey said. She was fairly bursting with all sorts of news.

"Danny J.?"

"Oh, Charlene, don't get that look. He is fine. You do not need to immediately assume the worst."

"Oh, I know." She straightened and raked a hand through her hair. "I do fight the habit. I simply haven't been able to get up enough strength to face Danny J. riding broncs. I should have followed up with Joey about the bucking horse. I should be the one to jump right in there and get him on the broncs, before he does it at some really inopportune time." Her eyes opened wide. "He didn't, did he? He hasn't been riding a bronc yet?"

"Yes. He phoned to tell you. He was on one over at his friend Curt's. And he is still alive to tell of it—quite happily so. "

"Oh...and I wasn't here to hear him."

"Charlene, you will call him back. It's okay. You can't be there every single minute. You were with Jojo this time."

"Well, yes, I was. And we had such a good time. This is the first year she has really taken part in choosing her school clothes. And she does not like the color green. That girl wants denim blue, and that's the end of it."

"So I noticed. It looks good on her, too."

"She may turn out to be one of those girls who can wear a feed sack and look good," Charlene said in an absent fashion and then studied her fingernails like she always did when thinking deep, sad thoughts.

Intent on pulling her sister up, Rainey said, "Guess what Daddy did now?"

"What?"

"He installed lights for his flag and speakers up underneath the eaves. Now, each morning at sunrise, he flips a switch and "Dixie" plays out. And he doesn't have to take his flag in, except in rain, because he switches the lights on it each night. Danny J. says it looks grand. Can you imagine?'' She laughed.

Charlene said, ''I just hope he doesn't get some ACLU fellas comin' into Valentine. You know the fuss a lot of people are makin' over things like that.''

''Oh, he's just an old man who loves his South. Lots of people do. Lots of older people know a country we don't, Charlene. One of Harry's patients, Mrs. Roth, she goes on and on about how her family was thrown out of their house by a big corporation that moved in and ran them off their farm back in the Depression. It happened all over out here. There's a lot of those older people over at the retirement home who sit around the radio and listen to these shows that talk all about the terrible acts of government. They're like a bunch of Senior Subversives.''

''Well, Daddy may not like the government, but his main objective is to get Everett's goat,'' Charlene pointed out.

Rainey nodded, thinking warmly of her father, a one-of-a-kind man. ''Their rivalry keeps them both going. It makes them happy, and there's no harm done.''

Then she went on to tell Charlene that Danny had reported the heat had been so bad as to open a crack right on Main Street, right out from the thermometer. ''Mildred says that's a sign they need to take the thing down for good. She's hopin' you'll come back and make Sunday dinner, by the way.''

Charlene was studying her fingernails again.

''And Mason MacCoy came by to see you.'' Rainey had been saving this for last.

''He did?'' Charlene's head came up so fast it almost snapped off.

''Yes,'' Rainey said, quite pleased to relate the information. ''The very evenin' after you left, but Danny J. forgot to tell you. He hopes you aren't mad at him.''

"Well, for heaven sake." Charlene looked flabbergasted.

"He came calling, Charlene," Rainey said, tickled by the phrase. "Isn't that what you wanted?" Laughing, she picked up a pillow and whacked her sister. She was thoroughly delighted at this turn of events and had questioned Danny J. very closely about the entire matter. "He brought flowers. Danny J. said Mason had flowers in his hand."

"He brought me flowers?"

"He said he wanted to come visit. What that means, Charlene, is that he is hot for you."

Charlene stared at her for a long second. "But I'm not divorced. I don't think I should start carrying on with some man who brings me flowers." She backed off the bed, as if backing away from the idea.

"Oh, Charlene, Joey has gone off. He has broken his vow before God. You don't get much more broke up than that. I don't care what the legalities are. And just because a man brings you flowers does not mean you are carrying on with him."

"Well, I am not ready to start dating," Charlene said, raking her hand through her coppery hair.

"You told him he could come see you."

"I didn't think he would bring flowers."

"What does that have to do with it?" Rainey was a little exasperated at Charlene, who could not seem to be pleased.

"I don't know. I should have explained that I didn't want to date. That I didn't want to start any sort of affair." She breathed the word *affair* in a low, furtive voice.

"You may just insult Mason by saying that. Just because he brought you flowers does not mean he wants an affair."

Charlene went to raking her fingers through her hair at a frantic rate, and Rainey told her to stop it, before she pulled her hair right out.

Charlene looked at her. "I don't know the least thing about dating nowadays. And I'm not sure I want to know."

"Mason sounds to me like he is a sweet, old-fashioned sort of guy. He came to visit you bringing flowers." She paused, then added, "And then, as Mason was leaving, Joey was coming in and saw him."

"He did?" Charlene seemed both shocked and dismayed.

"Yes. He asked Danny J. what Mason wanted, and Danny J. told him that he wanted to see you."

"Well, it does not matter what Joey might think about it," Charlene said in a snappy tone Rainey appreciated. "Nor does Mason coming to see me matter. I really don't want any involvement with a man right now."

Rainey asked, just for clarification, "Joey, either?"

Confusion flickered over her sister's face. "I still don't know about Joey and me," she said. "Right now I have to deal with myself and what I'm going to do."

At last, Rainey thought with relief, Charlene was returning to her stalwart self.

"Let me have the phone," Charlene said, motioning. "I want to call Danny J."

"Are you goin' to ask him about Mason?" Rainey asked wickedly.

Later that night, when Jojo was watching a Disney movie with Harry and Roscoe in the living room, Charlene brought Rainey a cup of warm milk, shoved the big flowered chair close to the bed and curled into it, and told Rainey about the white-haired woman who loved roses. She talked about first meeting the woman on Main Street that day, and then told of encountering her at church. She told about the woman's lively expressions and the way she gave Charlene a rose each time.

"I think she could be Mama," she confessed and watched Rainey's eyes get wide. "I know it sounds outlandish, but she just seems to appear and disappear."

Rainey said with skepticism, "If she is Mama, why didn't you recognize her right off? Doesn't she look like Mama? There shouldn't be a question here, Charlene."

"She resembles Mama," Charlene said, unable to say that the woman definitely looked like her mother. "Maybe she looks more like Mama did back when she was younger."

"Maybe she's an angel," Rainey said, obviously wanting to agree to something. "People have reported visits from angels."

To which Charlene said practically, "Rainey, if you can believe she is an angel, why would it be more outlandish to believe she is Mama? She sure talks like Mama," she added.

Charlene really could not be certain of her suspicion about the white-haired woman. And none of the theories made any difference, she decided. No matter if the woman was real, or a ghost, or even a hallucination, she had come to Charlene like a gift, at a time when Charlene truly needed her. So Rainey was probably right: the woman was an angel.

The next day Harry began his leave of absence in order to take care of Rainey, and Charlene knew it was time for her to go home. She could see that Rainey was getting irritated by her and Jojo's presence. Her sister wanted time alone with her husband.

Sitting on the side of the bed, wearing her new dress, she told Rainey, "I can't thank you enough for letting Jojo and me come up."

"Oh, honey, thank you for comin'. You've taken such

good care of me. It really did ease Harry's mind. And I've enjoyed visitin' with both of you so much."

They gazed long at each other, then Charlene said, "Well, I sure needed to get away...like Freddy hidin' in the hospital. Everyone needs to get away sometime."

"Yes," Rainey said, understanding bright in her eyes. "Everyone's on the way to somewhere, Charlene. You'll know when you get there."

Charlene blinked away sudden tears. "I guess I'm ready to go home and get started."

Rainey laid a hand on her arm, and Charlene looked down at it for a long second, then laid a hand over Rainey's. "We've wasted a lot of time," she said, her throat tightening. "All these years we could have been better sisters to each other."

"Everything in its time," Rainey said. "I guess we didn't really need each other so much when we had Mama. Now we do."

Charlene thought about Rainey's comment as well as many other sentimental things during the bus trip back to Valentine. She sat with Jojo's head resting in her lap and gazed out the tinted window at the scenery racing past, while what she saw were memories of yesterday and images of the possible future.

She sighed deeply. That was what visiting Rainey had done most for her—enabled her to breathe again. She had not realized until she had been at Rainey's and away from everything in Valentine for several days that she was finally breathing easily again. Change of scene, it was called. It was the oddest thing, how physical distance had helped her put her life back into perspective.

Somewhere along the way, she seemed to have lost her panic about the future, and, most blessed of all, she could pray again and felt that God heard her. That He was watching over her all along, even in her angry state, and was leading her to wherever it was she needed to go.

Plans began to flow through her mind like a vibrant river. She would immediately have Larry Joe help her with getting back to driving. She thought briefly that maybe her father could help, but of course that would very much be the blind leading the blind. She told herself that she didn't need to fear driving. She had driven for many years in the past, and likely it was a skill like bicycle riding, which, once learned, you just had to brush up a bit.

She would go to Dixie's to apply for a job doing nails, and if that did not work out, she would find something else. Something would work out. She just had to believe it would. To picture it unfolding and all working out. She would watch Danny J. ride a bucking horse, and she would speak to the bank about a loan to help Larry Joe with college and enable him to continue on to the school in Michigan. She had to let him go and be a man. She needed to go see Freddy; she had told her father she would and had completely forgotten. Maybe if she and Rainey could grow closer, she and Freddy could, too. Admittedly, given Freddy, this did not seem highly likely, but she needed to try.

She did not know what she would do about Joey. She still could not even think the word *divorce* without having a horrible pain. And there was Mason. My goodness, the very thought of him, who she saw with his brilliant blue eyes when he asked if he could come to call on her, started an excited twanging inside her.

She would get through all of it, she told herself. All she had to do was keep going down the various roads with faith that all would turn out.

The outskirts of Valentine appeared, and Jojo sat up.

Charlene looked over Jojo's shoulder out the window, watching homes and then the first businesses pass.

"Mama, look! The clock is working on the City Hall."

"Why, it sure is." The digital lights read 5:30, then the temperature at 100°.

The brakes whooshed, and the bus pulled to a stop in front of the Main Street Cafe. Charlene suddenly felt that she had been gone an entire lifetime, instead of just six days.

She and Jojo stepped off the bus onto the hot, dusty concrete. Then there were Larry Joe and Danny J. and her father. And they seemed as eager to see her as she was to see them.

"I tell you, Daughter," her father said, walking with his arm around her shoulder, "ain't none of us can get along without you."

"That is sweet to know, Daddy, because I need you all to need me." And she didn't feel afraid of that anymore.

Twenty-Two

The City Hall thermometer reads 90°

Charlene was sitting at the kitchen table, folding clothes—
a week's worth of laundry from Larry Joe and Danny J.
She heard Joey come in the front, and Jojo call out with
pleasure, "Hi, Daddy!"

She paused, holding a T-shirt, and cocked her head, listening to the voices in the living room, Jojo saying she
wanted to show her father her new clothes and Joey's low
answer. The voices faded to the far end of the house.

A short while later Joey appeared in the doorway, his
hat in his hand. When she raised her gaze to look at him,
she saw a startled expression on his face. She realized he
was staring at her hair, which he had not seen since her
new style and rinse.

After their initial greeting, he came in and sat gingerly
in a chair across the table, twirling his hat between his
fingers and bouncing his knee. She knew he had something
on his mind. That he might be trying to approach the subject of divorce occurred to her. He would have to begin the
subject, she thought, because she was not ready to do so.

He said, "Jojo sure is excited about her new school
clothes."

"Uh-huh. She picked all of them out herself."

Their eyes met, and then Charlene averted her gaze to the jeans she was folding.

He asked about Rainey and the new baby, and she told him. She questioned him about Danny J.'s bucking horse, and he said he had found three retired rodeo broncs at a ranch over near Frederick. They would still buck but were growing mellow. Charlene felt reassured, and pleased that Joey was having sense enough to look for such a horse.

"I thought I'd take Danny J. with me and he could choose," Joey said. "Uh...would you want me to keep it over with me?" He did not call the Arnett ranch by name.

"Bring it here," she told him instantly. "You can come to help him here, and that way I can watch, too." She definitely was not going over to that slut's place, and she did not like the idea of her children over there, either. "But I want the rule understood that if he gets on that horse without one of us there, the horse goes."

"Okay," Joey said with a nod, his gaze sliding down once more to his hat.

She then told him about Larry Joe's decision to start at the junior college that semester and his further ambition to go to automotive design school in Michigan. "I'm going to speak to Gerald down at the bank," she said, "to see what kind of loan we can get to help him. He can't be working long hours and keep his studies up, too."

"Whatever you think is best," he said, which annoyed her. She wished he would have an opinion or a suggestion. But then, seeing his frown of worry, she felt a little more tender. They already had a sizable loan at the bank. She thought about it as she smoothed wrinkles from a pair of Danny J.'s jeans.

When he said, "Your hair looks nice short like that," she looked at him, greatly surprised.

"Thank you," she said. His eyes were on her in an intent

manner that she had not seen in some time. In a way that made her glad and frightened at the same time. And he was bouncing his knee again.

She broke the gaze and stretched down to draw an armload of underwear from the basket, dropping several pieces.

Joey reached to pick them up, handing them to her—a pair of her panties and a lacy pink bra, starkly delicate against his thick, work-roughened fingers.

"Thank you," she said again.

He leaned forward and propped his forearms on his thighs and twirled his hat with his fingers. She cast glances at him as she folded the pieces from her lap and put each neatly in the appropriate stack on the table. He was still a very handsome man, she thought. She could understand Sheila's interest.

Joey said, "You know, I suddenly realized that last week was the anniversary of my daddy's death. I drove up to the cemetery and checked the date on the stone. It was Thursday."

Charlene dropped her hands and the T-shirt she had just folded into her lap and gazed at him.

He lifted his eyes and said with a puzzled look, "He was only two years older than me when he died."

"I know."

He returned his eyes to his hat, and she sat staring at him, feeling him tugging at her, requiring of her. Her heart felt resistant to giving. And she wasn't certain she had anything left to give him.

"I just began to feel that nothing was ending up how I wanted it to be," he said. "I felt like my life was runnin' out, and I wasn't getting anything done that I'd started out to do. It made me go a little crazy, and I couldn't seem to stop myself."

He sat there staring at his hat, and she saw lines on his

face that she hadn't noticed before. Her heart began to melt and run all over her chest.

He said, "I guess I've been runnin', Charlene, thinkin' that I was going to end up like my dad." He lifted his eyes to her. "Can you understand that?"

"Yes," she said, her voice thick. "Yes, I can, Joey."

"I went crazy, leaving here. I know that now. I just felt so lost and scared because of it. There didn't seem to be any way to fix it here."

She listened to this, to the sorrow in his voice mingled with the unasked and hopeful question. He wanted to come home, she knew as she sat there holding the T-shirt knotted in her fists. She thought she needed to tell him it was okay, but she could not.

The buzzer sounded from the dryer in the laundry room and caused her to jump. She got up and went to attend to the clothes. A moment later Joey came to stand in the door. She felt his eyes roaming over her body. Her breasts tingled, and her stomach quivered, and the memory of how his touch used to make her feel flashed through her mind. She couldn't bring her gaze to his.

He stepped closer. "Charlene, don't hate me."

"I don't hate you, Joey," she said, breathlessly, feeling tears welling up. "I've loved you for twenty-one years. I can't just turn that off." Then she stilled her hands and looked at him. "What are you wanting me to say? That now you can come home? I can't say it, Joey." Her heart thudded in her ears. "I just don't know if I can do that."

His eyes shifted, and he changed hands with his hat. After another moment he said, "I'll call about pickin' Danny J. up to go get that horse."

"That'll be fine." Their eyes met and held. She saw ripe questions in his, questions that she could not answer, and so she looked away.

"Well, good night," he said.

"Good night."

Then she stood there listening to his slow footsteps and the faint jingle of his spurs as he went back through the house, to voices as he told his children good-night, and then to the closing of the door.

She took a step and stopped, remaining stock-still, listening to the sound of his truck engine start and then fade away.

Guilt and panic washed over her. She had let him walk out. She might have missed her chance to stay a married woman and to keep her children's daddy for them. How could she have done that?

Charlene tossed and turned in the bed, while her mind tossed and turned with wondering why she had not jumped to make things up with Joey. She could not understand herself. She had her children to think of. She should do all she could to keep their daddy for them.

Hadn't she told Joey that she had loved him for twenty-one years? A person couldn't stop loving after that time. But, God help her, she wasn't certain she could be married to him anymore.

Something had gone wrong inside of her, she thought. Something had gone horribly wrong.

Finally, in the early hours of the morning, she fell asleep, only to be awakened by a startling clap of thunder. It was just after two, and with the next flash of light, she came fully awake. Immediately she switched on the bedside lamp, got the flashlight from the drawer and tested it to find it in working order. Then it was down the hall, peeking into each of the children's rooms to see them still fast asleep, despite the heavy crashes of thunder above them.

Another crash of thunder and more lightning so close

she thought that it surely had hit a tree, and she went back and unplugged the stereos in both Danny J.'s and Larry Joe's rooms, unplugged the living room stereo and television, then turned on the one in the kitchen to see the report that their county was under a tornado watch and flood warning.

Rain began with hard splats against the night black window, and wind rattled the panes. Then the rain came as fast as water rushing from a big open spigot.

The rain continued as she made coffee, all the while vigilant for the sound of a tornado. Of course, by all reports once one was heard, it was too late. She sat to watch an old movie and to monitor the weather updates by weathermen with rolled-up sleeves, loosened ties and eyes as baggy as her own. She wondered a number of times about Joey. When he had been living with her, he would remain sound asleep through any storm, relying on her to watch for a possible tornado. She wondered if Sheila watched for him.

By five o'clock the storms had moved on north. Charlene went out the back door, padded down the wet back steps and across to the rain gauge on the corner fence post. It had rained an inch and a half in three hours.

She stood there in the blessed moistness. The sky in the east was beginning to glow with morning, and the dark storm clouds could be seen to the north. It was a sight that stirred her, made her know how big and powerful life was, and that if she really knew the power of it, she wouldn't be able to stand it. Then she felt the first cooling breeze in two months touch her face.

The temperature had dropped, she thought, and Joey seemed to be at last coming to his senses. She was reminded of what her mother used to say: *This, too, will pass. Always does.*

The heat had passed, but it wasn't going to be something people forgot very quickly. They would be watching for it to flare up again before summer finished its run.

The City Hall thermometer reads 80°

"The ground is really soggy. Just make sure you stay on the gravel," Larry Joe told her on her first driving excursion. He sounded like she had never driven before.

"I only need to warm up," Charlene said. "I know how to drive." She felt a tiny bit of panic rising in her chest. She fought it, reminding herself she had practiced driving up and down the driveway. She could do this now.

As she made the turn onto the highway, however, Larry Joe started shouting at her to quit turning so sharply, and the next thing the right rear wheel felt like it hit a pothole.

"You went in the ditch," Larry Joe said, when she pressed the accelerator and the vehicle didn't move.

"Well, you scared me when you shouted."

Larry Joe was already out of the truck. She followed and found him staring at the truck's chassis, which was stuck on the culvert.

"I never did that with the Cherokee," she said, perplexed.

Larry Joe looked at her. "Mom, the Cherokee was a lot shorter than the Suburban."

With the help of the tractor, her sons got the Suburban out of the ditch, and Larry Joe said very uncertainly, "Do you still want to drive to town? I have to be at work at eleven today."

"You take me," Charlene said. "I really need to get groceries in this house." It was evident to her that, for some people at least, driving was not the same as riding a bicycle. One could lose the ability.

The City Hall thermometer reads 85°

She went to see Freddy with her father. As concerned as she was about his driving abilities deteriorating with age, she had to admit that her father easily negotiated getting out of the driveway and up on the highway.

The hospital shone blinding bright in the late afternoon sun. Her father said, "I hope he's dressed. I think they should make them get out of their pajamas by afternoon."

The interior walls were soft tans and blues, calming colors. The hall was even carpeted. Charlene, feeling tired, had a brief fantasy about lying down on one of the beds. Since she had let her husband go, let her dream go, she thought maybe she could use some therapy to get straightened out.

Freddy surprised her by seeming to be very pleased to see her. It had been a long time since she could recall Freddy being pleased about seeing her, or any of them. From his teens, Freddy had more or less separated himself from the family, seeming to come back only to get in a good argument with their mother at holidays or on a Sunday afternoon here and there, when he could fit it into his schedule as a fast-rising businessman.

Since their mother's death, Charlene could probably count on her fingers the number of times she had seen her brother. When he and Helen had come to Sunday dinner, it was always some business with their father that brought him, something Helen wanted from the house, or maybe just to check in to make certain they were still on the inheritance list.

"It's good to see you dressed," their father said, sizing up Freddy.

"Yeah." Freddy nodded and ran his hand over his head, his hair close-cropped, the way he always wore it. Charlene was a little startled to see how much Freddy had begun to resemble their father. She had never thought her brother looked like anyone in the family. Freddy himself had at times asked if he was adopted.

He was also freshly shaved, she noted, and although his clothes were just a touch wrinkled and he wore slippers, at least they were his own leather slippers and not the terry cloth ones given by the hospital and worn by a number of the other patients.

Since Freddy's roommate was lying in bed, his hands folded on his chest while he stared up at the ceiling—— "Looks like a dang corpse," their father said in a not-so-hushed whisper——they went down to the communal visiting room, a friendly place with big windows and a volunteer serving coffee and ice tea to the numerous patients and their visitors.

As Charlene got three paper cups of ice tea, she noted that a very thin man beside her didn't have a belt, and his pants looked precariously like they might fall down. Wondering if he were a patient, and if belts were prohibited, she looked around. Of the men who were dressed, a number did not wear belts. She wondered if this was some rule for the patients, or if they were simply poorly dressed visitors. It was a little disconcerting to realize she could not be certain exactly who were the visitors and who were the patients. She wondered if any of these people were violent.

Taking the cups of tea to her father and brother, who had chosen comfortable chairs in a corner, she noticed Freddy wore a belt. Possibly he was not considered a danger.

They conversed a little haltingly, sitting in silence between subjects while each of them thought of something to say, in the manner of the strangers they were, Charlene thought, saddened. She had come to the hospital with the high intention of encouraging a closer relationship with Freddy, but looking at him, at the three of them sitting there, she had trouble persuading herself that any such thing was possible. She was quite blue about how she had behaved at Joey's offer to reconcile.

They had fallen into silence for several minutes when their father suddenly said, "I'm gonna go get me a cold drink from the machine."

"You still have your tea, Daddy," Charlene said.

"I don't want it. Either of you want a Coca-Cola?"

Charlene and Freddy both said no, and their father headed out the door. Charlene's eye lingered on the bent and stiff set of her father's back, and when her eyes shifted back to Freddy, she saw he had been watching their father, too.

"He's really gonna go smoke," Freddy said.

"I know."

"I guess he isn't ever gonna quit."

"I guess he figures at eighty-seven there isn't much reason to quit."

Freddy nodded and looked down at his hands.

"You know, Daddy misses you," Charlene said.

To that Freddy said in a sharp manner, "Dad and I weren't never close. Don't try to change history. Dad didn't ever need anyone but Mama."

Charlene was surprised to see the hurt plain on his face for a split second, before he looked away. She had never realized her brother's hurt.

"I can agree with that, but now he doesn't have her," Charlene said, hoping to make her brother understand. "Rainey is gone away with Harry, and I have the kids, at least. Daddy has those women to keep him company, but mostly it is him looking after them, and a lot of times they drive him nuts. He's as sharp as he ever was, and he misses having someone to discuss real subjects with. All Mildred talks about is food, and Ruthanne hums a lot. Since Bill Yearwood passed away last spring, Daddy hasn't had another close male friend. Most of the men die off before they get to Daddy's age.''

"It's just how things happen, I guess," Freddy said, a comment Charlene didn't find at all satisfactory.

"Maybe now you and Daddy could finally get to know each other. Before it's too late, Freddy." She was certain this was the silver lining that would help both men.

Freddy sat there looking at Charlene's expectant face. Then he said, "Our family is not the Waltons from television, Charlene."

Confusion flickered across her face, and then hurt. "I just think it would be good for you and Daddy," she said.

Freddy felt a bit of remorse pluck at his annoyance. The thing about Charlene that had always gotten on his nerves was that she always seemed to expect so much. The thing she expected the most was for them all to be like one big perfectly happy family. She would give those big family dinners and expect them all to show up and spend a couple of hours in a group hug or something.

Looking at his sister now, he could recall her as a girl, taking their mother's and father's hands to walk down the sidewalk, while he was always left to walk a little ahead or behind. From Charlene's birth, it had been as if his parents had pushed him aside. "You're the big boy now," he could remember both his father and mother saying. Even before Charlene came along, his mother and father had seemed taken up with themselves, leaving him in the care of a nanny. And then Rainey, who hadn't even been his father's child, had come along. His parents had pretty much dropped Freddy and Charlene and focused all their attention on the new, adored *late child,* as Freddy thought of his sister, and on themselves. They had not had time or energy left over for anyone else.

Or maybe it was him. That was what the doctor here had suggested to him, that Freddy himself had trouble getting close and letting others be close. The doctor had consulted his father, and though the doctor never really said, Freddy gathered his father had said something that led the doctor to conclude Freddy had from birth been aloof and different. That was a load of crap, and went to show his father's view that Freddy just didn't fit.

"Freddy?" Charlene said, a little worried.

"Charlene, it's too late." He thought for a bare instant that he shouldn't be so blunt, so hard, but it was the way he was, and he stubbornly had to cling to that right now. He had lost himself for a while and was finally finding himself now, and he was holding on desperately.

"Why would you say that? Daddy's still alive. He's still tryin' to be your daddy," she said, her voice sort of small. "Maybe he sees his mistakes in the past, Freddy. Every parent does, and he's tryin' to make up."

He saw he'd hurt her and was moved to be a little more tender. "I know he's alive, Charlene. And I am, too. And we are still the same people we always were." He leaned forward. "I guess maybe I could try to be the close son to Dad now. Maybe he does need that, but my time for being that son passed years ago. *He* was the one let it pass, Charlene. He never needed me, or you, as long as he had Mom and then Rainey. Well, now I need somebody, and it isn't Dad. I need Helen. And I'll do what I have to do to keep her, just like Dad did to keep Mom. I understand that much now."

They gazed at each other, Charlene searching his face with her green eyes.

"I'm sellin' the store," he told her then, speaking of the

dealership. "The IRS hasn't found enough to seize it. They've tried to find problems with my real estate and well-service businesses, too, but they haven't done it," he said with satisfaction. "I'm sellin' the dealership before anything more comes up. As soon as my lawyer can fix it, me and Helen are movin' out to California."

"California?" Charlene came up straight with this piece of news.

She had understood about his resentment of their father and his determination to hold on to his wife. She had followed him up to this point, but to move away from his home, where he had lived for all of his fifty-plus years, and where his family lived and his father would surely die, was a foreign thing to Charlene. She would have understood if he had said he was moving to Dallas. Lots of people moved down to Dallas, not more than three hours drive away. But California was a half the country away, and filled with smog and loonies.

"Helen wants to go to California," he told her. "Out to Palm Springs, where it never gets cold. She wants to belong to one of those nice country clubs."

"Palm Springs? Where rich people live?" She had once read an article on the place in a travel magazine at the doctor's office.

"I have plenty of money," Freddy said.

Charlene, the first of her shock abating, had to admit she could picture Helen in such a setting. "I guess you'll be getting out of the hospital soon, then," she said.

Freddy nodded. "This last week has been mostly to give my lawyer time to set a few things up."

That was Freddy—use being in a mental hospital to set up business.

Charlene could not think of much of anything else to say to any of it. Her father rejoined them, bringing his can of

Coca-Cola, and she noted the age in his hands and on his face. She knew he had never expected to outlive their mother.

She wondered if she would live to be old, and who would be there for her when her skin was like wrinkled paper. She thought of how she had let Joey walk out of the house and felt guilt settle on her again.

They left Freddy at his room and walked silently down the hall and out into the sunlight. As they were getting into the Oldsmobile to leave, there came Helen, in a brand-new champagne-colored Lincoln, whipping into a parking place several cars down. She had to see them, yet she never looked their way, did not give a call or wave or any notice at all to her father-in-law and sister-in-law.

Charlene stared at her, amazed to see that in slim pants and a long-sleeved T-shirt, wearing dark glasses and with a pale scarf wrapped around her head and neck, Helen looked amazingly young.

"She looks like she's practicin' for California," Charlene said.

"What?" Her father shot her a puzzled expression.

"Oh, Daddy. Start the car. I'll tell you on the way home."

When she had done with the telling, her father's only comment was, "It'll be perfect for Helen. She likes modern."

After a minute of looking at the passing scenery, Charlene said, "What about Freddy, Daddy? Will it be perfect for him?"

"I expect so, or he wouldn't be doin' it. Freddy isn't one to do what doesn't suit him."

Twenty-Three

The City Hall thermometer reads 88°

The bell jingled over the blue door as it opened, and she stepped into the blue world.

"Welcome, Charlene," Dixie Love said, sweeping forward with her familiar smile and long strides.

There were two women under the dryers and two in the chairs, and all of them were looking at Charlene. She came closer to the counter and said, "Would that offer of a job still be open?"

"Well, yes!" Dixie smiled a warm, lovely smile. "We'd love to have you. You can start right now, if you want." And she gestured toward the manicurist table, which sat as if ready and waiting.

Charlene stared at her and finally got out, "Oh. Yes, I can."

She had been sitting there, feeling as if she had stepped into another world and looking over everything for twenty minutes, when she remembered she had left Larry Joe waiting in the Suburban. She jumped up and raced out to tell him, "I have a job. I'll call you to come get me!"

"Way to go, Mom." He gave her a thumbs-up and backed out.

Her gaze lingered on him and then the Suburban as he

drove away. She thought that she needed to quit leaning on him so much. And she was awfully glad Larry Joe was her son, and not like Freddy. Maybe it was because of the mother she had been, she thought with a start, feeling a little disloyal to her own mother.

The City Hall thermometer reads 94°

She did not have very many customers that day, but that was okay, because she spent time getting familiar with the points of working toward her license. She would be working under Dixie, who was a registered instructor and taught at the beauty college up in Lawton. She kept telling herself that getting started at something was the main thing at this point. She found that while she had dreaded the thought of getting a job, she was now very excited about it. It was perfect for her, right there in town, and Dixie agreed Charlene would only work school hours.

She realized that when she had left the house that morning, she had left behind so many of the worries and regrets that plagued her. Here in the shop those concerns seemed almost like bad dreams, of no importance. A number of times through the day, as she arranged her station to suit her, she would glance up and see herself in the mirror and wonder just who that woman was and how had she come to be where she was.

Early in the afternoon, when the shop was momentarily empty of customers, Oralee suggested Charlene make herself useful and go around to get them all fountain drinks from the cafe. "It'll give you somethin' to do, and bein' the new girl, you get the job of goin' out in the heat, and I don't have to."

Charlene was not quite certain of how to take Oralee, who very often seemed quite bossy and ill-humored.

"Oh, that would be nice, Charlene," Dixie said, in the pleasant manner she always employed. "Oralee does not like canned or bottled soft drinks."

"They don't agree with me," Oralee said.

"She gets quite cranky when she has not had a Coca-Cola about this time," Dixie said, handing Charlene several bills.

Charlene tried to refuse the money, feeling very indebted to the woman already, but Dixie pressed the bills in her hand, saying the shop always bought.

"You had better take what bonuses you can, workin' in this place," Oralee said.

Charlene didn't know what to make of that.

She stepped out the door into light so bright she wished she had her sunglasses. She realized she was still wearing the pale blue smock Dixie had given her. She walked to the corner and turned down Main, glancing at the thermometer on the City Hall building. It read ninety-four. It was hot, but not as hot as it had been, thank goodness.

"My gosh, gal, what are you doin' here in the middle of the day?" Fayrene asked her when she approached the counter at the cafe.

"I'm workin' down at the Cut and Curl. I just started," she added, not quite feeling like a full working woman yet.

"You are?"

"Uh-huh. I'm doing fingernails. Hand massage, too."

Fayrene's gaze went to Charlene's nails. "Well, I might just come down. I've always wanted nails, and Judy here wears those acrylics. She says they wear like iron."

"They do. I could do them for you." She stopped short of mentioning the price, feeling it might not be polite.

She ordered the drinks, and Fayrene said, "Oh, yes, it is time for Oralee's Coke. She gets testy when she doesn't have her daily Coca-Cola."

Charlene paid, and Fayrene handed the drinks over in a paper sack. "Make sure you hold the bottom, too," she cautioned.

Charlene went happily out the door, thinking so hard about being a working woman, that she apparently wasn't watching where she was walking. She turned onto the sidewalk and ran right into Mason MacCoy.

"Oh!"

He took her by the upper arms to steady her. "I'm sorry."

"No, it was my fault. I wasn't watchin' where I was going."

And then they were standing there looking at each other, Charlene staring into his blue eyes. Very blue eyes. And then the question of why he had not been to see her came to mind.

He averted his eyes. "I was just going in for something to drink, too," he said, indicating the sack of drinks she held.

"Oh." She couldn't think of a thing to say and came out with, "I'm taking these around to the beauty shop. I'm working there now, at the Cut and Curl."

"You are?"

"Yes."

He rubbed the side of his nose and began, "I was—" but then he was cut off when two women came out of the cafe and one bumped his back.

"Excuse us," Charlene and Mason said in unison. The woman who had bumped Mason said she was sorry, but she was frowning in irritation.

Then they were standing there looking at each other again. Charlene waited for Mason to continue with what he had been going to say. She hoped he was going to say something about coming to see her, a thought she immediately stuffed down.

"I was just goin' in for a late lunch," he said.

"Oh."

"I guess you've already had lunch."

"Yes." She felt a little silly, and disappointed. Maybe he had been going to ask her for lunch. "Well, I'd better get these back to the shop. The sack's startin' to get wet." Realizing she'd forgotten, she put her hand to the bottom of the sack. "Bye," and she walked away along the sidewalk.

Then, in a moment of instinctive boldness, she looked over her shoulder to see if Mason was still standing there watching her.

And he was.

Jerking herself straight, she walked quickly to the corner and around it, and there, out of his sight, she stopped to take a deep breath. *Ohmygosh, he had been looking after her.*

She grinned, still standing right there on the sidewalk. A movement in the window to her left caught her eyes, and she realized there was a woman at a desk on the other side of the window, in the offices of the *Valentine Voice*. The woman was looking at her.

Charlene headed on up to the beauty shop, wondering why Mason would gaze after her like he had and not come to see her. Quite suddenly visions of making love with Mason, their naked bodies all entwined in passion, filled her mind. *Dear Lord, if you didn't want me to have such thoughts about a man, naked, you should not have made humans with sexual desires.*

Jerking open the door to the beauty shop, she determinedly wiped the thoughts from her mind. She did not think she was up to sex with a man, no matter her desires.

The only man she had ever slept with had been Joey. The thought of starting fresh in the sexual department was very daunting. How could she let a man see her naked? Everything might still be there, but it had definitely shifted.

And she certainly had enough mess in her life caused by one man without beginning a romance with another.

After work, Charlene was waiting on the sidewalk, when Larry Joe drove up and stopped for her to get in the Suburban. Just outside of town, she told him to pull over. "I want to drive the rest of the way home." She had a job; surely she could manage driving.

Her son looked uncertain, and she pointed. "There, that looks good." So he pulled to a stop on the shoulder, and they changed places, each getting out and going around the hood of the Suburban, getting back in and slamming the doors. Charlene sat there a moment, fighting down the panic that seemed to be in her bones. Then she shifted into gear and pulled out onto the highway. She drove slowly but smoothly, gradually increasing speed. She could feel independence welling up inside her.

She cast a grin at Larry Joe, and he gave his slow grin back. "Let's roll down the windows," she said, and they did, letting the warm wind blow their hair, while still running the air conditioner. *She was driving!*

The entry to the driveway came up, and she slowed, turning.

"Mom...Mom, you're cuttin' too close!"

The back left wheel went in the ditch this time.

Out and looking at it, Charlene said, "We have to make this entry wider."

Without a word, Larry Joe strode away down the driveway to get the tractor.

* * *

That evening on the telephone, Charlene told Rainey, "Well, I went to see Freddy, I've gone to work, and I've put the Suburban in the ditch twice. I guess I am at least doing something."

She told Rainey all about Freddy and his plans to move to California. The most Rainey said was, "Oh, well," and Charlene did not find this adequate, but before she could fully address Rainey's attitude, or lack of one, Rainey said, "So, what about Mason?"

"What about him?" Charlene said, feeling a little stubborn.

"Well, has he come around?"

"No, not really. I saw him at the cafe today, though."

"And?"

"And he said hello." After a moment she said, "He watched me walk away."

"That's something, I guess," Rainey said.

Disappointment echoed in Rainey's tone and seemed to come over the line and slip into Charlene. She thought of how she had been home for several days, and now all evening, and Mason had not called.

"I guess Mason has changed his mind about being interested enough to come visit."

"Well, you said you didn't want any involvement with a man," Rainey reminded her.

Charlene was annoyed at what she saw as Rainey changing sides of the fence. She said smartly, "Yes, and I still don't. If I can't judge distance enough to get into my own driveway, I don't think I'm going to be able to judge things like breaking up with one man and taking immediately up with another."

"You have a good point," Rainey said.

Charlene thought Rainey should have bolstered her, rather than agreed.

* * *

Danny J. got his bucking horse, a bay, very stout, and no matter that he was graying around the nose, he was a lot bigger than Charlene had expected him to be. A monster next to Danny J., who was short for his age. She didn't like it at all, but she kept quiet.

With her eyes shaded by the brown cowboy hat she'd had since she was nineteen, she stood at the training pen fence with Jojo, who was standing on the second plank up for the best view. Joey held the bay horse against the fence, while Danny J. climbed carefully aboard.

Danny J. stayed on for four full bucks, before he was flung loose like a discarded bandana and landed with a definite thud in the dirt. Charlene wanted to run to him, but she held herself at the fence with Jojo, while Joey slipped through to help their son to his feet. She heard Joey say, "Are you all right, son?" and saw with immense relief that Danny J. was able to get up, to move everything. *Oh, thank you, God.*

He waved to Charlene and called, "I'm okay, Mom."

"I see!" She waved back.

He prepared to get on the horse again.

"Mama, you're squeezin' me," Jojo said.

"Oh, I'm sorry, honey."

It would not do for her to get sick. She had to stand there and smile and encourage. Her fear would harm him, but her faith would hold him up.

Jojo's small warm, moist palms came to her cheeks. "Mama, it's okay. You can open your eyes. He'll be okay."

She hugged her daughter and cheered for her son as he went bouncing across the pen atop the bucking horse. *Looks like a bundle of rags up there. Oh, God, take care of him.*

Three good bucks, and down went Danny J. again. This

time he was up quickly, watching for the horse as his father hollered at him to do. The horse appeared to consider this a well-known game. He trotted off to the far side of the pen, as if saying, I know my part, you don't know yours. Five times the pattern was repeated, and each time, Joey would slip through the fence and go over to instruct his son, laying a hand on his shoulder as he spoke.

For the final try, Larry Joe drove up and joined them, standing beside Charlene, hooting and hollering. "Hang on, buddy! Yeee-haaa!"

And Joey joined in jubilantly, "Yeee-haa!"

Danny J. took a bad fall this time, and instantly both Larry Joe and Joey were beside him, helping him up. Charlene tried to find her breath. She saw Danny J. was smiling, if a little crookedly.

Then she saw her husband standing with both his sons in the dusty, golden glow of the setting sun, and her throat got thick.

"That's enough now," she told them firmly. "It is time to get some supper." After a minute, she said, "Joey, do want to have a bite with us?"

He looked startled. "Yes. That'd be nice," he said, and a slow grin spread across his lips.

She turned from his warm expression and strode away to the house, all manner of emotions twirling around in her chest and propelling her to fly around the kitchen, throwing together grilled ham and cheese sandwiches and fruit salad, fresh ice tea, and a table set for five places as it had not been in a long time.

Once she happened to look at the television, which had been left on CMT, and there was a sexy young woman singing and dancing her wiles all over the screen.

Charlene picked up the remote and clicked off the television with great satisfaction.

The children came bursting in the back door, Joey following more slowly and quietly behind. Laughing and poking, they fought for the sink to wash up. Jojo tried to squeeze between their legs, and Larry Joe lifted her up to stick her hands under the faucet. So very much like it used to be, Charlene thought, a sharpness crossing her chest. She avoided looking at Joey.

Then they were all at the kitchen table, sharing the meal. Danny J. and Joey did most of the talking, discussing the finer points of bronc riding. Larry Joe put in that he'd heard of a couple of colleges with rodeo teams and that Danny J. should think ahead about getting a scholarship. Joey's eyebrows went up at this, and then he quickly agreed.

"I'm gonna ride broncs, too," Jojo said, wanting attention and doing her best to look like a boy right there in the chair, with her legs wrapped around the chair legs.

The boys and Joey chuckled, and thus encouraged, Danny J. said, "You're a girl."

Charlene said, "Girls can ride broncs. There have always been women riding broncs and bulls. Your grandmother did."

Jojo gave them a "See there."

"Well, I gotta go, Mom," Larry Joe said, pushing back his chair. "I got to get over to Mason's and work on his engine." He kissed her cheek.

"Oh," she said, wondering what engine, her eyes following him as he ruffled his sister's hair and waved goodbye to them.

Joey's questioning gaze met hers. Averting her eyes, she rose and got the pitcher of ice tea, refilling Joey's and Danny J.'s glasses. Just as Jojo was wiggling onto her father's lap, his pager began to buzz.

"Uh…I'll use the phone in the living room," he said, moving Jojo so he could rise.

Charlene said, "Danny J., you'd better get out there and feed and water the horses," and Jojo went racing after her brother.

Charlene cleared the table, and when she picked up Larry Joe's plate, she suddenly paused, realization crawling over her shoulders.

Larry Joe had been sitting in the place that Joey used to sit. Sometime in the weeks since his father had walked out, Larry Joe had started sitting there and had naturally come and sat there tonight. And Joey had sat in Larry Joe's place. She remembered then seeing Joey standing for a moment, looking perplexed, before sitting down.

Everything was changed, she thought, her heart sliding heavily downward.

She was standing there, staring at the table, when Joey appeared in the doorway. "I have to go," he told her. "I had a horse come in." He looked uncertain, as if torn in two.

"Yes, of course you do," Charlene said quickly. She wasn't going to be the one left waiting again. "Oh, don't forget your hat." She grabbed it from the hook near the back door and shoved it at him.

When he heard the rumble of Larry Joe's pickup, Mason was in the barn, working on fixing a dent on the rear fender in the light from a fluorescent lamp he'd hung from the rafters. He had to keep swatting away moths that fluttered down in front of him and stuck to his hot skin.

"Why don't you turn on the fan?" Larry Joe said and went over and switched it on. Mason felt silly for not thinking of it.

"I've got to meet Neville in a couple of hours," he said.

"That's cool." Larry Joe took up a wrench to work on the engine they now had out of the car and hooked on a stand. "I'll work as long as it takes to get this thing apart. I don't have to get up early."

"When do you start school?" Mason asked.

"Next week."

Mason continued sanding. Only firm conviction kept him from asking about Charlene. What did he want to know? He knew she had come home, had seen her in town. There was nothing else he needed to know, he thought, working the flat board with fury.

"If I get this thing apart tonight, you want me to take the head to the machine shop?" Larry Joe lifted an eyebrow at him.

Mason nodded. "Yeah. Just have them do what needs doin', and tell them I'll pay for it."

He paused and watched Larry Joe stand back and look at the engine for a minute, about like Picasso studying a painting. As soon as they had gotten the engine out of the car, they had agreed to leave it to Larry Joe and the body-work to Mason. Mason preferred the bodywork. He liked filling and sanding the dents.

Just then Larry Joe said, "My mom came home last week."

The hair prickled on the back of Mason's neck. He nod-ded, saying "Hmmm," while again pushing the flat board at a rapid rate and thinking of Charlene the afternoon before on the sidewalk. Of her warm green eyes and creamy skin, and how her son would surely laugh if he knew Mason's mushy thoughts.

"And she got a job this week."

"Oh?" He didn't look up.

"Down at the beauty shop. Dixie Love's."

"Ohh."

"She's decided to start drivin' again, too." He threw

aside one socket and got another. "She's put the Suburban in the ditch at the driveway twice."

For a long minute there was only the squeaking of the socket wrench turning bolts and the shooshing of the hand sander.

Then Mason said, "Sounds like you need to widen the driveway."

"That's what she said," Larry Joe said with a bit of surprise. After a long second, he added, "But I don't think the whole town is goin' to want to widen their intersections."

Mason laughed aloud at that.

Their eyes met, and Larry Joe's were so ripe with a question that Mason could hear it clearly: What about you and my mother?

Mason broke the gaze and stood up, laying the flat board aside. "I'll go get us a couple cold drinks."

Larry Joe watched Mason walk out into the night. Then, with a shake of his head, he once more bent over the engine. Whatever did or didn't go on between his mother and Mason was not his business. And he wished her taking up driving again wasn't any of his business, either.

He worked the socket wrench with expert turns. Things were easing inside of him. Maybe he was coming to accept that he and his father were never going to be close, that he could take it as it was and not be too disappointed. Maybe a lot of the acceptance he felt was because he was able to come over here with Mason. Maybe he was growing up, because he had come to realize that adults didn't have all the answers. The preacher had said that there was only One with the answers, and that was God. Larry Joe would have to go along with that—it sure wasn't any human on this screwy earth.

It was well after one o'clock when Larry Joe got home

and found his mother had fallen asleep on the couch where she had been waiting up for him.

"I was a little worried," she said, sitting up sleepy-eyed. "You said you were working on an engine for Mason?"

"Yeah. Out of an old Chevy that belonged to his grandfather. He's paying me five hundred dollars."

She blinked. "Oh. I hope it isn't too hard a piece of work."

"Mom, I've rebuilt three engines before this one." He hugged her. More and more he was beginning to feel that she was so small in his arms. He was beginning to see that he wasn't a child anymore, and it was unsettling to know, especially because it caused him to have some wild fantasies about Iris MacCoy.

Twenty-Four

The City Hall thermometer reads 75°

Vella came down to poke around in the rosebushes again in the gray light of dawn. Winston saw her because he had for the third time in a row been awakened by Ruthanne climbing into his bed. This time not at the foot but right up beside him. He just about had a heart attack, because he was having a bad dream about being crushed in a crowd of people at a cafeteria where Mildred had insisted on going. When Ruthanne's arm flopped on him he came awake with a start, breathing hard.

He slid out of the bed, got his slippers on and stood there in his striped pajamas, scratching his head and wondering exactly what to do. What if someone came by and saw this? He would be in a fix. Although some down at the Senior Center might think more highly of him.

Deciding to see if he could get Ruthanne back to her own bed, he went around and shook her until she responded. He succeeded in getting her to her feet and walking back to her own bedroom, and he didn't think she ever came fully awake.

He was fully awake, however, so he went on downstairs. As he passed the dining room windows, his eye caught movement. He went closer. Yes, it was Vella again. He had the disconcerting thought that maybe she was walking in her sleep, like Ruthanne. But if she was, she was also clipping roses in her sleep.

She did not look asleep.

He decided to go out and investigate the matter and was headed for the kitchen when an idea stopped him in his tracks.

Only a moment's hesitation, and he was heading for the living room, walking on tiptoe so Vella would not hear a floorboard squeak, so thoroughly pleased with the notion that he could hardly contain himself.

He pressed the button on the little stereo and was sprinting for the dining room window when the first strains of "Dixie" hit the air. Through the window, he saw Vella hotfooting it across the misty pasture to home.

A flutter of guilt touched him at having frightened her. He should be ashamed, and he was. *But, Lord, it was pretty funny.* And he still wondered what she was up to.

Feeling energized, he went to check out the sky to decide about putting out the flag. Despite having the lights, he had taken to bringing the flag in before he went to bed, in case of rain, now that the drought was abating. Neville Oakes said he thought it was okay anymore to let the flag fly in the rain, especially since Winston had the lights, but Winston believed perfectly good traditions had been going to hell in a handbasket ever since Roosevelt had gotten in office. And he didn't care to have a good flag ripped to smithereens by a storm, either.

He was going to have to get him a freestanding flagpole, he thought, as the strains of "Dixie" died away and his gaze moved from the dark clouds gathering above to his neighbor's front porch. He wasn't going to wait for Everett to make the next advance.

The City Hall thermometer reads 81°

"Oh! Oh, I'm sorry," Mildred said. Each time a clap of thunder sounded, she would jump, and Charlene would mess up with the polish.

"It's all right, Mildred. We'll get it by and by." Charlene took a tighter grip on Mildred's fingers, which were a little greasy because she kept eating Fritos out of a little blue Tupperware container.

Oralee, trimming Odessa Collier's beautiful white hair, was also watching the report on television of the damage done by the early morning storms down in Texas. "Thank heaven it was them and not us," she said.

"Oralee, what a thing to say," Dixie Love said. "It's a shame it is anyone."

"Well, it does have to be somebody," Oralee said practically. "That is the way the storms go in this country. And we're lucky we are just gettin' the leftover. I don't know why I don't leave this hick town and move back up to Chicago, where they don't get tornadoes."

"They get snow. Piles of it," said Odessa Collier. "And, Oralee, please look more at my hair than at the television."

"I believe I've heard of a tornado up there," Dixie Love put in. "Tornadoes are possible in every part of the world."

"Well, all those prayin' for rain can please stop," Oralee said.

The thundering had passed by the time Mildred's nails had finished in the UV dryer. As Mildred admired the results and went over to show the other ladies her bright fingernails, Charlene put the lid on the container of Fritos for her. Mildred dropped it carefully into her purse and then went over to sit in Dixie's chair for her hair appointment, without thinking to pay Charlene.

Charlene would not ask her. It would have been like asking an aunt. A rather destitute aunt.

The thing was, Charlene was beginning to feel a little destitute. She had been working for almost a week now, and despite the rosy financial picture Oralee had proposed, she was not earning much of a living.

It was only ten-thirty, and with no customers scheduled for the rest of the day, Charlene felt a little blue. She comforted herself by arranging all the bottles of polish at her station. She loved to see so many bottles of color, even if she did owe Dixie for them. She loved to be sitting at her manicurist station, waiting and ready to improve someone's nails in an almost instantaneous way, as she had not been able to improve her marriage.

By the second day, when she had experienced an appalling dread upon going home, Charlene realized that her job at the beauty shop was not so much about earning money as it was a way for her to escape the sense of disappointment that haunted her at home.

Each evening, when she went home from the shop, she would wait on the front step for her children to come down the drive from where the bus let them off. She would not go into the kitchen until they arrived, at which point they would go in together, and she would bring out every good snack she could think of to please them. She wanted to do nothing else but hang around in her children's bedrooms, asking them to tell her about their day or if they needed her help with homework. She wanted to be with her children because, she felt, at least with them she had not failed. When they would finally give her that look to shoo her away, she would go to arranging their closets and drawers.

At night, after the house was quiet, she would find herself once again listening for Joey to come home, knowing she would be disappointed. She would listen, too, for her very self, and be disappointed in not finding that, either.

Then each morning she dressed with a sense of eagerness and was ready for Larry Joe to drive her into town the instant Danny J. and Jojo left on the school bus. And the instant she stepped into the shop, she would experience both a sense of peace and a sense of possibility. Here she was not a mother or a discarded wife, not somebody's daughter or sister, but purely a woman, with other women, discussing things of importance to their lives as women and making a difference in the lives of other women.

Oralee, observing Charlene wearing herself out arranging all the bottles of polish, said, "Things are slow right now because of all this rain, but they will pick up—and so will the tips," she added loud enough that Odessa Collier lifted her eyes and told her to stop hinting.

And Oralee said, "I am not hinting. I'm sayin' it straight out."

Charlene said to Odessa, "She needs the money to feed the kitten she saved from drowning in the alley this morning," and caught Dixie Love's smile in the mirror. Charlene had learned that Oralee went to great effort to appear hard as a hazelnut, while, like the nut meat, she was sweet and tender inside.

Oralee flashed black eyes at her and pointed the comb at the tiny calico now sleeping on a towel in an emptied curler tray. "I just wanted to hush the critter up. It was makin' enough noise to wake the dead. I'm takin' it over to the animal shelter when I leave here." Then she added sweetly, "Unless any of you ladies want to do the good deed and give it a home."

They all remained quiet and averted their eyes.

"Uh-huh. That's what I thought," Oralee said.

When the bell over the door jingled, Charlene looked up

expectantly, smiling in preparation for a customer, hopeful to greet someone who, if she didn't plan to have her nails done, would see Charlene sitting there sweetly and suddenly decide she could not do without a manicure.

Charlene's smile froze, as she saw the woman who came through the door and over to the counter like she meant business, her tight tan jeans flashing with each stride, her hair like glossy black silk and the curve of her cheek like fine porcelain.

It was Sheila Arnett, right there in front of Charlene's eyes, and she said to Dixie, "I need to have a nail repaired."

"Why certainly," Dixie said with all her customary pleasantness. "Charlene would be glad to fix it."

Then Sheila Arnett was gazing right at her with deep blue eyes that widened with shock.

Charlene had already gotten to her feet. For the space of five taut seconds she and Sheila Arnett stared at each other. Then Charlene did what seemed the only thing to do. She stepped forward and asked, "Do you want silk overlay or acrylic?" She held her hand out to accept the other woman's.

Sheila glanced around at the others watching them, then back at Charlene. "Acrylic," she said in a low voice, although she did not display the damaged nail but kept one hand at her side while with the other she smoothed hair back behind her ear.

Charlene pulled the chair out. "Please have a seat."

Slowly Sheila slipped down into it, sitting on the edge. Charlene sat in her own chair and reached for her reading glasses and then looked at the woman.

Sheila Arnett laid her hand on the towel atop the table in a careful manner, as if expecting the towel might burst into flame any minute.

Charlene took the woman's hand just as carefully into her own. It was like picking up an ice cube. And the skin was like smooth porcelain, too. But her nails were not her own, and for that Charlene felt a small slice of gratification.

She worked on the nail with perfect calm. She actually felt in control, and feeling such, she could be magnanimous and have no ugly thoughts about the woman at all. It was a delightful feeling.

In a few minutes she had the nail cleaned, had a tip in place, formed and filed and looking exactly like a genuine nail.

"Do you know the color of your polish?" she asked. "I may have it. It looks very much like Passion Rose."

"Don't bother," Sheila Arnett said, jerking away her hand and coming up out of the chair. "Thank you."

Charlene saw the green twenty-dollar bill flutter to the table. The woman pivoted and was out the door.

In an instant Charlene snatched up the bill and ran out the door. Sheila Arnett was three cars down, getting into her Lexus. With firm, swift steps, Charlene ran down the still-damp sidewalk and reached the driver's door just as it slammed closed. She stood there, waiting, so determined it was as if her thoughts came out and pounded on the car roof, until the darkly tinted window finally slid down.

"Yes?" Sheila said from behind dark glasses.

"It's on the house," Charlene said and tossed the money in the woman's lap. Jamming her hands into the pockets of her smock, she strode back to the shop, where she went straight past everyone staring at her and into the bathroom.

As she regarded her reflection in the mirror, seeing very good bone structure and a lovely complexion, for which she could thank her mother, but with forty-six years of creases growing around her eyes and lips, she began to cry. But then she thought of the shocked look on Sheila Arnett's face, and she started to laugh.

She breathed deeply and heard the murmur of voices through the door. Murmurs of support and concern.

Oralee's voice was never a murmur. "She showed that slut what a real lady is."

Friends, Charlene thought.

A knock sounded on the door. "Charlene, honey, I really have to use the bathroom." It was Mildred.

Charlene opened the door, and Mildred gazed up at her, her expression anxious. Very quickly Mildred hugged her, then darted into the room and shut the door.

Odessa, just then leaving, cast her a smile and a wink. Dixie came over and hugged her.

After a few minutes Oralee said, "How much did she give you?"

"A twenty."

"Uh," Oralee said, frowning. "That woman is definitely cheap. If she had wanted to make a point, she should have used a hundred, at least."

"And if it'd been a hundred, I'd have kept it," Charlene said, which earned her an honest-to-goodness wide smile from Oralee.

A few minutes later the bell jingled again, and Charlene jumped, automatically thinking of Sheila.

It was Iris MacCoy, looking like a model out of a Victoria's Secret summer catalog, who came straight over to Charlene and said, "I just saw Odessa's nails. She said you did them. Could you do mine in that shade, too?"

Her first referral, Charlene thought, happily sitting Iris down.

The City Hall thermometer reads 86°

Joey was in the barn, examining a horse's swollen leg, when Sheila came blowing in like a wild wind, saying, "Why didn't you tell me?"

"Tell you what?" he said, straightening and feeling the need to defend himself. Sheila was leaning forward and looked very much like she might smack him.

"That your wife is workin' at the beauty shop. The least you could have done was tell me, Joey. I felt so stupid."

"Charlene's working at the beauty shop?" he said, feeling thrown into confusion by the surprising information, as well as Sheila's accusations.

"Yes, she is. The one time I decide I can get something done in this town, and there she is, acting all righteous. I don't need that, Joey. She has no right to treat me like that."

She pivoted and stomped away, seeming to take the wind with her, and Joey stood there watching her go, wondering if he should go after her and apologize, although he wasn't certain what he would apologize for.

It wasn't like Charlene to be rude to anyone. Sheila, though, was likely to be rude. Sheila didn't have much patience.

Then he thought, Charlene is working. She isn't at home.

Within an hour, the entire town knew about the meeting between Sheila Arnett and Charlene at the Cut and Curl. Charlene was fairly certain the story was carried by Mildred, who had gone straight to Blaine's to pick up a bottle of milk of magnesia, which she made certain to say was for Ruthanne, and had told Belinda Blaine and everyone else within hearing distance of the checkout counter about Sheila Arnett coming into the beauty shop, "bold as brass," and Charlene, "like the lady she is," fixing Sheila's fingernail. From the drugstore, Mildred had gone on to the Senior Center, where she again told the story, a Paul Revere of gossip.

Such good gossip went like wildfire through the town, and as with all repeated stories, it got embellished until one version had Charlene slapping Sheila and throwing her out of the beauty shop, and another had Charlene broken down in tears so bad a doctor had to be called.

Early in the afternoon, when Charlene made the trip around to the cafe to get the fountain drinks, it seemed that everyone in there turned an eye to her. She told herself this was her imagination, but she couldn't fully shake the sensation of being stared at.

Then Fayrene, while ringing up the drink order, asked in a hushed voice, "I hear Sheila was over there at the shop this morning."

"Yes," Charlene said, handing over a bill.

Fayrene handed back her change. "We heard that you slapped her."

"No, I didn't. I fixed her nail."

"Well, I would have slapped her," Fayrene said and closed the register drawer with a hard bang.

Charlene was certain when she left that half the people in the cafe were indeed watching her. She paused with her hand on the cool chrome door handle, then turned and said, "The true story is that Sheila Arnett came into the shop and I fixed her nail. That is all, sorry."

And then she left, appalled at making a spectacle of herself and laughing at the same time. She felt suddenly lifted and carried along. As if she had made it over some difficult and rocky hill. As if during those few minutes when she had faced Sheila, she had turned some corner.

Charlene had this thought just as she turned the corner of the street, and it caused her to pause a moment. Her gaze drifted over, and through the large tinted window she saw the same woman at her desk in the *Valentine Voice* offices. Giving the woman a smile, Charlene waved.

The woman looked taken aback, and then she tentatively waved in return.

The City Hall thermometer reads 88°

When Charlene came out of the shop, she found Joey parked right in front.

Seeing her, he hopped out. "I told Larry Joe I'd give you a ride home."

"Oh, okay," she said, squinting a little in the sun that had burnt off the clouds.

He surprised her by hurrying to open the passenger door. As she slipped into the seat, she saw a bouquet of flowers wrapped in red tissue paper lying in the middle. The sight jolted her so much that she slipped, and Joey had to grab her.

He slammed the door closed. She watched him round the hood, and then she looked down again at the flowers, wondering at them and at his peculiar behavior. She supposed she should not consider it peculiar behavior. Doing a good turn for one's wife and son and making a special effort to be polite should not be considered peculiar.

"These are for you." He picked up the bouquet and held it toward her, his expression so shy and hopeful it went clear to her heart.

"Thank you," she said, accepting the flowers.

She smoothed the tissue paper. The thing was that she had gotten used to him having left her. For him to pop back into her life now, offering rides and flowers, caused almost as much stress as when he had abandoned her. She wasn't certain how to act, what to say. All the way to the house, she held the flowers in a death grip, vacillating between hitting him over the head with them and breaking out in tears. The most conversation she could offer was to respond to his questions that yes, she was now working at the beauty shop, and Dixie had agreed to hours that allowed her to get home to be there when the children got home from school.

When they stopped in front of the house, they both sat there for a silent moment.

Charlene said, "Thank you for the flowers, and the ride."

Joey shrugged. Then he said, "I think I'll go get the horses ready for when Danny J. gets home," and raised an eyebrow at her.

"He'll like that," she said. He started to get out, and she said, "Joey."

He looked over at her.

"I think we need see Jaydee Mayhall about a divorce." She had meant to be more diplomatic. It was her fear that made her say it like that. She made herself look him in the eye. The pain she saw there took her breath.

Staring straight at the steering wheel, his jaw tight enough to break, he nodded. "I guess, if that's what you want."

Charlene was struck to the core. She wanted to scream at him that here he was again putting it on her. She saw very clearly in that second that this was how it was between them, how it had been for a long time, and no amount of yelling and screaming was going to change it. She looked at him and felt great sorrow for him.

"Joey, I still care for you. I will always care for you, but it's just too late. I'm not the same person, and neither are you."

"Yeah, I guess so," he said heavily.

Again silent seconds ticked away, and then she asked, "Do you want me to speak to Jaydee, or do you want to?" knowing full well what his answer would be.

"You do it."

He got out and slammed the truck door. She saw him in the dusty side-view mirror, striding away toward the barn.

Carefully she laid the flowers in the seat, got out of the truck and went inside. She thought she might cry, but the tears did not come. She supposed she had cried herself out over Joey and her failed marriage weeks before. She had, she thought with a great deal of surprise, moved on down the road. She didn't know where she was going, but she knew she was headed in the right direction.

The sun was far to the west when Joey unsaddled his horse, throwing his saddle and sweat-soaked pad in the back of his truck. Joey was sweat-soaked, too, and wished fall would finally arrive. He was tired of sweating.

He turned and saw Danny J. standing at the entry of the barn, watching. "When are you comin' back, Dad?" his son asked, his gaze moving to the saddle in the truck and back to Joey.

"Not till next week, I guess. I got a horse show down in Fort Worth this weekend, and I gotta get ready for it," Joey said, looking over at his roan gelding tied to the fence. "You look after Blue for me until I get back, okay?"

"Okay."

"You know," Joey said, putting his hand on his son's shoulder, "you're doin' just great with your bronc ridin'. You got the fundamentals down now. What you need is to find your own seat, and it will take practice to do that. Your mother can watch you ride when I'm not here."

Danny J. nodded, keeping his head down.

Joey said, "Hey, give me a hug," and opened his arms,

holding his son tightly for a brief moment, before turning away to get in the truck.

Seeing the flowers on the seat, he handed them to Danny J. and told him, "Give these to your Mama and Jojo for me. They're a little wilted now, but your Mama can probably bring 'em back. You know she can fix just about anything."

Then he got in the truck and drove away, squinting with blurred vision and thinking that Charlene *could* fix just about anything, except him.

Danny J. carried the bouquet into his mother, who was in the kitchen with Jojo, putting sandwiches on the table. He noticed there were only three plates.

"Daddy said to give you these. He said they were for you and Jojo." Carefully watching her expression, he held out the flowers wrapped in the red paper and saw her eyes jump. As she took the bouquet, he said, "They're a little wilted, but Dad said he thought you could fix them."

His mother's eyes came to his. "I'll try," she said.

He watched her take the bouquet over to the sink, where she unwrapped the paper and put the flowers in a big jar of water.

Danny J. said, "Dad says he can't come back until next week, but he left his horse. I have to go take care of it."

As he went out the door, Jojo came after him. "I'll help," she said.

On the way to the barn, Danny J. told his sister, "Dad's gone, and he's not comin' back."

"How do you know?"

"I just know." He clamped his jaw closed, to keep himself from crying. He thought that when he grew up he wasn't ever getting married.

Charlene got out a green vase and mixed the little packet of preservative that had come with the flowers in the water.

She cut the stems and arranged the flowers in the vase and set it on the table. By the time she went to call the children to come have supper, the flowers had perked up. She wished she could have done the same for Joey and her marriage.

Joey went by the house of a man who owed him two thousand dollars. The man scraped up five hundred in cash and gave him a check for the rest. From there Joey drove over to the Texaco to get his truck filled up. He was relieved to find Larry Joe still working. While Larry Joe pumped the fuel, Joey got out and washed his own windshield in the glow of the yellow lights coming on above. When he left, he handed Larry Joe three hundred dollars and said he hoped that helped with his school bill.

His son looked at him with wonder.

Joey said, "I know where I can come when I need a good mechanic. You know, lots of people tell me all the time how good you are."

Larry Joe looked from the money to Joey and said, "Thanks, Dad."

His son's look and tone made Joey feel really good. He put a hand on his son's shoulder and said, "Take care of your Mom."

Driving to the Arnett ranch, he thought about packing up and leaving, but then Sheila was sitting on the porch, and she called to him, as she had been doing every night for weeks. This night he went with her. He had a strange feeling of needing her arms around him. Maybe he would stay put, if she held him. He also felt guilty about owing her so much. She had given him a great chance, and she'd given him her heart, too, however much she was able.

They went up to her room, and he made love to her in her big bed. She had lots of soft pillows on her bed. "Are

you goin' to move into Daddy's room now?'' she asked
when they lay together all sweaty on the smoothest sheets
he had ever felt.

"I don't know. Maybe.'' He didn't mean that, but he
didn't want to get in an argument. He didn't want to talk
at all. His head was spinning, and he felt as if he could
hardly breathe. He began to get worried that he might have
a heart attack, like his father had done.

Sheila fell asleep, and Joey lay there for some time, fighting with himself, but then he gave in. He thought that the
only one who would understand would be Charlene.

He slipped out of the bed and dressed, waiting until the
front porch to put on his boots. It was dark, and he got the
wrong boot for the wrong foot and had to switch. He went
to his trailer and packed his things into two large duffel
bags. Then he hooked his truck to his old three-horse
trailer, loaded the three horses he owned into it and drove
away. At the road he headed south, thinking of Fort Worth.
He could sell that one good horse he had there. He sure
hoped that check that old boy had given him was good.

The City Hall thermometer reads 87°

It was Jaydee Mayhall who told Charlene that Joey was
gone. She had seen Jaydee about the divorce proceedings
the first thing in the morning, and that afternoon he called
her at the beauty shop to tell her that he had learned Joey
had taken off.

She stood at the counter, clutching the receiver to her
ear, with the scent of the permanent wave solution Dixie
was using wafting around her, listening to Jaydee say in
his long drawl, ''Sheila Arnett says when she got up this
morning, Joey was gone. That he left in the night, truck,
trailer and horses. And nobody knows to where.''

No one needed to tell her Joey had gone. She had known
he was going the minute Danny J. had brought her the
flowers, and she had awakened in the night and lain there
with the knowing, probably at the same minute he had
driven away.

"Does it matter for gettin' a divorce?" Charlene said,
speaking low.

"Well, no. No, I can go ahead. It may take a little
longer."

"I don't think I'm in any hurry," Charlene said. "I'm
about as single as it gets now."

She told the children that night after supper. They were
not surprised, either.

When his brother and sister had left the table, Danny J.
said, "Will you watch me on the bucking horse, Mom?"

"Yes, I will. Your father has given you a good start.
This is probably what he was thinking, that he has you
started and now all you need is practice."

Danny J. nodded, dropping his gaze to the table. Charlene went over and laid a hand on his shoulder. She started
to say she was sorry, but that seemed like condemning
Joey, and that would hurt her son even more.

She thought of Joey driving down the highway, while
here she was with the responsibility of keeping these young
hearts and lives on track. *Please help me, Lord, to give my
children what they need.*

She said, "We have a light out there if it gets dark. Why
don't we go out now, while your brother is here to help,
and you can ride that horse?"

They got Larry Joe and Jojo, and all four of them went
out. Charlene caught Joey's roan and saddled him and took
her place on him in the pen. Apparently, while she couldn't
drive, she had not forgotten how to ride a horse. She didn't
intend to fail at this, she thought, kicking her heels into the

gelding with determination. She had seen Joey do this a hundred times, and she would manage. Both she and Larry Joe helped Danny J. to get on the bucking horse, while Jojo cheered enthusiastically from the fence rail. After Danny J.'s third go-round on the bucking horse, Charlene wasn't squinting so hard anymore.

With the kids down to bed, Charlene lay in her moonlit bedroom and spoke to Rainey on the phone, telling her about her decision to divorce Joey, and his decision to run off for good.

"You aren't surprised, are you?" Rainey said.

"No. I guess deep down I knew this would happen. It's one of the reasons I couldn't go back with him. I was afraid I would end up like Sheila and wake up one morning, and he'd be gone. He's running from himself, and once he started that, he couldn't seem to stop."

She thought of him driving down a highway somewhere right now, his truck the only one on the road in the night.

"I'm worried about him, Rainey. I keep thinking that if I had taken him back, maybe I could have helped him."

"And that is exactly what he wanted you to do, too. Fix him. But do you really think it would have worked? My first two marriages are pure examples of the failure of this thought. Robert and Monte both expected me to make them right. Robert wanted me to praise his every move, and Monte wanted me to be his mother. Well, I couldn't do it. Nobody can save another person. That is God's job.

"You did the right thing, Charlene," she added.

"I know I did, but thank you for sayin' it."

When Charlene hung up, she lay for a long time, thinking of being a divorced woman. It no longer seemed the nightmare she had thought.

She was not afraid, she realized with surprise. *The Lord is my shepherd....* And he was Joey's, too.

Twenty-Five

The City Hall thermometer reads 88°

With her reading glasses perched on her nose, Charlene studied the shelves of vitamins and herbs at Blaine's Drugstore. One could learn a lot more at the beauty shop besides who dyed their hair, who was not a natural blonde, who bleached her mustache.

Rainey's swearing by vitamins E and C had been confirmed by Dixie and so many customers with youthful appearances that Charlene had put those on her list first. Iris MacCoy had told her to be sure and get a potent vitamin B mixture, saying, "It is the thing for a woman. Keeps my complexion like this. That and zinc." Iris was awfully pretty, but Charlene knew her own complexion to be one of her best features. Charlene had always attributed it to genes inherited from her mother, that and the butter and olive oil she ate.

There was some argument about the zinc. Someone said that was for men's sexual prowess. Charlene decided she would need to read up, but right now, when her nerves were so strung tight, she thought she should get a start. Then, seeing the prices of everything, she decided on getting only the calcium and cod liver oil tablets, which Oralee had said she absolutely must get, and all the woman had backed her up.

Somewhat daunted by the many brands and types to choose from, however, Charlene stepped over and asked Belinda Blaine to recommend some. Belinda was sitting behind the prescription counter, eating a candy bar and reading a *People* magazine.

"Mama, what type of calcium is it that you take?" Belinda said over her shoulder to Vella, who Charlene only just then saw through the doorway to the storeroom. To Charlene, Belinda said, "It's the one Paul Harvey recommends. Lots of the women your age take it."

Charlene didn't think Belinda needed to say "your age."

Vella came out from the back and picked out the bottle for her, saying, "Charlene, I know you are under a strain these days. This calcium will really help you sleep better." She put the bottle in Charlene's hand and picked up a small box from another shelf. "And if I were you, I'd start drinkin' ginseng tea."

"That's chamomile tea for nerves, Mama."

"Chamomile's good, too," Vella said, "but the ginseng will help your vitality. You know, that Larry King says he takes it."

"You might want to get that ginkgo," Belinda said, looking up over the top of her magazine. "It's supposed to help your memory. Of course, you have to remember to take it in the first place."

Charlene carried the calcium, cod liver oil tablets and the ginseng tea over to the checkout register before Vella could manage to give her anything else. She couldn't afford anything else. She was annoyed with herself because she had allowed Vella to sell her one more thing than she had decided on. She was absolutely not spending another penny.

As Vella rang up her purchases, she said, "I heard that Freddy and Helen packed up and left for California, too."

Charlene caught the "too" and knew the inference was to Joey leaving town. It had been the hot topic for the past week, made even more so because Sheila Arnett had reportedly been so mad, she had taken a .357 Magnum pistol and shot holes in the trailer that Joey had been staying in.

"Yes," Charlene said. "They're movin' to Palm Springs."

Vella was shaking her head. "I hear that Freddy and Helen haven't even sold their house yet. They just packed their clothes and left everything. That must have been a real surprise to you all, and comin' right on top of Joey and all."

"No, it wasn't a surprise," Charlene said. She didn't want Vella thinking their family did not share confidences. "We knew for some time that Freddy and Helen were moving. They'll come back to get some things when the house sells, but they just needed to get out and have a vacation." She accepted her change from Vella and took up the small bag.

"It sure was a shock to think of Freddy putting his car dealership up for sale. I didn't believe it when I read it in the *Voice*. Then Perry told me he had heard it from Freddy himself. How is your daddy takin' this move?"

"Daddy's happy for Freddy being able to retire young." That was the best Charlene could do. The entire situation was too complicated to discuss. She headed for the door.

"You let me know how you feel after a few days of drinkin' that ginseng," Vella called after her.

Walking back to the beauty shop, Charlene gave thought to her family. They had sure become the great topic of conversation in town, first Freddy threatening an IRS agent and ending up in the mental hospital, and now up and leaving town as if his shoes were on fire. Then there was Joey going crazy, and then even crazier, and being the cause of Sheila taking a gun to an innocent trailer.

The gossip, which Charlene knew not to trust, was that after shooting the trailer, Sheila had driven off in a mad fury to find Joey, but had returned and shut herself in her house.

"Do you mean to tell me that woman is so stupid that she would lose her mind over a man?" Rainey said, when she had telephoned. She was telephoning Charlene every other night, to bolster Charlene's spirits. Rainey was a really good sister. She went on and on about how stupid Sheila Arnett was. That left Charlene free to feel sympathy for the woman, who had, like Charlene, been disappointed by a man and life in general.

Her thoughts moved back to Freddy. She had been at her father's house when Freddy and Helen had stopped by. They had their car all packed, and Helen had not even gotten out. She had sat there behind her sunglasses, with her head wrapped in a scarf. Charlene had imagined her drumming her frosted fingernails on the seat, impatient to get out to Palm Springs and start being Californian.

At the very moment of parting, Freddy had suddenly given their father a big hug. Charlene thought a lot about that hug. How such a small touch could make things so much better.

As she went around the corner of the *Valentine Voice* building, Charlene remembered she was supposed to bring Oralee her fountain drink. She turned around to go get it.

Oralee was fixing Fayrene's hair, and Dixie was going over a supply order, when Charlene came from the back room with a cup of the ginseng tea. She sat in her manicurist chair and propped her feet on another chair and sipped the tea.

"Well, what do you think of that tea?" Oralee asked.

Charlene sipped some more and thought a minute, then said, "I think it tastes like what I imagine cat pee with sugar in it would taste like."

Oralee laughed so hard she doubled over, and Fayrene said, "Oh, let me taste that."

The City Hall thermometer reads 83°

The UPS delivery man brought a package to Charlene at the shop. While large, it was not heavy. As soon as she finished up with a customer, she went in the back to open it. Mildred, whose hair Dixie had just finished, came back to see what was in the box. After a minute, Oralee appeared, too, saying, "Well, let's see what your sister has sent."

Charlene got the tape cut and opened the flaps. Inside was a bunch of foam peanuts. She dug around in them and pulled out a box of ginseng tea.

"Oh, for heaven sake, that will take forever," Oralee said, producing a shopping bag. "Put those peanuts in here."

With Oralee helping, Charlene emptied the peanuts into the bag and then began pulling out the rest of the contents: colorful and fragrant boxes of herb teas, bottles of every vitamin known to man, and containers of health powders claiming to cause rejuvenation. Charlene pulled them out and looked at each one, tears filling her eyes. At the bottom of the box she found a bright blue ball cap, and on the front it said, "Go Girl."

"Where are you goin' to go?" Mildred said, looking

vaguely worried. "You aren't movin' off, too, are you, Charlene?"

Touched, Charlene kissed Mildred's cheek. "No, I'm not moving off. But I'm goin' along just the same, I guess." She put the hat on and went to see how she looked in the mirror. She thought she looked quite youthful, even vibrant.

Charlene reflected that her life had changed very little with Joey out of it from when he had been in it. When she discussed this during one of her late-night talks with Rainey, her sister was quick to point out, "I could have told you that, but you wouldn't have liked hearing it."

Charlene continued to see to the meals and clothes and well-being of her children, to all the household tasks of cleaning and bill-paying, even the lawn upkeep, all that she had done when she had been married to Joey. The major change now was that she was no longer waiting to hear his step through the door or waiting for him to come to her in bed.

It was an immense relief to have given that up. She thought that if she had realized what a relief it would be, to have given up waiting breathlessly and to have given up on trying to change herself into the perfect wife so he would love her, she would have done it the first week he had walked out on her, and not put herself and everyone else through all the strain.

It came as a shock to her when, after a number of days, she threw out the flowers Joey had given her, which were now dead, and she realized, upon seeing them lying in the trash, that she had not thought of Joey the entire day. It was then that she realized she had gone so far down the road that he was only a small figure in her rearview mirror.

She was, she knew, on a road that was leading to herself. To the woman she really was. Sometimes she watched herself and was amazed. She discovered that she had a talent for soothing people. Customers would come in invariably looking frazzled and strained, sit at her table and give her their hands and soon be pouring out their hearts. It was therapeutic to listen to everyone else's troubles, because it took her mind off her own.

Charlene would listen and nod and get ice tea, and massage lotion into dry skin and brighten fingernails, and the customer would leave relaxed and smiling. Charlene would imagine at times that she had given mothers hope for their children and wives patience for their husbands.

One afternoon a woman of about her own age was brought in by her husband. That the woman was very ill was readily apparent. Her skin was translucent, and the woman looked, standing there, holding on to her husband, as if she was about to crumple at any minute. Dixie had that day, which was a rare busy one, begun Charlene washing hair. Charlene's initial reaction was one of hesitancy to touch the woman, indeed, to run and hide in the bathroom. She had never been very good with sickness. Her mother and Rainey had been the nurses in the family, and Charlene never felt adequate to deal with a sick individual. She knew so little of medications, always calling Rainey to double-check when she needed to medicate the children.

The woman was thrust upon Charlene, however, and she did what she knew to do, which was to lay her back in the chair and start warm water running over her head. She watched the woman's eyes fall contentedly closed as she gave out a large sigh.

"Oh, that shampoo smells lovely," the woman said, smiling softly. "And your hands feel so good."

"I'm washing some starch into you," Charlene said, and then she saw Oralee smile at her.

When she helped the woman to Dixie's chair, the woman

admired her nails and asked if Charlene could do hers, too. "I'd like that red color, too," she said, seeming to perk up. "Tom, you don't mind if I get my nails painted red, do you?"

Her husband said, "Honey, you get them any color you want." Charlene thought they should give him a badge of honor.

Although short, the woman's nails were well-formed. Charlene filed them and moisturized them and painted them bright and shiny, pointing out that the color matched the bits of red flower in the woman's cotton skirt. She doubted that the woman had ever had her nails painted before. The woman left smiling and strong enough to walk unaided beside her husband, who was smiling, too.

Charlene had to go to the back because she was crying. Dixie found her there.

"I think she's going to die," Charlene told Dixie. "I felt for a minute the life running right out of her. My mother used to say that was what happened, that life slipped away to heaven well before the body knew it, and I felt it today."

Dixie smiled tenderly and said, "You gave her what she needed. You have a gift for that, Charlene. I like to think that we have a ministry here, and it is to make women feel better about themselves so they are happier and can give to others. I don't think it is any less a service than doctors and nurses."

Oralee, never one to dismiss herself, said, "I know I have saved lives. I have had women in this chair that were wrought up enough to kill, and I've laid hands on them and prayed while I've fixed their hair, and I know I kept them from going home and either stickin' their heads in their own gas ovens, or beatin' the tar out of their children and slashing their husbands' throats."

Charlene believed that Oralee was not far off in her estimation. Quite a number of their customers came in saying they were so tired of the heat of this summer that seemed to go on forever that they were about to pull their hair out and decided instead to come to the beauty shop, where they could spend some idle time being tended in the air-conditioning. From Charlene's own experience, she knew a new hairdo or manicure could save a woman from a breakdown.

She found greater satisfaction in her work than she could have imagined. Often Dixie would say, "I do not know what we did without you, Charlene." To which Oralee would reply, "I know what we did—*I* did it, and I was worn to a frazzle from it, too."

What was lacking, however, in the job was money. Thus far, despite Dixie's assurances that business was picking up with the addition of Charlene's services, and Charlene was making a little more money each day, she did not at this point and time come anywhere close to earning the imagined sums Oralee had led her to believe possible. Oralee said that she ought to report Joey as a runaway father, but Charlene would not consider this. It would cost money to seek legal action, even if anyone knew where Joey had gone.

What Charlene made at the shop was enough to buy food and incidentals. She was not making enough to pay the house payment, utilities and insurance, too. Her worry about what she was going to do increased daily. She wondered if Joey would send money, but she had little hope that he would. She had visions of being put out of the house and having to go live with her father, of her children crying at night because of being jerked out of their home. Sometimes she cursed Joey, and each night when she went to bed, she would pray, "God, please give me strength and send the money we need." And she wished she didn't have so much doubt.

The City Hall thermometer reads 85°

Gerald was a second cousin on her mother's side. Although only thirty, he was balding. He looked, Charlene thought, exactly like a banker. Indeed, his father had sat in exactly the same place in the tall-backed chair behind the wide walnut desk, as head loan officer of the First Valentine Bank. She had never particularly liked Gerald, and this did not help now, when he told her that he could not give her any money.

"You and Joey have a loan here now," he reminded her. "If you can't pay on that, I don't see how we can give you any more."

"What people come to a bank for, Gerald, is to get money because they need money."

"I'm sorry, Charlene. I just can't do it." He sat back and looked at her, waiting for her to leave.

The City Hall thermometer reads 78°

She got Larry Joe up early in the morning to drive her to Lawton, to the state aid offices. It poured rain on them the entire drive, making Charlene's spirits sink even lower. She had been told that it would take weeks to get the aid started.

A bored-looking woman called her name, "Darnell."

Charlene went over and sat in the chair in front of the white metal desk, while the woman asked her questions and jotted down the answers on a form. Then the woman opened a drawer and started pulling out forms. She handed the stack to Charlene. "You can go over to one of those tables and fill these out, or take them home and mail them to the address indicated.''

"Thank you."

The woman was already turning her attention to another person.

Charlene took the papers and sat at the big table. She scanned the papers, and after a minute, she got up and left. It was still raining. She wanted to throw the papers in the big puddle in front of her, but instead she rolled them and tucked them into her purse, then held her purse close as she ran across the parking lot to the Suburban.

Larry Joe, who had been leaning back, napping, came sitting up with a start.

"I have a bunch of papers to fill out," she told him. "I'll do it at home."

That night she sat at the table and spread out the forms. She wrote her name and address in the blanks, then looked at the questions. There were a million. They could not ask her religion, but somewhere on there they probably asked what brand of soap powder she used.

Pushing herself up from the table, she went to the refrigerator and gazed into it for a long time, finding nothing that would do. With a sense of desperation, she tried the freezer, and let out a, "Hallelujah!" By some miracle a box of Ding-Dongs had been overlooked. She tore into the box, then turned it up and emptied the little cakes out onto the table and immediately snatched one, unwrapping it quickly and taking a big bite. As she ate the cake, she switched on the television and tuned to CMT. Then she unwrapped another chocolate cake and ate it as she settled herself to fill out the forms.

Twenty-Six

The City Hall thermometer reads 85°

When Charlene came out of work and laid eyes on the Suburban, she went around to the driver's door and told her son she wanted to drive.

"Are you sure you want to drive in town?" Larry Joe asked.

"Yes." She motioned him to move over, throwing her purse in the seat. Seeing his look of doubt—mild doubt, but doubt just the same—she added, "It's only a few blocks." They were not headed home as usual at this time, but to her father's house. Both Danny J. and Jojo had after-school activities, and Charlene needed to speak with her father.

Charlene felt determined to progress in her driving. She had managed to grab hold of this determined mood, after having struggled all day to keep her spirit from sagging into a low ditch where it seemed to perpetually lie these days. She got behind the wheel, carefully adjusted the seat for her shorter legs, and shifted into gear. Since she was already out of her own driveway, she felt confident she could navigate the wide streets.

About halfway through the Main Street intersection, despite having taken her B vitamins and drunk a cup of cham-

302   *Curtiss Ann Matlock*

omile tea, the panic attack started. She felt her breath coming short, and heat sweeping her from head to toe. She let up off the accelerator and went slower, and kept thinking of pulling over, but she could not reveal her foolish panic to Larry Joe. A mother could not be panicky in front of her child.

At her father's street, she inched around the corner, and then, seeing the big Victorian house come into view, she pressed on the gas, confidence returning that she was indeed going to make it without mishap or acting a fool.

There was a workman's van sitting out front. And the curious sight of a metal pole being erected in the front yard.

"What do you suppose that is?" Charlene said, turning into the driveway.

"I don't know, but you are gonna run over the lilac bushes."

"Oh!" She braked and twisted to look, then got out and saw the smashed limbs of the bush, where she had run over half of it. "It really needs pruning back," she told Larry Joe. "It's grown right into the driveway."

She had driven through town and the only casualty was half a lilac bush. She found that acceptable, and her determined mood rose once again. She turned from the truck and walked with her son across the yard toward the men.

They discovered that the pole was a flagpole. "Twenty feet," her father told them smartly. "What'd ya think, Larry Joy?" he said, using his pet name for his grandson.

"Looks like it ought to fly a flag, Grandad."

"Oh, yeah, it's gonna fly a heck of a flag."

Charlene thought to caution her father about flying the Confederate flag in these modern times of political correctness. But then she saw his face. He was an old man whose delight was a lovely thing to see. He carried with him wounds from World War II and had always struggled to do the right thing by his family and his country. She was not going to dampen his little bit of fun in his old age.

The two men from Goode Plumbing finished tapping the ground solid around the pole. "Now, you can't fly that flag for a few days, Mr. Valentine," one of the men said, standing back and wiping sweat from his brow with his sleeve. "You gotta let the concrete in the ground set up good. We'll come back tomorrow like we said and lay the pad around it, too."

The other man was nodding, and then he said, "You might want to catch your vehicle."

Because of his monotone voice and expression, it took several seconds for Charlene to realize that he was talking to her. It was Larry Joe taking off running that made her turn and see the Suburban slowly rolling backward.

"Ohmygosh!"

Charlene threw down her purse and took off after her son, hollering, "Let it go! You'll get run over!" One of the flagpole workers came running past her and got up beside Larry Joe, who had reached the Suburban, which had gained speed and was rolling at a pretty good clip backward across the street toward the Northrups' front yard.

Charlene saw Larry Joe grab for the door and miss, and then grab again. She hollered for him to get out of the way.

The worker from Goode Plumbing put his hand on the Suburban's fender, as if he could slow it down. It did slow as it bounced up over the low curb. Larry Joe got the door open, threw himself inside and jammed on the brakes to stop the truck halfway along the Northrups' neat brick walk. A few more yards and it would have rammed their porch.

Gasping for breath, Charlene reached the Suburban. It seemed very strange to be standing in the neighbors' front yard, gazing at her son behind the wheel of the truck.

She and her son looked at each other.

"Mom," Larry Joe said, quite calmly, "you have to put the lever in park when you stop, not in neutral. Especially on a hill."

"I thought I did," she said, experiencing a sharp stab of regret for her failure. It was more than regret at her carelessness with the gearshift, but regret that she seemed to repeatedly be leaning on her son. Now he was jumping into moving vehicles to save her.

Charlene sent Larry Joe on to the Texaco, saying, "I'll walk down to the station after I visit awhile with Daddy."

"Don't forget I have class tonight," he said, furrowing his brow in a way that she wished to ease.

"I haven't forgotten. I won't be long."

She watched the Suburban head away down the road, driven by her eldest son.

Then she went over to her father, who was instructing the two workmen about where to reposition the lights when they returned the following day. She thought, as she spied her purse on the ground and retrieved it, that she might pour all her worries out to her father as soon as the two workmen left. She really needed to talk. They could sit on the front porch, and she would talk to him and tell him all her worries over Larry Joe and money and everything.

As she stood waiting for her father, Mildred came out the front door and called to her. "Charlene, did you bring those coupons you said you've been saving up for me?"

"Oh, yes, I have them." She dug into her purse. "Oralee gave me some for you, too. For the mayonnaise and Kellogg's."

"Well, wasn't that nice of her," Mildred said, reaching eagerly for the envelope and looking inside of it to pull out the one for the cereal. "I just love to get those little boxes of cereal. They're really good to keep in my purse for if we get stuck somewhere. Like that time we had the flat at the rest stop and Larry Joe drove out to fix it. I had these two boxes of cereal for Ruthanne and me. Your father doesn't like them.''

"What do you do for milk?" Charlene asked.

"Oh, we just used water. It's just about as good. And I always have a bottle of water in the car. Bottled water is too heavy to carry in my purse, though. Makes my arms hurt tryin' to carry it. You want to come in out of the heat, honey?''

"No, I'll just wait here. I want to talk to Daddy when he's finished.''

"Well, okay.'' She started back inside, then stopped. "Are we havin' Sunday dinner at your house this week?'' Mildred's face was very hopeful.

"Yes.''

"Oh, good. Can we have ham?''

"Why don't I call you later, and we'll make up the menu together? You jot down some things you'd like to have.'' Charlene's spirits sort of fluttered back up with the knowledge that she had always been able to nurture her family with food.

Mildred was thrilled with the prospect of giving recommendations and went in the house to get started on a list of her favorites.

The two men were leaving in the plumbing truck, and her father was standing there looking up proudly at his flagpole. Charlene went to capture him, but then Everett Northrup came pulling into his driveway across the street.

"What do you think, Northrup?'' her father hollered, when his neighbor was standing and staring across at them. "Twenty feet. It ought to fly a dandy flag.''

Charlene's urge to speak to her father about her worries

fizzled. He was a man so enamored with a flagpole that likely he would not hear what she had to say. And she didn't think she could explain, anyway. Suddenly she could not speak of any of it.

Northrupt went into his house, letting the screen door slam, and her father continued to walk around and look up at the flagpole and smile happily.

Charlene took that moment to force herself to ask her father for five hundred dollars. "I want to pay Larry Joe's college bill. Joey left him some money, and we've paid some, but I want it all paid. I don't want Larry Joe to have to think about earning money. He needs to focus his attention on his studies."

Her father, still distracted with checking the pole for straightness, immediately pulled bills from his wallet, three hundred dollar bills, and handed them across to her, telling her to wait a minute and he would get the rest from the house. That he would carry around so much cash did not surprise Charlene. He had done so as long as she could recall, had been known to carry over a thousand dollars in big bills. She used to get onto him about the danger of carrying around so much money, but his answer was that the most that could happen was he would be robbed and the thief get a good haul. He wanted to carry the money to be prepared in case the opportunity to get a good deal on something came along.

"I don't know when I can pay you back," she told him, when he handed her the rest from a drawer in the desk in the hallway.

He gave a dismissing wave and said, "Let me show you the flag I bought to go on the pole. Northrupt's gonna go green as grass."

She admired the flag at great length, and then made her goodbyes and left, pulling the door closed behind her with relief that she had not given way to her irritation. It was not her father's fault that she felt overwhelmed but was too reticent to speak of the things weighing on her mind. He would have made the effort to be supportive, if she had talked to him. Still, with lingering frustration, she acknowledged there was an enormous gap between making an effort and succeeding.

In that moment, feeling terribly disloyal, she nevertheless felt a little of what Freddy had obviously always felt, that their father, despite great strides, remained mostly unavailable and always would be. It was a hard truth, and an even harder truth was that their mother had loved her children and at the same time had in her own way been unavailable. It was for Charlene, herself as a mother, a very depressing thought. She had wanted to be the perfect mother, in order to make up for those years when she had felt motherless. She was now coming face-to-face with the fact that being the perfect mother was impossible.

Just then, reaching the end of the driveway, Charlene looked down and saw the lilac bush, squashed by her truck tire. Bending, she gathered the crushed limbs and tried to tuck them back with the rest of the bush. You failed in that turn, she thought. She had not meant to run the bush down. She had been doing her level best to succeed in driving, and yet she had made a mistake and squashed something. This was the way of life for all mothers and fathers, who tried to do their best but left behind little mistakes and failures, squashed places in their children.

Continuing on down the hill, she considered that the only cure for the unseen wounds was forgiveness, and it was sad that forgiveness so very often was one of those things beyond the reach of successful endeavor. She was simply very blue, and every thought was blue, and had she not been walking out in public, she might have had a good cry.

Just then, giving her a little start, a vehicle pulled up beside her.

It was Mason MacCoy's truck.

She stopped on the old concrete sidewalk, and the truck stopped on the patched tarmac street. Mason, all thick-shouldered and blue-eyed, hopped out the driver's door and looked at her across the hood.

"Would you like a lift?" he asked, his expression quite excited, she thought.

"Yes. Yes, I would. Thank you."

He grinned widely and ducked back into the cab. She opened the passenger door and slipped into the seat. It was cloth, red. The truck cab was dusty but not dirty.

He put the lever in gear and started slowly down the street. "Where are you going?"

"To the Texaco," she said, smoothing her skirt. Then she saw one of the books stacked in the middle of the seat start to slide. She grabbed it, an old book with the gold title halfway worn off. *"Huckleberry Finn."* She cast him a questioning eye. "Is it an early edition?"

"No," he said, shaking his head. "I bought it at a used bookstore. Used hardbacks don't cost so much, and the paper is a lot better. That one's pretty old because I bought it a long time ago."

"Oh." She set it carefully back atop two others and some magazines and rested her hand on them to keep them from sliding.

"Are you going to see Larry Joe at the station?" he asked.

"Yes. He gets off in half an hour." She wondered if she should say she was going home, if then Mason would offer to take her.

"Are you heading home? I'd be glad to drive you," he said.

"Oh. All right. Thank you. But I'll need to go over to tell Larry Joe."

"Sure."

He smiled at her, and she smiled at him, thinking again that he had the most beautiful blue eyes. And then she whipped her face forward, focusing her gaze firmly out the windshield.

"Did you know you're running the air conditioner?" she asked after a minute.

He looked a little surprised, and then he nodded. "Yes. I like the windows down for fresh air. Are you hot?" he asked quickly, pressing the button to raise his window. "We could put the windows up."

"Oh, no. I like it. I run the air conditioner and have the windows down a lot myself."

"You do?" He lowered his window again.

"Uh-huh. I like the breeze. I got in the habit because Jojo, my youngest, used to get carsick, and having the fresh air helped her."

"I got in the habit because of riding around with Neville at night on patrol, and he just about freezes me to death with the air-conditioning."

"You ride around on patrol with Neville? Are you a deputy?" She had never seen him wearing any kind of policeman's uniform.

"I'm the part-time help," he said. "No uniform or weapon required. Basically what I do is provide an extra body to keep Neville and sometimes the other fellas from having to drive around alone every night."

"Oh," she said, imagining him riding in the patrol car, eyes surveying the town, getting out and dealing with speeding drivers or front-yard fights.

Forgetting to be self-conscious, she looked him over, thinking he could deal with toughs, noting the T-shirt that stretched tight across his chest and shoulders. His elbow rested casually on the open window. The wind fluttered wisps of his short, sun-touched hair on his forehead. She could see the sort of man he was, a solitary type, a man of deep contrasts, who would lift heavy feed and grain sacks all day and ride shotgun in the patrol car in the dark night, and possibly sit in the early hours of the morning on his porch, drinking thick, black coffee and reading classic literature from old books while dawn came on.

They pulled into the Texaco, underneath the portico, and the bell dinged. Larry Joe came out from the garage, wiping his hands on a rag. A look of surprise passed over his face very quickly, as he came to Charlene's side of the truck. Then he said a casual "Hey" to Mason through the window.

"Mason's goin' to give me a ride home, honey," she said quickly, intently studying him for his reaction. That he had once told her he believed Mason was interested in her meant little. Sometimes there was small correlation between the head and the heart.

He looked down at his hands as he wiped them some more, and nodded. "That's cool," he said. "I probably won't be home until after eight, then. After class."

He still did not look her full in the face, and this worried her.

"What about supper? You need to eat, Larry Joe."

"I'll get a burger or somethin', Mom," he said, with patent patience, his eyes only grazing hers.

A car pulled up on the opposite side of the island. Larry Joe glanced at it. "Gotta get to work. See you later."

Then, for an instant, he paused and laid his hand on the open window, and cast her a broad grin, a grin that jumped over and lodged in her heart, while his eyes met hers fully, and she knew his thoughts completely without words: *Enjoy this, Mom...it's all okay.*

Mason pulled away. Charlene's eyes followed her son, and he cast her a wave.

As Mason headed down the street at a good clip, Charlene had to grab her hair against the brisk breeze blowing in the open window. Only a few minutes ago she had felt so very discouraged about her life. Now she suddenly felt very happy. She felt, she thought, glancing at Mason, quite a bit reckless.

All the way to her house, he worked the question over in his mind. When he pulled to a stop in front of her house, he said, "I heard about Joey leaving town."

She looked a little startled. "Yes, he did."

"I probably should say I'm sorry, but I'm not."

She gazed at him, possibly a little startled. Then she tilted her head, looking at him with her green eyes, as if she was trying to figure him out.

He said, "I was wondering if you would like to have dinner with me tonight."

She continued for a long second to study him, and then she shook her head. "I'm sorry, but I can't. My children will be home soon. I have to fix their supper. And I really can't leave them alone."

"It's okay. I should have asked ahead, so you could plan. How about tomorrow night?" he added. Since he had started, he was going to go for it.

"A number of weeks back, you told me you wanted to visit me," she said, startling him. "Danny J. told me you brought flowers one day while I was visiting Rainey."

"Yes, I did."

"Why didn't you come back when I came home?"

The conversation had taken an uncomfortable turn. He was not prepared for explanations. Finally he said, "I decided maybe it wasn't such a good idea."

"Do you think it is a good idea now?"

This made him a little annoyed, and he said, "I guess maybe I don't care if it is a good idea or not. I'd still like to see you." Although he was beginning to question his reasoning.

She looked down at her hands for a few seconds in which he wondered what he should do or say, and then she was looking at him again. She said, "My children are capable of staying for a few hours by themselves, but they aren't ready for their mother to go off on a date, and I'm not ready to leave them to go off on a date. We simply aren't ready for dating." She gazed at him as if to study his reaction.

He said, "Okay. Then how about if I go get pizza or fried chicken and bring it back? I don't think that's really a date. That's more a friend bringing supper by."

"Well..." She stopped, then said, "I had planned fried chicken for supper. It's my daughter's favorite. Would you like to join us?"

"Yes, I would like that," he said, grinning broadly, thrilled at having won the invitation, although the next second he wondered why she couldn't have said that in the first place.

They got out of his truck, and he followed her, his gaze flowing from her shining hair to her slim ankles. Then, at the door, he hesitated. What if their relationship didn't work out at all? What about his cherished dreams then? At least now he had dreams to comfort his loneliness. If things went wrong, he would be left even without dreams.

"Please come in," she said, holding the door open and looking at him with a quizzical expression.

He stepped over the threshold and into the dim coolness, alone with her, the woman of his dreams.

Twenty-Seven

The City Hall thermometer reads 81°

She asked him if he liked tomato pudding.

"I never had it," he said.

"You never had tomato pudding?"

"No, ma'am." There was something touching about the way he said ma'am. Like he was giving her a pet name. And his blue eyes twinkled in a sensual way that made her breath catch in the back of her throat.

"Then I think it is high time you had some," she said, pivoting quickly away from him and his blue eyes that were threatening to turn her into a fool.

He asked her what was on the menu, besides tomato pudding and chicken, and she told him green salad, rolls and potato salad, which she already had made. When she set out the large cutting board and chopping knife, he offered to make the green salad.

"I'm pretty passable as a cook," he told her. "I used to cook for my grandpap. For the last year he had a restricted diet, and I even made him salt-free bread."

Charlene asked, "Did you take care of your grandfather by yourself?" What she was wondering was if he had been married.

"Yep," he said, slicing a tomato as deftly as a gourmet

cook. He reached for the second tomato and said, "I haven't been married since I was twenty-two, when my wife and I got divorced."

"Oh." She didn't think she should be so glad at that bit of information. What difference did it make if he had been divorced one year or fifteen? *Charlene, you are acting like a hormonal teen.* And it felt delightful.

While she flitted around, frying the chicken, and mixing and popping the tomato pudding into the oven, he finished putting together the salad, then went on to whip up a vinegar, oil and herb dressing. It was quite apparent he knew something about salads, anyway.

He had her taste his dressing concoction for approval, and she properly made a fuss over it. Then their eyes met.

"I've never had a man help me in the kitchen," she said, only just then realizing the strangeness of it.

"I hope I'm not bothering you." He raised an eyebrow.

"Oh, no. You aren't." After several long seconds, she added, "I like it."

He looked pleased.

He washed the knife and cutting board and then worked to get the faucet to shut off.

Charlene went over to do it for him. "You have to get the cold knob set just right," she said.

"I can fix it. Do you have tools? Never mind, I have some in the truck." He said all this quickly, and Charlene barely got in a protest before he had the water to the sink cut off and was working over the handle.

He and Charlene, who was watching him, were bent over the sink, shoulders touching, when Jojo and Danny J. arrived from school.

"Mom?" Danny J. said, and she whipped around to see him and Jojo staring at them from the doorway, their round eyes moving from Charlene to Mason and back to Charlene again.

Immediately Danny J. made it very plain that the advent of Mason in their midst was not at all okay. Like Larry Joe, he did not say a word, but from a lifetime of familiarity, Charlene easily read her son's thoughts, which were more or less screamed by his angry expression. *I do not like this. He needs to go.*

The first thing Danny J. said after laying eyes on Mason was, "I'm gonna go take care of the horses. I have a lot of homework to do later."

Throughout dinner, Danny J. retained his sullen expression, while beside him Jojo continued to watch Mason with avid interest, all the time swinging her legs and kicking the table leg in a rhythm of sorts that seemed to have something to do with the conversation going on between Mason and Charlene. The more rapid the conversation, the slower the kicks, but when Mason and Charlene fell silent, gazing at each other, Jojo's kicking picked up tempo.

While Charlene noticed the less than polite behavior of her children, she was incapable of responding to it in an annoyed fashion. The thrill of having a man unable to take his eyes off of her—and she had become convinced she was correct on this point—made her so delighted that there was simply no room inside her for annoyance. Delight edged out every other emotion, except for wonder at what was happening to her, and about the man who was causing whatever was happening.

Thoroughly fascinated as she was with what was going on between herself and Mason, it probably would have taken God Himself, coming in a cloud of glory and trumpets, to get her attention.

She watched Mason taste the tomato pudding and smile, saying, "This is delicious."

"You like it then?" *Silly, silly.* She blushed, averting her eyes.

"Oh, yes, it's great." He took another bite, definitely enjoying it.

"Yuk," Danny J. said.

"Danny J. doesn't like tomato pudding," Charlene said mildly. "He loves my potato salad, though, don't you, hon?"

Danny J. scowled at her.

"I like tomato pudding…a little bit," Jojo said. "Can I have some, Mama?"

"Of course, honey. Here. You just eat what you want and leave the rest."

The table jiggled as Jojo kicked the leg, and Charlene was about to remind her daughter to stop, but at that moment she heard the front door open. Seconds later, furthering her pleasure, Larry Joe joined them.

"Aw, Randy had to go see some new girl he's met," he explained. "Got any left, Mom?"

Charlene raced into the kitchen to get her son a place setting and glass of ice tea, thoroughly enraptured at being in her home surrounded by all three children and an attentive man.

After the meal, Larry Joe made talk with Mason and his mother for a few minutes and then excused himself from the table, strode through the dimly lit living room and down the hall to his brother's room. The door was closed, music playing on the other side, light shining underneath. He knocked, and when Danny J. said, "Yeah," he went in.

"Hey, kid," Larry Joe said.

His brother was sitting at his desk, hunched over one of his schoolbooks. Larry Joe threw himself on the bed. He looked over at his brother and saw him furtively wipe his eyes. Larry Joe looked up at the ceiling. No guy liked to be caught crying. If anyone had to catch you, it was best if it was your brother, but if a brother was smart, he didn't let on about knowing.

Danny J. said, "What are you doin' in here? Don't you have a room?"

Larry Joe sat up, stared at his brother's profile a minute and then said, "Look, kid, don't screw this up for Mom. She's happy. Don't ruin it for her."

Danny J. glared at him with red eyes. "And what about Dad? You don't care anything about him, do you? You always hated Dad."

His brother's accusation stabbed hard and deep, touching already broken and wounded places Larry Joe didn't even know about. "That's not so," he said quietly, feeling near tears himself. "But I'll tell you somethin', if they can be happier apart than they have been together for the last year, I say they shouldn't waste time goin' for it." Then he added, "He's run off, Danny J. What do you want her to do?"

"He would have come home, if she would have let him. And he still might."

Larry Joe shook his head. "He wasn't ever here half the time, Danny J....even when he was here, he wasn't here." He shouldn't get angry. He couldn't help his brother if he was angry.

"Maybe he wasn't ever here because she never did anything to make him want to be."

"Oh, come on, Danny J. The truth of it is that horses always come first with Dad, and they always will. Mom and us have always come second. You may think he is somethin', but I'll tell you, it was Grandma who had to come drive Mom to the hospital when you were born. Dad was off buyin' a horse."

Danny J. came up out of the chair and lunged at Larry Joe. Taken by surprise, Larry Joe, although stockier, went stumbling backward on the bed, with Danny J. punching him for all he was worth. Larry Joe twisted his head, trying to avoid the blows, and tried to grab Danny J.'s fists. "Stop it…" he hissed, but Danny J. was in a fury. He was gritting his teeth and crying and punching. Blows caught Larry Joe in the jaw and the nose, and lit his own fuse, yet he held himself back from hitting his brother. He just couldn't do it. They rolled onto the floor and over into the desk and the chair, knocking it over onto themselves.

Then Jojo was there. "Stop it!" Her shrill voice cut through their huffing and puffing. "I'm gonna tell!"

This last caused Danny J. to quit fighting and look up. With a curse, Larry Joe shoved Danny J. away, scrambled to his feet and raced after his sister, catching her in the middle of the living room and lifting her clean off the ground. He clamped a hand over her mouth and carried her kicking and squirming back down the hall and into Danny J.'s room. Danny J. shut the door and locked it.

Larry Joe sat Jojo on her feet and kept hold of her by the wrist. Danny J. was picking up the chair and some papers that had somehow gotten strewn on the floor.

"You're bleeding," Jojo told Larry Joe, gazing up at him with her big eyes.

He felt the tickling in his nose then, wiped with his fingers and brought away blood. He stared at it, somewhat stunned. Without a word, Danny J. slipped out and brought back a wet washcloth from their bathroom, holding it in front of Larry Joe, who took it and dabbed it beneath his nose.

"I'm sorry," Danny J. said after a few minutes.

"It's okay."

"You can let go of me," Jojo said. "I'm not gonna tell."

Larry Joe had forgotten he still held her firmly. He let go of her, feeling like a stupid kid instead of the man he almost was. He was so often these days finding himself doing something like a kid, when he was trying hard to be adult.

He eased down on the side of the bed, and Jojo sat beside him, scooting close enough for her little hip to touch his and laying her hand on his thigh. It felt so small and warm through his jeans. Then she put her other hand, palm up, out to Danny J.

Danny J. slipped a glance to Larry Joe, and then gazed at Jojo's palm a moment. With a reluctant grin, he smacked his palm on hers. After a minute, he said, "You guys want a Coke?"

Mason's initial hesitancy to enter the house that afternoon had not been lost on Charlene. There had been a moment when she had wondered if he was going to turn and run back to his truck and drive away at top speed. For her part, she had almost closed the door in his face.

But from the moment he stepped over the threshold, he had seemed to settle on definite intentions. It had been a very long time since a man had had intentions toward her, and she was somewhat excited to discover exactly what Mason's might be. All her womanly wiles, which had seemed to have been put to death with the difficulties with Joey, suddenly came back to life in a rush that almost astonished her. She found herself gazing at Mason, as attentive as a woman can be to a man who interests her. To a man who stirred the woman inside of her.

"Thank you for helping me clean up," Charlene said, closing the dishwasher with her hip.

"Thank you for the supper," he said, drying his hands

on a towel. "You're a great cook, and it's better than what I normally have—a ham and cheese sandwich."

He grinned, and his blue eyes came up and rested on hers in the manner of an intimate touch.

She said, "You said you can cook, and you proved tonight that you know your way around a salad."

"Cooking just for me never seems worth the trouble."

He glanced downward. There was a loneliness about him, she thought.

"I find it difficult to believe that you could not have any number of women who would enjoy your cooking and your company," she said, listening intently to discover what he would say about women in his life.

"Not so many," he said, with a sad grin. "I guess most women think I'm a pretty boring guy."

"Now, why is that?" Realizing she was flirting, she pulled back a little, putting a hand on the edge of the sink, grasping it, as the urge to move toward him and press herself against his hard male body swept her.

"I don't much like to go to clubs. I don't dance, and don't care much for parties, either."

"I don't either—go to clubs or parties, I mean. I do like to dance, but I don't like to go where there is dancing. I don't care to be around a crowd of people." His gaze roamed over her face, seeking, caressing. "I like music. Country music mostly, but I like some classical."

"I play a guitar."

"You do?" She immediately imagined him holding a guitar, his fingers on the strings, and for some reason this affected her in an erotic manner.

"Yes, ma'am. Folk ballads mostly. Simple ones." He smiled softly. "My grandfather taught me."

"Oh? And who taught you to cook—your wife or your mother?" She wondered about those women in his life.

He blinked and looked away, and his warm expression was suddenly gone. Charlene had a little panic, wondering what she had said wrong, her mind racing with the disturbing suppositions that perhaps he was still in love with the divorced wife, or maybe still attached to his mother.

And then his gaze came to her again, and he said in a low voice, "I learned to cook in prison. I worked in the kitchen a lot there, with my roommate. He'd been a chef, and he liked to talk recipes. He liked to go over them, just like he was cooking in the cell, to pass the time."

There was hurt in his voice and in his eyes that stared at her, searching for her reaction.

She said, "I had heard the rumor, but not what happened."

Turning and bracing himself with both hands on the counter edge, he took a deep breath and told her that he had gone to prison for killing his wife's lover with a boot.

When he paused, she said, "A boot?" She might have laughed at the ridiculous image that popped into her mind, but there was no laughter in her as she stared at his thick shoulders that seemed in that moment to struggle with the weight of sorrow and shame.

"Yeah," he said. "I found them in bed together and I hit him with his boot, and he fell over and hit his temple on the corner of the night table. I didn't get charged with murder because I'd used a boot, and even though he was pushed by the dead man's family, the prosecutor could not manage to get anyone to believe a boot could be considered a lethal weapon. I was a wild, drunk boy, not insane. I got five years to pay my debt and grow up, and I was out in two."

Charlene looked at him, at his face, tanned and lined from the weather and hard work, at the silver showing at his temples, at his eyes, blue and clear and straight on hers in the way only a strong man can look.

"You haven't been a boy for a long time," she said.

With a wry smile, he said, "No, ma'am. Not for at least twenty-six years."

It seemed then that they put that subject behind them, because they gazed at each other, both of them smiling and shimmering with desires that surely, had they been anywhere else, would have left them no choice but to fall together.

Just then Jojo appeared in the kitchen doorway to say she was ready to get a bath. "You said you wanted to wash my hair tonight, Mama."

"Oh, yes, honey. I'll be right there. You go ahead and run the water and get in."

"O-kaay," Jojo said, turning very slowly as she gave Charlene and Mason a highly curious going-over that made Charlene wonder what impressions her daughter might have been picking up.

Mason, feeling very self-conscious, said, "I'd better be going. I have to meet Neville in a few hours for patrol."

She said she would walk out with him. He wanted to take her hand, but he didn't. He thought fleetingly about all he wanted to do with her.

Luckily, he saw now, he had stopped his truck under the shadow of the elm tree, where the light from the porch and pole lamps couldn't reach.

She thanked him again for giving her a ride home and said how she had enjoyed his company at supper. He told her he had enjoyed it, too.

He could feel more than see her eyes. Before he knew what he was doing, he slid his hand up to cup the back of her neck and kissed her.

She was clearly surprised, and he was, too. It was like a

jolt went through him. The next instant desire overrode every other emotion, and he went to kissing her, and she went to kissing him. A warm and moist and eager kiss, and even a moan in her throat that shook him to his core.

When they broke apart, he thought he heard her whisper breathlessly, *"Ohmyheaven."*

He stared into her eyes for long seconds. His heartbeat was pounding in his ears and in his groin. He grappled for and found coherent thought, along with the handle to the truck door.

"Good night," he said, opening the door.

"Good night," she said.

She slowly turned and went into the house and shut the door, and Mason drove away with the taste of her on his lips and in his heart.

The City Hall thermometer reads 78°

As Charlene lay in bed in the dark, looking at the patterns the moonlight made on the walls, she went over the events of the evening, dwelling on Mason's blue eyes and his smiles and his intense looks of interest, until she came to his kiss, which still lingered on her lips.

She had, she only just now realized, wanted that kiss badly. Had he not taken the initiative—and she was very proud of him for that—she might have thrown herself on him and wrestled the kiss from him. She had wanted desperately to know if she were capable of feeling passion, of sharing passion with a man.

She thought back, counting the months to the last kiss she recalled Joey giving her. She had tried so often to kiss him passionately, trying to draw him back to her, but every time he had eased away, saying he had to do something or other. The pain of it came fresh upon her.

With sudden clarity, she realized that she had built a wall around the pain of Joey's rejection. It wasn't a new wall. It was an old one, first built when she had to learn to deal with the heartache caused by her parents withdrawing into their own turmoil. With each heartache since, she had added a row of bricks. She had been adding rows for many years, shutting herself into her own cell of loneliness into which only the children could come and go.

And in shutting out the pain, she had also shut out a great deal of hope and promise and joy that seemed too precarious to believe in. She'd been afraid of feeling. Feelings hurt.

She lightly touched her lips with her fingertips. They seemed to tingle, and with the memory, her body recalled the wanting, too. It was a good feeling, desire all full and exciting. It frightened her, too, made her feel vulnerable in a way that she lay thinking about until she began to ache with sweet passionate longing of a sort almost forgotten.

When the telephone rang, she jumped and let out a gasp.

Grabbing for the receiver, she fumbled and dropped it, grabbed it up and said a breathless "Hello?" along with a prayer that it was not her father or Rainey having an emergency.

Mason, in the old phone booth at the corner of the IGA, said, "I'm sorry. Were you asleep?"

"Oh, Mason." She sounded relieved. "Oh, no, I wasn't asleep. I was just layin' here. I got startled by the phone. I always think that it's bad news when the phone rings in the night. I think it may be Rainey or Daddy, you know."

"I'm sorry. I guess I shouldn't have called so late." It was almost eleven. He felt stupid for getting carried away and calling her at this time of night, and more stupid because he was standing there in a lit-up phone booth, in plain sight of Neville, who was waiting in the patrol car, the engine running and air-conditioning going.

"It's fine," she was saying. "I wasn't asleep yet. Did you forget something? Are you missing a tool?"

"No. I got all those," he said quickly. He turned his back on Neville and faced the wall of the building. "I just wanted to tell you again that I had a really good time tonight."

"I did, too," she said, and her voice sounded warm.

"I was wondering if maybe you would go out with me tomorrow. I know you said you weren't ready to date," he said quickly. "But maybe you and your kids would like to go to dinner with me tomorrow."

"It's kind of you to think of it, but I don't think my kids are ready for anything like that. It's just too soon."

"Yeah. I can understand that." He leaned against the phone booth door. "Can we start with lunch? Would you have lunch with me tomorrow at the cafe?"

"Well, okay." She sounded hesitant. He wished she didn't sound so hesitant. "But I have to check my appointment book in the morning to make certain what time I'm free. And if I have a walk-in, I might not be able to get away right on schedule."

"That's okay. I can go anytime." He arranged to call her the following morning about a time for lunch, and then he said good-night, hung up and opened the phone booth door. The light promptly went out, and he wished he had thought of opening the dang door earlier, and then he wouldn't have stood there in a spotlight. He should get himself a cell phone.

"Well, is she going out with you?" Neville asked, as Mason climbed back into the patrol car.

"How do you know I asked her?"

"You said you wanted to call her. What for, but to ask her out?"

"I'm havin' lunch with her tomorrow." Mason said and grinned, feeling terribly foolish but unable to quit smiling.

Twenty-Eight

The City Hall thermometer reads 76°

Winston switched on "Dixie" and went out on the porch to put up the flag. He looked at his newly set pole in the middle of the yard with rising anticipation. By Sunday, the Stars and Bars would be flying in the sky. His neighbor would be green with envy, and Winston didn't think there would be any way Northrupt could top him now. His neighbor might get a taller pole, but that wouldn't amount to much.

He looked across to his neighbor's porch. With surprise, he saw the porch was empty. Possibly Everett had overslept, Winston thought, slowing his motions as he set his flag in the holder, expecting his neighbor to step out the door at any moment.

But his neighbor had still not appeared when the flag unfurled and the last strains of "Dixie" died away. Winston stood there feeling disappointed and a little worried. This was the first morning in the nine months since they had begun raising their flags at dawn that Everett had not shown.

He went down his steps and across the yard and peered down the Northrupts' driveway. Yep, the Mercedes, all repaired now after the wreck, sat at the end of the drive, in front of the garage Northrupt used only during storms. He looked back at the still empty porch, annoyance rising.

The paperboy came pedaling past, tossing the paper right into Winston's hands. "Hi, Mr. Valentine. Mr. Northrupt's late this mornin'."

"Mornin', Leo. Yes, 'pears so."

Carrying the paper, he went around to the roses. He didn't need to water them, since they'd had some good rain. They were blooming bountifully, giving off a light scent in the cooler morning. He pulled clippers from his back pocket and began cutting blossoms, the entire time keeping an ear out for music from his neighbor's porch.

Likely Northrupt had slept clean through, he thought. He couldn't go barging over there, banging on the door, just because the man didn't show his face at dawn. Sometimes when a person butted into another person's business, a person found out stuff they would just as soon not know. Northrupt had never even invited him in for coffee. He didn't think his neighbor would take kindly to him going over there and asking why he had not come out at dawn, especially if his neighbor was sleeping in.

Then, like a lightbulb coming on in his head, Winston thought, maybe this was a new tactic on Northrupt's part. Maybe he was planning some really big new move, and he was just throwing this "nonhanging" of the flag in for the time being to irritate Winston.

Determined not to be irritated, he walked around the corner to go in the back door. There was Ruthanne sitting on the back steps, bundled in a long wool coat.

Winston said, "Good mornin', Ruthanne."

She regarded him blankly for a second and then smiled with recognition. "Good mornin', Winston. I was just sitting here enjoying the birds singing. I think they sing so much clearer in the mornin'."

"Yes, they do seem to." He was judging her to see how much she was in her mind. That he was having to do this more and more saddened him. A sudden weariness came over him, and he edged down on the step beside her.

He handed her a rose, telling her to be careful of the thorns. Her gaze was on the trees. He pulled the pack of Camels from his shirt and lit up, blowing the smoke to the side.

She said, "We had lots of tall trees like this around our place in Creek County. They had so many birds in them, and I started learning their names. Then we had to move all the way out to the west, and it was so flat and no trees, only a few Mama planted, and they never grew very well. We sure had some drought back then, didn't we, Winston?"

"Yes, we did," he answered, his own thoughts traveling back to what a lot called the "good ol' days," but when he had been a boy he remembered dust seeping in the windows and having to sleep on the porch, being eaten by mosquitos while trying to escape the hot house.

"They couldn't drive Daddy out of town today," Ruthanne said, "like they did then, just because he was colored and Indian and a good businessman. 'Course a lot of it was because Mama was so light skinned and beautiful. There was this one powerful white man who wanted her," she said confidentially to Winston. "But Daddy loved Mama, and she was crazy about him. He said he would go out where a man could have his own land, and he'd make her proud. Then he went to work in the oil fields, you know, and after a while we lived nice, so I guess it worked out, but I still want to go to college. I'll have to go back to Tahlequa for that and stay with my Aunt May. I want to be a teacher. I'll teach about birds."

Winston gazed down at the grass, thinking of how Ruthanne had been a teacher, before quitting and giving over her life to take care of her parents and her sister's family. She was the only one of her family left, besides a few nephews who had no thought of her.

"I...I *was* a teacher, wasn't I?" He glanced up to see a doubtful and confused expression play over her face. "I just have a lot of trouble keeping things straight these days," she said, almost apologetically.

"Well, I wouldn't let it bother you," Winston said. "You are happy, and that's a lot more than most people in their right minds can say."

She smiled. "Oh, yes, Winston, I am happy. I just let myself be," she said simply.

He thought that most definitely Ruthanne was more in her right mind than any of them. Everyone sought happiness their whole life, but few could figure out how to just let themselves be happy.

Stamping his cigarette butt in the damp soil, he got to his feet and helped her up. As they came into the kitchen, Ruthanne said she felt a little woozy.

"Well, you are probably goin' to have heatstroke," Mildred said, speaking in a loud voice. She was in her customary place at the table, eating a fat sweet roll. "You had better get out of that coat. Why in the world are you wearin' a coat?"

"I wanted to be ready," Ruthanne replied.

Winston wasn't going to question that. He tossed aside the newspaper, plopped the roses in their vase of water, and left the women to their nonsense conversation, going off to hang Ruthanne's coat in the hall closet. As he shut the door, his gaze swept the hall and living room, and he realized the house had gotten pretty messy since their housekeeper had skipped the previous week. He needed to make a stab at straightening up.

Then he went to the front door, opened it and looked across the street. Northrupt still had not hung his flag.

He slammed the door, rattling the glass pane.

The City Hall thermometer reads 80°

Vella filled in the holes the armadillos had dug with composted zoo manure she had ordered from her gardening catalog. The manure from wild predators, animals such as lions and tigers, was supposed to both fertilize and keep away annoying critters. Vella wondered if armadillos unfamiliar with lions and tigers might not simply ignore the strange smell.

Finished with the last bush, she got stiffly to her feet, stood back and surveyed her plants with frustration. Even though the extreme heat had abated, the blooms on her bushes were puny and scant compared to Winston Valentine's.

She looked in the direction of the Valentine house, at the rosebushes that were overflowing with big, bountiful blossoms, more than ever, if that was possible. Feeling defeated, she went inside and took a couple of Pepto-Bismol tablets.

The City Hall thermometer reads 84°

Mason telephoned at ten-thirty. Oralee answered, then called Charlene to the phone.

"It's a man for you," she said, her hand over the receiver. "If it's your husband, he sounds good, so get prepared." She handed Charlene the phone and then stood at her elbow to listen.

Charlene, thinking surely it was Mason but now worrying about Joey, took the phone. "Hello?"

"Hello, this is Mason. Are we on for lunch?" He sounded eager.

"Yes," Charlene said, relieved it was Mason. Glancing at Oralee, she refused to call him by name. Oralee frowned and went back to her customer.

Charlene squeezed up to the counter and spoke so low that Mason had to ask her to speak up. They arranged to meet at the cafe at noon. "I might be a few minutes late, if I get delayed here," she told him.

"I could come by the shop and wait for you," he said.

"I'll meet you at the cafe," she said quickly. "That way you can save us a table." The idea of him coming to the shop unnerved her. It made her feel pressed, as if it was a date and he was picking her up. Since waking up in the clear light of day, she had begun to have doubts about seeing him at all. There was not only the technicality of her marriage, but she simply did not feel up to a relationship with a man, no matter how wonderful his kiss. The very wonderfulness of his kiss at this precarious time of her life was frightening. She thought meeting him at the restaurant would help to put them more on the scale of two friends simply having lunch together. And she would pay for her own meal, too.

Fridays were normally busy days at the Cut and Curl, and on this particular one they were taking care of the bridal party for a big wedding to be held at the Methodist church. They were doing not only hair but nails and facials. They also had the mothers and the pastor's wife and a number of relatives and guests. Charlene was kept booked all morning with appointments and walk-ins, and in between nail jobs she helped Dixie and Oralee by welcoming customers, passing out ice tea and shampooing hair. It was by far the best morning she had had thus far, and her spirits were up with hope for enough money to make headway on her bills.

Into this full shop arrived Muriel Porter, a middle-aged spinster and the domineering owner-publisher of the *Valentine Voice*. Ms. Porter, as she made certain everyone knew to address her, had a standing appointment with Dixie each Friday at eleven to have her hair done to her exact specifications, which left her hair looking the same when she went out, mannish, as when she came in: with three waves on top. This Friday she surprised everyone by wanting a manicure, too.

"I'm going on a cruise," she said. "I think I should like to try to have something new done." She wanted the manicure while Dixie was doing her hair, so as not to waste time.

"Don't waste Ms. Porter's time," Oralee said in a whisper as Charlene passed to get her tray of supplies. "She's liable to cut off your head."

Raising even Oralee's eyebrows, when Charlene had just about finished shaping the cuticles and filing the ends and was about to apply lotion and massage, Ms. Porter said she wanted color on her nails. "Think you got a color that I could wear and not look foolish?"

Charlene said, "I don't think you could look foolish at any time, Ms. Porter."

That comment didn't seem to please the woman. Charlene hurried to choose colors and brought them back for the older woman's inspection. Ms. Porter looked at the colors and then gave Charlene an assessing eye. "You think about it, don't you?" she said with a faintly approving tone.

"I think the color of the nails should represent the woman," Charlene said.

"I'll take that one." Ms. Porter pointed to a muted rose color that Charlene thought would go with most shades of blue and brown—the colors the woman was wearing at the present.

Charlene carefully applied the polish and the glaze, and when she had finished, Ms. Porter examined her nails thoroughly. "I like them," she pronounced and paid Charlene, including a generous tip.

Then, with her handbag still open, she said, "Would you be willing to go out to the nursing home and do my sister's nails?"

"Well…" Charlene said, taken by surprise. "Is that all right, Dixie?"

"Yes, I think that would be okay. Charlene's working toward her license," she said to Ms. Porter, who waved such a technicality aside.

"How about fifty?" The woman held forth a fifty dollar bill.

"Oh, no, that's too much. Twenty is sufficient," Charlene protested, and Oralee poked her in the back.

Ms. Porter said, "Sister's nails may be work. I'm sure no one has touched them except to cut them in years. Take the fifty and do what you can. Can you go tomorrow afternoon? It would be nice for her, since I'll be missing my normal visit with her."

Charlene said she would go tomorrow, and Ms. Porter nodded and stalked out of the shop in her heavy shoes.

Oralee shook her head, "Umm-um, I cannot picture that woman on a cruise."

Charlene, who had kept one eye on the clock, jerked off her smock, dabbed on lipstick and grabbed her purse.

While she was at this, Oralee said loudly, "Uh-huh, the girl is seein' a man." As Charlene raced out the door, Oralee called, "Don't you forget to come back, girl, and bring me a fountain Coke."

* * *

He was waiting for her, his eyes on the door, and when they saw her, they jumped with pleasure in the manner that every woman dreams of. Charlene's eyes met his, and she felt herself gliding across the room. His expression one of pure gladness, he rose out of the booth and greeted her, then waited for her to slip into the seat before he sat back down.

Charlene sat, and had to catch her breath. They gazed at each other for a minute in which Charlene was remembering his kiss and wondering if he was remembering it, too. If he was, he seemed happy about it. Then Fayrene appeared with two moist glasses of ice tea, bringing them back to reality when she thrust out her hands to show how long the color Charlene had put on her fingernails was lasting.

"They keep on goin', through all I do here," Fayrene said, thoroughly pleased. "You-all ready to order?"

Charlene ordered a hamburger, and Mason had a cheeseburger with fries. Fayrene said, "Have a good time, kids," winked at Charlene and left.

Again the two stared at each other.

"Thank you for coming," he said.

"Thank you for asking."

She wondered what they could talk about and tried to think of some safe, friendly topic. What she came up with was, "Well, how was your morning?"

"Long," he said, his blue eyes on hers. "How was yours?"

"Busy," she said, and happily.

With him sitting there listening intently, even when Fayrene slipped their hamburgers in front of them, she went on to tell him about her encounter with Muriel Porter, and how Ms. Porter had engaged her with the exorbitant sum of fifty dollars to go tomorrow afternoon and give Ms. Porter's sister a manicure in the nursing home.

"Larry Joe is probably working all afternoon," she said, suddenly thinking of it. "Well, I can go any time. I'll have him drive me over before he starts work, or on a break. If I have to, I can get Daddy to drive me. That's what I should do," she said, although hesitant to encourage her father to more driving. "Daddy goes out there to visit friends anyway. He can have one of his visiting days."

"I'll drive you," Mason said.

"Oh, no, I can't ask you to do that." The idea perturbed her. First she was having lunch with him, and then she would be riding around with him. It was much too close, too fast. When a man started driving a woman around, he tended to think he had some sort of control. The thought made her a little annoyed at him. She stirred her ice tea briskly, sending the ice chunks into a spin.

"I would be glad to drive you, Charlene." Mason watched her face, and saw her guard come up.

"I could probably drive myself," she said. "I can drive," she added, not wanting him to have the idea she was a helpless woman. "At least, I *did* drive, and then I had a wreck with Rainey that caused her to lose her baby. After that, I kept putting off driving until I felt enough courage to tackle it, and before too long it was easier just not to try. Joey could always take me, or Mama or Daddy, and then Larry Joe. I know it seems silly now, but it just happened."

"I don't think it seems silly. There are some people who never drive. Muriel Porter doesn't drive."

"She doesn't?" This was a surprise; the woman didn't seem the type to rely on anyone for anything.

"She has someone, usually her secretary, drive her around. I've never seen her behind the wheel of a car."

"Well, I can't hire a secretary," Charlene said. "I've got to begin driving again. I didn't think it would be so hard to pick back up. It probably wouldn't have been, but I put the Suburban in the ditch twice while tryin' to get out and in the driveway, and it's ruined my confidence." She could not tell him about the panic attacks.

She thought about the driveway, and how the Suburban had looked in the ditch. She would hate to let Ms. Porter down because she went in the ditch again.

Seeing her discouragement, and the way she was now preoccupied with driving, annoyed Mason, who had been enjoying her attention and sparkling eyes.

"I'll come over tomorrow, and if you want to drive, I'll ride along with you. How about that?"

She blinked and looked up at him, saying earnestly, "Thank you. That really would be better than having Daddy drive with me. I'm a little afraid that if I have an accident, it'll cause him to have a heart attack or something." She turned to motion for Fayrene, calling for a fountain Coca-Cola to go.

He had solved her problem, and that made him feel good. But he wished she sounded a little more enthusiastic about seeing him tomorrow. He was disappointed, too, when she insisted on paying for her own lunch.

The City Hall thermometer reads 76°

Charlene sat on the side of Jojo's bed and bowed her head, while her daughter lay on the pillow, folded her hands and said her nightly prayers.

"Now I lay me down to sleep, I pray thee, Lord, my soul to keep," Jojo said in her little voice. "If I should die before I wake, I pray thee, Lord, my soul to take."

Charlene's eyes popped open. That really was such a

morbid prayer, she thought, gazing at her daughter, who was now praying, "God bless Mama and my daddy, wherever he is, and Danny J. and Larry Joe, and my grandpa and our horses, Dog and Bo and Lulu, and..."

Charlene ran her gaze over Jojo's pale, angelic features, the long eyelashes, creamy cheeks, flaxen hair, and her heart swelled and tears threatened. Jojo finished her blessing, and Charlene said, "And thank you, Lord, for sending me Jojo." She smiled at her daughter and bent to kiss her cheek.

Jojo looked up at her with a solemn expression. "Mama, I did something today."

"What did you do?"

Jojo got out of bed and slid down on her knees and reached under the bed, pulling out a pile of papers. Pieces of papers. "I tore them up."

Charlene's heart thudded. "What are they, honey?" She took the pieces of paper to look at in the lamplight. They were schoolwork papers, done in Jojo's neat little handwriting, marked all over with slashes of red.

"They are all bad grades," Jojo said then, beginning to cry. "I didn't want to show you."

Charlene's heart cracked, and she swept Jojo into her arms. "Oh, honey, it's all right. You don't have to hide the papers from me."

"I just got so mad, I tore them up."

"That's okay. It's okay to be mad. It's okay to be upset." She held Jojo and tried to put her love into her daughter by touch and kisses. Jojo cried, and Charlene made herself not cry.

After a few minutes, when Jojo began to sniff and Charlene felt she could talk normally, she said, "Okay, let me see."

Matching the pieces of the pages with Jojo's help, she

scanned them. They were mostly English papers. The red marks seemed to carry screams. She looked over at Jojo, who sat beside her small and hurt, with hanging head and slumped shoulders.

Gathering the ability of all women who are naturally born mothers to say exactly what needs to be said and with exactly the right assurance, she said, "I'll tell you what. I will take these papers and tape them back together, and you and I will go over them this weekend. Honey, bad grades are nothing but bad grades. We'll fix everything. Don't you worry."

She soothed Jojo with more caresses and kisses and tucked her into bed, closing her eyes and saying, "Thank you, God, for always taking care of Jojo." Turning out the lamp, she sat there and smoothed Jojo's hair off her forehead in rhythmic motion until her daughter drifted into sleep. Then she took up the torn pages of schoolwork and left quietly.

In her steps somewhere between the bed and the hallway she became highly irritated. She would teach Jojo a different bedtime prayer straight away. Why had she ever taught her that traditional bit of Puritan morbidity? She did not remember having gotten it from her mother, so she could not lay blame there.

It was a little startling to realize she was having such new and rebellious thoughts. Questioning things she had never before questioned.

The door to Danny J.'s room was open, light falling out into the hall. She stopped and looked in. Her son was at his desk, tapping his pencil on his knee. Charlene went in and asked him how school was going. She asked him about each course in turn and about each teacher. She talked to him about the bronc riding and about the possibility of going to a college with a rodeo team. He seemed to have looked into this, and she was thrilled at his interest.

"If you have any problems at school," she told him, "I want to know, so that I can help."

He looked at her as if she had gone off the deep end and said, "I will, Mom."

Then she did what she probably wasn't supposed to and caressed his hair and told him she loved him, receiving a shy grin and mumble in return, which she could clutch to her heart.

Passing Larry Joe's dark bedroom, she sighed, reminding herself that her son was grown, as was supposed to happen. On impulse she went back and entered Larry Joe's room, turned on the bedside lamp and folded down the covers and plumped the pillow, thinking, "Mom loves you, Larry Joe."

In the kitchen, she spread the pieces of Jojo's schoolwork on the table, got invisible mending tape from the drawer and carefully smoothed and taped the pages back together.

Twenty-Nine

The City Hall thermometer reads 79°

Saturday was the third day that Everett Northrupt did not hang his flag. Winston had not seen hide nor hair of the man, either. At mid-morning, he marched himself across the street and rang his neighbor's doorbell.

Doris Northrupt came to the door. "Hello, Winston." She folded one hand over the other and regarded him through the screen. She wasn't known for hospitality, but this was generally excused because she wasn't from this part of the country and didn't know any better.

"I haven't seen Everett hanging his flag for a few days now," Winston said. "I was wonderin' if something was wrong."

She pursed her lips and then opened the screen door. "Come in."

He stepped into the entry hall. It was bright and gleaming, like a picture in a magazine, and smelled faintly of lemon wax. Doris told him, with a surprising bit of desperation, that Everett had "taken to bed" at the sight of Winston putting in a flagpole. "He says he doesn't feel well, and I can't get him out of bed. Since you started this, maybe you could talk to him."

Winston did not see that he had started anything, but she

was already heading up the steps before he could say yes or no.

Everett was propped up on a bed in a large front bedroom, watching television. The man was twelve years younger than Winston, but at that moment he looked at least five older. Doris said, "Look who's come to visit," and left Winston standing there. Everett didn't appear very thrilled.

Winston saw a chair near the dresser and brought it over to sit nearer the bed. "Doris said you haven't been feelin' too good."

"I'm just tired," Everett said, seemingly enthralled with the television show, one of those fishing shows. Winston found them boring.

"I've missed you at flag raisin' time."

"I haven't felt much like luggin' it out there. My bursitis has been actin' up."

"You could get a flagpole. It would make it easier."

"Foolin' with it at all is a lot of trouble every mornin' and evenin'."

"Yes, but it gives you somethin' to do, though. A good reason to get up in the mornin' and start the day."

"You got a flagpole," Everett said flatly. "One fool in the neighborhood is enough."

Winston thought for a second, then said, "Now you tell me what is more foolish—puttin' a flag up a pole or vegetatin' in bed," and got up and left.

The City Hall thermometer read 82°

"Have a good time, honey." Charlene waved Jojo off in Mary Lynn Macomb's van. Mary Lynn was taking her Sara and Jojo to the library and shopping up in Lawton. Danny J. had gone off for the day with Curt Butler and Curt's rodeo bronc-riding brother, and Larry Joe was working all day, as Charlene had expected.

With her children all securely placed, she raced back into the house to dress in a chambray blouse and skirt, do her hair and put on makeup, using a new lipstick Rainey had sent her. When Mason drove up, she walked out to meet him with her supplies fixed up in a carrying case.

His smile and thoroughly appreciative look sort of rattled her, and she quickly jutted the Suburban keys at him, saying, "You drive to the nursing home. I wouldn't want to have a wreck on the way there and end up disappointing Ms. Porter and her sister."

What she was mainly thinking about was getting stuck in the driveway ditch on the way out.

They left the windows down, and the air felt fresh and lively. Mason smiled at her, and she smiled at him, and noticed the wisps of short hair that fluttered over his forehead. Suddenly she was struck with the realization that she was on her own without her children for an entire afternoon. And here she was, she thought, leaving an attractive man to go spend her precious time at a nursing home.

Mason pulled into the parking lot and into a spot shaded by a tall cottonwood. He said he would wait in the Suburban and read. He held up an old battered book upon which Charlene read the title: *Leaves of Grass* by Walt Whitman.

Charlene looked from the book to him, wondering at the contrasts he presented.

She said, "I shouldn't be but forty-five minutes to an hour." She saw him opening his book and settling back in the seat before she even got out.

Inside at the nurses' station she found a nurse who appeared in charge and explained to the woman what she was about for Ms. Porter's sister.

"Oh, I'll bet Sister will like that. Her room is number twenty, all the way down that corridor at the end on the right," she said, pointing.

"Sister is her name?" Charlene asked.

"Uh-huh. That's how she's listed. She's a doll. You'll find out."

Charlene went down the carpeted hallway. Pains had been taken with color coordination and soothing pictures on the wall, although there was the antiseptic smell above it all. Several patients in wheelchairs and walkers looked her over, and a couple of them greeted her politely. There were names beside the doors, Charlene saw. The name at number twenty was Sister Porter.

All the rooms she had passed coming down the hallway contained two beds, but this room had only one, and it seemed a very large bed, or else it was that the woman in the bed was so very small and frail looking. Her voice was that of a child when she said, "Hello. My Mimi said you were coming. Oh, this is exciting."

Charlene could not imagine Ms. Muriel Porter being called "My Mimi." Then she noted Sister's hair. It was white, mostly, and sort of flying out, but with a second look she saw it was very long. It was caught at her neck with a tie and was long enough to disappear into the sheets. The next thing she realized was that Sister was watching Roller Derby on television and had, the greeting dispensed with, returned her attention to the screen.

"I love Roller Derby," the tiny woman said. "I like to see the fights those girls get into." The woman's eyes sparkled. "Oooh...look at that number nine. Get her!" Her small, pale-as-milk bony fist jabbed the air. It was a startling sight.

Charlene brought the bed tray over and adjusted it low over Sister's lap, settling herself on the side of the bed away from the television, so as not to block Sister's viewing of Roller Derby, which Sister continued to watch avidly, while Charlene set up and went to work, one hand at a time, as Sister needed one free to jab imaginary punches.

The woman's hands were so small and delicate that Charlene was a little worried. She pushed her glasses down the bridge of her nose and bent close, trying to see carefully. Sister had little to say for the following ten minutes, until Roller Derby went off, and then she watched Charlene's ministrations and began talking.

"I wish I could have been in Roller Derby," she said. "I did skate. And I did some of that marathon dancin', too. I did a lot of things, but that was a long time ago. I'm thirty-one years older than Mimi. My mother was Daddy's first wife, and Mimi was from his third. I got married, but my husband died in an oil well explosion. I never married again. Are you married?"

"Yes. Well, divorced." She supposed that was close enough to be accurate.

"Daddy would have died if I had been divorced. It is a sin. Mimi never got married. Daddy didn't want her to. I don't think Mimi ever wanted to. There is just us now. Daddy and Mama are dead. I would like my fingernails painted. Mimi said you would pick a color for me. My favorite color is yellow. That's why I love forsythias when they come out every spring. They are so yellow. Don't you think they are lovely?"

"Yes, I do. Would this color be okay for your fingernails?"

"It isn't yellow, but I imagine it will be pretty." She gave a smile, and then she didn't say another word.

Charlene thought of the fifty dollars Ms. Porter had given her and felt a little guilty. It had not taken long to give Sister a manicure, and the old woman was so sweet.

"Would you like me to comb your hair and braid it?" she asked.

"That would be nice." She fell asleep before Charlene finished the braiding.

As she quietly gathered up her things to go, a rather robust woman with bright blond hair and swinging earrings, and wearing a flowered kimono, came rolling into the room in an electric wheelchair. She stopped in front of the doorway, as if to block it.

"I've been watchin' you do Sister's fingernails. I would like you to do mine, too. I used to always have wonderful fingernails, kept them perfect. I was a dancer," she said with pride, and then her expression dropped. "But now..." Her one arm lay limp in her lap, and seeing it, there was no way Charlene could refuse.

She followed the blond woman—Annabelle—to her room, and before she got out of there she had to quickly file Annabelle's roommate's fingernails. The woman wanted polish, too, but Charlene explained that she did not have time.

"I have someone waiting for me," she said, feeling somewhat torn. She was eager to get back to Mason, yet she was happy to be with these women and to find she could be of use in lifting their spirits. Annabelle waved a bill at her, but Charlene said it was on the house, and it felt good to do that, too. She thought that Ms. Porter had paid for a lot more hands than she had imagined.

When she came out of the glass double doors, she saw Mason sitting on the passenger side, his head bent over the book, an expression of deep concentration on his face. She stopped there at the sight of him, gazing at him. She watched him turn a page and never take his eyes off the book. He was thinking so hard, she could feel the energy.

She wondered what was on the page that could make him do that.

A rolling swell of tenderness welled up in her at the look of him, which was warm and alive and very male.

As if sensing her attention, he lifted his head and saw her. "All done?" he called through the window, sitting himself up.

She walked over. "Yes. I'm sorry it took longer than I had anticipated. I ended up doing two other ladies, too."

"No problem," he said, giving a grin. And then he sat there, showing no sign of moving, other than to set his book aside. "I thought you could drive home," he said. "You don't need to race home to see to the kids, and I'm in no hurry. You can take your time."

"Okay," she said, because there didn't seem any way to counter his reasoning.

She felt him watch her round the truck. She stuck her case in the back seat, got in behind the wheel and slipped on her sunglasses. He reminded her to buckle her seat belt. She started the engine, and then she sat back. She looked over at him, and then, her gaze focusing on his chest, she confessed her fear to him, something she had pushed into an inner pocket.

"It's like a panic, really, more than a fear," she said. "I feel it jump into my belly and then rise up my chest." From the shelter of her dark glasses, she watched him for a reaction. He would probably think she was nutty. "I have a couple of times felt this when I haven't been driving, too, but when I have been driving, it comes so strongly. The memory of the wreck sort of flickers, and then this panic comes over me. It's as if I can't control it."

His answer was, "That's very natural, and it'll go away once you get to driving all the time," and he motioned for her to get on.

She was a little annoyed that he did not seem to fully appreciated her plight. Taking a deep breath, she made her shoulders relax, put the Suburban in gear and headed for the road. Mason suggested she turn away from town. "Get out on the open road for a bit."

The entry onto the highway was plenty wide, so she made the turn quite easily. Then she was heading away from town, no traffic at all. She pressed the accelerator, picking up speed. The smooth motion of the Suburban, the fresh breeze blowing in the windows, felt delicious. Her spirits rising, she flashed Mason a smile.

With a wink, he said, "You're doin' just fine, ma'am."

The City Hall thermometer reads 58°

They drove in a wide circle to the edges of Lawton and then back to Valentine. It was lovely, the smooth rhythm of the tires speeding along the open road, the warm sunshine and the fresh wind. She had only two panics, one that seemed to have no reason at all, other than she suddenly thought, *I'm driving sixty-five,* and another when meeting two enormous trucks loaded with hay bales that appeared in danger of toppling over onto the Suburban. Mason seemed to sense these little panics and each time laid his hand on her shoulder.

When they came upon a small country store at a crossroads, Mason suggested she pull in, and Charlene did, quite expertly, she thought, enjoying the sound of the tires halting on gravel. They went inside and bought Drumstick ice-cream cones out of an ancient freezer and ate them while leaning side by side against the Suburban fender and talking about everything and nothing.

There in the sunlight, seeing the light shine on Mason's blond-brown hair and reflect in his sparkling eyes, she thought, I am enjoying the company of a man, and I am driving.

Back in the truck once more, they headed for Valentine, coming into the town from the opposite end of Charlene's home, passing the MacCoy Feed and Seed. Here there was traffic, and Charlene felt a little panic swirl in her stomach. She breathed deeply, telling herself she was calm. She had driven only a few days ago through town to her father's house, and the only casualty had been a smashed lilac in the driveway.

Mason's hand came upon her shoulder, and he smiled at her.

When they stopped at the Main Street light, Charlene noticed people staring at the City Hall digital sign.

"Looks like its gotten a little cooler than we'd all thought," Mason said.

Charlene saw then the lights on the sign blinking 58°. She was staring at it when a horn honked behind her, making her jump. She let up off the brake and continued down the street, watching carefully, breathing quickly. With each block that she passed, confidence seeped back into her, however, and then she was going along quite well, and her own house and buildings came into view.

Her gaze fell on the mailbox and narrow driveway.

She slowed, and then she stopped right there in the road. "I have done wonderfully. I don't want to ruin my confidence. You take it into the drive."

He looked startled at her pronouncement, but she began scooting over, so there was nothing for him to do but get out and come around to get behind the wheel and drive the Suburban into the entry and down the drive the rest of the way.

For a number of seconds after Mason stopped the truck, they regarded each other. Then Charlene asked if he cared to come inside for a little while, and he said he did. She went up the walk toward the door and used the key to open it. She felt as if Mason were close enough to breathe on her neck. She wanted him close enough to breathe on her neck. That was the train of her thoughts.

The house was quiet. They were alone.

She hurried on through to the kitchen. "I always seem to be bringing you to the kitchen," she said to him. "I do have a comfortable living room."

"The kitchen is your place. I like it."

She turned quickly from him and his warm eyes, and jerked open the refrigerator. "I don't have any ice tea made...but I could easily brew some fresh."

"Coke is fine," he said, right at her ear, causing her to jump. "I'll get the glasses, you get the ice."

She thought that the very air seemed to whisper, *You are alone here...you are alone here....*

She brought the ice container and two cans of Coke to the counter, where he set the glasses. She dropped the cubes in the glasses, while he popped the tops on the cans. He poured the glasses full, as she returned the ice container to the freezer. He handed her a glass, and he said, "You're welcome, ma'am," in that tender fashion that melted her heart.

She looked into his eyes, and then set her glass on the counter, just before he grabbed her into his strong arms and went to kissing her in a most fiery manner, taking her breath and all of her senses.

He kissed her and kissed her again, and she welcomed him and tugged him back for yet another kiss when he would have pulled away. She put her hands into his hair and bared her neck to his lips, glorying in the wild and wonderful sensations pulsing through her body. His back, his shoulders, all of his muscles, were hard and hot beneath her palms. She whispered his name, and he whispered hers. She inhaled the musky, manly scent of him and found his pulse in his neck with her lips. He pressed her against the counter, lifting her up and holding her there so he could move against her, causing sexual desires of every exquisite nature to whip and pound from her head to her toes.

For the briefest few seconds they hovered there, just on the edge of sinking onto the floor, because they never would have made it to a bed, or even the couch. But then they both stopped. It was as if a calm voice of reason penetrated the passion.

Charlene opened her eyes, and her lashes fluttered against the hot, moist skin of his neck. His breathing came fast, as did her own. His hand was on her breast, and he moved it ever so slowly.

They parted and gazed at each other, each one asking if maybe they could possibly continue, finish it, and come to reason afterward.

Her hand lingered on his chest. The pressure of his wild kisses lingered on her lips.

"I can't do this," she said, dropping her hand. "I have my children to think of. And it's too soon."

"I know," he said, seeming to search for his breath at the same time that he caressed her cheek.

Raking a hand through her hair, she moved away, averting her eyes. "I haven't had sex in a very long time," she said, forcing herself to speak her mind, a little embarrassed at the rawness of her tone. "And maybe that's all this is, and I don't want that. I really just don't know anything right now. I can't trust my emotions." Very near tears, and very near throwing herself upon him again, she dropped into a chair.

A minute later he plunked the moist glass of cold soda

on the table at her elbow. She looked up to see him take a long drink out of his own glass, as if swigging back whiskey. She drank, too, relishing the cool liquid.

Then he said, "This isn't just sex."

"No," she said, finally able to regard him levelly. "No, it isn't, and I don't want it to turn into that. I want it to be the result of knowing each other. I hardly knew my husband. Twenty-one years together, and we talked, but we could not truly speak to each other. I was always afraid of saying the wrong thing, and he was always afraid of saying anything. I don't want that kind of relationship with a man again. If I ever get involved again, I want to share my heart with someone who can share his with me."

He searched her eyes and nodded with what she thought was understanding. Then he gave a dry smile, saying, "I don't think right now is a good time, though. I think I'd best go."

He sat his half-empty glass on the table and hesitated. Then he bent and kissed her softly, tenderly, and moved to the door.

She jumped up and said, "I'll walk you out," which she thought was a very brave thing to do.

Thirty

It was well after dawn when Winston attached his new flag to the rope of his flagpole and hoisted up the Stars and Bars, with "Dixie" playing in the background, low because Mildred especially liked to sleep in on Sunday mornings. He didn't feel nearly as much of a thrill as he had anticipated, because Everett Northrup's porch post remained empty of a flag and no "Star-Spangled Banner" rang out.

He got the Sunday paper from the yard and continued halfheartedly on with his morning routine. Passing the roses on his way to the back door, he cut two. Coming into the kitchen he tossed the newspaper on the table, jammed the roses into a jelly glass with water and then poured himself a cup of coffee.

When he turned around to the small table, there was Coweta, sitting there, roses in her hair and wearing a rosy sort of dress. He blinked.

"You're in a mood this morning, aren't you, Winston?" she said.

"Yes, I am." He plunked his coffee cup on the table and sat himself down heavily. "I haven't seen you in a while. To what do I owe the honor of this visit?"

"You haven't missed me," she said, lifting a knowing eyebrow.

"I knew you weren't here." He felt a little guilty because it was true that he had not missed her so much. He wondered at that, at what it said about him.

"You've been getting on with things. Having fun with your flag. You haven't thought about me hardly at all."

"I never stop thinking about you, Coweta," he said and meant it, in his own way.

"Well, I've come to say goodbye." She whipped a rose out of her hair and laid it on the table. It was bright red against the creamy tablecloth.

"You said goodbye a year and a half ago, when you dropped dead," Winston said. He still got irritated at her for leaving him like that.

"I mean that the time has come for me to move on. Freddy has rallied and made a necessary change in his life, Charlene has made her difficult decision and is starting down a new road, and Rainey has finally found herself and all she needs. You have your flag and your purpose with these old women. Just as all of you are getting on with your lives, I have to get on with mine." She looked at him solemnly. "I mean that I won't be back, Winston."

He gazed into her eyes for a long moment. "Will I ever see you again?"

"Yes," she smiled lovingly. "I'll greet you when you come over, my love."

She blew him a kiss, and then it seemed like he blinked and she was gone. Winston's gaze dropped to the rose, still lying on the table. He swallowed and wished a thousand things that could never be, such as to be a young man again and to hold his wife in his arms and time in his hands. He felt, for an instant, great anger at having to grow old and lose the life he loved.

With heavy muscles, he got up, retrieved the jelly glass and brought it to the table and plopped the red rose in with the pink and white ones. He gazed at the blossoms for a long minute, resignation coming slowly but as inevitably as his hair going white and his skin getting blotchy. He knew this was life and was glad to be a part of it.

Then he snapped open the *Sunday Voice* and sat with the roses' scent around him to read the headline, which stated: Mayor Rips Out Clock-Thermometer. It appeared the thermometer had gone haywire again, and Kaye Upchurch, the mayor's wife, had just about gotten run down by somebody who was distracted by the false reading of 58°. Calls had been flooding the City Hall office, and the mayor had gotten so aggravated, probably at his demanding wife, Winston thought, that he had torn out the wires to the computer. The city council had agreed to take the sign down permanently.

Joey, on his way to Houston, stopped at the tiny post office of a small town. It was closed on a Sunday, of course, but he knew the lobby would be open, and he could get stamps for his letter from the machine.

He pulled his rig into the gravel lot next to a two-tone Chevy that had the hood up and steam coming out of the engine.

As Joey got out of his own truck, the fellow bending over the engine came up, and Joey, surprised, saw that the fellow was really a young woman.

"Hey, cowboy," she said, brushing hair out of her eyes with the back of her grease-smudged hand. "I don't suppose you carry a spare radiator hose around with you."

He stopped and then walked over. "No, 'fraid not. I don't know a thing about engines. That'd be my son's department, but he isn't with me."

"Oh, yeah?" She wiped her hands on a rag in a way that said she knew a little something about what she was doing. Then she was looking at Joey with golden eyes that caused him to stare at her, while she gave him a going-over in a way that made him both pleased and nervous. Young women these days were bolder than he was comfortable with.

Shifting his gaze to the steaming engine, he said, "I saw a station open a little ways back. I could give you a lift."

"How 'bout the other way?" She cocked her head. "Could you give me a lift home? On down this road another five miles and then east three. I probably got parts at home. I save a junk car just for parts for this one."

"Well, sure," he said. He couldn't just leave her there. Then he remembered why he had stopped and pulled the envelope out of his jacket. "Let me just drop this in the mail."

He strode into the lobby of the post office. At the machine, he deposited coins, pushed the button, and a little packet of stamps came out. He put one on the letter and stepped over to the mail slot.

For long seconds he gazed at the letter, at Charlene's name. He pictured her at home in her kitchen, the kids around her. The well of loneliness inside him seemed to get deeper.

Then, quickly, he dropped the letter in the box and strode back out to find the young woman already sitting in his truck, a move that caused him a little shock. The way the sun hit her face, he thought maybe she wasn't as young as he had first estimated. This made him feel a little better.

As he pulled out on the road, she asked him where he was headed, and he told her Houston. She asked where he was working, and he said he hoped to get a job in Houston.

"We're lookin' for help at our place right now," she said. "There's just my grandmother and me. We run some cattle and put up hay. My grandmother broke her leg, and I have two sections of hay to get baled and loaded on a flatbed, and cattle to get moved. Why don't you stop and have a look around? I can offer you Sunday supper, and my grandmother is the best cook in the county.''

He glanced over to see her regarding him with those golden eyes, steady and inviting.

''All right,'' he said. ''If you have a corral for my two horses.''

''We have a couple of corrals just sittin' there waitin' to be used,'' she said, smiling.

Joey focused out the windshield, squinting a little in the sunlight, staring down the blacktopped road ahead.

Mason displayed the seat covers he had purchased for his Grandpap's old car, and Larry Joe, finishing tightening the last nuts and bolts on the engine that was once more set in the car, gave them a skeptical look.

''What's wrong with them?'' Mason wanted to know.

''Nothin', I guess. If you like ugly.''

''Hey, I ordered these from a hot rod catalog. This is what was popular back when this car was made.''

''That's the problem, then,'' Larry Joe said and returned his attention to the engine.

Mason looked at the young man stretched under the yawning hood and grinned softly. He had sure enjoyed Larry Joe working with him on the old vehicle. He was almost a little sad that the car was about ready to run, he thought, as he stretched the cover over the front seat. He thought he would drive it for a while, and likely he would have to have Larry Joe work on it from time to time. He intended to find things like this that they could do together.

''Y'all want to take a break for somethin' cold to drink?'' said a feminine voice. Mason recognized his sister-in-law Iris's tone at the same instant that he straightened up to see her standing in the wide doorway of the garage.

He saw Larry Joe come up from the engine so fast that he
bumped his head against the hood.

"Hello, Iris," Mason said.

"Hello."

She came forward. Dressed in a silky blouse and short
skirt and heels, she came forward on tiptoe, carrying a tray
and glasses. She barely glanced at Mason. She was grinning
at Larry Joe, who mumbled, "Hello, Mrs. MacCoy."

"I took the liberty of goin' into your kitchen and gettin'
us all somethin'," she said, stating the obvious as she set
the tray on a corner of the battered work bench. "Adam's
showin' a buyer over the pasture, but I was still in my
church clothes and wasn't about to go trompin' through all
those weeds."

"A buyer? For his half of the land?"

"Yep. Some housing developer. He lost the juvenile de-
linquent center to Freddy Valentine. Now here, hon, have
a glass of tea."

She passed Larry Joe a cold glass, leaving Mason to pick
up his own. Mason downed half of his and then decided to
go see Adam and the buyer. "You can keep workin'," he
told Larry Joe, who dove back beneath the car hood.

Adam was out in the middle of the big pasture with a
rotund man. He gestured this way and that. When Mason
reached the two, he was struck by how much the men re-
sembled each other. He thought it had to do with a shared
expression of wheeling-dealing. Adam's cordiality to him
and eager introductions let Mason know that this sale would
be very profitable to his brother.

"Mr. Wrigley is thinkin' of building a housing devel-
opment here," Adam said. "Three- and five-acre tracts."

"Ah." Mason watched the developer look over the land

like he was placing his houses. "Think there's a good market for that way out here?"

Wrigley's eyes stopped on him for a second. "Depends. Could be." Then, "And you own that house and how many acres over there?"

"Forty."

"Maybe we could build a little lake over there," Wrigley said, pointing east.

"My creek," Mason said.

"I imagine we could work somethin' out," Adam said, shooting Mason a fiery glance. Then he led Wrigley away to find the surveyors' stakes and just where the property lines ran.

Mason walked back across the pasture. At the gate he turned and watched Adam and the developer. Then he looked at his house. Suddenly it looked very small and old, even shabby. There sure wouldn't be room for a woman and her kids here.

The thought struck him hard. He had not realized he was moving along those lines with Charlene, but he supposed he was. Quite suddenly he was imagining marrying her, and he realized, without ever consciously knowing, he had been fantasizing about this for some time.

When he walked into the garage, it took his eyes a few seconds to adjust, and then he saw Iris bending over the fender, displaying her cleavage while talking to Larry Joe, who was pretty much trying to crawl into the engine.

"Iris, Adam would like you to drive over to the pasture gate and pick them up," Mason told her.

"Pick him up?" Iris said, then sighed. "Oh, all right. It was nice to see you boys." She touched Larry Joe's arm as she left.

When she was out of sight, Mason said to Larry Joe, "Just enjoy what that woman is bestowing upon you, son."

Larry Joe looked embarrassed. Mason winked at him, and Larry Joe grinned sheepishly. "I don't think I could do anything else with her," Larry Joe said, causing Mason to laugh.

Then he said, "The tires I put on are old, but they appear to be holdin'. If you can start this thing, let's see if we can drive it out of here. Adam never said for Iris to go get him, and I imagine she'll be back."

Larry Joe told him to get behind the wheel, while he dove into the engine for another few adjustments. Then he called, "Fire her up."

Mason, his heart actually picking up tempo, turned the key. The engine chugged and sputtered. Larry Joe hollered at him to give it gas. Mason pumped the accelerator and tried again. The engine chugged and sputtered harder, almost caught, then died.

"Let me do it," Larry Joe said, motioning impatiently for Mason to get out of the way.

"I can do it," Mason said, adding, "It is my car." He felt like a kid, and Larry Joe's doubtful expression made him all the more determined.

He turned the key, pumped the accelerator and willed the engine to turn over. It did, with a sudden great roar.

"Aw-riight!" Larry Joe shouted, slammed the hood and ran around to jump into the passenger seat.

With a "Yahoo!" Mason revved the engine and then put it in gear. As he started out of the garage, the engine threatened to die, but then it caught and they went shooting out into the sunlight. As he turned onto the road, Mason pulled out the bills he had ready in his pocket and handed them over to the young man, who repeated, "Aw-riight!"

They got two miles down the road to town, and the engine quit. They had run out of gas. They were arguing about who was going to walk in to the gas station when Adam and Iris came by and gave them a ride. Adam talked to Mason about selling his property to the developer, while Iris smiled and showed her stuff to Larry Joe.

Thirty-One

When Oralee drove up in front of the elementary school, children were bursting out. "Looks like a swarm of wild bees," she said to Charlene, who had one foot out of the car. "Don't get stung."

Charlene carefully made her way through the racing children, some who called hello, and entered the school. It was already empty, and her footsteps echoed in the hallway. She felt self-conscious of her footsteps, almost like a child being where she was not supposed to be.

Jojo waited at the doorway of her classroom and raced forward to greet her, taking her hand and walking her into the room to present her to her teacher, Mrs. Norwood. The teacher rose from behind her desk with a smile and extended her hand for a firm shake, saying, "Very nice to meet you."

Mrs. Norwood was around thirty, so she had some experience, and was quite attractive, with frank brown eyes, hair cut in an easy-care bob, and comfortable cotton clothes. Charlene was sufficiently impressed with the woman. She immediately formed the opinion that children would adore this teacher and possibly learn something, too.

"Honey, Oralee is out front," Charlene said to Jojo. "Would you go out and keep her company while Mrs. Norwood and I chat?"

"I know," Jojo said, taking up her school bag. "So you two can talk about me."

"Yes, that is the idea." Charlene hugged her quickly.

Jojo gave a roll of the eyes and walked out the door, which Mrs. Norwood closed behind her.

Charlene sat in a chair beside the teacher's desk, and the woman said, "I'm very glad you took the time to come in," while the two of them further sized each other up.

Charlene said, "Jojo is my daughter. I want to make certain she is getting the best attention."

That made the woman sit back a bit. Charlene then launched into her view of Jojo's difficulties with lessons and questioned the woman for her understanding of the situation. The woman knew, of course, of the breakup of Jojo's parents.

Her observation was that Jojo's reactions to the circumstances were of a fairly normal nature. "She's having a little trouble concentrating," Mrs. Norwood said. "She doodles and gazes out the window a lot. When she is outside on the playground, rather than take part, she keeps to herself. I did speak to our student counselor, and she agrees that this is a way of coping by losing herself in daydream fantasies, and that this is fairly usual. It can be an effective way of coping with stressful situations, if not taken to an extreme.

"Although…" the teacher's eyebrows came together in a puzzled frown as her gaze shifted "…I have to admit that I can't explain away this rose as a fantasy."

Following the teacher's gaze, Charlene saw a red rose in a bud vase.

Mrs. Norwood said, "I was glad to know you were coming this afternoon, because Jojo may be developing more serious problems. She brought that rose to me this morning and told me an angel gave it to her."

"She did?"

"Yes. She asked to go to the girls' room, and she was gone some time. Actually, I didn't really realize how long she was gone because I got distracted by two of my students getting into an argument. When she came in the door, she had this rose, and wanted me to put it into water and keep it on my desk. I asked her where she got it between here and the girls' room, and she made up this story about an angel, who stopped to speak to her in the hallway and gave her the rose.

"I've asked all the teachers, and no one has been given any roses. I'm certain she must have gone out of the building and near the street. She knows that is not allowed, so of course she would lie about it. But that's the only way she could meet with some woman. At first I thought she must have gotten the rose from someone's bush, but no houses nearby have rosebushes."

While the teacher had been talking, Charlene picked up the rose and held it beneath her nose. Then she said, "Jojo doesn't lie."

Mrs. Norwood blinked. "Well, I don't know where she got it."

"I imagine she got it exactly how she said, from a woman with roses in her white hair. Just because no one saw this woman doesn't mean she wasn't there."

"Jojo didn't mention roses in the woman's hair, or that it was white." Mrs. Norwood stared at Charlene, who inhaled the scent of the rose again.

"I just imagined an angel would have that," Charlene said. "It's not uncommon for young children to report seeing angels, you know. I've seen and read a number of reports about this, haven't you?"

Mrs. Norwood stared at her in a manner that indicated her thoughts: *And the pecan doesn't fall far from the tree.*

"I am aware of the phenomenon of children reporting seeing angels, but this usually stops by the time they are five, when they get more aware of reality. I could have the county counselor speak with her. She comes Tuesdays and Thursdays, and she is a qualified child psychologist."

"Many people report seeing angels. I do take Jojo to church and have read many a Bible story to her, so I don't think her belief in angels is so far-fetched." Charlene, suddenly feeling much better about her daughter, set the rose back on the teacher's desk. "And only a few weeks ago she spent a great deal of time with her uncle, who is a physician and psychiatrist, and he finds she's doing just fine."

"Well...that's good."

"Please be assured that I will contact him, should I grow concerned with Jojo's ability to cope." She rose. "Enjoy the rose. It smells lovely."

She thanked Mrs. Norwood for her time and then left. All the way down the wide hallway, her footsteps again echoing on the tile, she listened and kept an eye out for the white-haired woman. At the front doors, she paused and wistfully looked back down the quiet, shadowy hallway, but no one was there.

When Charlene joined Jojo and Oralee in the car, she said, "Your teacher showed me the rose the angel gave you."

"She did?" Jojo regarded her with suspicion. "She didn't believe me, that an angel gave it to me."

"Did the woman *tell* you she was an angel when she gave you the rose?"

"Nooo...but she was all white and shimmery. And she was sort of old." Jojo frowned in thought. "But I still think she was an angel. She told me that angels watch over me all the time, and that God loves me. I told her I knew that, but she said she wanted to tell me.''

She regarded Charlene, as if to see Charlene's true thoughts.

Charlene smiled and said, "And she is absolutely right. God loves you, and so do I.''

After a minute, Oralee said, "I wouldn't go tellin' just everybody about the angel, though, Jojo. You might as well learn right now that it's easier to keep some things to yourself.''

Charlene was trying to think of a way to contradict this negative statement when Jojo said flatly, "I think I already found that out.''

During the drive home, Oralee said, "I speak from experience, you know.'' She hesitantly went on to tell of seeing what she thought were two angels when she was a child weeding the vegetable garden. "That was when we lived down in Tennessee. My legs were all tired, and I sat in the dirt, and about that time, here come these two girls with long dark hair out of the edge of the woods and floated past the end of the row of corn. I guess they didn't see me. They were talking, and it seemed to me they were arguin'. I blinked and they were gone. I went runnin' in to tell my mama, and she told me I'd fallen asleep in the garden and dreamed it. She said no angel had dark hair, for one thing, and that telling such tales wasn't goin' to get me out of weedin'. She put a hat on my head and sent me back out. Maybe I did fall asleep and dream it," she said, wonderingly.

Jojo said her angel was no dream, she was just one woman, and she didn't float.

Charlene, puzzling for some minutes, asked Oralee just how many places she had lived, since she had mentioned living in Chicago, and now Tennessee.

Oralee blinked and then said, "Well, I've moved some. I'm from St. Louis, but we got around."

As they approached the drive to Charlene's house, Jojo looked ahead and pointed. "Look, Mama!"

Charlene was looking. She saw a large truck with a flatbed trailer and big dump truck parked along the side of the road at the driveway entry. And there was Larry Joe, working their tractor, digging out the ditch.

"What are they doin', Mama?"

"Well, I don't know."

There was Mason's truck, and there was Mason himself, directing the lowering of a big galvanized pipe into the ditch Larry Joe had dug. And Danny J., helping with a shovel in hand.

Oralee edged the car up closer, and then she started laughing. "What they are doin', honey, is makin' your mama a wider driveway entrance."

The next morning, after her children had left for their various schools, Charlene drove the Suburban up the drive and out onto the road, happily passing the ditch and the mailbox with plenty of room to spare. With the window down and the breeze batting her hair, she drove into town and continued on through it to the MacCoy Feed and Seed store, driving smoothly up to the warehouse loading dock.

Mason appeared and crouched down to say, "Well, good mornin', ma'am," his blue eyes twinkling in a way that made her insides flutter.

"I owe you an immense kindness," she said. "Would you let me make you supper Friday night?" It was all she had to offer.

He grinned with a delight that split her heart. "You don't owe me anything, but I sure won't say no to a home cooked meal, especially one of yours."

"Six o'clock," she told him and drove away.

She went on to the Cut and Curl, and her only mishap was to bump over the curb when pulling into the very narrow entry of the shop's parking lot. She found that acceptable for her first totally solo drive.

Charlene left the shop a few minutes earlier than usual. It was very freeing to drive herself home. She stopped right in the middle of her widened entry, got out of the Suburban and got her mail from the box.

In the kitchen, she poured herself a glass of ice tea and then sat, taking her shoes off, to go through the mail, anxiously viewing each bill and looking somewhat desperately for a letter from the State Department of Human Services for a confirmation of her eligibility for aid.

Then she came to a plain white envelope. The moment she recognized Joey's handwriting, her heart leaped into her throat. There was no return address, but it was postmarked from some town in Texas.

She tore open the envelope, finding a single sheet of notebook paper. She read: *Dear Charlene, I'm sorry for running out, but I know you can handle everything.* It sounded like an accusation and excuse rolled into one, and Charlene wished she could smack him. *I have sent five thousand dollars to your account at the bank.* Startled, eyes widening and bringing a hand to her neck, she read that sentence over twice before going on. *Please tell the kids I love them. I will send more money for them when I can. Thank you for taking good care of them. Joey.*

Grabbing the telephone, she called the bank to check to see if five thousand dollars had gone into the account.

"Yes, Miz Darnell," a young voice told her. "That money was posted to your account this morning."

Charlene hung up and sank back down into the kitchen

chair. She looked over at the stack of bills. She thought of how she had been falling into bed at night and praying for strength and for money to keep the electric and water turned on and her children fed.

"Thank you, Lord," she whispered.

She thought of Joey, seeing him alone somewhere on the road. She knew the only way he could get this much money at once was to sell his one really good horse. Smiling, with tears beginning to flow, she thought, And Mrs. Norwood didn't believe in angels. Joey, at that moment, surely qualified.

When the children came in that evening, she had the letter on the table for them to read. When Danny J. read it, he said, "I guess this means he isn't comin' home real soon."

"No, he isn't," she said. "But he hasn't forgotten you. He's trying to say he loves you."

"I'm driving again," Charlene told Rainey during their telephone chat.

"Well, hallelujah," Rainey said. "Now you'll be able to drive up here and see the baby when he is born."

"Yes, yes, I will," Charlene said, and her mind raced ahead nervously down the road to Rainey's, mentally checking places where she might have problems. The only narrow turn would probably be into Rainey's house. She would probably be better at turning by then. "You tell Harry to call me the instant you go into labor...after he gets you to the hospital, I mean."

"We have some weeks yet," Rainey reminded her.

"Yes, but I want to be ready." She was already thinking ahead to having Larry Joe tune up the Suburban and to keeping the gas tank full. She always liked to be prepared. When she hung up, it occurred to her that for some things, like a marriage breakup, there was simply no preparation. One had to just go along with faith.

Thirty-Two

Cool fall came in as it always did—abruptly. The previous day the temperature had risen to a warm, humid 80°, and overnight storms came through, bringing rain and temperatures dropping into the fifties. By early afternoon, when Charlene went around to the cafe to get hers and Oralee's fountain drinks, the sun had warmed things to the high sixties, but the air remained brisk. Strolling along the sidewalk, Charlene enjoyed the fresh-feeling air and sunshine, and just about everyone she encountered seemed to have a smile on their face. Fayrene even said, "Isn't this weather wonderful? I am sure glad to be shut of that awful summer."

Charlene agreed the summer had been awfully tough.

As she pushed out through the chrome and glass door, she thought of that day when she had confronted Joey in front of the feed store, in the blazing heat. It seemed a lifetime ago. She had thought she would die, yet here she was, she thought, catching a glimpse of her reflection in the plate glass window. That was her. She recognized herself now and no longer felt a stranger.

"Miz Darnell!"

Turning, Charlene saw a teenage girl with glossy black hair and wearing a midi-T-shirt and jeans hurrying out the door of the cafe.

"Could I get an appointment to have my nails done this

Friday? I have a date, and I want them to look really nice." The young woman held out her hands, showing fingernails that were mostly bitten off. "I thought maybe I could have tips put on, and that would help me to quit biting them."

"Yes, that often helps." She checked the small appointment book she'd taken to keeping in her smock pocket for just such occurrences and wrote the girl's name—Pia Sanchez—in for just after noon on Friday.

Then the girl said shyly, "The date I have...it's with your son, Larry Joe."

"Oh." Giving a polite smile, Charlene held out her hand. "Nice to meet you, Pia." The girl's shake was firm, while her expression remained shy. Charlene saw a dark-eyed beauty, but one with the open face and lively expression of a still young and innocent heart. Her smile widened. "I look forward to seeing you on Friday."

She walked back around the corner of the shop, casting a wave at the woman on the other side of the *Valentine Voice* window, who had taken to waving back, and thinking about her son and the young woman with a mixture of gladness and fear. She wished she could prevent Larry Joe from suffering any heartache at all. But there was no way she could. Larry Joe had to make his own way and learn his own lessons, even those of the heart. What she had to do was to trust. Easy words to say, hard to actually do.

The entire week, the weather remained balmy and dry, and everyone agreed it was perfect weather. It had the effect of stirring people's enthusiasm for life, and as a result, more women than usual came to have their hair and nails done. The shop fairly "sizzled," as Oralee put it, and for the first time Charlene's schedule was crammed. It was most fortuitous that she was driving again, because twice she had to go to school to pick up Jojo and bring her back to the shop to wait while Charlene fulfilled late appointments. It was also fortuitous that she was earning money, because any aid from the state would not be forthcoming.

She learned of this on Friday from a woman from the State Department of Human Services who called the shop to tell Charlene that her assistance was being canceled because their investigation showed that she had five thousand dollars in the bank. The woman made it sound as if Charlene had been lying about her needs. Charlene was furious. She only barely remembered to switch to the phone in the back room, and then she asked the woman just what assistance she was speaking of.

"There never has been any assistance. My children could have been thrown out into the street by now. You take weeks to provide any aid, yet you discover money in my account immediately. Did your investigation happen to show that that money just arrived from my husband?"

The woman ignored the question and said, as if taking notes, "The money is from your husband. It says here that you don't know where he is. Well, since he is now providing such good support, your state aid will be canceled."

"You can't cancel what you haven't started!" Charlene yelled into the phone and hung up.

She felt only slightly ashamed of hanging up on the woman, who had sounded like an automaton. Perhaps the woman could not help that, given all she saw and heard in her position, but Charlene thought that she herself put up with a lot in life, too, and yet she managed to be able to drum up interest for her customers who needed her to be interested.

The woman introduced herself as Nancy Scott. "Head nurse at Shady Elm...the nursing home," the woman added, when they all looked at her blankly. She was a serious-looking woman with short auburn hair. She put Charlene instantly in mind of a television news commentator.

"How may we help you, Ms. Scott?" Dixie Love asked.

"I believe it is your manicurist who came out and did three of our ladies' nails recently?" She looked at Charlene. "I'm sorry, I don't know your name."

Charlene introduced herself and said that, yes, she had been the one. The woman looked so solemn that her heart leaped into her throat, wondering what she had done wrong. Perhaps she had managed to kill one of the women by filing her nails.

But then the woman, in the same solemn fashion, went on to explain that the ladies whose nails Charlene had done had so enjoyed their manicures that it had picked up morale considerably.

"Therefore, we have decided that having a beautician for the ladies should become a weekly event. We have created positions for a hairdresser and manicurist to come once a week, in the afternoon, to do our ladies," the woman said. "The nursing home will be picking up the tab. I'm sure we can come to an arrangement to suit us all, if any of you are interested." She mentioned a fee sizable enough to cause Oralee's eyes to widen.

"I think we can arrange it," Dixie said, and Oralee said, "Yes, ma'am, we'll be there."

When the woman left, Charlene had to sit down a moment. She thought about the older women whose nails she had done at the nursing home that day, and how she had apparently managed to bring happiness to them by something that was easy for her to do. Something she enjoyed doing—most days—anyway. It thrilled her beyond measure, bringing tears to her eyes.

* * *

Oralee took over her last customer, saying, "You get on and get yourself up for your prospect."

"He isn't my prospect."

"What would you call him, then?"

"Well, not a prospect," Charlene said, finding the idea disconcerting as she hurried out the door to drive over to the IGA, where in her haste she turned too sharply into the parking lot and, with little notice, bumped up over the curb.

Dashing inside, she raced up and down the aisles like a driver in a road race. Then she headed home, dropped the grocery sacks on the kitchen counter, stuck the pork roast that was waiting in the refrigerator into the oven, checked the ice maker to be certain there would be enough ice, and hurried to shower. She put on fresh makeup, choosing night-time colors, and went to the closet for her chambray dress, old, but pretty and comfortable.

"He is not a prospect," she mumbled. He didn't have to be a prospect for her to want to look nice. She wanted to look nice for herself.

Just then her eye fell on an apricot-colored knit number she had not worn in several years because of added pounds. In a bold moment, she pulled it out and put it on, just to see how it looked, calling herself crazy.

But an astonishing image was reflected in the long mirror on the closet door. She turned this way and that, making certain what she saw was true from every angle. Amazed and thrilled, she put on earrings and a bracelet, quickly combed her hair and spritzed on Éstee Lauder, then hurried into the kitchen, where she switched on the television to CMT, hummed along with the music as she tied on an apron and set to work making supper, beginning with to-mato pudding.

Danny J. and Jojo came in from school. "What's goin' on?" Danny J. asked, frowning at her.

"Supper," she said. "I told you Mason was coming to have supper with us tonight."

"Yeah," he said, and slouched from the room.

Charlene paused, gazing at the empty doorway after him, wondering if there was anything she could say to him to make it better.

"I'll help, Mama," Jojo said, her expression that of peacemaker.

Charlene kissed the top of Jojo's head and told her to set the dining room table with grandma's tablecloth and the good dishes. Jojo surprised Charlene by questioning the wisdom of this move.

"Is Mason company or a friend?" she asked in the manner of one getting rules straight. "Is this a date or having a friend over?"

"Well...tonight he is both, I think. Use the good dishes."

Jojo went off to do her job, and Charlene turned the heat on beneath the fresh lima beans and started the sauce to put over the pork roast, humming happily with joy that really seemed foolish, but too precious to let pass.

Larry Joe came in. "Mom, did you wash my good jeans and blue plaid shirt? I have a date." Glancing around at her cooking efforts, he winced. "I forgot to tell you, I won't be here for supper."

"I know." Charlene, bending over the stove, tasted her sauce. "I did Pia's nails this afternoon."

"You did?" He looked a little uneasy.

"She's very pretty. And you should compliment her nails. She wanted to look pretty for you. Your pants and shirt are hanging in the laundry room."

He disappeared into the laundry room and came back out holding up his shirt and pants, tossed her a thanks and a kiss on the cheek, and hurried away to get himself ready.

Charlene checked to see how Jojo was doing in the dining room. Jojo had set two candles in crystal candlesticks on the table. "I thought it would be nice," she said matter-of-factly.

When his truck pulled up, she hurried to the door, then paused and composed herself. He was not a prospect.

She opened the door and found he had brought flowers, purple mums and white daisies and little irises and rosy carnations that smelled like spice, and the loveliest little silver box of chocolates. He had dressed for the occasion, too, in a crisp yellow shirt and sharply creased jeans and shiny snakeskin boots, and he looked a little nervous. Every bit of it touched the soft place in her heart, and she buried her face in the flowers for long seconds, thinking, He is not a prospect.

Then she put her arm through his and, rattling off the menu, escorted him eagerly through to the dining room, where she sat him at the head of the table. As if on cue, Jojo appeared with a glass of ice tea for him and sat down to entertain him, while Charlene went to the kitchen, where she hurriedly put the flowers into water and then got the roast out of the oven and set the rolls to browning. She was glad to do these familiar things. She kept telling herself that Mason had had supper with them before.

This time, however, was different. This time they were making it an occasion. This time it was a date, she thought, pausing to check herself in the glass cabinet door and make certain she did not have flour or something on her face.

"You look fine," Larry Joe said, coming up behind her and startling her.

She straightened his shirt that didn't need straightening and told him, her throat getting thick, that he was so handsome. Then, suddenly, she threw her arms around him in a fierce hug. Letting him go just as suddenly, turning away so he could not see her face, she said, "Have a good time."

"Mom...I've had dates before," he said, with a mixture of puzzlement and tenderness.

"I know." She waved him away, saying again, "Have a good time."

He bent over her shoulder and kissed her cheek and said he wouldn't be late; then was gone.

Why in the world she felt like crying, she couldn't say. It was her children changing, growing up, she thought, and herself, too. Just that day she had tried a sample of a new lipstick from a supplier and found that the shade, decidedly more sedate and decorous, suited her much better than her old favorite. And at sometime, without realizing, she had given up the frosty shades of fingernail polish for calm, deep and smooth colors. These changes felt right and a little disconcerting at the same time.

She let the heat of the oven blast her face as she removed the tomato pudding, thinking that would camouflage red eyes and blushing cheeks.

Then came Jojo's voice. "We'll help, Mama." And Mason stepped over to slice the roast, and Jojo began ferrying serving dishes out to the formal table.

While not so openly rude this time, Danny J. clearly was not pleased with Mason's presence. Refusing to look at anyone, he plopped himself in a chair, at the same time informing Charlene that he had arranged to go over to Curt Butler's house, where a few of the guys were gathering to watch rodeo on ESPN. "Curt's dad will come get me and bring me back home," he said, "so you won't be interrupted."

Charlene sucked in a breath. "All right," she said, refusing to scold him for not consulting her. "I will expect you home by eleven."

He flashed her a sharp look, but said nothing. He had barely eaten a few bites when a horn honked outside, and he threw his napkin down, racing out of the room as if making an escape, with Charlene calling after him, "Remember, eleven o'clock."

The door slammed before she finished. She looked at Mason, who slowly raised a piece of meat on a fork and said, "This is really good pork roast. Tell me how you make the sauce."

The rest of the meal was quiet and decidedly intimate, and Charlene felt a rare contentment as she listened to Mason tell Jojo stories of when he had been a roustabout in the oil fields.

After helping to clear the table, Jojo left Charlene and Mason doing the dishes together, shaking a mindful finger at them and saying, "I will be popping in here from time to time," causing Charlene to chuckle and Mason to shake his head in disbelief.

"How old is she?"

"Nine going on nineteen," Charlene said.

They finished the dishes and then sat for coffee at the kitchen table. Mason said he liked the kitchen table best, that he felt more at home in the kitchen. They drank the coffee and ate chocolates out of the silvery box, and talked quietly about everything and nothing, just sitting and looking at each other and not at all embarrassed about it. Charlene kept marveling at how Mason paid such close attention to her, to everything she said, every question she asked. She marveled at his easy laugh, and the way he made her laugh.

"Oh," she said at one point, "I have not laughed like this in a long time."

"You should," he said, looking intensely into her eyes. "You have a wonderful way of laughing."

They again looked long at each other, raising such a fluttering inside of Charlene that she jumped to her feet. "I should check on Jojo. She's been quiet for an awfully long time."

Jojo was asleep on the couch in front of the television. Charlene turned off the set and then scooped Jojo up and carried her to bed. When she straightened, she found Mason standing in the doorway, gazing at both of them with a bleak expression.

Silently she took his hand. It was warm and moist against her own as she led him back to the kitchen, where he said, "I really wish I'd had children."

Charlene wasn't certain what to say to that. There was a loneliness in his voice that cut to her core.

She poured more coffee. He didn't sit down, though, but went over and turned the sound up on the television. A soft country tune played out, and he pulled her into his arms, tenderly, seductively, and danced her around the room and over to the overhead light switch, which he flipped off so that they danced in the dim light from above the sink.

Around and around they went, to the song and then the next one, too, and all the while he gazed down at her the way every woman wishes the man in her life would look at her, as if she were the most beautiful and precious woman on this earth.

"Where in the world did you ever learn to dance like this?" she asked, amazed.

"You know that cook I told you I shared a cell with?"
She nodded.

"Well, he liked to dance." At her skeptical expression, he added, "True, I swear. He earned money givin' dance lessons, and I figured I should use my time wisely." He winked.

She chuckled and then pressed her cheek against his, felt

the hard muscles at the back of his neck and his belly moving against hers. She inhaled the seductive scent of him and said she found it so, and he said it was some cologne from the Wal-Mart. She threw back her head and laughed, and he whirled her around and around, and she clung to him, savoring the sweet passion stirring inside her.

The music stopped, and so did Mason. He kissed her, seeking her mouth softly with his own. Tasting the sweet-saltiness of him, she told herself to be careful, but then she was melting against him and kissing him and wanting him. When they broke apart, he held her carefully, tenderly, kissing her forehead and into her hair. She saw the pulse beating hard in his throat.

"Oh, Mason," she whispered, daring to raise her eyes to look at him. "You have the most beautiful eyes I have ever seen."

"That sounds like something I should say to you."

She grinned. "I said it first."

"Then I must get to say that you are the most beautiful woman I have ever seen."

"Now that sounds like some sort of line." She would have pushed him away, but he held her.

"Why?" He looked genuinely perplexed.

"Oh, I don't know." Uncomfortable, thinking of how Joey had left her, she shrugged. "I suppose because I am forty-six and things aren't exactly in the same place anymore and my heart feels a lot like it's been run over by a Mack truck."

"Well, ma'am, I imagine that is what attracts me," he said, with that way that made her warm all over. "I surely know that feeling."

The music changed to a faster tune, but Mason stayed with both arms around her, only swaying back and forth, his warmth seeping into her.

He said, running his gaze over her face, "What I see is a full woman. I don't have an eye for any little girl without experience. I want a woman with full capacity."

"Capacity?" She raised an eyebrow. "Sometimes I feel so dry, like the holes in my soul are so big that air just blows right on through."

He nodded. "It's the heart's way to survive. Just give yourself time. You'll get through it."

He swirled her around then, and dipped her backward, gazing into her eyes. "You ever heard the saying 'From now on is all that counts'?"

She shook her head.

"Well, it's like this," he said, straightening and whirling her around. "Everybody alive gets some dents and scratches along the road of life. That whole trip, though, is what makes us who we are. When I got out of prison, a guard told me to remember two things—that everything we go through makes us who we are, and that with each new day, it was from now on that counted."

"You are a rare man, Mr. MacCoy."

"I'm a rare, lucky man who's holdin' a beautiful woman," he said immediately and in a very seductive tone.

She laughed and danced around the room with him. "Right now, I do feel as if I have capacity," she dared to tell him.

He smiled and waltzed her around the room, then pinned her against the counter. "I think I should tell you something."

She propped her arms on his shoulders. Their warm bodies touched intimately, separated only by threads of clothing and discipline, while their thoughts ran wild every which way.

"What?" she asked.

"I've been in love with you since the first time I ever saw you."

She didn't know what to say. His expression was serious and anxious, studying her for a reaction.

"I came to deliver feed, and Joey was gone. You showed me where to put the feed. You were pregnant."

"With Jojo?" She gazed at his shadowy features with wonder.

He nodded. "Yes."

She stared at him, searching for the truth and knowing she had heard it.

Struck to the core, she pulled away from his embrace and raked a hand through her hair. "Oh, Mason."

"I wanted to tell you so you would know how I feel. That this isn't some passing attraction. I love you, and I want to marry you."

She raked her hand through her hair harder, growing angry. He reached for her, took hold of her wrist and turned her to face him. "Talk to me."

She had to find her voice and the words. "Mason, I am not even legally divorced," she said, pausing to try to sort out the feelings that roared around inside.

"Look, here's how it is." She shook her arm free of his grasp but faced him squarely. "I was married for twenty-one years. I'm just now beginning to find the pieces of myself that I immersed in Joey. I have a long way to go before I will be able to be in a partner relationship again. It wasn't a healthy relationship, and I'm not sure I know how to have a healthy relationship. I have to learn. Right now I'm simply not ready to deal with love, romance and sex. I may never be ready."

She spoke hard and fast and angry, and then they were staring at each other. He did not look perturbed at all, and this perplexed her, as she felt plenty perturbed and she thought he *ought* to.

Then there was noise at the back door, causing them both to jump and turn. The door flew inward, and Danny J. was there, bursting into the room, yelling in panic. "Mom...it's Blue. Call the vet! Call the vet now!"

"What is it, Danny J.? What's wrong with Blue?"

"He got into the grain. I forgot to tie the gate closed." His face was smeared with tears and his voice was cracking. "He's bad, Mom. Call the vet, *please.*"

She strode to the phone, and punched the number on the speed dial. Mason said, "Show me the horse, son."

The rings came across the line as Charlene watched Mason hurry out into the night after Danny J. The ringing went on. Normally Parker Lindsey's calls were automatically switched over to his home and mobile numbers. When an answering machine picked up, she left a quick message and hurried out to the barn.

The horse was in the pool of light on the ground at the entry, squirming, making a grunting noise. Danny J. was with him, kneeling, and the other three horses on the far side of the gate, securely fastened now, looked over the fence with avid interest. Charlene looked around for Mason and saw him in the barn, looking into the grain barrel.

"Parker's out," she told her son. "I had to leave a message."

"He'll die, and it's all my fault," Danny J. said in a broken voice. "I didn't fasten the gate with the bailing wire. He can open the gate unless I do that, and I forgot. I told Dad I'd look after him."

Charlene reached for him, but he jerked away from her.

Mason came then with a halter and lead rope. "Was the barrel plumb full?" he asked as he knelt to get the halter on the old gelding.

"I don't remember...I don't think so," Danny J. said angrily, watching Mason.

"He didn't have that much...he's just takin' on like some do. We got to get him up."

And with that Mason went to tugging on the lead rope and shouting, "Get up. Get up, you old sissy...get up!" and started kicking the horse in the hips. Charlene stared at him. "Hee-yaa...get up, you mangy old critter!"

Danny J. flew at Mason, and with the boy tugging on his arm and yelling at him that he couldn't treat his dad's horse like that, Mason kept kicking the horse and shouting at him to get up, while Charlene and Jojo stood there staring at both of them.

Then the gelding began to get to his feet.

Danny J. let go of Mason and stepped back. The horse got partway and acted as if he might lie back down again, but Mason didn't give him a chance, and now Danny J. joined in kicking and screaming at the horse to get up. The big old gelding got to his feet. Mason didn't give him a chance to go back down. He began to run and tugged the horse after him out into the dark yard. Over his shoulder, he hollered at Charlene to check in Joey's medicines. Charlene caught the word Bani-something. Danny J. raced off after Mason and the gelding, and Charlene ran into the tack room, jerked open the refrigerator.

There were several tubes of wormer. She found a clean needle and syringe, then went through the couple of vials. She thought she found what Mason had asked for and hurried out to where he was making the horse walk quickly around the yard.

"Is this it?"

Mason handed the lead rope to Danny J. and said for him to keep the horse moving. He peered at the label in

the silvery light from the pole lamp. "No...but it'll do."
And he began to load the syringe.

Danny J. came trotting past Mason with the horse, and
Mason quick as a wink injected the horse. "I don't think
he got enough of that grain to make him all that sick, but
some horses can fold at the least pain. Keep him up and
movin'," he said.

Parker Lindsey came and tended Blue with mineral oil
down a tube to his stomach. He said the same as Mason.
"This old fella just got a little uncomfortable, is all. I've
seen their sides so tight their stomach bursts." Then he
assured Danny J. that the gelding was too old to die young
and that it wouldn't be that night, in any case.

Leaving Danny J. in a corral with the gelding, Charlene
and Mason walked the veterinarian to his truck and waved
him off. Then Charlene walked Mason to his own pickup,
there in the dark beneath the stars.

"Thank you for saving the horse," Charlene said. "It
meant the world to Danny J. It's his father's horse."

"I gathered that."

He reached for her hand. While they spoke in low tones
about the events of the evening, they rubbed each other's
palms with their thumbs.

Then Mason said, "About what I told you earlier in the
kitchen..."

He gazed at her.

"Yes?"

"I wanted to tell you, so you would know where I stand.
That's all. I'm willing to wait for you as long as it takes.
I wanted you to know how I feel."

Before she could recover from that statement, he bent his
head and kissed her softly but fully, taking her breath.

When he lifted his head, she stared at him, unable to do anything else.

A movement came out of the darkness. It was Danny J. Charlene immediately let go of Mason's hand, even as she thought that her son must have witnessed the kiss.

"I wanted to tell you thanks," Danny J. said to Mason in a halting tone, "for savin' Blue."

"Glad to be able to help," Mason said.

Then he got into his truck and started the engine and began to back up.

Charlene hurried up beside the open driver's window and said in a low voice, "You are really a piece of work, Mr. MacCoy. I want you to know that I can't make you any promises, even if you are a hero. I'm not up to promising to a man. You may be waitin' till hell freezes over, if you wait for me."

"Yes, ma'am," he said, and drove away.

Thirty-Three

W hen Vella went outside at dawn, felt the air and saw the heavy dew all over everything, she had to go back inside for her gardening sweater. Her daughter, Belinda, who was up amazingly early—upset stomach, she said—reported that the paper called for an overnight low of fifty-eight. "High of seventy-two expected," she said.

All Vella could see of Belinda was her hands holding the newspaper and one fuzzy slipper. She went back out the door, wondering if Belinda were still talking to her.

Her feet left footprints in wet grass. Vella loved these fall mornings. Spring was nice, too, but she loved fall best. Surely now, with the cooler temperatures, her roses would bloom well for at least a month, and then she had that one garden rose that would bloom well after Thanksgiving. She surveyed each bush anxiously and was thrilled to find many new swelling buds. At last. This was as it should be.

Then she slipped her binoculars out of her pocket and looked up into the trees to see what birds she could find. She walked around, aiming the binoculars upward, until she'd reached the large lilac bush. Belinda could see the bush from the kitchen, but likely she wouldn't look out from her paper until coffee made her have to go to the bathroom.

Vella pushed her way into the lilac and sited the binoculars on Winston's rosebushes. She studied each one of his bushes in turn, all the way from back to front and then back again. Her bushes were picking up in production, but still, they could not seem to match the Valentine rose-bushes.

Just then the faint strains of "Dixie" reached her. She moved the binoculars to see Winston coming down his front steps with his flag. She checked over at the North-rupts', but there was no movement there. She had heard that Everett was in a depression about Winston's flagpole. She shifted the binoculars back to Winston and saw that he was not only attaching the Confederate flag, but another, too. When he pulled the rope, up went both the Confederate and United States flags.

She watched him get his newspaper, and, making up her mind quite suddenly, she slipped the binoculars into her pocket and started across the little meadow toward the Valentine house.

"Yoo-hoo, Winston!" She waved, not wanting him to get in his back door before she got there.

"I guess we're the only two around here who get up at sunrise," he said, taking her arm to help her through the fence on his side.

"Dixie..." she said, then had to stop and catch her breath, before saying that Dixie Love was awake and usu-ally doing yoga. She offered no more about that, since how she had seen Dixie clearly in her living room was with the binoculars.

She spoke of liking the cool weather and then asked if Winston had very much trouble with armadillos.

"A little," he said, and pointed at fresh holes. "They can be a nuisance."

Giving up working around to the subject, Vella said, "Your rosebushes bloom so heavily, even all through that awful heat, Winston. How did you keep them blooming so abundantly, when my bushes just seemed to hang on?'' She gestured, the words pouring out, now that she had started. "I've done everything I can find to do, but even now, my bushes don't match this. I tell you, I've done everything, watered, lit 'em up, fertilized. What do you do, Winston?''

He looked at her, blinking behind his glasses. "Well, I didn't do anything, Vella. I guess it was Coweta. You know how she was about roses.''

"Coweta?'' Vella said, somewhat taken aback. She looked at the rosebushes.

"Coweta had a green thumb,'' Winston was saying. "She would be out here talking to these plants, and singing and praying over them, and then she'd come in and we'd have coffee and talk about what was in the paper. And ever since she died, well, these bushes just seemed to keep bloomin' more and more. I think she still sings over them.''

Vella stared at him, realizing he had pretty much forgotten he was talking to her. Why…why, he's lonely, she thought, the knowing hitting her sharply. He was lonely just like she was, came the next thought.

"Winston,'' she said, "would you like to come have coffee with me? I don't mean this in a forward way.'' She lowered her eyes, fearing how she might have sounded. "I am a married woman…'' she gathered herself "…but I'd enjoy hearing you tell me what else Coweta did with the rosebushes.''

He was surprised for only an instant before he looked very pleased. "Well, now, that is a nice invitation. Thank you.''

They both went stiffly through the fence, across the little pasture and through the fence on the other side, where Winston suggested they have their coffee outside, so the neighbors would not start gossiping. Vella, remembering Belinda, quickly agreed. She was also thrilled that he thought anyone would gossip about her in that manner.

"Oh, Winston…I'm an old woman."

"Don't mean you aren't a woman," he said firmly. "And I am a man."

Blushing, she turned quickly, telling him over her shoulder to have a seat. As she went in the back door, she was shocked to realize that she was having what could be considered lusty thoughts.

They had their coffee while the sun came up, and each discovered the other had a keen mind and bent for conversation. Vella found it refreshing to talk to someone who paid attention to her and didn't listen with half a mind into the newspaper, as her husband always did, and to whom she did not have to explain things, as she had to do to Minnie and every other old woman she knew. Winston was delighted to find a woman who talked about subjects other than food and days gone by.

He said as much to her when he left forty-five minutes later.

Winston went down the hall, saying, "I'm comin', keep your pants on," to the incessant ringing of the doorbell.

He opened the door to find Everett Northrupt standing there, his sparse white hair standing on end, his eyes furious, and while he had on dark slacks, Winston was fairly certain the man was still wearing his pajama shirt.

"How dare you fly both the United States and Confederate flags together!" Northrupt said without preamble.

"Somebody has to fly the United States flag, since you quit," Winston responded, then added, "And they don't seem to mind flyin' together."

"Are you crazy?"

"No more than you."

"You cannot fly the United States below the Confederate flag. It is an insult to the flag of this country, and it is against the law."

"Then you better go to see Neville. And at least I am flyin' the flag, which is more than you are doing. Good day to you, sir."

With that, he flung the door closed in the man's face. Then he turned with a satisfied smile, thinking that he had succeeded in provoking Northrupt out of his bed. Life was good.

Charlene drove Danny J. to a bronc riding clinic at a ranch where a number of young bronc riders gathered to practice on fresh stock out in a small, sandy arena, where men and boys in big hats and dusty jeans sat atop the fence rails and yelled their enthusiasm.

She had gotten herself up in full makeup, slim jeans and a silky shirt with the top buttons undone, an experiment to discover men's reactions, and her own. She was quite gratified to note the interested glances of quite a few men. Some, there alone, boldly looked her over and smiled, and others, accompanied by wives, furtively slid their eyes to her, believing their wives did not notice, when surely they did, evidenced by the number of frowns Charlene received from the women.

Charlene, the only single woman in attendance, received gallant treatment, cold drinks put in her hand, space made at the rail for her, a lawn chair suddenly produced, and all the while she looked the men over, too, very discreetly, testing herself for reaction. She did not think that she should confine herself to Mason so quickly. She needed to sample before getting attached. The only problem being that there were so few eligible men in Valentine. This had been Rainey's problem, too. As Rainey said, "Well, if there are any good men, they are taken."

To her frustration, Charlene quite quickly found that none of the men there aroused her in the least. She tried to be aroused. Heaven knew several of the men were drop-dead handsome, most especially a man at least ten years younger than herself, who stayed by her side the entire time and made eyes at her. She regarded him boldly and tried to get her spirit to respond, yet nothing happened.

She thought perhaps a bucking bronc practice was not the place to try to drum up interest in a man, because she was distracted by worrying over Danny J. She had to hold on to the fence rail to keep from running out there each time he landed in the dirt.

When she returned home with Danny J., whose clothes were dirty enough to prove a detergent commercial but whose spirit was flying and body quite safe and sound, she went straight to the answering machine. The green light was blinking, three calls, and she pushed the button eagerly, her mind racing ahead to Mason.

But Mason had not called. The messages were not at all what she expected. The first one was Everett Northrupt's angry voice, which started off saying, "Winston has gone off his nut," and went on to tell her that her father was illegally flying the United States flag below the Confederate flag.

The second message was from Larry Joe, working at the Texaco, who sounded a little worried about the same subject. "A few customers are talkin' about it, Mom. Maybe you should go see Grandad and make sure he is okay."

And a third call was from some man Charlene did not know, and who did not identify himself but said in a low voice, "I think you should know your grandfather is a subversive."

The news that her father was upsetting people was a little disturbing, but she had trouble giving it her full attention. She was quite disappointed and annoyed with Mason for not calling. She felt that after telling her what he had the night before, he should have called.

Having left Danny J. and Jojo watching a movie for the short time she would be gone, Charlene enjoyed driving in the twilight by herself with a Don Williams tape playing out loudly. When she arrived at the big old house, she was a little dismayed to skim the poor lilac bush that she had half flattened before, but she told herself she was getting better all the time.

Her father was just taking down the flags. He handed her the United States flag to carry.

"I thought you could leave them up, since you had lights, Daddy."

"Weather report says there may be storms. I don't want to take a chance."

"And you like raising it every mornin', don't you?"

He shrugged.

"You feelin' all right, Daddy?"

"Fair to middlin'."

"What's this I hear that you're flyin' the Confederate Flag above the United States flag? I had three telephone calls about it."

He stepped into the foyer to lay the flags on the table there.

"Everett's in a snit, isn't he?" he said, coming back out, looking pleased.

"Him and a few others are in a snit, the way I'm hearin' it."

"Makes you wonder, doesn't it?" he said, sitting heavily in the porch rocker.

"What?" Charlene took the swing.

"About the quality of people's lives. They get so wrought up about the protocol of flyin' a flag, then they'll do all manner of other low-down, mean and rotten things. Do you know one of those sons-o'-a-buck who called to yell at me was that no-'count Ragsdale fella, who I know has cheated people, sellin' sick cattle. He's even bragged about it."

Charlene shook her head. The swing chains squeaked softly as she pushed her foot on the floor. Through the window came the glow from the living room and the murmur of the television. Her father said Mildred and Ruthanne were watching *Wheel of Fortune*. Charlene watched the lights coming on in houses across the street and down at the corner. She saw Dixie come out with her little dog, but she was too far away for Charlene to call to her.

"If people can take the flag and put it on their coats or drag it out in the street and burn it, I figure I can hang it south of the real flag," her father said.

"Daddy, you are a mess."

"People need to get shook up sometimes. I've had as many calls supporting me as yelling at me, you know."

"Really?"

"I put a notepad beside the phone to keep track. I thought I might write up a report for the paper."

Charlene thought her father was having a good time. He was a little tired, but he was okay. A least he was keeping busy.

Mason telephoned just as she was getting ready for bed. "How was your day?"

"Interesting," she said.

"Interesting?"

She could not say, I tried to be interested in other men, but all I could think of was you.

Curling herself into a ball, she said, "Blue is as good as if he'd never been sick."

"That's good," Mason said.

"And I took Danny J. to a bronc riding clinic. He did real good and returned all in one piece. And Daddy has upset people because he is flying the American flag below the Confederate flag."

Mason laughed, then said, "My day was pretty boring. I cleaned out old books all day."

And she said, "So tell me about the books you found."

They talked for thirty minutes about anything and everything that mattered to each of them. When Charlene hung up, she sighed and stretched and snuggled down in the bed. After several minutes, she pulled a pillow over to hug. She wondered about how she would handle sex.

The erotic pictures that came through her mind caused her to toss and turn for some time.

Thirty-Four

The cool of fall brought out the appearance of sweaters and sport coats at church services. Charlene wore her tall dress cowboy boots with a flowing skirt. Jojo wore tights under her dress. The talk was about the possibility of an early winter, while the roses and mums in everyone's gardens went into riotous blooming, and the wild sunflowers along the sides of the roads grew bigger than ever.

Charlene had just settled her family into the pew when Mason appeared, in a tan sport coat that made him look like a million dollars and slipped in beside her, laying his arm along the back of the pew behind her, in a companionable manner which she allowed.

A few minutes later, her father and Mildred and Ruthanne came to sit in their accustomed place in the pew directly behind, and whispers ran rampant around the sanctuary.

"Good mornin', Daddy."

"'Mornin', Daughter," he said, his head high and satisfied.

They stood for the first hymn, and Mason held a hymnal to share with her. She told him to hold it out farther so she could read the words. He laughed and then pulled reading glasses from his pocket, handing them to her. She took them in a good-natured manner.

Her gaze slid off the book and focused on his strong

hand holding it. The same hand that had caressed her. The same hand she longed to feel on her bare skin all over her body. Throughout the sermon, her mind repeatedly strayed to thoughts of the virile man sitting beside her, from his hands that drew her eyes to the sense of his strength there beside her, to imagining what his body looked like without clothes—all thick muscles of a man in his prime, a man who would make love the way a woman longs for, all tenderness and strength and thorough delight.

She thought that maybe she was assuming a great deal.

Crossing her legs and giving a sigh, she supposed God understood a woman's heart. When Mason's hand strayed down to her shoulder, she sat there, feeling the weight and warmth of it, and battling the longing. Thank heaven she was in church. It gave her an edge in the battle.

After the service, Neville caught Winston in the parking lot and said, "I've gotten several complaint calls about your flag-flyin', Mr. Valentine. I don't suppose you're gonna change those flags around, are you?"

"No, sir."

"That's what I thought," Neville said and went off with a great sigh.

Winston said, "Let's everyone go out for Sunday dinner. Larry Joe's here and can drive us up to Lawton. My treat."

Monday morning Mason took a box of Louis L'Amour books over to Neville at the sheriff's office. Everett Northrupt was already there.

"I'm makin' a formal complaint about Winston Valentine flyin' the U.S. of A.'s flag in an improper manner," Northrupt said with vehemence, and continued on in this vein for a few more minutes, ending with the flat demand, "I expect the law to do something about it."

"Just what is it that you expect me to do?" Neville asked, rearing back in his chair.

"Well, go over there and make the man do right."

"How? You want me to arrest him?"

Northrupt looked startled. "Well, no...unless you have to, to bring him to his senses."

Neville shook his head, then sat forward. "I appreciate what you are sayin', Mr. Northrupt, but we have never had this sort of situation around here, and frankly, I'm not exactly certain of my jurisdiction in this area. More to the point, I don't really care. There's no way in hell I'm goin' to go to Winston Valentine's house and tear his flags down, and I'm certainly not goin' to arrest the man, who I've known all my life, who has been an upstanding member of this community and who isn't hurtin' a dang soul. If you don't like seein' the flags, don't look."

Northrupt left in a huff, pushing around Mason, who was standing in the doorway with his box of books.

"He was a little upset," Mason said, coming into the room.

Neville looked exasperated. "I've had eight calls this weekend. Bunch of malarkey. Winston is an old man. Do you know he has medals from World War II? He saved a bunch of lives once, my dad told me. Seems as if he ought to be able to do what he wants in his own front yard. Whatcha' got?" He nodded at the box Mason carried.

Mason set the box on Neville's desk. "I've decided to clean out some, and I know you like these Louis L'Amour books. Got a few hardbacks...maybe a couple you haven't read yet."

Neville looked surprised. "You mean you are actually gettin' rid of books?"

"Well, the urge hit. My place has gotten to be a real messy bachelor house."

Neville raised an eyebrow, but Mason said he had to get on to work. He wasn't about to talk about the feelings pressing him to suddenly start cleaning out his house and make room for what, he wasn't quite certain.

Tuesday evening, seizing on what he thought was a good excuse to go over to Charlene's, Mason drove his Grandpap's old car over to show her what he and Larry Joe had accomplished.

"I have one more dent to fix, and then I'm gonna get it painted," Mason said, as they all walked out to look the car over.

Larry Joe got in and started the engine and revved the motor, listening to it, then hopping out and making adjustments in the engine, then getting back in and revving it again. Jojo climbed in beside him and ran her hands over the seat covers, which she said she liked. Danny J. stood there, off to one side, and said, "It'll be neat when you get it painted."

In an effort to continue in the right direction with everyone, Mason suggested driving everyone up to the Dairy Freeze for an ice-cream cone. Danny J. got in the back seat. He was quiet, but he was back there, and Mason was satisfied.

They went to the Dairy Freeze and had a good time, and then Mason stayed awhile with Charlene in the kitchen, taking every opportunity to touch her, inhale her scent and generally act very juvenile.

Before he left her that night, Mason dared to ask her for a date Friday night. "It's the final weekend for the Little Opry. I was wondering if you might want to go." The Little Opry always closed for the season the weekend before Halloween. "We won't stay out late. Maybe to eleven, if that would suit you."

He really expected her to say no and called himself a

fool for asking, and when she said, "Yes. That'd be fun," he wondered if he'd heard right.

"You will?"

She nodded. "I should be home early, like you said, though." He saw her already having second thoughts.

"Okay!" And he kissed her quickly before she could change her mind, then drove away whistling and feeling as spirited as a teenager.

Quite a few people went driving up and down Church Street to see Winston Valentine's flags that were causing so much fuss. A number of people stopped to take pictures. Kaye Upchurch was almost run over when she stood in the street to get a good shot.

Flags began appearing all over town. Some flew the Stars and Stripes and some the Stars and Bars, some flew both, and after Neville stuck the Oklahoma flag in his yard, saying, "That's the only damn flag that counts as far as I'm concerned," a lot of people followed suit.

Blaine's Drugstore put out a Rexall flag, and Grace Florist put out one with the FTD emblem on it, and Dixie Love produced a flag with a great big red heart on it that she fastened to the eave of the Cut and Curl. The *Valentine Voice* came out in an editorial and said they would hang both the American and Confederate flags, but in the correct order, the U.S.A. flag on top. Saying he was really siding with Winston, but thought he had to be patriotic, Jaydee Mayhall hung both the Confederate flag and the American flag, one on either side of the door to his law office. At the Texaco, Norm Stidham had Larry Joe and Randy got up on the roof and stuck flags all along the front of the portico—a Texaco flag, the American flag, the Confederate flag, the Oklahoma flag, and a flag bearing the Stidham coat of arms.

The mayor, Walter Upchurch, got a flag made with the city seal on it and had it hung off the city hall building, then went around asking people if they thought it was a good idea to begin presenting their town as the flag town of the U.S.A. "It's a darn sight more personable than a digital thermometer."

Early Wednesday morning a crew showed up at Northrupt's house to put in a flagpole. Winston and Vella saw it all from her side yard, where they were enjoying coffee. Vella, to Winston's surprise, whipped a pair of binoculars out of her apron pocket. "The van says T&S Flagpoles," she said and handed him the binoculars.

Winston took a look through the binoculars and said, "Why, those are the two guys from Goode Plumbing who put in my flagpole." Another minute and he said, "Let's go down and have a close-up look."

Northrupt appeared to ignore them, so Winston followed suit and went to talking to the workmen, finding out that the flagpole was only going to be fifteen feet in the air.

"I want people to see my flag," Northrupt said, finally jumping into the conversation. "People have to crane their necks up to see yours, but mine's gonna be right here near the road, where people can see at first glance."

"You know, Mr. Valentine," one of the workers said to him when they stood to the side, "you really started something with this flagpole business. We've been called all over town, so we thought we might as well leave the plumbing for a bit and ride this wave of opportunity. We can always go back to stopped-up sewer lines."

About that time Minnie Oakes came driving by and showed them all the picture of Winston's flags that was running in the Lawton newspaper that day.

Thirty-Five

"I'm going out with Mason tonight to the Little Opry," Charlene said at breakfast.

Three pairs of eyes looked her over. Larry Joe's eyes grinned at her, Danny J.'s skittered away, and Jojo's stared levelly at her.

"Larry Joe, could you stay home with your brother and sister?"

He nodded. "Sure."

"I ain't no kid," Danny J. said. "I don't need no baby-sitter."

"No, you don't. You need English lessons."

Danny J. made a bland face, then he sort of grinned. A grin that said he might be hesitant, but he thought it was all okay.

Charlene lifted her coffee cup and thought for a minute. "Look, it's me that needs reassuring. I know you don't need a sitter, and Jojo really doesn't, either. But she is too young to be left in case an emergency should happen. I couldn't enjoy myself if I was worryin' about you and Jojo."

"Then don't go," Danny J. said, again with that grin.

"Aw, I'll take you both up to Lawton for a movie," Larry Joe told his brother and sister. "Maybe I'll even let you drive, kid." He punched Danny J. lightly as he rose.

"Larry Joe?" Charlene said, alarmed. Her eldest simply gave her his warmest grin and kissed her cheek as he left.

Danny J. got up and quickly followed his brother, while Charlene called after them, "Don't you let him drive, Larry Joe."

Jojo said, "It's okay, Mama. Larry Joe has taken him out on the dirt roads and let him drive a bunch of times. He does just fine." She calmly jellied her toast and took a bite.

"How do you know?" Charlene wanted to know. "Have you been with them?"

Jojo realized she had let more out of the bag than she'd wished. "Only once. He did good, too." She put down her toast and went to get her schoolbooks.

Charlene sighed. Did a mother have any control, or was it all illusion?

Dixie squeezed in time to do Charlene's hair, and Oralee gave her a facial and an eyebrow waxing. Charlene did her own nails in between customers, painting them with Autumn Passion, all the while having thoughts of a passionate nature.

She could not go to bed with Mason MacCoy, she told herself firmly. For one thing, there would not be time; she had said she would be home by eleven.

There were a lot of hours before eleven, she thought.

She had children to think of. What was hidden eventually came to light, especially in a small town. Larry Joe was old enough to understand about the nature of things between an adult man and woman, but Danny J. and Jojo were not. All they would see was that their mother had been with a man who was not her husband or their father. No telling what this would lead them to.

Yet she was a woman of flesh and blood. She had needs, just as her children did.

"What are you wearin' tonight?" Oralee wanted to know, sitting down and propping up her feet during a lull in customers.

"I don't know. I'd like to wear my floral sundress that shows what I should have and hides what I shouldn't have, but it really is for summer."

"It gets warm in the Opry with all the dancing," Dixie said, passing them with an armload of fresh towels. "You could wear something over the dress and then be able to take it off."

Later, Dixie ran home and brought back a little white cardigan that would go perfectly with Charlene's dress.

Mason telephoned at noon in an overwhelming moment of needing contact with her. "I'm goin' to get a haircut for tonight," he told her, feeling silly. "Just thought you'd like to know you'd be goin' out with a properly groomed man tonight." He could have kicked himself. Why couldn't he say suave things?

She laughed, though, and his heart expanded. "I got my hair done today, so I guess you'll be going with a properly groomed woman."

Mason, sufficiently boosted, said, "I'll be going with a beautiful woman. I'll pick you up at six. We can get a hamburger before the Opry."

"You know how to sweep a girl off her feet." Her voice was decidedly sensual, causing his mind to run rampant and his heartbeat to pick up tempo.

"You don't know anything yet," he told her. He hung up, then went to whistling as he picked up the stack of invoices waiting for him, until Iris, coming out of Adam's office, said, "My gosh, you sound like a man in love."

She regarded him with wide eyes, and he said, "Yep,"

and left her standing with her curiosity, while he walked away, his mind filled with lusty thoughts of the woman he loved.

Winston was sitting on the porch smoking one of his daily allowed cigarettes when a dark green Buick pulled up in his driveway. Two women got out and came up to the porch. They were of the same size and shape, one in a brown sport coat and skirt and the other in black. The woman in black looked long at his flags flying, and when she turned her gaze to him, she looked at the cigarette clamped between his fingers with a deep frown, while the woman in brown asked, "Are you Mr. Winston Valentine?"

"I'm him, if that's who you're lookin' for."

The woman smiled a thin smile and nodded. "Yes, we are. We'd like to come in and talk to you a bit, if you don't mind."

There was something about the two women that caused him to sit up and look them over closer, just as the woman added, "We're from the State Department of Human Services, and we'd like to visit with you about your situation here."

The woman in black was looking up at his flags again, and then she looked at him.

Winston said, "I don't think I have a situation."

"You do have a..." the woman checked a notebook from her purse "...Ruthanne Bell living here in your care, don't you?"

"Yes, if it's any business of yours." He stabbed out his cigarette in the flowerpot filled with sand.

"It is our business, Mr. Valentine. We'd like to visit with you and Mrs. Bell for a bit."

Winston felt a niggle of fear. "It is *Miss* Bell, and she

has been layin' down for a nap, like she does whenever we get back from lunch down at the Senior Center.'' He rose then, thinking he had best put forward a good foot. ''We can see if she's gotten up yet.''

As he led them inside, it jumped into his mind that they might think he was some sort of pervert or molester. He'd made a few joking cracks about the women being after him, which Mildred and a few from down at the Senior Center were, but nothing beyond normal women finding a live man their own age who could actually walk and hear.

''Who made the complaint against me?'' he asked.

''This is just routine checking, Mr. Valentine,'' the woman in brown said.

Her eyes were running rapidly over everything. They stopped dead when they came to Mildred, who had risen from where she'd been watching her afternoon soap on television and eating jelly beans. Her lips were black; she liked the black jelly beans best.

Mildred was thrilled to greet the women, pressing her hands together and saying, ''Oh, my golly, company!'' as if she never had any, and proceeded to invite the women in for ice tea, saying that Winston would get it because she couldn't, since she had to use a cane. When Winston explained who the women were and that they'd come to see Ruthanne, Mildred said, ''Oh,'' and seemed to fall dumb, which at any other time might have been a blessing but now left Winston annoyed at feeling deserted. He needed support.

There didn't seem to be anything else for him to do but to go up and wake Ruthanne. These women were not about to leave until they had seen her.

The woman in brown startled him by saying, ''I'll go with you,'' and followed him up the stairs.

As she obviously wanted to see everything, Winston

pointed out the rooms. "That's the bathroom for the ladies. I have my own. That's Mildred's room, and that's mine, and that's the guest room, and that is just a little sittin' room. We usually have a cleaning lady once a week, but she went down to Mexico to see her family for a month."

The door to Ruthanne's room was open. She lay atop the spread, fully clothed, thank heaven, sleeping like an angel. She came awake when he touched her shoulder. "Hello, Winston. Is it morning?"

Winston went out on the porch with the two women, shutting the door behind them. "I would like to know who made a complaint against me," he said, his anger having reached a high point.

The woman in brown looked at him a moment, then said, "We aren't authorized to discuss any of our sources." Apparently the woman in black had come as a second pair of eyes. She had yet to say a word.

"Well, you see Ruthanne is okay here. She doesn't want to go anywhere else. She told you herself."

"Mr. Valentine, I can tell you that I am satisfied that your relationship with Miss Bell is truly in a friendly manner. But you are an elderly man." She paused, staring at him as if to make certain he comprehended. "Miss Bell needs more care than she can get here."

"What more does she need? She is content here. I make certain she eats and has clean clothes and a good time, and we get her to her doctor appointments. Have you talked to him? He knows how she is, and he's the one that has told us to keep her in familiar surroundings and her confusion will stay at a minimum."

"We will be speaking with him," the woman in brown said, then added, "I know you mean well, Mr. Valentine, but really, Miss Bell is a great responsibility."

"I don't find her a responsibility. I find her a friend. When she came here the past spring, after bein' dumped on neighbors by her nephew, she would hardly talk and couldn't remember what time of day it was. Maybe she still don't chatter, but she smiles, and mostly she knows what house she's in. This has become her home, and if you so-called experts come in and jerk her out of here, you're goin' to take from her what mind and peace she has left."

"We sometimes have to do hard things for the best for all involved," the woman said with irritating detachment, not even looking at him. "We'll get in touch with you when we've made arrangements."

"You can make arrangements until hell freezes over," he said. "The only way you'll take her out of here is over my dead body."

The woman said something in response, but he didn't hear her, because he went in the house and slammed the door.

He went into the living room for a minute, where he exchanged worried glances with Mildred but tried to control his anger. Ruthanne got upset if anyone around her got angry.

"Think I'll go for a walk," he said and headed for the stairs, to go to his room and put on his walking shoes. He had just put his hand on the newel post when a dizziness struck him. He felt himself sinking, and then blackness closed in.

It was Everett Northrupt who saw Mildred come running out of the house like only a chubby crazy woman with a cane can, screaming for help. He rushed over and gathered from Mildred's ravings that it was Winston, and even as he went to find the man collapsed at the bottom of the steps, with Ruthanne patting him and telling him everything was going to be okay, Everett was commanding Doris, who had followed him, thank goodness, "Nine-one-one. Call 911!"

Winston appeared to be breathing, if shallowly, and his heart was beating, if weakly. "Well, buddy," Everett said helplessly, while Ruthanne kept patting him.

The emergency squad came and took Winston off in a wail of sirens, and by then Doris holding both Ruthanne's and Mildred's hands, with Mildred the one seeming to come totally undone. Everett read Charlene's number posted next to the phone and dialed.

Charlene was just out of a relaxing soaking bath and wrapped in a soft robe and beginning to paint her toenails, which she had neglected, when Jojo spoke in a tight voice through the bathroom door. "Mama, Mr. Northrupt's on the phone, and he says he has to talk to you now."

"Ohmygod, not again," Charlene said, knowing it was her father and at the same time praying it wasn't and for strength to endure.

Everett Northrupt's clipped accent said, "It's your daddy. They've already got him goin' up to the hospital. He ain't dead yet," he thought to add firmly.

Thirty-Six

Charlene sat alone in the emergency waiting room. That she sat there in her sundress was something she would never forget. The dress had been lying out on the bed, and she had jerked it on as the first thing she saw. In the same manner, she had also stuffed her feet into her open-toed sandals, so now she stared down at three painted toenails and seven bare. It made her feel as if her eyes were out of focus.

It seemed as if her dress and her toenails revealed how askew she was inside and how her entire life seemed to go. Just when she thought she got a handle on it, she would find herself hitting a pitted road and be bounced all over.

Only an hour ago she had been anticipating dancing in Mason's arms, anticipating his chest brushing her breasts and his lips enticing passion on her bare neck in a hot embrace out back in the alleyway like lovers often did. She had been worried about letting herself get carried away and making love with him.

She had been worried for nothing, she thought with a sigh.

Lifting her head, she saw the small television in the corner flicker in black and white. It was *Father Knows Best* coming on. She looked for the remote to turn up the sound, but she couldn't see it anywhere. A nurse passed the window to the hall, and Charlene watched her expectantly to see if she would come in the door, but the woman continued on.

The clock on the wall said six-twenty. She could almost hear it ticking, there alone in the room.

Larry Joe would explain to Mason. And here she was, missing out on the Little Opry again.

She was instantly ashamed of the thought. *Oh, I really didn't mean it like that, Lord. I am just so scared.* How was she going to do it? How was she going to take care of her father and Mildred and Ruthanne and her children? What would happen to her now? How was she going to do it all?

"Charlene."

She turned to see Mason coming through the door. She stared at him. He opened his arms, and she went to him and laid her head on his chest, which was bigger and stronger than she had ever realized.

"They think it's a stroke," she said, when she could speak. Getting hold of her good sense, she pushed away from him and grabbed a tissue from the box someone had thoughtfully set on the table and blew her nose. She did not intend to do something as silly as to cry in front of Mason. "They still don't know a lot yet. It's only been about an hour," she added, to encourage herself.

"You're cold. Have you had anything? Coffee, Coke?" he asked, looking her over.

She shook her head, and he went straight to the little coffeemaker and got her a cup, brought it back and sat close to her, holding her free hand. She gripped his hand, despite not wanting to need him.

Then suddenly there was Everett Northrup. "Don't worry. Doris is with Mildred and Ruthanne," he said immediately. "She's fixin' them supper, and she'll stay the night with them. I just thought I'd come up and sit with you a bit and see how Winston is doin'. I hear he isn't dead yet.''

That made Charlene smile. ''No, he isn't.''

Then here came Vella Blaine, her purse strap tight on her arm. She pressed Charlene's hand, then sat herself in a chair. Another ten minutes and Dixie and Oralee showed up. Mary Lynn Macomb telephoned and said she had told Larry Joe she was there if he needed her. And then here came Lila Hicks, in full blue eye shadow, saying, ''Pastor Weeks is at another hospital. He sent me over here to bring comfort, so I brought chicken salad sandwiches from the cafe.'' Dixie and Oralee went out and returned with fountain soft drinks and ice tea and a sweater for Charlene. Oralee sat down to paint Charlene's toenails. ''Heaven knows you don't need the distraction of half-painted toenails,'' she said with perfect understanding.

Charlene looked around at all these people, and then clutched Mason's hand tight. ''Thank you for being here,'' she said.

Mason drew her head down onto his shoulder, and she let herself go there, for just a few minutes.

''Hi, Daddy.'' She laid a hand on his arm and fought down the panic that tried to choke her at the sight of him with tubes in his nose and in his arm and the beeping of the machine. She wished powerfully for Rainey, and then made herself straighten up.

He gazed at her with a bit of confusion, and then his pale eyes moved anxiously, and his mouth worked, noise but not words coming out, while his arms tried to move, too, as if to get up. Charlene pressed his shoulder.

''Just lie here, Daddy. You have to lie here right now. You know you're in the hospital. The doctor talked to you.''

To her relief he settled, but his eyes were so filled with anguish she felt like crying.

"You've had a stroke, Daddy, but the doctor said it is going to be okay. That you will get better." *What did better mean here, anyway?* "You will be out of here soon. You're under medication, that's all. You're supposed to rest. Don't worry about Mildred and Ruthanne. Doris Northrupt is over there with them. They are fine. There, that's what you were worrying about, isn't it. Well, you don't need to. We're goin' to take care of them until you get out of here. Oh, Daddy, I love you."

She laid her head down then, her cheek on his hand, and she felt him move his hand against her. Every bit of hurt from her childhood faded away.

At dawn, Everett Northrupt went out and put his new flag on his flagpole for the first time. He pulled the cord, raising up an enormous American Stars and Stripes, with a very small Confederate Stars and Bars below it that he had bought at the all-night Wal-Mart on his way home from the hospital.

He gave a sharp salute to the flags, and then he went across the street, got his neighbor's flags and lifted them up on his neighbor's flagpole. Standing at attention, he gave a sharp salute to the Confederate flag flying high, although he was squinting with one eye.

"Look after that old fruitcake, Lord."

In honor of Winston Valentine, Perry Blaine went out and stuck a Confederate flag in his front yard, Jaydee Mayhall took in his American flag and left the Confederate fluttering. Oralee stuck a Confederate flag on her car antenna, despite her brother having something like a seizure over it, and the secretary at the *Valentine Voice*, who had begun waving at Charlene through the window, stuck a small Confederate flag on her desk.

The sun was streaming in the kitchen windows. Charlene, bleary-eyed and sipping strong coffee, worked up enough energy to dial Rainey's number.

"I'm comin' down," Rainey said at once.

"No, you aren't. You know you can't. Do you want to risk that baby?"

After a silent moment, Rainey said, "Oh, Charlene, you're all alone."

"No, I'm not. I have you on the phone, and I have the kids, and good friends and neighbors. And I have God with me, Rainey. There isn't anything you can do for Daddy right now, honey. But take care of his grandbaby. Oh, and call Freddy for me, okay? We ought to tell him, even if he can't be any help."

Silence hummed between them on the line. And then Rainey said, "I'm sending Harry down there to make sure the doctors know what they're doin'."

Rainey had a tendency to send Harry here and there.

Larry Joe had to work, so Charlene was forced to rely on Mason to stay with Danny J. and Jojo and to take them around to where they wanted to go on Saturday, while Charlene checked on Ruthanne and Mildred, bought groceries for both houses, took Mildred to the hospital, leaving Vella to stay with Ruthanne, consulted with the doctor and visited with her father, who had some moments of wakefulness and was able to say a recognizable "Daughter."

Harry did indeed show up, wearing new glasses that made him look more than ever like a stockbroker. With his customary tender but commanding manner, he looked over his father-in-law and then took himself off to talk to the doctor. He returned a half hour later to assure Charlene that her father was in good hands. Before leaving, he gave her his cellular phone. "You use this to call Rainey regularly from here, or she is going to have a hissy fit," he said. He had from the beginning taken careful care of Rainey.

Charlene looked into her father's room and saw Mildred sitting there, holding his hand. "Can I stay awhile?" Mildred asked, her face a mass of tears.

Struck to the core, Charlene said, "Of course you can, Mildred. You stay as long as you like." As she drove home through the late afternoon golden sun, she kept picturing the older woman beside her father's bed. It made her cry tears she did not understand, tears both happy and sad. She thought of her mother in a similar bed in a similar room, and her father sitting there beside her, his face awash with tears. Was that what life came down to—old hands holding on atop a white hospital sheet?

When she walked into her kitchen, there stood Mason wearing a dish towel apron. "I made you tomato pudding," he said, showing her the bowl. "It may be a little burnt."

She instantly told him she liked it that way, and she ate a big helping.

Mason drove her back to the hospital to see her father and to get Mildred, who had begun to show amazing strength. On the drive home, Mildred said, "Oh, yes, I should tell you about the women from the state. They want to take Ruthanne away and put her in some nursing home."

Charlene let Mason ask the questions. She was not up to it. She was still seeing hands holding on atop the white sheets.

During the following days Charlene ran a course from her house to her father's to the hospital. Her mind filled with worries of the days and weeks ahead, she ceased to worry about running over things when she turned into drives. She was trying to hold up the world, and with such a responsibility, she began to drive as if everything and everyone had better get out of her way.

Vella amazed Charlene by working with Lila Hicks and organizing a squad of ladies from the church to take turns staying with Ruthanne and Mildred. Charlene juggled Danny J. and Jojo around between letting them stay by themselves for short periods, or with Larry Joe or, when she absolutely had to, with Mason, who seemed to spend way too much of his time at Charlene's, watching Danny J. and Jojo and cooking and cleaning.

Monday evening, Charlene came in from the hospital to the most surprising sight of Iris MacCoy, an apron over her formfitting little mini-dress, in Charlene's kitchen helping both Danny J. and Jojo at the table with their homework, while Larry Joe did the dishes.

"Mason asked me to come over. He has some problem down at the feed store." She pushed hair out of her face and looked shy and sexy at the same time. "I told him I'd see what I could do with supper and homework."

"She can sure do algebra, Mom," Danny J. said.

"I always helped my daughter, Ellie, when she was in school," Iris said shyly, again pushing at her hair. Then, "Oh, here..." and she pulled a plate of food out of the oven. "Come on and have some supper, Charlene. Mason cooked this before he left. I can't cook worth beans. Y'all move your books now and give your mama some room. There."

Charlene slowly sat at the table. Iris brought her silverware and coffee, and Charlene ate, running her gaze from the amazing sight of her son at the sink doing the dishes to the equally amazing sight of the sexy woman in platform heels, patiently and expertly helping her younger children with their homework, while her eldest kept giving her glances from behind. Charlene thought that people never were quite what they seemed, and it didn't pay to make hasty judgments.

She thought this again as she sipped the coffee and discovered it was the best coffee she had ever had in her life.

They were propped up on pillows in Charlene's bed, and Charlene was reading *Misty of Chincoteague* to Jojo, when the telephone rang. It was Mason.

"What are you doing?" he said.

Charlene found the question vaguely silly for almost ten o'clock at night. "Jojo and I are reading in bed," she told him, feeling annoyed at the interruption, then guilty for feeling annoyed, so she added quickly, "Thank you for sending Iris over. She got the children fed and helped them with their homework."

"Despite appearances, she's really smart. She was going to be a teacher once," he said.

For some reason that made Charlene feel dumb. She didn't say anything.

He said, "I asked her to come over when I got the call about the feed mixer. We have to get out a pretty big order tomorrow. She was glad to do it. She loves kids."

"Yes. She seems to." Charlene thought of Larry Joe. She felt a stab of inadequacy in caring for her own children.

"How's your father?"

"He's okay." She suddenly felt very overwhelmed. "I'm really tired, Mason, and Jojo's waiting for me to read. I'll have to talk to you tomorrow."

"Oh, yeah. Sure. Good night."

"Good night."

She was too tired and pulled in too many directions, she thought, picking up reading where she had left off. She automatically read the words on the page, while thinking that she had no energy left for a relationship with a man.

Mason telephoned her at the shop the following morning. She laid her customer's hand on the cloth and excused herself a moment.

"I thought maybe I could take you to lunch," he said.

His chipper voice annoyed her.

"I don't have time for lunch," she said. "I have to go over to get Mildred and Ruthanne and take them to the Senior Center for lunch." She didn't know what she was going to do about the two older women. Every time she thought of them, she felt a growing panic. "Odessa Collier will bring them home, but I have to take them."

"Want me to drive them for you?"

"No. I can do it. I have to check the house, anyway, get whatever groceries they need. Vella has a list."

"I can do that for you."

"No, I have to do it, to get the right brands and stuff." She did not understand why she felt so annoyed with him. "Thank you anyway. I have to get back to my customer now."

"Okay. I'll come by tonight."

"Well, we won't be home. I'm takin' the kids up to the hospital with me, and then we can go by the Wal-Mart and get some school supplies they need."

"When can I see you?" he asked, his voice serious.

"I don't know, Mason. Right now I just don't have time to know anything."

And she sure thought he should know that.

From down the hall, she saw the doctor coming out of her father's room. She hurried to catch him and get a report. He assured her that although it didn't seem like it, in another day or so she would see definite improvement in her father's condition. He was calling in a therapist to begin with her father tomorrow.

"I believe he will regain sufficient speech capability and will eventually get around quite well using only a cane. Right now it looks like he'll be transferring to the nursing home at the first of next week, so he'll be closer to home."

"The nursing home?" she said, tightening her hands in the pockets of her smock that she had not removed.

He nodded. "Yes. He can get the necessary therapy there. If all goes well, he will be home again within two months." He touched her arm and then hurried away to other patients and life and death.

Charlene turned and walked down the hall and out the doors into the sunshine, the doctor's words, "…two months," echoing in her mind.

Two months of trying to take care of Ruthanne and Mildred and see to her father, too. Two months of splitting herself in a half-dozen ways. Two months of being a daughter and caretaker, a mother and provider. What would happen to the woman she had begun to find inside? The woman who had just begun to grow? There did not seem to be any time or space or energy left for her.

She had slipped behind the wheel of the Suburban before she realized that she had not visited her father. She laid her head down on the steering wheel and cried. After a full ten minutes of tears, she blew her nose, jerked the mirror around and repaired her face, then went back in to smile at her father and tell him that the doctor was positive that he would recover and that she was so glad to have him. She held his hand as she told him this, and she sat there a few minutes, wondering just who was holding on to whom.

Thirty-Seven

When did everyone get so all-fired set on coming to MacCoy's to get grain and seed and cattle feed and pet food? Mason couldn't get a break from filling orders to call Charlene until just before lunch. He paced as he dialed on the warehouse wall phone.

He didn't want to think it, but had it begun to appear as if Charlene wouldn't return his phone calls.

Dang, he'd called her house by mistake and gotten her answering machine. Of course she wouldn't be home. He hung up and dialed the beauty shop. At least there he did not get an answering machine.

"Umm...I'm sorry, Mason," Dixie said, "but you've just missed her. She's on her way to see her father. Just gone out the door."

"Well, please tell her that I called...and to call me back. I'll be at the warehouse until five today."

"I will, Mason," Dixie assured him in her calm, graceful voice.

He hung up and stood there a minute with his hand on the receiver, while disappointment washed over him.

Hearing footsteps and catching sight of his brother coming through the side door, he let go of the phone and moved to his desk, getting ready for whatever concern his brother was fixing to throw at him.

"I want to talk to you about your part of Grandpap's place," Adam said.

Mason raised an eyebrow.

"Look, that fella that was out there the other week, he's makin' a huge offer, but he wants the entire section, not just my part of it. He wants the creek. It's a good deal, Mace. It'll set you up for life."

"I am set for life," Mason said.

"Aw, geez, there is no talkin' to you," Adam said and turned to storm off.

"Wait," Mason said.

Frowning, Adam looked over his shoulder. "Wait for what? For you to send me to the poorhouse?"

"Look." Mason considered with a great deal of hesitancy, knowing how he and Adam had never gotten along. "I have an idea about the land, if you want to hear it."

Adam looked skeptical, but then curiosity edged in. "So?" He came slowly toward Mason.

"If I throw in with you, we could sell all but twenty acres to your big developer. Would he go for that? We could give him control of the creek and keep the front part where my house sits next to your pasture at the road."

Adam folded his arms. "Why keep that? I know he isn't gonna want to build his fancy houses and have your dump sittin' there at the front."

"We'll take the money we get from the sale of the land and build a senior living complex up front."

"You want to build a nursin' home?" Adam looked disgusted. "Valentine already has one of those."

"Not a nursing home. A real nice living complex, duplexes, with places for gardens, and pets allowed. Walking pathways…one of those arboretums, maybe. There can be a section for assisted living and a section for those people who are really active. Swimming pool and hot tubs…fancy, but not so fancy it can't be affordable." He stopped, watching his brother's face.

"You know why those cost so much? Because a place like that costs a lot to build."

"We could do it. We could plan it affordable, not luxurious. We'd still make money," he added, although Adam's expression was not one to give hope.

"Why do you always have to make things so difficult?" Adam said and walked away.

"It's an idea that could make money long-term," Mason called after him in a voice so tight with anger that it surprised him.

It surprised Adam, too, because he stopped and looked at Mason for a long minute, before continuing on back to the store.

Mason thought with frustration that this was the first idea he had ever shared with his brother, and it went to show why he had never shared before.

His afternoon was as busy as his morning, but he kept glancing at the phone, hoping for Charlene to call. When she did not, he called one of the boys from back at the elevator to come stand in for him, and he went over to the Cut and Curl. He wouldn't give her a chance to avoid him.

But the manicurist table was empty.

"Charlene and Oralee went over to the nursing home to do some ladies," Dixie told him.

He had Neville pull over to the pay phone at the IGA for his third call to her house that evening. He got only her answering machine. He opened the door of the pay phone, shutting off the glaring light above, and stood for a minute looking at the last pale light of a golden setting sun. He thought of having Neville drive him over there and leave him to wait on her front porch, but he couldn't do it. He thought, *If she doesn't want to talk to me, I'm not going to push it. I'm not being stubborn, Lord. She is.*

Charlene listened to the answering machine click, no one speaking. She knew it had been Mason. She went into the kitchen and got a glass of ice tea. She stood there with the glass in hand and gazed out at the setting sun. She wanted to call him, but she could not. She thought, *I can't, Lord. What will I say to him? I can't need him. I can't need anyone ever again.*

Mason was stopped at the light on Main Street when Charlene's faded Suburban passed across in front of him, going so fast that the truck sort of went airborne for a second. The light turned green, and Mason whipped his truck around the corner, as fast as a one-ton flatbed delivery truck stacked with grain sacks can be whipped, and followed her up Church Street, to her father's house. Her speed amazed him. She took out a lilac bush as she pulled into the Valentine driveway beside a dark green sedan.

He pulled up at the front of the yard and got out. She stopped on the steps and looked at him. "I'm busy right now, Mason. I'm sorry but I can't talk to you."

"So I see," he said, striding across the yard.

She was at the door when he reached the stairs. She looked at him as if he had lost his mind. Then she said in a lowered voice, "It's those women from the state human services department that Mildred was telling us about. I have to see what I can do about keeping Ruthanne."

She opened the door. He went in right on her heels. She cast him an impatient frown but kept on going.

Vella strode out of the living room toward them so fast the hem of her dress flew out behind her. "I've held the floor until you got here," she told Charlene in a righteous whisper.

To Charlene's quick, whispered questions, Vella replied, "Ruthanne's hiding in her room. She is terrified. I have tried to tell this to these women, but they…" She cast Mason a surprised look. "Hello, Mason."

Charlene continued on into the living room, where Mildred sat gripping her cane, and two official-looking women stood in front of the sofa. "Hello, Mrs. Darnell. I'm Pamela Browne, and this is my colleague, Louise Tallman."

Charlene shook the women's hands. Mason saw immediately which woman was the one in charge; he had the impression of a small but implacable rod of steel. No one volunteered to introduce him, and he stayed in the background. The rod of steel spared him one glance and then seemed to dismiss him as she explained her mission to Charlene, which basically was to take Ruthanne, as a ward of the state, out of the care of an elderly gentleman who had been showing signs of mental deterioration and was now incapacitated. "I'm sorry about your father, Mrs. Darnell. I didn't know about his illness, or I would have made a point of coming earlier in the week." There was a vague accusation in the condolence. "We have a place for Ms. Bell in a state-monitored home."

Charlene said, "Shall we sit down?" causing Ms. Browne's eyes to jump.

The women sat. Mason remained leaning against the entryway jamb.

"When you speak of removing Ruthanne to a home, do you mean a nursing home?" Charlene asked.

"Well, yes," Mrs. Browne said. "Ms. Bell will have care there."

"Ruthanne isn't sick," Charlene said, emphasizing *Ruthanne*.

"Nooo, but you must concur that Ms. Bell is not in her right mind."

"Ruthanne may often be confused and not what we all term in her right mind, but she is not crazy. She is not harmful. She is right now quite afraid and hiding in her bedroom. She is afraid of you and being taken from this home. I don't know how that can be better for her."

The rod of steel did not like having her plans questioned. "Ms. Bell is not a relative of yours, Miz Darnell. Why should you care whether she stays here or goes?"

Charlene looked at the woman for a long minute in which Mason wondered if he might have to break up an out-and-out fight. Although a much softer woman, Charlene had steel inside her, too. She said, "If you think it is because of her social security, let me assure you that that bit of money barely covers her expenses. I surely could not get rich off of it. I care because in the months she has been here, Ruthanne has become a friend, a part of our family. Her welfare is important to my grandfather and to Mrs. Covington, so therefore, it is important to me. And it seems to me quite silly to jerk someone out of where they are happy and put them through unnecessary misery."

Charlene had the woman's attention. Mason watched her tilt her head and listen to Mrs. Browne, who no doubt knew she had made an error in judgment of Charlene and possibly the entire situation, but who was not a person to readily admit to errors. The two talked around the situation. Ms. Browne pointed out that the women needed help in the home, and that a responsible person was needed to watch out for Ruthanne. Charlene explaining that she could not move her children from their own home to live here with her father, but that she would be looking in on a constant basis.

Finally Mildred stuck in, "Well, if you take Ruthanne,

I guess you'll have to take me, too," which caused the other women to stare at her. "I am not crazy. I can look out for Ruthanne." She lifted her chin.

After that Ms. Browne got around to admitting what she had wanted to admit five minutes after Charlene started talking. "I can see that Miss Bell has some good friends here."

"Well, she certainly does," Vella put in. "We take care of each other around here in Valentine. We'll all keep helping out, too, until Winston comes home, and then his insurance and medicare will pay for a day nurse, if he needs it."

Mason stepped forward. "Ms. Browne, would a day nurse right now be something that your offices could help with?"

All the women looked up at him with surprise, apparently having forgotten his presence.

"It would cost the state a lot less to have some temporary help come in here for these ladies than to put Miss Bell in a home, when she doesn't need a home. If someone could come a few hours each day, Miz Mildred here is capable of making certain Miss Bell eats and is kept clean. All she needs is some help."

"That's true," Mildred said instantly, glancing around at all of them. "Winston did that, but I can do it until he comes home. I can do it for as long as I have to. I just can't cook," she said directly to Ms. Browne.

It was arranged. Vella and the squad of church ladies would check on the two women and help out as required, the Senior Center could send a hot meal each day, and Ms. Browne would send a practical nurse to check three times a week.

"That is the best I can do," Ms. Browne told Charlene

and Mason on the front porch, "and that is bending rules all over the place, and I don't know how long I can get away with it, either."

Charlene watched the two women go down the walk to their car. Ms. Tallman, who never uttered a word the entire time she had been there, glanced up at the flags flying high and shook her head.

Glancing over her shoulder, Charlene saw through the screen door into the foyer that Mildred was hugging Ruthanne, who had come out of her room when told the "State Lady" was gone.

Charlene looked at Mason. "Thank you for the suggestion of the practical nurse. It gave Ms. Browne some way to keep control."

He inclined his head in acknowledgment, then said, "I've been trying to reach you."

"I know." Her gaze rested on his blue eyes. Her irritation wasn't at him. It was at herself. But how could she tell him that?

"Why haven't you returned my calls?" he asked, hurt in his voice.

She raked a hand through her hair. "I am up to my ears, Mason, in kids and my father and these old ladies and trying to earn a living so my kids don't starve."

She looked at him and felt badly. "I'm sorry" was all she could think to say. "That's how it is, Mason. You've been such a help to me, but the more you help, the more obligated I feel. The more I feel…caught. I'm not ready for such a relationship where you're helping me so close. I can't deal with you and me right now. Everyone else needs me."

"Well, that's all I wanted. An explanation."

"And now I've given you one." She headed away to her truck.

The next thing she knew he had followed her. When she
opened the truck door, he grabbed it. "You're runnin' from
me."

She felt trapped and was angry at him for it. "Maybe I
am. I think that's my choice."

She got into the Suburban and backed out. Suddenly she
was crying. Her vision was so blurry that she backed over
the lilac bush before she realized it.

Thirty-Eight

Mason turned out the warehouse lights and shut the door,
hardly aware of doing so. He had not been able to keep his
mind on anything all afternoon, since his argument with
Charlene. He didn't suppose it was much of an argument.
It was more like her telling him to get lost.

As he opened the door of his pickup, Iris called to him
and came hurrying across the lot in a ridiculously short skirt
and idiotic platform shoes. "Adam told me about your
idea," she said, a little breathless. Breathing deeply made
her prominent breasts move up and down in a noticeable
fashion. "The idea for the senior living complex."

"Oh."

"My parents live in one, you know, up in Kansas City."

"No, I didn't know."

"Well, they do, and they love it. It's really expensive.
Most all of them are like that. My parents searched a lot
of places, and they were all expensive. But they can afford
it. I think your idea for one around here that would be more
affordable is really good, and I told Adam so."

Mason looked at her, waiting politely for her to finish.

She lifted her chin. "I told Adam that I'd like to work
on something like that. I could do a lot of the information
gathering and figuring the costs. I'm really good at shopping for bargains. Adam said he'd think about it. Would it

be okay with you if I work on it, too? It'd be something Adam and I could do together, you know.''

Mason was startled by both her anxiousness and the proposal. ''Well, yeah...if Adam goes for it.'' He couldn't imagine his brother coming around to the idea.

Apparently Iris could, though, because she smiled big and said, ''Thanks, Mason. This, well, this would give Adam and me something to work on together. He's real good with investing, and I'm real good with spending.''

He shook his head, grinning, and started to get into the pickup; then he stopped. ''Iris?''

''Yeah?''

Now he felt really foolish. ''What should a guy do about a woman when she starts running from him, but he's pretty certain she likes him?''

''You mean Charlene is givin' you the run-around?''

''Yeah, something like that,'' he said. He was in it now, so he might as well get through.

Tilting her head in thought, Iris walked slowly back toward him. ''Well, Mason, put yourself in her shoes. Her husband leaves her for another woman. That's gonna make a woman feel like an awful failure. And she has to provide everything for her kids. And now her daddy is sick and everybody is leaning on her. Don't you think that'd make you a little crazy? She's just got to sort it out. You might just need to give her some time.''

It wasn't really what he wanted to hear. He wanted to know what he could do.

She laid her hand on his arm, and she asked in her warm, liquid voice, ''Have you told Charlene how you feel? I mean, straight out.''

''Yes.'' He nodded, feeling embarrassed, but saying, ''And I've tried every way I know to show her, too.''

''Then there isn't anything else you can do. You let her

know you are here when she's ready, and you leave her to herself. Have faith in her to know what's right for her. If you don't have faith in her, have faith in the Divine Spirit inside her. Don't crowd her. And don't do for her what she has to do for herself.''

She looked down at her platform shoes. "Don't do to her what I did to Adam. I kept after him so hard that it was me controlling everything. I controlled him right into marriage, and he's always felt a little maneuvered. He loves me,'' she said quickly. "It's just that sometimes he feels resentful, and it's because I wouldn't let him do his part. I was so scared he wouldn't do what I thought he should that I did it for him. Controlling like that, well, it just takes away a person's pride.''

He was struck then, seeing her eyes get teary. He put an arm out, and she came against him.

"I meant it with love with Adam, but trying to control somebody just never works,'' she whispered shakily.

He didn't know what to say. It was a relief when she sniffed and pulled away, because he'd suddenly gotten a little worried about Adam catching her against him.

Iris patted his chest. "You just let Charlene know you're waitin' and then give her space. If it's right, then it will work out.'' She smiled bravely at him. "Not everything depends on us, you know. God is there, and He'll do his part, if we let him.''

He managed a thanks and then got quickly into his truck, before she could go to touching him all over again. He had shifted into gear when he was surprised once again by Iris appearing at his open window.

She said, "There's something else. Something people forget. People have needs, Mason, you know?'' She arched her eyebrow in a sexy manner. "We are human bodies, but a lot of times people won't admit that and deal with it. And when we don't face it, it just makes us so terribly grumpy.''

Then she turned and walked away, leaving him feeling a little as if he'd been through a wringer. He knew about needs. He was having a whole lot of them himself. It amazed him that for all these years he could have managed to not really have any needs, but since his hope for Charlene had taken wings, he'd been having all sorts of needs he had not thought of for a long time.

The next morning, upon passing down Main Street, it struck him to pull into Grace Florist. He walked right in, hardly realizing why he was there, saw a sign for roses and ordered a dozen roses to be delivered to Charlene. Yellow roses, he decided on impulse, when the girl told him their yellow roses had a scent.

He took so long to write the card that the girl gave him an impatient look.

There, he thought, when he had come out. He had done something. ''I guess it's up to you now, God,'' he said.

That afternoon, at the shop, Charlene received a florist delivery—a dozen yellow roses. Magnificent roses. ''Fresh this morning,'' the young girl who delivered them said.

''Well, hurry up and read the card,'' Oralee prodded.

Charlene opened the small envelope with shaking fingers. It read: *I want you to know I care for you. I'm here if you need me for anything. Love, Mason.*

Charlene pressed the card to her chest and stared wide-eyed at the roses for several long seconds, and then she burst into tears, right there in front of a room of customers. Mortified, she raced to the back room.

Oralee followed and hugged her. ''Why, that SOB! Sending flowers. We'll get him for that.''

''Oh, Oralee,'' Charlene said, laughing and crying. She

handed Oralee the card; she read it and passed it to Dixie, who had joined them, leaving all their customers wondering.

Dixie read the card and said, "That is some kind of man."

Charlene took the flowers home and put them first on the dining room table, and then she moved them onto the kitchen table. The rest of that day and into the next, she kept looking at the flowers. She came in from shopping for Mildred and Ruthanne and saw the flowers. She came in from visiting her father, and she saw the flowers. She cooked supper, she saw the flowers. She rose and made coffee, and she saw the flowers.

"I'm afraid, Lord," she said aloud as she sat to drink her morning coffee in full view of the roses.

She went about her busy Saturday, forgetting the flowers. Until that evening she came into the kitchen, and her eyes fell on them. Quite suddenly she realized the most amazing fact that she was alone. Larry Joe had a date with Pia, Danny J. was off with a bunch of his friends, and Jojo had decided to stay awhile with Ruthanne and play checkers.

The idea hit her to drive over to see Mason. By the time she got into the Suburban, however, she was having great doubts. Of course she couldn't go see him. She was too confused to explain things to him. She didn't know what she would say.

She drove all over town, until finally she was driving into Mason's yard lit with the warm glow of a setting sun. She stopped the Suburban and shoved it into park, and then sat there, not turning it off.

Mason came out on the porch. He stared at her, and she stared at him.

He came up to her window and sort of crouched down. "Are you going to come in?" he asked.

"I don't know," she said, feeling at a loss. "I don't even know for sure why I'm here."

He grinned that wonderful, warm grin. "Why don't you come in and maybe you'll figure it out."

She looked at him and then turned off the engine and got out, looking around. She didn't know when she'd found out he lived here. It suited him. Old-fashioned, warm and homey. A big mimosa tree in the front yard.

He held the screen door for her, and she went inside. The first thing she saw were books. Books on shelves lined the walls and seemed stacked everywhere.

"Ah...I've been going through them. Cleaning out." He pointed to boxes.

She went around the living room, scanning the books, touching her fingers lightly to titles like *The Hound of the Baskervilles* right next to *A Cowboy Dictionary*. For a minute Mason stood there, watching her, and then when she looked around he was gone. She heard him at the back of the house, heard the clink of dishes. She continued to peruse the books, all covered with fine dust so that she could see Mason's fingerprints here and there.

She went all around his house, into the rooms, just standing there and looking around. She liked the scent of the house. It was Mason, musky and warm and sweet and salty. There was a desk in the small room adjoining the living room, an old rolltop desk, papers covering it, slipping off and to the floor. In his very old-fashioned but neat and tidy bedroom, his bed, an old iron bedstead, was made with a lovely quilt. Books on the night table. A clock with big alarm bells, as if he needed that to wake him. Her gaze went back to the bed, and she stared long at it, thinking of being snuggled there.

On into the bathroom, which had the fifties green and white tile. The terrazzo on the floor was a real surprise.

A small rear room that must have once been a porch was lined with windows. Things were stored there now.

She came to the door into the kitchen and took the room in at a glance, seeing the enameled cabinets, the green checked curtains at the windows, the welcoming yet lonely feel of it. The house was lonely, she thought quite suddenly.

Mason's back was to her. His T-shirt was stretched tight over his shoulders. Feeling her gaze, he turned. She went toward him. He watched her come, and then he reached for her and drew her against him, breathing a great sigh when she pressed against the length of him.

"Charlene," he whispered in a warm and welcoming tone.

She wrapped her arms around his neck and kissed him deeply, until she began to feel weak in the knees. Weak all over, so that she clung to him and said, "Please hold me. Just please hold me."

He held her tight and kissed her eyes and her cheeks and her neck down toward her breasts that she bared for him, while running her fingers through his silky, thick hair. And then he laid her head against his chest, and he massaged her back while she listened to the steady, hard beating of his heart. They stayed like that, listening to each other's heartbeats, absorbing certain knowledge of each other's bodies, for uncountable minutes.

Finally, having absorbed enough of his strength to stand on her own, Charlene pulled away.

"I made coffee," he said and indicated the steaming cups on the table.

"Thank you."

She sat at the table. Seeing her shiver, he moved to shut the back door, but she said quickly that she would rather it be open. "I like to see the sunset light fade. It's so beautiful."

So he went out of the room and came back with a thick, soft corduroy shirt that he placed around her shoulders. His scent surrounded her.

They sat at the table, not talking at first, until finally Charlene managed, "I'm trying to figure out what I need to say," and he told her, "Take your time."

Grinning at that, she asked him if he had always been this patient, and he said that he had not and that he really wasn't right then, but he was trying to be.

She shook her head, feeling teary, and said, "Oh, Mason...thank you for the roses. They are beautiful. They smell so good. So many roses have no fragrance. Very often the ones from the florist don't. They're bred for beauty, not for scent. I love the ones with scent."

"Something told me that," he said.

She gazed into his eyes, which were clear and warm. They smiled at each other. A warm sensation like water washed over her.

"I apologize for my attitude toward you the other day," she said.

He told her he understood, that it was okay.

She shook her head and told him, "I want to explain, as best I can." Then she took a deep breath and continued. "I have been running from you, Mason. I failed in my relationship with Joey. I tried as hard as I knew how to try, and I failed. I think if I had not tried so hard, that failing wouldn't hurt so badly, but to know I gave it all I had and I still came up deficient is very hard to take."

"Why do you not think Joey had a big part in the failure?" he asked.

"That is something I have to work through. I can see that logic now, that it wasn't all me, but I have not gotten to the place where I can deal with it. You see, I am terrified that I will repeat all the mistakes I made with Joey. That's why I need time to find out who I am, not who I am with someone, but who I am by myself as a woman. I lost that knowledge somewhere along the way.

"And you don't know me, Mason," she continued. "Not really. You are in love with someone you've made me out to be in your mind. I don't want you to wake up one day and find I don't in reality match up to that fantasy woman. I want you to love the real me."

"Tell me about you, then," he said, in an earnest fashion that caused a great thumping in her chest.

"I like to see sunsets and sunrises," she began. She told him a dozen things she liked, and then asked him what he liked, and he told her so many that she laughed and asked if there was anything he did not like.

"Yes," he said. "Cold winters and toll roads."

They fell quiet, so quiet she thought she could hear his heart beating. He laid his hand on the table, palm up, and she slowly put her hand into his. A shiver of pure desire went up her arm and down her back to land deep in the recesses of her belly.

"I am so attracted to you, Mason, that it scares my socks off," she admitted, facing him fully, watching the warm light grow in his eyes and the crinkles at their corners as he smiled.

"Scares me, too, I guess," he drawled.

"But I don't want to let my body dictate my life. My soul. I don't want to make love with you, because I'm afraid I will lose myself. I don't want to go in that deep, until I can commit my total self. Can you understand?"

He nodded. Yet his hand stayed tight around hers, and hers tight around his.

"I'll wait until you're ready," he said. "But can you be my girl?"

"Oh, Mason." And then she got up and went to him, and he pulled her into his lap.

"Yes, I can be your girl," she said with a teary whisper into his ear.

She wrapped her arms around his neck and kissed him.

And while the golden setting sun sent deepening shadows into the warm kitchen, they kissed and explored each other with hands and lips and voices, and Mason displayed an amazing understanding of her needs right at that moment.

Six Months Later...

It was the second Saturday of the month, and Mason did as he had been doing each second Saturday, he drove into town to the florist to get Charlene a vase of yellow roses. This Saturday it was also his turn to help Winston Valentine raise his flags, so he drove in at the crack of dawn.

"You're late," Winston said. Despite the chilly, damp morning, he was waiting on the porch.

"I am not. I'm on time. Sunrise is in exactly one minute, according to the weatherman this morning."

Winston always had to tell him he was late. It was part of the ritual. Mason came two mornings a week, Larry Joe one, and Northrupt the other four. It was hard on Winston's pride, but he said he would put up with it in order to keep up the standard of the flags.

Mason, carrying the flags, helped Winston, who used a cane, down the stairs. He walked just behind the older man over to the flagpole. He attached the flags, and Winston managed to pull the ropes, sending the flags into the air, while "Dixie" played out from the house. Mason, slightly behind Winston, followed suit in saluting.

Then Winston said, "You are askin' her to marry you again today, aren't you?"

"Yes, sir," Mason said. He asked Charlene the second Saturday of every month, the day he considered something of their anniversary.

"Good luck," Winston said and waved him away.

Mason looked over to see Vella coming across the pasture. She would join Winston for morning coffee.

"Nobody hardly lets me pee alone," Winston muttered as he walked in his halting gait off across the yard.

Mason went into town, had coffee and the regular argument with his brother Adam over their joint project on the senior living complex that was nevertheless progressing, and then went down to get the vase of yellow flowers that now always awaited him at Grace Florist.

"Good luck today," Fred Grace told him.

Mason took the roses and drove back to his old house, which sat upon a foundation that was currently being dismantled. They had decided not to tear down the old house but to move it to five acres three miles down the road. This had been Charlene's idea.

"Oh, Mason, you can't tear it down. It is…well, so *you*." She loved the house, she said. It had become *their* hideaway.

He set the roses on the kitchen table, and for the rest of the morning hours and into the afternoon, cooked a stew, sorted and dusted books, which appeared to be a lifetime's work, and prepared the table for their Saturday evening supper.

When Charlene arrived, she brought him his favorite tomato pudding. It was her part to put candles on the table and light them, even though they always ate just before sundown, when the long buttery rays of the sun slanted across the yard and in the windows.

He told her she looked beautiful in the candlelight, and she told him he looked good, too.

"The roses smell especially lovely tonight," she added.

"Mr. Grace makes sure he orders these for us once a month."

Then he gazed at her for a long minute. "Are you going to marry me?" he asked.

And she said, "Yes."

She sat there, knowing he had not really heard her.

He picked up a bowl to serve, and then he looked at her.

She grinned broadly, every womanly cell in her body dancing.

He put down the bowl. "You said yes?"

She nodded. And, laughing, she threw herself into his lap and kissed him with an abandon that she had never before allowed herself to display.

After a minute of that, he jerked her away from him and said in an eager voice, "You said yes?"

She put her palm against his dear, tender cheek and said, "Mason, you are some kind of man. I will be your wife, here and now."

Then she rose and took his hand and said boldy, "Mason, I cannot wait another minute to have you."

And she led him off into his own bed, where the flame of their passion flared quickly, burning away their initial bit of shyness. The ticking clock seemed to beat in time with their hearts as, fully naked, they stared at each other, a man and a woman with trembling hearts and hungry bodies. Her breasts were creamy mounds of flesh more beautiful than he had imagined, and his hips more narrow and man part more eager than she had imagined.

Then, with a great smile and breathless sigh, she extended her arms, and he came fully to himself and took her as a man does the woman he has longed for, mating with her in hot desire and wanting and piercing happiness, where the cries of two hearts melding into one floated on the evening breeze.

Afterward they lay damp in each other's arms, caressing, kissing lips and skin, and whispering words of praise and love such as only two souls can who have at last found their mates.

"Let's do it again," she whispered, and he laughed a great laugh and covered her body with his.

SHERRYL WOODS

*H*eather Reed thought she was making the right choice when she decided to raise her daughter, Angel, on her own. But five years later Heather realizes that she needs help. It's time to track down Angel's fahter.... The only problem is he doesn't know Angel exists.

*I*f Todd Winston is dismayed to see his old girlfriend show up in Whispering Woods, he's horrified when he looks into the angelic eyes of the little girl who is clearly his daughter.

*N*either Heather nor Todd count, though, on their unexpected desire to become a family. The only question: Is it too late?

ANGEL MINE

Available mid-August wherever paperbacks are sold!

MIRA

Visit us at www.mirabooks.com

MSHW600

From the *Los Angeles Times* bestselling author

NELL BRIEN

When architect Joel Stanton returns from a business trip to
Kenya in a body bag, his twin sister, Cat, doesn't accept
the official explanation of his death.

Heading to Nairobi, Cat retraces her brother's footsteps across
the rugged and heartbreakingly beautiful terrain of Africa and
embarks on a journey that will change her life…and put
her in the same kind of danger that got Joel killed.

LIONESS

A "powerful debut novel…this romantic thriller…explores the
complexities of culture as well as those of the human heart."
—*Publishers Weekly* on *A VEILED JOURNEY*

On sale September 2000 wherever paperbacks are sold!

Curtiss Ann Matlock

66499   LOST HIGHWAYS   ___ $5.99 U.S. ___ $6.99 CAN.

(limited quantities available)

TOTAL AMOUNT $_____
POSTAGE & HANDLING $_____
($1.00 for 1 book, 50¢ for each additional)
APPLICABLE TAXES* $_____
<u>TOTAL PAYABLE</u> $_____
(check or money order—please do not send cash)

To order, complete this form and send it, along with a check or
money order for the total above, payable to MIRA Books®, to: **In
the U.S.**: 3010 Walden Avenue, P.O. Box 9077, Buffalo, NY
14269-9077; **In Canada**: P.O. Box 636, Fort Erie, Ontario, L2A
5X3.

Name:_____
Address:_____ City:_____
State/Prov.:_____ Zip/Postal Code:_____
Account Number (if applicable):_____
075 CSAS

> *New York residents remit applicable sales taxes.
> Canadian residents remit applicable
> GST and provincial taxes.

MIRA